MYSTERIOUS THREADS

MYSTERIOUS THREADS

A Virginia Davies Quilt Mystery
Book Six

By
David Ciambrone

Names, characters, businesses, places, events, and incidents are either the products of the author's imagination or used in a fictitious manner. Any resemblance to actual persons, living or dead, or actual events, is purely coincidental.

No part of this publication may be reproduced,stored in a retrieval system, or transmitted in any form or by any means, electronic, mechanical, photocopying, recording, or otherwise, without the written permission of the publisher.

Text Copyright © 2022 David Ciambrone

All rights reserved.
Published 2022 by Progressive Rising Phoenix Press, LLC
www.progressiverisingphoenix.com

ISBN: 978-1-958640-17-3

Printed in the U.S.A.

Book and Cover design by William Speir
Visit: http://www.williamspeir.com

This title was originally published by
White Bird Publications
ISBN: 978 1 63363 487-9
eBook ISBN: 978-1-63363-488-6
LOCN: 2020947548

ACKNOWLEDGMENTS

I would like to acknowledge the following people who were critical in the production of this novel.

The Williamson County Coroner's for their support and critiques.

My great wife Kathy for her support and understanding.

My publisher, Amanda M. Thrasher, at Progressive Rising Phoenix Press.

I would also like to thank my contacts at DARPA for the insight into some of the special equipment that Virginia and her friends used in this novel.

CHAPTER 1

Virginia Davies Clark, with her blonde ponytail sticking out of her baseball cap and dressed in a tight, red T-shirt and denim shorts, hung onto her seat belt as bushes, trees, and fence posts appeared to fly by. She glanced at Natalie. "You do remember we're going to a quilt and sewing retreat, not to a stock car race?"

Natalie North, a blonde, semi-retired movie actress, who resembled Melissa Rauch, Bernadette of the Big Bang Theory TV show, and now a rancher chuckled. "Yes."

Virginia glanced at the speedometer. "Just how fast are you going? Mach 2?"

"Close, but not quite. You're a big chicken."

"I'm not chicken," stammered Virginia "I just want to live long enough to get to the retreat."

Natalie continued to fly toward the Mayfield, an historic ranch in Williamson County northwest of Georgetown, Texas.

Virginia adjusted her sunglasses and consulted her map. "The entrance to the Mayfield is ahead a couple miles on the left; you might want to start your descent for landing."

"Okay. Landing gear down, flaps down, engine slowing. By the way," she asked, "who's the owner of this ranch we're going to?"

"Colin Carswell owns the ranch, and when he's not hosting events like our retreat, he does historic and archaeological/haunted tours. He also has a large herd of longhorn cattle. I think that's for an agriculture exemption for property taxes."

"Historical and archaeological tours? What's historical about the joint?"

"It's not a joint. It's a humongous ranch. And there is some old history attached to it, and artifacts from people who once lived there. I'm sure we'll get the full story from him."

"Humongous, huh?" Natalie frowned. "Did you say the place is haunted?"

"There is a legend about it being haunted, and an ancient curse."

"Sounds fascinating. How old is he? Is he sane, or does he think the ranch has fairies and dragons, too? Curse?"

"I don't know exactly how old he is, but from talking to him on the phone and seeing pictures, I'd guess in his late fifties to early sixties." Virginia chuckled. "Not sure about the fairies and dragons. But I'm sure if there are any, they're friendly. Yeah, there is supposed to be a curse. I'm sure he'll tell us about it." Virginia pointed ahead at a large stone edifice and black-iron gates. "Looks like we've arrived."

Natalie slowed her white Toyota land Cruiser, turned into the ranch entrance, and rolled to a stop. She straightened and squinted out the window. "Where's the ranch house?"

"Up ahead. The ranch is huge; remember? This road looks a little rough, so please try to stay under the sound barrier. My kidneys will thank you."

"Very funny." Natalie drove up the slightly inclined gravel road a mile to the crest of the hill. She spotted a cluster of buildings in the distance. "This place is big. That Victorian must be the main house."

A Victorian mansion of fourteen to sixteen rooms with a towering gabled roof stood nestled in oak, elm, and fruit trees. They gazed at the upstairs balconies and downstairs porches on the south and east sides. Two palms stood at the far side of the building.

Virginia nodded. "According to Mr. Carswell's directions, you're correct. Those buildings on the right may be where we're holding the retreat. There are a few cars parked around them."

"Think any members of our Bee Hive Quilt Bee will be attending?" Natalie continued driving down the slope toward the buildings.

"I don't know. There are about thirty women registered, so it's possible." Virginia tugged at her denim shorts. "I just want to get signed in, find our rooms so we can unload our stuff for our classes, change clothes, and see what the schedule looks like. We can meet the other people then."

"You said this is kind of a first. Did you mean both quilting and knitting at the same retreat?"

"Yeah. A lot of quilters are knitters, too. Putting the two subjects together like this is a first. That's why a lot of people signed up for your knitting and felting classes. Showing them how you do it and make those gorgeous handbags should be interesting." Virginia pointed to some signs "Looks like we park over there and go to that smaller ranch house to sign in."

Natalie pulled the SUV up in front of what looked like a blacksmith's shop and parked under an old, sprawling, oak tree. She furrowed her brow. "Did I see a ghost painted on that sign back there?"

"Yes." Virginia paused before swinging her legs out of the car. "I wonder why? Maybe the history, ancient curse, and histrionics are starting already."

Natalie released her seatbelt. "Curses, haunted houses. Here I thought quilting and knitting were safe hobbies. After our last adventure with a quilt, I mean wall hanging, and me getting shot, more drama I don't need." Natalie gave Virginia a conspiring look. "Maybe a new hobby would be nice. You ever consider skydiving? We could do it together."

"No!" Virginia's eyes widened. "I'd never jump out of a perfectly good airplane. I don't see the fun in that. And, if the chute doesn't open, the State of Texas stops you… flat, and painfully. No jumping from airplanes."

Natalie held up her hands in surrender. "Okay… okay, just kidding. No jumping out of airplanes."

"Good." Virginia patted her arm. "Anyway, we're at a quilt and sewing retreat in the middle of Nowhere, Texas with about thirty women. What could go wrong?"

"We were in a cursed place the middle of nowhere, which also just happens to be haunted. 'What could go wrong?' she asks."

CHAPTER 2

Virginia finished unpacking her suitcase and teaching materials when the phone rang. She settled into an overstuffed chair near the window looking out over the ranch and answered. "Hello?"

"Hi. Unpacked yet?" Natalie asked. "Just finished. You?"

"Yes. Did you read the brochure about this place they gave us at registration?"

"Not yet. I was going to look at the official schedule–"

"We can do that later. Let's go to the… the food court, or restaurant, or whatever they call it. You're going to love this place."

"Okay. I'll—"

Virginia turned at the knock on her door. "Someone's at my door; got to go."

"It's me. Get off your butt and let's get hopping."

Virginia answered the door. Natalie, now in jeans and a red blouse, paced in a circle in the hall. "Ready?" She stopped and looked at Virginia. "You're going ghost hunting in shorts?"

"I ahh… hadn't planned on ghost hunting quite yet."

"Plan on it." Natalie pushed Virginia farther back into her room. "Go get some ectoplasmic hunting garb on and hurry."

Virginia gave Natalie a quizzical look. "What's got you so excited?"

Natalie handed Virginia her iPad. "Take a look but change first."

"Why don't you tell me about it while I do?"

"Fine." Natalie took her iPad back. "As you know the Mayfield is an historic ranch in Williamson County. The ranch has a… a history that dates back well over a hundred years. Back in the day, the owner died under mysterious circumstances. His widow, Mrs. June Cochran, took over the place." Natalie walked to the window and peered out, then back at Virginia. "There was a neighbor, Mr. Derwood Noble, who coveted the land and tried to drive her away. The reports said he just disappeared one night. There was speculation that he ran off to Chicago with a bar girl. But, in Mrs. Cochran's diary, she said she got him drunk and enticed him into the smokehouse. She tied a rope around his neck and hoisted him up with a pulley. She let Mr. Noble hang in the smokehouse along with the rest of the meat, but she didn't do it right. He died a slow death and was… well… he was smoked, along with some beef."

Virginia pulled her new T-shirt on. "Sounds rather grizzly."

"Remind me to find out where they get the steaks we're having tonight at the barbeque."

"We're having barbeque?"

Natalie gave her a quizzical expression. "Didn't you read the schedule?"

"I was going to until you–"

Natalie looked at her iPad and scrolled the page. "Where was I?"

"Derwood Noble being hanged and smoked."

"Oh, yeah. She buried him somewhere on the ranch." Natalie set her iPad on the desk. "According to the original story, his spirit haunts the place to this day, especially the attic of this house."

Virginia finished changing into a pair of jeans. "What's Mrs. Cochran's relationship to Colin Carswell, the present ranch owner?"

"She's like his great-great-great-great grandmother or something. Not sure about the number of greats."

"I'm sure Mr. Carswell's presentation tonight and tour will cover this. Why are you so anxious to go investigate now? We should check the sched–"

"Because we have time, and he may not mention the smokehouse or the death of the old neighbor. And why does the old boy haunt the attic instead of the smokehouse?"

Virginia tucked her hair under a University of Texas baseball cap and picked up a map of the ranch. She studied it while Natalie fidgeted. "There is no ranch smokehouse on the map."

"I know. But I found where it was on an old webpage. It gave a description of the ranch back then. Let's go." Natalie headed for the door.

Virginia followed Natalie down to the main parlor of the Victorian and out the front door. "We need to check when our classes are."

"Later. I'll show you where the smokehouse used to be. We can start from there."

Virginia caught up with Natalie. "Do you have any idea how to investigate ghosts? You know they aren't real, right? Ghosts are like fairies and dragons… not real. You've probably been out in the sun too long. Maybe you should be having some iced tea and be wearing a hat."

Natalie stopped and stared at Virginia. "How can you say that? I have two small dragons living at my house. I don't like hats."

"They're stuffed toy dragons."

"Details. They're cute and I love them." She pointed in the direction of a large barn. "The smokehouse was on the other side of that barn."

They walked around the barn and searched the area. They didn't see anything indicating a structure, even an old one. Virginia was about to get Natalie to return to the house when a voice startled her. She spun around. A man stood by the corner of the barn.

He titled his head and smiled. "Hello. I'm Colin Carswell, the owner of this ranch. What are two pretty ladies doing out in this heat looking at dirt?"

Virginia walked to him. "Mr. Carswell, I'm Virginia Davies Clark and this is Natalie North. We're instructors for the retreat."

He removed his cowboy hat revealing a head of wavy white hair. "Nice to meet you ladies. I know who you are, but what are you doing out here?"

"Looking just for the remains of an old smokehouse," Virginia said. "Is that okay?"

"Yes, of course it is. You're interested in the legend about the hanging of Derwood Noble?" His black eyes sparkled.

"Yes. It says he was hung in it and he haunts the ranch even today," said Virginia.

"Yeah. That's the story. I'll be telling the story tonight. But since you two are here, let me give you a short tour." He walked to the area Natalie was still exploring. "Miss North, you are standing in the middle of the old smokehouse where the alleged hanging took place."

Natalie jerked around looking at the ground. "I am?"

"Yes. There are bits of the foundation hidden in the grass." He motioned for them to follow. "Down here is the family cemetery. A number of my relatives are buried beneath these weathered stone tombstones. But a few graves have no markers. The original grave markers may have been wooden and decayed away many years ago. We know the graves and remains are here, but their identities are questionable. My guess is Mr. Derwood Noble is buried somewhere in here." He pointed at the iron, fenced-off area with knee-high grass partially concealing tomb markers in various states of condition. "Feel free to look around. I include this on the archaeological/historical tour of the ranch house, especially the attic, the old ranch buildings, this cemetery, the story about the haunting, especially the old curse."

Virginia and Natalie leaned on the decorative, old, iron, waist-high fence and looked at the cemetery.

Natalie turned to ask Carswell a question. Instead, she stood wide-eyed, staring at the empty ranch area behind them. "Where'd he go?"

CHAPTER 3

After a barbeque dinner in the converted barn cafeteria, Virginia and Natalie, along with the other thirty attendees, adjourned to the main meeting hall in another building.

They had settled into their seats when Helen Chandler, a sixtyish woman with light brown hair, stepped onto the stage. She picked up a microphone and spoke. "Ladies, welcome to the Seventh Annual Mayfield Quilt and Knit Retreat. In your welcome packet, you will find the class and event schedule and the instructor list. You'll notice we left free time during the week for you to explore the ranch, to mingle with the other participants, and to attend the entertainment planned for some evenings. We start with breakfast being served starting at seven in the morning and classes begin at nine. If you have any questions or issues during your time here, please contact me or our host, Mr. Colin Carswell. Now, Mr. Carswell will give you a short presentation about the ranch, its history, and what I know you're looking forward to... the haunting and the curse." She turned toward him. "Mr. Carswell." She handed him the microphone as he stepped onto the stage.

Carswell smiled at the crowd. "Good evening ladies, and welcome to Mayfield Ranch. I have a short slide presentation showing the ranch that you are free to explore. There are university people doing archaeological research at the ancient Indian village site, so please do not interfere with them. Then we'll go on an archaeological and historical tour, and I'll tell you about the ghost, his history, and the curse."

"After the lecture and tour of the ranch house, the old ranch buildings, cemetery, ancient Indian burial grounds; I'll show you the remains of the Indian village I mentioned." Carswell led small groups up into the musty attic of the main house. Virginia and Natalie were in the third group. Virginia glanced around at the large, rustic attic filled with dusty travel trunks, old paintings, furniture, vintage suitcases, dress mannequins, and wooden boxes, while she listened to Mr. Carswell.

Carswell narrowed his eyes and cleared his throat, then spoke in a slow constricted tone. "This is where the ghost of Mr. Derwood Noble, an old neighbor who coveted this property, is said to haunt. His ghost is not dangerous but has been known to cause trouble and scare visitors. There are a couple stories about him. One story said he ran off with a bar girl. But why would he leave a thriving ranch to run off with her? According to the diary of an old relative of mine, she drugged him, then hung poor Mr. Noble in the old smokehouse many years ago. He was hung but died in a slow and grizzly manner and was supposedly smoked along with the beef in the smokehouse. Where he is buried is still a mystery." Carswell nodded taking in the expressions of disgust on the women's faces." He chuckled. "No one knows. Witnesses place his ghost here in the attic, around the cemetery, and where the old smokehouse stood."

"How about the curse?" a woman asked.

Carswell turned toward her. "Yes, thank you. Now to the curse. There is a legend that old Mr. Noble cursed my relative and the following generations of her family to a painful and mysterious death by the age of sixty-five." He allowed a dramatic pause and lowered his voice somberly. "So far no one in my family has survived past sixty-five." He glanced at their wide-eyed expressions. "Are there any questions?"

Virginia, kneeling next to a vintage steamer trunk, raised her hand. "Yes. Did you know there are human bones up here?"

CHAPTER 4

The women on the tour turned and gasped. Carswell stuttered. "Hu... human bones? There are no human remains in this attic. You... you must be mistaken. An animal maybe? A Halloween decoration?"

Virginia held up a mandible. "This is a human jawbone."

Carswell frowned. "Where'd you get it?"

She pointed. "This 1940s wardrobe steamer trunk was partially open. When I leaned on it, the trunk opened more, and the bones fell out. They've been in this trunk for quite a while. Where they came from, I don't know, but they're here now."

Carswell maneuvered around the contents of the attic and the women. He stopped next to Virginia and took the bone. "How do we know this isn't a fake?"

"I've taken physical anthropology courses and work with anthropologists at a museum and I also work for the Smithsonian. It's real, trust me." She left out the part about being a special agent. "That mandible you're holding most likely belonged to a male."

He turned the bone in his hands examining it. "How do you know that? It's just a bone."

"The ramus is wide, sharply angled, and flared. The chin shape is square." Virginia picked up the skull. "Note the zygomatic arch. This is different than a female and the mastoid process is different." She put the skull back, picked up the pelvis, and showed it to the group standing around. "This is a dead giveaway. This skeleton is a male."

"My God." Carswell's hands shook. "I've been up here thousands of times and I never saw these bones before."

A woman warily stepped closer. "Could those be the bones of Mr. Derwood Noble?"

Virginia looked at the remaining bones. "He was old, well... older when he died. The sutures on the crown of the skull are fused, so he was an adult. His dental work is old technology. From the looks of these joints, I'd say he had osteoarthritis. He may have had some other diseases that affected his bones, but I'm not a forensic anthropologist." She looked up at Carswell. "How old was Mr. Noble when he… disappeared?"

He stared into the distance for a minute, then said, "I'm not sure exactly. I'd guess in his mid-to-late-fifties. He ran a ranch, so I'd guess he was in pretty good shape."

Virginia examined more bones then looked up. "This is the hyoid bone. It's intact, so my guess is this man was not hung or strangled. Also, from the condition of the bones, he was not used to a large amount of manual labor. And from the appearance of his bones and…" She reached into the trunk and pulled out a humerus with some decayed fabric attached.

A woman swallowed then stammered. "What's that?"

"A humerus. It's the bone in your upper arm. This fabric that is clinging to it is about seventy to eighty years old." She picked up a couple phalanges and metacarpals.

"These finger bones show signs of arthritis." Virginia climbed to her feet. "Where did this old trunk come from and how long has it been here?"

Carswell examined the trunk. "I don't recall seeing it before, but since it is over here out of the way, I may have not really noticed it. It's got a lot of dust on it, so the thing has to have been here quite a while. As you can see, this is a typical old attic with pieces of everything from furniture to paintings to boxes of old clothes…" He picked up a vinyl record. "The Wayward Wind. One of my favorite songs. This is from the early fifties. It's been here a while."

A short, white-haired, stout woman, with a name badge that read Clara Paterson, cleared her throat, and smiled. "This has been great. The bones look very authentic. You've done an excellent job making them look old. Do you two do this with every tour?"

Other women murmured agreement.

Virginia stared at her. "Mrs. Paterson, these bones are real. They belong to a man who died in the nineteen-forties or early fifties. We need to call the sheriff."

Natalie held her phone up. "I've called. The deputy I talked to said to keep everyone here until deputies arrive which should be shortly."

Another woman slid through the gathering and peered down at the bones. She pointed to a femur. "Is that one broken?"

Virginia picked up the long leg bone and examined it. She set it down, slid the wardrobe steamer trunk open more, and moved some cloth and a few more bones around. Then she held up a smashed piece of lead. "Bullet. He was shot in the leg. If he had any more gunshot wounds, they went through soft tissue. The bones don't show any more evidence of gunshot wounds, at least none that can be easily seen. Microscopic analysis may show more." She looked toward the stairs. "We'd better leave things alone now and let the sheriff's deputies do their investigation." She looked at the area by her feet. "I think I've done enough damage."

Natalie stepped to Virginia's side and whispered. "I hear sirens. Did you happen to bring your Smithsonian Central Security Service badge and credentials with you? That could help keep us... you... out of a jam."

Virginia patted her pocket. "Yes."

"Good. That way I won't have to visit you in the county jail tonight for tampering with evidence."

They all turned at the sound of footsteps pounding up the stairs.

Two uniformed deputy sheriffs entered the attic, stopped, and looked around. The older of the two stepped forward. "Mr. Carswell? Miss North?"

Carswell raised his hand. "Yes, Sir. I'm Colin Carswell."

Natalie stepped forward. "I'm Natalie North. I called your office and reported our find."

The deputy stared at Natalie for a second before speaking. "I see. Are you the lady who discovered the remains?"

"No. That would be Virginia." Natalie pointed at Virginia leaning on the wardrobe trunk.

"Okay. Where are the remains?"

Virginia pointed down at the floor next to the trunk. "Right here."

The second deputy motioned for them to all move to the far side of the attic and joined the group. He started to take down names and addresses in a notebook while his partner examined the bones.

After a couple of minutes the deputy with the bones stood. "Were any of you touching or examining these bones?"

Virginia nodded. "Yes. I looked at them when I discovered them. At the time, I didn't know if they were real or some Halloween decorations. But they're real. The bones are that of a man in his late fifties; he probably died in the late nineteen-forties to mid-fifties and was shot in the leg. He wasn't a farmer or rancher and had severe arthritis and maybe a few other illnesses that could affect his bones."

The deputy stopped taking notes. "You know all this how?"

"I work for a museum..." Virginia gave him a sheepish grin. "Well, a couple museums really."

"They would be...?"

Virginia took a breath. "The San Gabriel Museum in Georgetown and the Smithsonian."

He scribbled in his notebook. "San Gabriel Mus..." He looked up at her. "The Smithsonian? The one in Washington, D.C.?"

Virginia nodded. "Yes."

"Oh. Wow. What do you do for them?"

"I'm a curator at the San Gabriel Museum." Virginia pulled out her gold SCSS special agent badge and credentials and showed them to the deputy.

The deputy examined her badge, raised an eyebrow, and then asked, "Are you here in an official capacity, Special Agent Clark?"

"No. I'm an instructor at this quilting and knitting retreat."

The deputy turned toward the group of women and Carswell. "Mr. Carswell, will you step over here please?"

Carswell maneuvered around the items in the attic to the deputy. "Yes, Sir?"

"What can you tell me about this old trunk and the… the occupant?"

"Nothing." He wiped his hands on his pants legs. "I don't know how long that trunk's been here. I never really noticed it before. As to the skeleton inside, I've never seen it before either."

The deputy finished taking notes. "I've called for a forensic team and detectives. For now, I'd like you all to go downstairs and resume what you were doing, but don't leave the ranch."

"Thank you, Deputy," said Carswell. "We'll all be here for a week for the retreat. That is unless you tell us to cancel."

"No. Just don't leave the ranch. We'll have detectives and other people around here for quite a while and deputies at the entrance… so tell everyone don't plan on leaving. We'll need someplace to interview everyone on the ranch, guests, staff, the works. Can you help us out with that?"

"Yes, by all means. I'll set you up in the old hay barn. It's a conference hall now and the retreat isn't using it. It's air-conditioned, clean, and can be secured."

The deputy smiled. "Thank you, Mr. Carswell. Please take the women downstairs so we can continue our investigation."

Carswell led the group down to the main parlor.

When Natalie and Virginia started to walk toward the stairs the deputy called to them. "Not you two. I need a few words with you."

Virginia and Natalie returned to the deputies. Virginia smiled. "Yes?"

"This is a local matter and not federal. I know you're a federal agent and all, but I must ask you to stay out of this investigation unless we are asking you questions. Understand?"

Natalie shrugged. "Fine by me."

Virginia glanced at the trunk. "Right. Local matter. I think I've done enough damage anyway."

"Okay. Just as long as you two remember that, we'll get along just fine. Now, go back to your retreat."

They scurried down the stairs and into the parlor. The women were all talking at once but stopped when Virginia and Natalie entered. Clara Paterson moved to Virginia's side. "You were so knowledgeable and cool with that skeleton. That was something. Can you tell us anything else about the poor man?'

"No. And, the sheriff doesn't want my friend and me nosing around."

Clara looked around suspiciously. "I heard that deputy call you special agent. Are you police?"

"Federal. No jurisdiction in this matter." Virginia looked around. "Where's Carswell?"

"He left right after we came down. I can't wait to tell the other ladies what happened."

Natalie chuckled. "From the number of police vehicles coming, it won't be a secret long."

Virginia frowned. "I wonder where he went."

Harriet Fisher, who appeared to be in her fifties with white hair walked, asking, "What if we investigated ourselves? It would be fun."

Clara shook her head. "That could be dangerous. He was probably murdered, or he wouldn't have ended up in that old steamer trunk."

"If he was killed in the forties, the killer would be really old or dead. It would be fun," Harriet said.

"What if the killer put the trunk in the attic to hide it? Maybe the killer is still alive and around here?" added Natalie.

"Not you, too." Virginia shook her head. "You heard the deputy. We stay out of it."

"This is ranch country and... well I'm sure we could find answers they can't." Natalie turned to the women. "Let's get a small group together and start putting together a plan."

Clara bounced with joy. "Let's all meet in the cafeteria in an hour."

Harriet agreed and looked at Virginia. "You in, honey?"

Virginia stood. "Please don't call me honey. And..." She looked at their expectant faces and sighed. "Someone has to keep you guys out of trouble."

Harriet clenched her canvas tote bag in a death grip. "Great. Having a professional to help will be a big asset."

"But remember, ladies, the man was killed over seventy years ago. We don't know who he was, where he was from, or how he got here. All we know is he was probably killed in the forties or early fifties. The sheriff will most likely classify this as an unsolved murder and let it go. I still think we should let the sheriff do the investigating and we stick with sewing."

Natalie beamed. "We'll operate under the sheriff's radar. No one will suspect us of snooping."

Virginia chuckled. *Don't count on that.*

CHAPTER 5

Virginia took a seat at the table and motioned for the others to join her. "Okay, just what are you amateur sleuths going to investigate?"

Harriet stiffened in her chair. "The skeleton you found of course."

Virginia shook her head. "The police will not give you any information. You've seen only part of it, and they won't let you get another look. All we know for sure is that it is old, male, and was about forty when he died. He died maybe in the late 1940s or early to mid-1950s. He was not strangled or hung. He was not used to hard manual labor. He was shot in the leg. That's it. What are you going to do exactly?"

Harriet wet her lips. "I… I don't know. Maybe someone around here went missing back then."

Virginia leaned forward. "Good luck with that. He could have been a transient, hobo, or a local. The local police, meaning the sheriff, might have records about missing persons from that time. He may have been from somewhere else, so no one around here would report him missing. But if he died right after World War II, then there were a lot of discharged soldiers traveling home. He'd be hard to trace. They didn't have computers back then and files tended to be kept locally. Trust me, without a good reason the sheriff isn't going to cooperate with us. Don't even think about using the Freedom of Information Act."

Natalie shifted in her seat. "So, we're going to let the sheriff handle this?"

"Yep. Now if another body turns up, then we may have something. A fresh one would be best." She watched the horrified expressions on their faces. "But let's hope there're no murders while we're here."

Clara Paterson raised an eyebrow. "So, if there is another murder we can investigate?"

Virginia gave her an exasperated look. "We're at a quilting and knitting retreat, not a homicide investigation seminar." She looked at the women. "When are the first classes scheduled?"

"In the morning," said Clara. "But Mr. Carswell has another tour of the ranch planned shortly."

The women all started to talk at once but quieted when Carswell walked into the room.

Carswell smiled. "I'm sorry about this situation. The deputies are done talking to me, so, if you're still up for the rest of the tour and stories about the ranch, I'd be happy to do it now."

Everyone stood. Harriet gathered her satchel, "I think we're ready to go. Please lead on."

He eyed Virginia. "Mrs. Clark, please don't turn up more human remains."

She waved her arms dismissively. "I'll try not to. But it's your ranch."

Carswell led the women around the ranch telling them about each building, He discussed historical tidbits and told stories about the underground railroad, the ranch during the 1860s, and the raising of cattle. "In the mid-nineteenth century, early settlers in this area found a rich wildlife population of buffalo, deer, bears, mountain lions, alligators…" He looked at their startled faces.

Daniele Webley, in her late forties, rail-thin, with short red hair, raised her hand. "Alligators?"

He nodded. "Yes, They were in the San Gabriel River and some creeks. The alligators, bears, wolves, and most of the large predators here were hunted to extinction by 1900. Various kinds of small wild game including wild turkeys, fox, deer, raccoons, and small game are still around. We still have a few mountain lions."

Harriet waved her hand. "Did anything exciting ever happen?"

He eyed her skeptically. "Does violent crime count? In the later nineteenth century gunfights, horse and cattle thieves were prevalent. If they were caught, either they were lynched, or they were given a quick trial and hanged. Some of the more famous outlaws of the day, like Sam Bass and John Wesley Hardin, preyed on the citizens, robbed banks, and stagecoaches. Long-term family feuds and drunken brawls at the various saloons in the towns added to the toll of homicides." When he came to the area where the smokehouse had been, he stopped and explained what it looked like, its function, and told the tales tell of Derwood Noble's hanging and subsequent smoking.

Clara raised her hand. "Does Derwood Noble still haunt this place?"

Carswell gave her a questioning look, and then shrugged. "We have a resident ghost, as I'm sure you know, and some think it's him. Witnesses place Noble's ghost here where the old smokehouse was, in the attic where Virginia found the skeleton, and around the old cemetery." He turned. "If you will follow me, I'll now take you to the family cemetery." He led the group down a slight slope to a decorative, rusted, iron, waist-high fence enclosing an area with knee-high grass partially concealing tomb markers in various states of deterioration. "This cemetery dates back to the 1840s. A number of my relatives are buried beneath these weathered tombstones. As I mentioned earlier to Virginia and Natalie, a few graves have no markers. The original ones may have been wooden and decayed away many years ago. We don't actually know who's buried down there. I'm even not sure if Mr. Noble's remains are here or not."

Marlene Bauer, a woman in her early sixties, with gray hair and a round figure glanced around, and then frowned. "So, is it Noble who cursed your family or someone else?"

Carswell leaned on a tombstone. "To be honest, I don't know. My grandmother thought so, but an aunt said it was an old woman who lived in a hut at the back of the ranch in an oak forest. My aunt said the woman was a witch, but I don't believe that. A neighbor said there are stories about an old woman who lived in the area who made herbal medicines. Most actually worked. In any case, my aunt and my neighbor said the stories they heard were that my family did something to the old gal and she cursed us. So, whether it was Noble or the old woman who cursed the family, all we know for sure is, there *is* a curse on the family. It's the one I told you about in the attic before Virginia made her unusual find." Carswell looked at the women. "Any questions?"

Daniele Webley asked, "Could the old witch be buried here?"

"I don't know."

Natalie raised her hand. "Do you have any idea who Virginia's skeleton really is?"

Carswell shook his head and shifted his weight to his other foot. "The sheriff asked the same thing. None whatsoever. That was a total surprise. I'm not sure the sheriff deputies fully believe me, but Virginia finding it was a shock. At least it's an old skeleton, no one from the retreat." He glanced at his watch. "Getting to be time for dinner. Let's head up to the house and get ready." He led the women toward the main house.

Natalie poked Virginia as they followed the group up the slope to the house. "You buying his not knowing about your skeleton?"

Virginia wrinkled her nose. "No. And from where we were standing, did you notice the fresh disturbance of some of the soil in the cemetery?"

"Yeah. But only when I stepped closer to you. Where the others were standing, you couldn't see it. Maybe he's been looking for something."

Virginia looked over her shoulder at the cemetery. "Could be he's trying to figure out who the freeloaders are in the cemetery."

"Possibly. According to the Internet, this ranch wasn't here before 1840. Could the cemetery be older than the ranch?"

"Like I said, he could be trying to see *what* exactly is buried in the unmarked graves." Virginia chuckled. "Or, like the one at the Haunted House ride in Disney World, maybe the cemetery, story of Noble's hanging, and the curse are all for the entertainment of guests."

Natalie stopped and picked up a weathered arrowhead. "Looks like there were Indians around anyway."

Virginia stopped. "I just thought of something."

Natalie turned and walked a few steps back to Virginia. "What?"

"What if there is more going on here than anyone suspects?"

"Huh?"

"Fresh dirt in an old cemetery. A mysterious human skeleton in the attic. Strange stories from the late 1800s. Then, did you notice his expression when Daniele, Clara, and Harriet asked questions? Interesting."

"You're not thinking Carswell is a crook, are you?"

Virginia shrugged. "Probably not. Just my imagination having fun with me."

"You think there's something between Carswell and those three women?"

"Possibly. Maybe you and I should look into that. Let's catch up with the others. I'm hungry."

Natalie followed a few steps behind Virginia. She glanced at her arrowhead. "Maybe Virginia is on to something," she mumbled to herself.

CHAPTER 6

After dinner, Virginia went to her room to prepare for the paper piecing class she was teaching the next morning. She set up her display boards on the desk and bed. She carefully spread out her examples on the floor and reviewed her notes. "Okay, let's get this last-minute prep out of the way. It's been a long day." She cleared her throat and started to practice her presentation when the phone rang. "Now what?" She stepped to the phone by the bed and answered it. "This is Virginia."

"Guess what I found?" Natalie sounded excited.

Virginia plopped onto the bed. "What? More arrowheads?"

"No. I found out some interesting information."

"You going to make me guess?"

"Yes."

Virginia sighed. "Okay, Carswell already knows Harriet, Clara, Daniele, and Helen Chandler."

"You're good. But I discovered how he knows them. Clara is his cousin. Harriet worked on the ranch a few years ago, Helen is a close friend, and Daniele owned a country store that sold him supplies and equipment. She sold the business when her husband died, and she retired."

Virginia scooted up on the bed and leaned against the headboard. "How'd you come across all that in such a short time? The Internet?"

"Partly. I saw Helen Chandler in the parlor. She was quite upset about the skeleton and the sheriff's people being here."

"I bet. She and Carswell put this retreat on together."

"Yeah, and Helen confided in me that Harriet and Clara were last-minute sign-ups and told me who they were. Daniele is a yearly attendee. I verified it on Google."

Virginia sat straighter. "Wow. You've become a female Sherlock Holmes."

"Thank you. Now what do we do?"

"I'm preparing for my paper piecing class tomorrow morning. After class, let's get together and do some planning."

Natalie sounded hopeful. "You're going to investigate after all?"

"I didn't say that." She heard Natalie rustling some papers.

Natalie's voice lowered. "Shoot. It'll have to wait until noon. Tomorrow morning, I have two classes I'm registered in."

"Okay, see you at noon at the cafeteria." Virginia hung up. She leaned her head back and stared at the ceiling. *Okay, Virginia, there's more going on here than just a quilting and knitting retreat. But what? We have a skeleton no one knew about or won't admit to knowing anyway. Then there're the women in attendance who know Carswell. They might be quilters or knitters and being here is just something they wanted to do since they know Carswell. But why were they on the ranch tour if they've already been here? Then, this joint is supposed to be haunted, maybe by a neighbor who was murdered a century ago. Good story but ghosts don't exist. Strange digging in the cemetery? Maybe, maybe not. Something is funny, but what? The sheriff is looking into the skeleton so...?* The phone rang, jolting her back to reality. She leaned across the bed and answered it. "This is Virginia."

"Virginia." Carswell's voice sounded strained. "I need to see you. Can you come to the cemetery?"

She glanced at the clock radio by the bed. "It's eight-thirty. I'm preparing for my presentation tomorrow. Can it wait?"

"No. There's something I need to show you."

"It's not about that skeleton in the attic is it?"

"Yes, and... more. Please come, I don't feel well, and I'm afraid I may be next." He hung up.

Virginia sat staring at the receiver. *More? He may be next? Next what?* She slipped off the bed, pulled on a t-shirt and jeans. She grabbed a flashlight and headed out for the cemetery.

As she approached the dark cemetery, she saw two lights moving around. When she hurried toward them, one bounced toward trees in the distance and disappeared. The other light seemed to be stationary on the ground facing a tombstone.

"Mr. Carswell," Virginia called. She broke into a run, hopped over the rusty iron fence, and darted to the source of the light. *I hope there are no rattlesnakes still awake.* She stepped through weeds and around pieces of broken headstones, and then stopped. On the ground was Carswell, unmoving, a flashlight by his side. Virginia stepped carefully closer and knelt, feeling his neck for a pulse. *Shit, he's dead.*

She looked in the direction the other light had gone. It was dark. *Who was here with him? Why'd he call me?* Virginia swung the light at his outstretched arm. She opened his hand and noticed he was clenching an emerald the size of a tennis ball along with what appeared to be a very old lap quilt and an old coin. Rising, she swung her light around looking for footprints or disturbed earth. Nothing was visible. *Maybe there will be something when it gets light.* Virginia frowned. *I need to call the sheriff again, but what's with that jewel and the lap quilt? I think he was trying to tell me something. That's a huge emerald egg. Where did he get that?*

Virginia examined the tombstone Carswell's light was illuminating. The raised letters said Mrs. June Cochran. Born February 26, 1795 in Alexandria, Virginia. Died June 27, 1887. *The old gal lived to be 92, a real feat in the eighteen hundreds.* Virginia stepped away and paced. *Okay, Virginia, you've discovered a skeleton and a dead body in the same day. The sheriff won't like this. But you've got that feeling in your stomach again.* She pulled her cell phone from her pocket and pushed the speed dial for the Smithsonian Central Security Service Senior Special Agent Tom Mason's home phone.

He answered on the fifth ring. "Hello?"

"Tom, this is Virginia Davies Clark."

"Oh boy. Who'd you kill this time, or should I ask how many?"

"That's not nice. And, I didn't kill anyone. But I did find a dead body, and I need your advice."

"I'm sorry. Okay, you do sound distressed. Who died?"

"Colin Carswell." Virginia told Agent Mason about the retreat, the ghost, the skeleton, what Natalie had discovered, and about Carswell's body. She described the old lap quilt, the coin, the tennis ball size emerald, and Mrs. June Cochran's grave.

Agent Mason sighed. "Okay, that's interesting. That jewel. Does it look like it was mounted in something?"

"Huh? How would I know?" Virginia moved to the body and with a handkerchief, picked up the emerald and looked at it. "Yes, I guess so."

"Is it well polished?"

"Yes. It looks like it just came from Tiffany's."

"Virginia, that gem is rare. Hang on to it."

"Okay."

"Did you see any other gems?" Agent Mason asked.

"No. But it's dark out here."

"Be on the lookout for more jewels while you're at the ranch."

"Okay, I guess. Why?"

"The jewel is important. The quilt... describe it."

Virginia picked up the quilt and used the flashlight to inspect it. She described the quilt to Mason. "Is this important?"

"Yes." He mumbled what she thought was Nature's Jewel, then spoke again. "Both are important. Where you found them and the history makes me think the Smithsonian Central Security Service should take the lead in investigating this. You are my best agent and are on the scene, so you are now in charge."

"Where I found them? What history? Tom, I'm a reserve agent and I'm not on active—"

"As of right now you are on active duty, Special Agent Virginia Davies Clark. Is Ms. North there with you?"

Virginia hesitated. "Yes, why?"

"She's now officially deputized to assist you."

"Oh boy. She'll love that. By the way, the sheriff told me in no uncertain terms to bug off."

"Washington will inform the sheriff of your status and authority under several federal laws, and to give you all the cooperation you need. You are to investigate this crime, including the skeleton and… well… you know the rest."

Virginia wrinkled her brow. "If I may ask, why the sudden interest in all this? Again, what history?"

"It has to do with Emperor Maximilian of Mexico, and… well… let's say the laws about antiquities, international intrigue, and art smuggling, are involved. You'll sort it all out, I'm sure. And Virginia, please keep the body count down. Oh, you'd better call 911 and report the body, but keep the coin, gem, and quilt to yourself. I'll have the Smithsonian Central Security Service contact the local sheriff immediately. Let me know if I can help during the investigation. Have a nice evening." He hung up.

"Have a nice evening he says. It just went to hell and I've got a class to teach tomorrow morning. Goodbye sleep," she said to Carswell's body. Virginia gathered the quilt along with the coin and on her way back to the main house dialed 911. *This is going to get interesting. What's this all about? Emperor Maximilian of Mexico?* She shook her head. *How's Tom going to get the sheriff to let me investigate? He can't order them to stand down. And, I don't want to investigate, but I noticed no one asked me my opinion. My dear husband will blow a gasket. He thinks I'm at a nice safe quilting retreat with a bunch of women.*

The phone was answered on the first ring. "Williamson County 911, what's your emergency?" the voice said.

"Hello. I just discovered a dead body."

CHAPTER 7

The 911 dispatcher responded. "You found a... a dead... body?"

"Yes," Virginia responded.

"Are you sure the person is dead?"

"Yes." Virginia let out a frustrated sigh. "He's dead. Now I need the sheriff, a JP, and someone to take the body away. And probably the crime lab guys."

"What is your name and where are you?"

Virginia gave the dispatcher her name and the location. "I'll meet the deputies in front of the house and show them to the body."

"Are you safe?"

"Yes."

"I have deputies rolling. They'll be there shortly. Do not touch anything."

"Okay." Virginia heard the dispatcher hang up and looked around. *That went well. He didn't know the cops were just here about the skeleton. Probably won't get that lucky with the deputies when they arrive. Better tell Natalie and our organizer, Helen Chandler. Helen can figure out what to tell the attendees.* Virginia folded the gem into the quilt and stuck the coin in her pocket, then hurried back to the main house. She found Helen talking to a ranch staff member. She approached Helen. "Helen, may I talk to you for a minute?"

Helen smiled. "Of course, Virginia. What can I do for you? Need something for your class tomorrow?"

"No." Virginia pointed to a chair. "You might want to sit."

"Is there something wrong?" Helen asked as she sat in the upholstered chair.

"You could say that." Virginia swallowed. "There'll be sheriff's deputies all over this place shortly and probably tomorrow as well."

Helen looked confused. "Why?"

"I just found Mr. Caswell in the cemetery. He's dead. I called 911."

Helen stiffened. "He's dead?" Her eyes teared up. "What happened?"

"I don't know. He called me and asked me to join him in the cemetery to show me something. When I got there, I found him on the ground." *I'll leave out the part about seeing a second light, the big gem, and the quilt.*

"Ho... how did he die?"

"I don't know. I wanted to tell you before the police arrive."

Helen steeled herself and wiped a tear from her eye. "Thank you, Virginia. How did it happen? Heart attack? He was stressed lately."

"I don't know. Did he give you any idea as to what was wrong?"

Helen shook her head. "No. Not really. He just seemed uptight."

"I'll tell the sheriff's deputies when they get here. You sure you're okay?"

Helen took a deep breath and slowly let it out. "Yes, I'll be fine. I was thinking of the ladies here for the retreat. I think we should go on with the retreat if the sheriff will let us. The women have been looking forward to it, and I think Colin would have wanted us to continue."

Virginia nodded. "I agree. Also, you might want to tell Clara Paterson separately. She was his cousin."

Helen tilted her head. "Clara's his cousin?"

"Yes. His death might come as a shock to her, so telling her privately might be a good idea."

"Okay. I'll find Clara then call a meeting and inform the others."

Virginia nodded. "Good. I think I'd better go out front and wait for the deputies. While I do that, you can call everyone together and let them know what's happening."

Helen stood on shaky legs, and then gathered her composure. "You're right. That way we won't have hysterics or confusion." She smiled at Virginia. "Thank you again for handling this and telling me." She hurried to her office.

Virginia went to the house phone and dialed Natalie. When she answered, Virginia took a breath, and then said, "Are you sitting down?"

"Yeah. Why?"

"I just found Carswell dead in the cemetery and called the sheriff."

"You did what? Carswell? Dead? Two bodies in the same day?"

"Yes, Carswell. And only one actual dead body today. The other one was a skeleton. You might want to join me downstairs. I'm waiting for the sheriff and have some other news."

"Oh boy. By other news do you mean you've got a third corpse tucked away someplace?"

"No. I talked to the Smithsonian."

"Good grief. I'll be right down." Natalie hung up.

Natalie strolled into the front parlor a couple of minutes later. She stood next to Virginia who was watching the driveway from a picture window. "Okay, spill. What did the Smithsonian say and what about the retreat?"

"Helen is going to continue the retreat." Then she told Natalie what Senior Special Agent Tom Mason told her.

Natalie chuckled. "You're back in the saddle again. Can't wait for you to tell the sheriff. He's going to just love having you as the head investigative honcho now."

"Tom's going to do that somehow. Oh... there's more."

"You found the ghost haunting this place, too?"

"No ghost. You're now my deputy."

Natalie stiffened. "I'm your what?"

"Deputy."

Natalie shook her head. "I think I'll spend most of my time trying to control the ladies who wanted to investigate the skeleton. Now you've done it! You said, 'they could investigate if we found a fresh body.'"

Virginia's head snapped around. "I forgot about that."

"Not to worry. I'll go corral the ladies when Helen calls the meeting. You see to the local constabulary." Natalie looked out the window. "Looks like the boys in blue have arrived. Good luck. Oh, have you told Andy about this yet?"

"No. My dear husband isn't going to like it."

"You'll manage to sooth any troubled waters, I'm sure. Good luck with the cops." Natalie hurried out of the room.

Virginia walked out onto the front porch. She moved the emerald from the quilt to her pocket as she watched the police cars speed up the ranch access road and come to a stop with their lightbars, scanning red and blue streams across the building and trees.

When the first deputy stepped out of his car and looked at Virginia, he stopped. "You again? You make a habit of finding dead people? You found the body; right?"

Virginia gave him a big smile as she moved to the police car in the driveway. "Hello, Deputy. Nice to see you again. Yes, I found him. I thought you'd be off work by now."

He chuckled. "No such luck. I think you just like making me miserable."

"I like to spread good tidings around. As soon as your buddies come up here, I'll take you to the body of Colin Carswell."

"Carswell? The owner of this ranch? He was with us when we came to see the skeleton today."

Virginia nodded. "Yep. He's the guy."

"His body is in a graveyard? They have one here?"

"It's a cemetery, not a graveyard."

The deputy adjusted his service belt. "Same thing."

"No. A graveyard is attached to a church. A cemetery is free standing."

"You don't say. I didn't know that." The deputy looked around. "Okay,

Carswell's body is in the... cemetery that's on the ranch, right?"

"Yes, Mr. Carswell is there. At least he was when I left him." Virginia noticed the other two deputies coming up. "Get your flashlights, gentlemen. The body is this way." *So far so good.*

Virginia stood at the iron fence watching the deputies set up poles with large spotlights attached and run power cords from the nearest shed. The crime lab van had arrived. The technicians were busy taking pictures, picking up various things, bagging them, and taking measurements. Detectives were taking notes and had just finished interviewing Virginia when another sheriff's officer arrived. He had captains' bars on his uniform. He walked to the fence under the large lights the deputies had installed and motioned to the original responding deputy and another detective to join him. Virginia watched as a heated discussion followed. The captain waved a couple of documents and repeatedly pointed at Virginia. The detective motioned for Virginia to join them. She walked to the group. "Yes? What do you need?"

The captain handed her the documents he was carrying. "This is a federal court order, and these are documents instructing the Williamson County Sheriff to turn this investigation, and that involving a certain skeleton, over to the Smithsonian Central Security Service, and you, Special Agent Virginia Clark."

Virginia took the papers. "This wasn't my idea."

The captain glared at her. "You found the body, so I find that hard to believe."

"I called my superior because I found Mr. Carswell's body. I wanted to let him know so he wouldn't get blindsided." She glared at him. "And, Captain, I don't care what you believe."

His face muscles tightened. "I don't like your tone, young lady."

Virginia rested one hand on her hip. "Tough."

"You could be a suspect."

"Obviously, Washington doesn't think I'm responsible for the killing. And, according to the federal court and some obscure federal regulations, I'm now in charge; get over it." The Captain grumbled under his breath. "I'll have you know I don't like this one bit. But if you're now in charge, how do you want to proceed? I have the JP on the way. We do have jurisdiction on that part of the investigation."

"I know. He acts as coroner in this county." She narrowed her eyes. "Tell you what we're going to do. Since you have been so *nice*, Captain, I want your team to continue to do the investigation and work with me. I think I can do more good digging into things around the retreat and the ranch as a participant in the event being held here. These ladies will be nervous talking to the police and probably won't share as much with you as they will with me because I'm one of them. I'll also determine where they all were this evening. I can talk to the ranch hands, too, and move freely about without causing as much alarm as your deputies would. Also, we work together; your people give me everything they come up with and I'll share what I learn with them. When *we* get to the point of an arrest, the sheriff's department gets the arrest and the credit."

The captain stood silent, then stuttered. "We... work together and get the arrest and credit?"

Virginia nodded. "You also handle the press. I'm not good with that."

He looked at the detective and the uniformed deputy. "I like what she said and... we don't have much choice." He smiled at Virginia. "We can live with that. You're a strange fed. Usually they march in and want to take over and we have a major pissing contest. Sometimes we lose and get scraps. I like your plan."

Virginia sighed with relief. "Who will be my main point of contact?"

The captain motioned at the detective. "This is Detective Jon Alverez. He is the lead detective on this case and will work with you."

Virginia looked down at the documents in her hand, then back at the captain. "You know that skeleton I found this afternoon is included with this murder investigation."

The captain tensed. "We haven't determined that as of yet."

"You treat all suspicious deaths as homicide until proven otherwise, right?"

"Yes. After we look at the body, I'll ask the JP to get an autopsy. The Austin ME will do it. As soon as we get anything definitive from them, Detective Alverez will inform you."

Excited, Virginia's hair bounced around her shoulders. "Great."

The captain returned to his vehicle.

Virginia pulled a card from her pocket and handed it to Alverez. "Here is my cell and office phone numbers. I scribbled my home number on the back. Call me any time." Alverez slowly took her card then gave his to her. "We'll be back in the morning to get a better look at the crime scene in the daylight. Let's touch base then."

"Okay but make it about eleven. I have a class to teach in the morning."

"You have a class to teach?"

Virginia waved her arm at the main complex. "Yes. This is a quilting retreat. I'm an instructor."

"Oh. I was wondering why you were carrying that quilt."

Virginia looked at her hand. "Ahh... right. Quilting class." She turned as Natalie rushed to the yellow police tape and called her. "Please tell the deputy over there to let that lady in."

Alverez motioned to the deputy who raised the tape.

Natalie hurried to the group. "Helen has informed the ladies about Mr. Carswell. Things went pretty well. How are you doing?"

"I just made a deal with the deputies. We are now involved with the case."

Alverez tilted his head. "Wait. We? What does that mean?"

Virginia nodded. "She's my deputy. This is Ms. Natalie North."

"Deputy?" Alverez looked Natalie over, and then smiled. "Detective Jon Alverez. I'm the sheriff's lead detective on the case and will be working with Virginia, and I guess you, on this." He stared at her for a second. "Aren't you that actress that moved here a couple years ago? You caused a lot of commotion with some of the women and church groups around here."

"Yeah, that's me." Natalie yawned. "Can we let the JP and your folks finish what they're doing tonight and talk in the morning?"

Alverez cracked a smile. "Sure, but after Virginia's class in the morning." He looked at Virginia and Natalie. "Can I get a copy of your schedules so I can coordinate mine with yours?"

Virginia nodded. "Sure. We'll give you copies tomorrow along with a list of attendees at the retreat and the names of the ranch staff."

"Good. Do you want me to talk to the group tonight?"

"No. We took care of that already."

"You did? Okay. I'll get back to my people and see how we're doing. The JP just arrived. I'll see to him as well. See you tomorrow." He turned and walked toward the cemetery.

Natalie watched the detective walk away then looked at the quilt under Virginia's arm. "Where'd you get that? I don't remember you having it earlier."

Virginia sighed. "I took it from Carswell's hand along with a huge emerald. They thought this lap quilt was for my class. I'd better hide it and the gem before anyone asks questions."

"What Emerald?"

Virginia pulled the huge green emerald from her back pocket and showed it to Natalie. "This one. From what the Smithsonian said, it's valuable but also a clue to something. By the way, what do you know about old gems?"

"Not much, but I can learn." Natalie walked beside Virginia toward the ranch house. "Just a note, you stole the lap quilt and that jewel from the crime scene. That's not too legal."

Virginia glanced over her shoulder at the deputies in the cemetery. "Carswell obviously wanted me to do something with them, so I... liberated them."

"Right. Like I stole... liberated... an old Ford from under the nose of the police and feds in our last case, *Secret Threads*."

Mysterious Threads

"Yeah, like that." Virginia nodded. "I'm the lead investigator, so I can do that."

"You weren't at the time, but I guess all is well now."

Virginia chuckled. "Now, do *you* have new developments on this case since we spoke earlier? Oh, did I mention Tom said the skeleton I found in the attic is part of the investigation, too?"

"Simon is part of this?"

Virginia stopped and gave Natalie a questioning look. "Who's Simon?"

"That's the skeleton's name. Simon Cochran. He's related to the woman buried in the cemetery back there, and to Colin Carswell."

CHAPTER 8

The next morning Virginia moved around her classroom giving instruction on paper piecing of half-square triangles. She used her display board with detailed, step by step illustrations and provided a long strip of half-square triangle paper grids to each participant.

"You layer two fabrics, right sides facing together; then pin the grid paper on top through the fabrics. Be sure to pin in the blank areas so they don't cross the dashed or solid lines." She watched as the ladies followed the directions. "Okay, good. Now set the stitch length on your machines to about fifteen stitches per inch. This'll make it easier to remove the paper when we're finished." Virginia helped a couple of women with their sewing machines. "Now we stitch continuously along all the dotted lines following the direction of the arrows first. Unroll the fabric as you sew. When you get to the edge, stitch along the 1/8" edge to the next diagonal line." She watched as the women completed their sample. She had them move to the three cutting tables and rotary cut along all the solid lines. "Plan to cut the longest lines first leaving it all in place and cut as many sections as possible before separating."

Virginia looked at each quilter's progress. "Now separate pieces and finger press the paper along the seam line." Satisfied of their progress she continued, "Tear the paper from the center out to prevent loosening any stitches at the ends." She walked around the cutting tables looking at their work. "Good. Now move to the ironing boards and separate the pieces so the dark side is up. Lift the dark triangle and press on the right side. The seam will lay toward the darker fabric."

She continued to show them how to arrange the pieces and why it was important to oversize. The women practiced making more example pieces in different fabrics.

By eleven o'clock the class was finished. She remained to answer questions and was packing up when she noticed Detective Jon Alverez standing in the back of the room. "Hello, Detective, any news?"

Alverez smiled. "That was interesting. I do have a question. Why do it?"

"To get sharp corners and make designs with tight tolerances."

"Oh. Okay. I've admired quilts but didn't realize what went into making them."

Virginia chuckled. "My husband says we take fabric, cut it up, then sew it back together, and make designs."

"It's a lot of work. But the results are works of art."

"Thank you, Detective. That was a nice compliment for the quilters. Now, why are you here? Results from the Austin Medical Examiner already?"

Alverez shifted his weight to his left foot. "Where is your... deputy?"

Virginia looked at her watch. "She's getting out of her class about now. We were going to meet in the cafeteria. Want to join us?"

"Yeah. This way we can all catch up together." He walked beside Virginia.

He just wants to see Natalie again. "So, you've got the autopsy results? How'd you do it so fast?"

"My captain put a rush on it. I've got preliminary results. The full report is a day or two away. I've also got some information about that skeleton you found."

"You do?"

"Yes. It's the skeleton of a man in his late fifties with severe arthritis. The doc said he would have had a lot of pain in his neck, back, hips, and especially his hands. His right leg was broken at one time but had healed well. It was obviously treated by a doctor. He was shot, but that wound wouldn't have killed him. There are traces of lead and arsenic in his bones, but not of too high of levels. The medical examiner thinks, he died sometime in the late forties."

Virginia cracked a smile. "We already knew that."

Alverez frowned. "You did? The deputies who responded to the discovery didn't say anything."

"That's because they wouldn't listen to me. The lead deputy thought I was an interfering crackpot."

"I'm sorry about that." Alverez gave her an apologetic look. "I'm glad you are so observant."

"You know the skeleton case and Carswell's murder are related."

Alverez stopped. "They are?"

"Yep." As they exited the building, Virginia pointed. "There's Natalie." She waved and hurried to catch Natalie with Detective Alverez in tow.

Natalie stopped and waited for Virginia and Alverez to join her. "Hi. How'd your paper piecing class go?"

"Great. It was fun and the ladies did really well," Virginia said.

Natalie smiled at Alverez. "Hello, Detective. What have you learned so far?"

Alverez motioned toward the cafeteria building. "Let me buy you two some coffee. I'll fill you in and then you can explain what the skeleton has to do with this case."

Natalie nodded. "Sounds good to me." She reached into her knitting bag and pulled out a set of papers. "Here are our schedules and the lists of participants here for the retreat and the list of staff and ranch hands." She handed it to Alverez.

He took the papers. "Thank you, I'll examine them later." After getting coffee and finding an empty table, they sat. Alverez folded and put the papers in his jacket pocket and pulled his notebook out. He cleared his throat and then explained to Natalie what the Medical Examiner found out about the skeleton, and that they sealed Carswell's office and the top floor of the house where he lived. He then continued, "Do you want to go through the office and his home?"

Virginia nodded. "Yes, we'll do that, and then have your forensics folks go over it, too. We'll wear the jumpsuits, booties, hairnets, and plastic gloves your boys left for us last night."

"Okay. Now to the business at hand. The M.E. said Carswell was murdered."

Virginia raised an eyebrow above her cup as she sipped her drink. "We already knew that."

"Yes, but now it's official."

"How was he killed?" asked Natalie.

"He was stabbed, but that's not what killed him." Alverez looked at the women's vacant expressions. "You don't seem surprised."

Virginia set her cup down. "He was face down in the grass when I found him. I obviously couldn't see any wounds to his chest or abdominal area. If he was shot, I would have heard gunshots. And there was no exit wound. Small caliber possibly, but that would require a head shot to kill him quickly. Also, when I went to check his pulse, there was no pool of blood or any blood for that matter on the ground. But he had phoned me just shortly before his demise and said he didn't feel well. I figured something else had to be in play."

Alverez glanced at Natalie. She shrugged her shoulders. "The M.E. said he was stabbed. There was massive internal hemorrhaging."

Natalie nodded. "Stabbing could do that. Was the knife still in him?"

"Yes. It was a six-inch single-edged knife. A common kitchen knife. Before you ask, we checked, and no knives are missing from the kitchen. But that's not what caused the bleeding."

Natalie's eyes narrowed. "Okay, what killed him then?"

"When he was stabbed, he was already dying from poison."

Virginia stared off into the distance, then leaned forward. "Colchicine?"

Alverez sat back. "Yes, he had been given a lethal dose of colchicine. He also had cranberry juice and ginseng in his system. The M.E. said those two substances will enhance the effects of the colchicine. He was surprised Carswell made it that far before dying. What made you guess that?"

Virginia let out a sigh. "He said he wasn't feeling good when he called me and said he was afraid he was next. Also, s simple stabbing probably wouldn't cause a major internal hemorrhage unless the weapon hit an artery or a big, blood-filled organ like the liver, spleen, heart, or a kidney. A knife wouldn't affect a lot of organs at once either. The lack of a lot of blood on the ground meant the knife was still in him or he would have bled all over the place where I found him. The knife acted like a cork. Is the ME checking on his medical history to see if he was taking that drug already and someone just increased it?"

"The ME is checking. I'll let you know what he finds." Alverez finished his coffee. "So, we've got someone stabbing the poor guy in his cemetery while he's hemorrhaging internally, and his organs are shutting down from the effects of the colchicine. He was concerned about being next. Why?"

"It's related to the skeleton," Natalie said, pacing Alverez jerked around. "How? We don't know who the skeleton is or why it was here."

Natalie rested her hand on Alverez's. "The skeleton's name is Simon Cochran. He was related to June Cochran and to Mr. Carswell as well."

Alverez stared at her. "You... you found this out about the skeleton since last night?" He turned to Virginia. "You guessed Carswell was poisoned by colchicine? Who are you two? I thought I'd surprise you with what the ME said so far. You two are already ahead of me on this."

"Yes." Natalie patted his hand and smiled. "That's why we're helping you, Detective."

He swallowed. "Do you two happen to know who stabbed him?"

Virginia shook her head. "Not yet. But this implies there were either two killers or one who was very impatient. Another question is why?"

"I agree." Alverez scribbled in his notebook. "How was the skeleton, Simon Cochran, related to June Cochran and to Carswell? I see the connection to June."

"Don't know that either."

Alverez looked at both Virginia and Natalie. "Do you know where I can find June Cochran?"

"Yes." Virginia pointed toward the rear of the building. "She's buried in the cemetery out back. That's where I found Mr. Carswell. June Cochran died in 1871."

Alverez set his notebook on the table. "Wonderful. That lead goes nowhere."

"Not necessarily. Carswell's cousin is also here at the quilting and knitting retreat."

"His cousin?" He made an entry in his notebook. "Who's that?"

"Clara Paterson. She was in my class this morning," Virginia said.

"We need to talk to her."

Natalie leaned back in her chair. "Why don't Virginia and I talk to some of these ladies who've had a relationship with Carswell, both personal and professional. You start with the staff and ranch hands?"

Alverez pulled the papers Natalie had given him out of his pocket and looked at them. "Okay. We can cover more ground this way." He finished his coffee. "Anything else we should do at this time?"

Virginia slid her chair back. "Natalie and I are going to take another look at the cemetery. Your folks are done back there. I saw them taking down the crime scene tape earlier."

He chuckled. "Okay, but there isn't anything to find."

Virginia stood. "We'll see about that."

CHAPTER 9

Virginia and Natalie trudged through the tall grass, keeping an eye out for snakes.

Natalie eyed a thick patch of weeds near a small headstone and pointed. "I'd stay clear of that. I think something moved." She followed Virginia around a tree to the large, partly moss-covered, gray tombstone marking June Cochran's grave. She stopped and looked at the ground. "By the looks of the disturbed soil, this must be where you found Carswell."

"Yes. He was lying here facing the big monument with his flashlight aiming at it. He said he wanted to meet me here to show me something, but what?" Virginia stepped closer, knocked, and poked on a couple of the raised letter and number reliefs. She stood back and eyed the whole tombstone when she realized Natalie was missing. She glanced around then called out. "Natalie. Where'd you go?"

"Back here. Behind the grave monument. I've found something."

Virginia scooted around the large stone structure and found Natalie on her knees poking at the base with a stick. A loud cracking sound came from the foundation. A small rectangular block of stone popped a short way out. Natalie looked up. "I think I broke it."

Virginia rushed to Natalie's side. She scooped out dirt and tufts of dead grass and yanked on the piece of stone. It slid out about a foot. "How about that? The forensic folks missed this." Virginia and Natalie peered inside the hollow cavity. It contained a small leather bag and a sealed metal tube about six inches long and two inches in diameter. She looked at Natalie. "From the looks of these, they could have been here since 1887. I wonder if this was what Carswell wanted to show me."

Natalie sat back on her heels. "I don't know, but shouldn't we photograph this before we do anything else?" She jerked back hastily. "Do something about that enormous spider, will you?"

"Okay." Virginia swatted away the spider and the web. "You're afraid of spiders? It wasn't that big."

"You have no idea. I was bitten by a black widow when I was a teenager living in San Diego. That spider put me in the hospital, and it hurt like hell. I have no love for the critters. I don't like bugs of any type. And it was huge."

"I didn't know that. I'm sorry for teasing you." Virginia looked closer at the cavity. "There's something else in there." She slid the tube to the side and revealed a beaded object. "Maybe it's from some tribe of Indians."

Natalie eyed the beaded leather band. "This may be Iroquois or Mohawk, maybe Delaware Indians. The design and materials used doesn't appear to be the type of thing a local band from around here would use."

Virginia frowned. "You know this how?"

"I did a movie a few years ago that took place during the Revolutionary War in upstate New York. One of the technical advisors was a professor from Cornell University and a Mohawk. He told me about the Iroquois Nation and their history. I think he said they were all Algonquian. Not sure about that but that's what I recall. He took me to a couple of museums to see items from the Iroquois. It was quite interesting."

Virginia nodded. "I agree. I spent a lot of time in the Northeast with an archeological expedition my museum led. From what I saw there, this does look like Iroquois or Algonquian. One of the researchers said some of the Delaware joined the Algonquians and Iroquois a long time ago. I can have one of my archeologists from the Georgetown Museum take a look later. If necessary, we can send photos to the Smithsonian."

"Better photograph all this." Natalie held up her iPhone and took pictures of the monument, the stone box, and the contents in the box. She showed the images to Virginia then said, "I'll email them to you. I think we could call this documenting the find. Let's take these and vamoose."

Virginia nodded as she carefully removed the contents. "Let's get these to my room. We can examine them after we talk to the women who knew Carswell."

Natalie stood as Virginia slid the stone back into the monument. Natalie took the bag and the beaded band from Virginia. "Aren't we supposed to take them to the… war room the detective is setting up in the old barn? He called it a war room, didn't he? This stuff is evidence in a crime scene: right? And we're removing it? Is that kosher?"

"Yes, he did call it a war room. But I want to look at these things first. As for kosher… we aren't eating them."

Natalie frowned. "You know what I mean."

"Yeah. Removing them like we did is probably a police type no-no, but we did document finding them. I am the lead investigator and you are my deputy, so we're okay as long as we note where we found them, who has them, when we took custody, what we did with them, and document the actual location and the objects. You know, chain-of-custody stuff." Virginia looked around, then started for the house.

Natalie fell in step. "We'd better hide them well."

"We will. But first, we need to be discreet getting them to my room. Can't let it out that we found anything, at least not yet. We'll conceal them now and do a more detailed examination after we interview the ladies who knew Carswell. Maybe their comments will throw some light on these artifacts."

They hurried across the field to the main house. Virginia and Natalie entered through the kitchen door and gathered towels and metal trays with food items stacked on them to hide the articles from the grave. They nonchalantly walked through the first floor to the stairs and climbed to the second floor undetected. Then their luck ran out.

CHAPTER 10

Virginia stopped at the top of the stairs.

Natalie bumped into Virginia and looked around her. "Why'd you stop... oh, hi, Detective."

Detective Alvarez raised an eyebrow. "Now what have you two sleuths been up to?" He eyed the trays they were carrying. "Something you want to show me or are we having a snack in our rooms?"

Virginia brushed an errant piece of hair from her face. "We made a discovery, but we don't know what it means yet. We were going to examine the items, then bring them to the war room, especially if they pertain the Carswell's murder."

Natalie nodded. "Right."

He narrowed his eyes. "Where did you make this... this find?"

"In the cemetery." Natalie moved around Virginia. "It was inside June Cochran's tombstone monument. Your people missed it."

"Inside the stone monument?"

"Yep."

"I see. How did you... never mind. Why don't we take them to the war room now, and we all take a look at your— "

"Artifacts," said Virginia.

"Right. Artifacts. You two discover a new dinosaur or a lost tribe of Indians while you were at it?"

"No." Virginia sighed. "Okay, let's go to the war room and see if we can figure out if this stuff means anything to our case." She turned and followed Natalie down the stairs with Detective Alvarez behind her. They hurried out the rear door to the old, converted barn and to the large room Detective Alverez had made into a war room. A uniformed deputy opened the door for them to enter.

Natalie stepped into the well-lit room and glanced around. "Wow. What a transformation in such a short time. Mobile whiteboards, tables, computers, file cabinets, evidence lockers, storage lockers, crime scene wear, flashlights. Portable radios. Nice."

Mysterious Threads

Alverez leaned closer to Virginia. "Does she always talk like she's making a list?"

Virginia moved inside. "When she's impressed or stressed, yes."

"Oh." He took a breath. "Ladies, shall we spread out what you found on that table over there and download any photographs of the discovery site I'm sure you took?"

Virginia went to the indicated table and set out the items from the tombstone while Natalie downloaded the pictures from her cell phone into a computer on a desk. She moved the digital file to a folder marked Carswell Homicide and a case number.

Virginia placed the six-inch, sealed metal tube on a white plastic mat in the center of the table. On the right side, she placed the beaded-leather object. She set the small leather bag on the left side of the tube. "Okay, Detective, this is what we found."

He looked at the objects. "You didn't wear gloves."

Virginia swallowed, then straightened. "From the looks of the stone container in the monument, I think these items are over a century old. I don't think any fingerprints you would find on them are in any database."

Alverez shook his head. "You never know."

Virginia nodded. "Okay. We'll wear gloves."

Virginia turned as Natalie, wearing green rubber gloves, strolled up and handed Alverez and Virginia blue rubber gloves. "Thought you two might want these." As Virginia and Alverez put their gloves on Natalie retrieved a red toolbox and brought it to the table. She opened it and removed a small digital camera.

Alverez watched her then said, "How'd you know that camera would be in there?"

Natalie pointed at the label on the side of the box. "I read the label. I figured we might want to take better pictures and document what we find when we open this stuff."

Alverez eyed her. "You're good. Were you ever in law enforcement?"

"Me? No. I helped Virginia in the past with some of her cases. But I've been in a number of mystery movies and played cops, villain's girlfriends, suspects, and a witness. Some parts I got were better than others. I guess I picked up a few things along the way."

Alverez's breathing became shallow and quicker. "I bet you were really good in them."

Natalie chuckled. "I tried to be. Sometimes people remembered my lack of costumes more than my acting."

"Huh?"

"My directors gave me the skimpiest or tightest uniforms they could get away with. They didn't spend a lot of money on my costume design." She winked at him.

"Oh." He smiled. "Maybe I should rent some of the movies... for background."

Natalie leaned close. "Detective, you get a lot of back and front in them, trust me. Now, do you want me to act as photographer while you two open this stuff?"

Virginia leaned against the table and crossed her arms. "If you two are done with the movie talk, let's get to work." She peered into the toolbox. "Any masks in there?"

Alverez frowned. "Masks?"

"When we open that tube, no telling what might come out. Maybe nothing or germs that have been waiting over a hundred years to make someone sick."

Alverez turned toward a cabinet. "I'll get surgical masks."

With their masks and gloves on, Alverez picked up the length of beaded leather and examined it. "What do you make of this? Indian?"

Virginia nodded. "Most likely Algonquians or Iroquois. Maybe Delaware Indian. I can take it to my museum and have one of our anthropologists who is an expert in this area take a look."

Alverez pursed his lips. "Okay, but you must follow established chain-of-custody rules."

"Right." Virginia looked across the table at Natalie taking notes. "You're our scribe?"

"Yeah." Natalie held up a tape recorder. "I didn't see a digital recorder, just this small tape recorder, and its batteries are dead. I thought about using my phone but that means it would need to be kept as evidence. Ain't going to happen."

"Okay. Let's see what's in here." Virginia pulled the leather bag toward her and carefully undid the ties. She turned it and slid the contents onto the table. An old Mexican Peso rolled around before coming to rest next to a thick folded document. A medium-size ruby rolled a couple of inches away next to a gold Maximillian gold coin. "That's quite a combination."

Alverez looked at the collection of items. "That it is. Large ruby, a Mexican Peso, a gold Maximillian coin, and some old documents. What's all this got to do with our murder and the skeleton?"

Virginia rubbed her forehead. "I don't know. Maybe the documents will shed light on it."

He cocked his head. "Virginia, your agency, the Smithsonian something or other jumped on this like a fly on—"

"I know. What do they know that we don't?" Natalie started photographing the items on the table.

He crossed his arms. "Yes. What are you holding back?"

Virginia cleared her throat. "Okay. The Smithsonian Central Security

Service told us to get involved. They knew I found the emerald and stuff at the time of Carswell's death. I'm guessing it has something to do with the Maximillian's lost treasure, and... well... the laws about antiquities and art smuggling." She waved her hand over the items on the table. "According to my superior at the agency, it has great significance to the United States and Mexico. This may be more information that could be the reason for the murders or be something entirely different. I'm guessing whatever we find we must keep secret until we complete this investigation."

Alverez's jaw dropped. "Significance to the United States? Secret?"

"Yes. And Mexico."

He shook his head as if to clear cobwebs. "What emerald? What other stuff? There's more you haven't told me about?"

Virginia gave him a blank stare. "Oops."

Natalie stopped taking pictures and moved closer to Alverez. "We have a coin and the huge emerald, Detective. It was with Carswell in the cemetery when he was killed. That, and a quilt. We have them in our rooms. We haven't had time to examine them yet. They might not have anything to do with this case. He may have had the quilt because of the retreat."

Alverez plopped onto a chair. "This is getting... complicated. You two are... exasperating to say the least. Those items are evidence in a murder investigation." He flexed his fingers. "Okay, one of you go get the other gem and the quilt and let's all look at them here. They, and this stuff on the table will be locked up here under guard when we're done." Virginia started for the door when he stood. "Maybe I should send a deputy with you."

Virginia looked over her shoulder at him. "Not necessary. I'll be right back." She rushed out the door.

Alverez glanced at Natalie. "With you here, I doubt she'll do anything too crazy."

Natalie grinned. "Don't bet on it. Why don't you come and sit on that sofa over there with me while we wait for Virginia?"

Alverez swallowed. "Okay." He followed her and sat. "Tell me how you found a way into that tombstone and the things inside."

"I found a section of the base that looked funny. Like it was a separate piece of stone. I found the trigger that opened it. Virginia wrestled it the rest of the way out. A stone box slid only partway out, and we examined it. The materials on the table were the contents."

"I see. Well, good job." He fidgeted in his seat. "When Virginia gets back with the jewel and quilt, we'll add them to our collection and take a look at all the evidence at once. Maybe there's a correlation."

"Maybe we should just document them for now and spend our time talking to the people here at the retreat with a direct link to Carswell before they change their stories or get together and come up with some plausible group fiction."

"Good idea. Are you always such a skeptic?"

"No, but I watch detective shows on TV and worked with Virginia before. Anything can happen when she's around."

"I've noticed." After another few minutes, he glanced at his watch. "What could be keeping Virginia?"

Natalie started to get up when they heard a shot fired outside.

CHAPTER 11

Natalie and Alverez dashed outside. Near the corner of the building, Virginia and a uniformed deputy stood looking at the ground, both with guns in their hands.

Virginia glanced at Natalie running toward her and pointed at the ground. "Rattlesnake."

Alverez reached them and looked where Virginia pointed. A large, coiled, dead rattlesnake rested in some ankle-high grass. Alverez looked at Virginia. "You shoot it?"

She shook her head. "No. The deputy saw it as I was approaching. He shot it. It looked like it was ready to strike, and I was its intended target. It didn't rattle." She looked at the deputy. "Thanks. You saved my life." She replaced her pistol in her tan, LL Bean messenger bag.

The deputy holstered his weapon and nodded. "No problem, ma'am. That's why I'm here."

Alverez cleared his throat. "Now that's over, let's get that emerald and the quilt you're carrying into the war room." He smiled at the deputy. "Thanks."

The deputy straightened. "Glad I saw it before the lady got closer."

They all turned as women hurried out of the main house and ranch workers headed toward them.

The deputy stepped into their paths. "It's all over, folks. Just a rattlesnake. It's dead now. No one was injured. You can go back to what you were doing."

The ranch people turned and dispersed into various buildings.

Talking to each other, the women stood around in small groups. Virginia stepped over to Helen Chandler. "Helen, the deputy is right. Take the ladies back to whatever they were doing. The snake had me in its sights when the deputy shot it. There's nothing to see. I'm fine."

Helen took a breath. "Okay. I'm glad everything worked out and you're not hurt. Anything new in the investigation?"

"We have some leads, but we don't know what they mean yet. I'll keep you posted when we have something we can divulge. Now escort the ladies back to the retreat, please."

"I will." Helen rounded up the women and herded them back inside.

Alverez led Virginia and Natalie inside and watched Virginia place the gem and folded quilt on the table. "This is what Carswell had with him when you found his body?"

Virginia nodded. "Yes, the quilt and this emerald. It's another gem like the ruby from the tombstone."

"Did he have a cell phone on him when you got there?"

"I didn't see one, but I didn't search him. Your people would have it if he had one on him. They didn't find one?"

Alverez shook his head. "No."

Virginia patted the quilt. "Want to unfold it and see what it looks like?"

Alverez flexed his fingers. "Yes. This could be critical."

He reached for the folded quilt when Virginia slapped his hand.

He jerked his hand back. "What did you do that for?"

"It's old and it's a quilt. It's been folded for a long time. We need cotton gloves and we must be careful, or we could destroy the threads used in the quilting or the fabric."

Alverez sighed. "Okay. Natalie, will you see if there are any cotton gloves in that cabinet, please?"

Natalie rummaged through three boxes before finding the gloves. She handed Virginia and Alverez theirs and she slid hers on. "Looks like we're ready. Virginia, you're the quilter, do the honors."

Virginia carefully unfolded the old quilt. The vibrant purple, green, turquoise, yellow, red, and blue colors seemed to leap off the fabric. The large quilt covered the top of the table and slightly hung over one side. Virginia gasped. "This is the Nature's Jewel. It's also known as the Fiesta Jewel quilt."

Alverez frowned. "The what?"

"It's an old design, but this one was made for the emperor of Mexico, Maximilian." Virginia bent closer examining the quilt. "I've seen paintings of it."

"This along with the gem and coins must be what Carswell wanted to show you." Alverez kneaded his forehead. "But what does it mean? What does this have to do with his murder?"

Natalie cleared her throat. "It is probably related to Simon's death, too."

"Who?"

"Simon, the skeleton we found in the attic."

"Oh yeah, right. But why would these things cause a… make that two murders?"

The uniformed deputy who had been guarding the war room stepped closer to the table and looked at the quilt. "This quilt was actually made for Empress Carlota, Maximilian's wife. Some of the threads are made of gold and silver. See? It is very valuable." He pointed at the elaborate quilting.

"Emperor Maximilian made arrangements to get his vast wealth out of the country. At the end of his reign, he knew that the ports were in rebel hands and the countryside was rife with banditry, so he thought it too risky to take his wealth directly out of the country overland or by sea by normal routes. Instead, he chose four Austrian officers and about a dozen Mexican loyalists to take the loot up north and through Texas to the port of Galveston. It was part of fifteen ox-pulled wagons full of ten million dollars of gold, silver, and jewels. The wagons took a zigzag course while heading north to avoid pursuit. They sent the caravan to Texas for safety. But they never made it to Galveston or any place else. The fortune was hidden someplace and never recovered."

Alverez titled his head. "How do you know this?"

"I am originally from Morelia, Michoacán in Mexico. I learned about it in school."

"Oh. Thank you, Deputy Sanchez. That's good information. Anything else?"

"No, sir."

Virginia refolded the quilt. "This will need more study, but now we have some other things to do."

Natalie stepped around the table and touched Alverez's arm. "Why don't Virginia and I go talk to the ladies? You talk to the ranch hands and some of the volunteers with the retreat. We can lock this stuff up for now. Also, you might want that nice young deputy, who is probably bored to death, to follow up with your forensics folks and find out what they may have learned."

Alverez raised an eyebrow. "For a civilian, you sure know how to get these procedural things in order fast."

Natalie smiled at Virginia. "I learned from the best. Shall we have the nice deputy who shot the snake lock this stuff in the cabinet while we get started?"

"Okay." Alverez gave the deputy instructions as Virginia and Natalie headed for the retreat buildings.

They walked across the open area between the buildings. Virginia mounted the steps to the rear porch and turned toward Natalie. "I'll start talking to the women. Why don't you send their names and addresses to Senior Special Agent Tom Mason at the Smithsonian Central Security Service for a background check? Also see what you can find about them on social media and the rest of the Internet."

Natalie gave a slight nod. "Okay, but wouldn't the sheriff's office be doing that?"

"Probably. But Tom can get the information faster because the SCSS is a federal agency. You're good with a computer. Being a knitter and quilter, you might spot something the police would miss. Maybe something about Empress Carlota's quilt that will turn up."

"Budding quilter. I see what you mean. I'll get right on it."

Virginia smiled. "Be sure to preface your message to Tom with the fact that I haven't requested any bodies be removed... yet."

Natalie chuckled. "I'm sure that'll motivate him. Where are you going to be?"

"In the parlor. I'll go round up the ladies. Come down when you're through."

"Okay." Natalie hurried through the door and up the stairs.

Virginia walked into the building and found the women just leaving their quilting class. *I'm glad there are only thirty women here for this retreat. Makes finding someone easier.* From the signs next to the doors, Virginia could tell which class each woman had taken. Helen Chandler was leaving the class on resizing quilt blocks. Down the hall, Clara Paterson exited the room where they were discussing and demonstrating the various uses of quilt notions, tools, and supplies like rotary cutters, threads, and quilt rulers. Harriet Fisher walked out of a room carrying a stack of papers and cloth where they were learning how to design a quilt on graph paper. Daniele Webley and Marlene Bauer were studying the Accordion Fabric Wallet. They were all heading in Virginia's direction. She hastily attached her SCSS gold badge to her belt, and then stopped the group. "Hello, ladies. Can we all go to the parlor? I need to speak with you."

Clara Paterson frowned. "Now? I want to call my husband."

"Yes, now. You can call him later. I have you all together now and there aren't any classes for an hour."

"Well, this is quite an—"

"I can call the deputy outside and have him take you to the sheriff's office in Georgetown until we question each of you. That will take a lot of time and will be more inconvenient for you. And, I'm sure you wouldn't like the accommodations."

"I don't see why you're trying to make Virginia's job harder, Clara," said Harriet Fisher. "We could be facing the sheriff's detectives for the questioning in Georgetown and miss other classes. At least Virginia is one of us and is trying to make it easy on us." She looked back at Virginia. "Your paper piecing class was great. I was afraid to try it, but not anymore."

"Thank you." Virginia gestured with a small spiral notebook she had taken from her bag. "Shall we all proceed to the parlor?"

They all shuffled down the hallway into the parlor and sat in upholstered chairs facing the fireplace. Marlene Bauer glanced around. "Good thing this room is empty. Otherwise we might be on our way to the sheriff's office."

Virginia stood in front of the stone fireplace and cleared her throat. "Okay, now, where was each of you all last night between eight-thirty and nine o'clock?"

Clara spoke in a soft voice. "Was that when Colin died?"

Virginia nodded. "Yes."

"I was..." She frowned. "I was in the kitchen, getting something to eat about then."

"Was anyone else in the kitchen with you?"

"No. Wait... the cook came in as I was leaving. I remember because she seemed upset about something needing replacing."

Virginia made some notes. "Good."

Marlene twisted in her seat. "I was in my room with Daniele Webley. We're roommates. We were preparing for the class we will be jointly teaching."

Virginia turned slightly. "Okay. You Harriet?"

"I was... where was I? Oh, yeah, I was in the barn with James Doughty. I was helping him fix a tractor."

Virginia made more notes then glanced curiously at Harriet. "Are you a mechanic?"

"Not really. I was raised on a ranch and we had a couple fussy tractors. My dad taught me to fix them. I was giving James a hand. The carburetor just needed cleaning."

Virginia scribbled in her notebook then looked at Helen Chandler. "Your turn, Helen."

Helen stiffened. "I was in the office doing paperwork."

"Can anyone vouch for you?"

"Like an alibi?"

Virginia sat on the fireplace hearth. "Yes."

"I... no." She slumped in her seat. "I was alone." She gazed up at Virginia. "I had the small TV on for company. There was a show on the Hallmark Murder and Mystery Channel I liked. It was Murder 101. It was the episode where Amy Winslow goes to Seattle to give a talk. It's my husband's favorite series on that channel. He likes the star who plays Amy."

Virginia smiled. "Thank you all for your cooperation. I'll talk with each of you individually soon. Do not leave the retreat early without my permission. Now I need to check on something." She rose. The others followed suit and meandered out of the room.

Virginia started to leave the parlor when Natalie walked in. Natalie strolled to a couch and plopped down. She patted the seat. "Sit. I've got news."

Virginia stepped to the couch. "That was fast."

"Yeah. I talked to Special Agent Tom Mason like you asked. He's thrilled you haven't killed anyone yet."

"Very funny. What else did he say?"

"I gave him the information I had on the ladies and he said something about running them through NCIC, CODIS, the U.S. Marshal's Warrant Information Network or WIN, the FBI, Homeland, the CIA and INTERPOL."

Virginia stared at Natalie, then coughed. "CIA and INTERPOL?"

"Yes, and Homeland, too."

"I can understand NCIC, CODIS, FBI, and WIN, but why Homeland and especially the CIA and INTERPOL? That seems like over-kill."

"I asked the same thing. He said he's being thorough as there are national security issues at play. I think he knows more than he's telling us at this point. He said he'd forward what he gets to both of us."

"Okay. Did you have time to do your own computer check on the Internet?"

"Yes. Before we came, my boyfriend, Professor Jeff, put more memory and new search software on my laptop computer. I just entered their names and told the new program to do a background check on them."

Virginia sat waiting.

Natalie leaned back and smiled. "Hey, this couch is really comfortable."

"Natalie!"

Natalie's emerald-green eyes sparkled. "You want to know the results of the search?"

Virginia rubbed her head in exasperation. "Does the sun rise in the east?"

"Last I checked." Natalie chuckled. "Okay, here's what I found on each of them." She wiggled in her seat. "I need to get one of these couches. You know something, if you dig deep enough, no telling what'll turn up on someone."

CHAPTER 12

"I guess you're right. We all have skeletons in the closet." Virginia chuckled. "And skeletons in the attic, like here. What did your new computer program find? Anything useful?"

Natalie nodded. "For starters, I ran a check on Mrs. June Cochran. I didn't expect much as she died in 1887. But I got some information I thought was interesting."

Virginia leaned forward. "What was it?"

"She was a personal friend of both Presidents Lincoln and Andrew Johnson."

"She was? Interesting since she lived in Texas, but so what?"

Natalie sat back and grinned. "In 1864, Emperor Maximilian was installed as the monarch in Mexico by the rich, elite class and with support from Napoleon III of France."

Virginia lifted one shoulder in a semblance of a shrug. "What does it matter? We already know Maximilian was removed from office and shot after he tried to get his wealth out of Mexico. We have what may be Maximilian's wife, the Empress Carlota's quilt locked in the war room."

"Right. I'm getting there. Remember what Deputy Sanchez told us about Maximilian's treasure? Old Max was rich when he went to Mexico, but while his rule was brief, he managed to obtain a lot more wealth. An American blockade of the Mexican Gulf ports in 1866 initiated by Andrew Johnson was an attempt to drive the French out of Mexico. Napoleon III capitulated to the Americans and left Maximilian in Mexico to fend for himself. The emperor had very little support among the people outside the few aristocrats, and without French military support, his days were numbered. After the French withdrawal, Empress Carlota went to Europe to seek assistance for her husband's regime among the various crowned heads of Europe. She even went to Pope Pius IX. She found no one to help her. Carlota never returned to Mexico and suffered a mental breakdown. On June 19, 1867, Maximilian was shot by firing squad."

Virginia arched a speculative eyebrow. "It doesn't sound like Carlota knew where Maximilian's treasure was hidden."

Natalie rubbed her palms on her pants. "No, Carlota didn't know. No one in Mexico knew. Now comes the real interesting stuff. Our little lady, Mrs. Cochran, was a secret emissary for the United States and President Johnson. During her confidential dealings with France and Mexico she discovered that the treasure was believed to be somewhere in the U.S. Both Mexico and France wanted it. President Johnson said if it was in the U.S., it was ours. He needed it so he could repay the treasury for the Civil War costs. He commissioned her as a U.S. Marshal, to find the treasure. She was seventy-two when she started looking."

"I'm surprised she could get around very well at her age in the middle 1800s." Virginia wrinkled her nose. "The president made Mrs. Cochran a U.S. Marshal? Why didn't he use the Secret Service or the army to locate it?"

"I don't know. There are no records of them looking. Maybe the president wanted to keep it secret and by having her look for it alone allowed him to maintain secrecy better. Anyway, U.S. Marshals had a lot of authority in those days."

"Makes sense. And, U.S. Marshals still do."

"There's more. Later, she died in New England and her body and possessions were sent back to Texas per her prior instructions to her son. There were rumors in Washington about it, but the treasure was never found. Copies of her diary and field notes mysteriously vanished."

"Where did she die in New England? She left burial orders with her son? Did she expect to die?"

"In western New York State. Someplace along the Genesee River. As to her health and subsequent death, yes, she knew she was dying. Mrs. Cochran had consumption or tuberculosis as we call it today. She even pre-ordered her headstone. In a letter, she told her son to put the things we found into the hidden compartment. She didn't tell him why, but I think he knew."

"Oh. That may explain the Iroquois or Algonquian beaded article we have. She went that far north knowing she was dying? That's dedication." Virginia sat back spellbound. "Wow. This sounds like a thriller or spy novel. Here I thought she was just an old Texas gal who was born in Virginia. Did she find the treasure?"

Natalie grinned. "Now comes the really, really good stuff. There was a note sent to her son that hinted that she had located it."

"Who would have guessed? She found it?" Virginia sat quietly for a moment, then grinned, opened her notebook, and scribbled. "Did the note give any ideas as to the location? Maybe it's where she died."

"No. I thought it would be in Texas, not New York. But the note did say she'd take the information to her grave. She didn't even tell her son."

Virginia frowned. "To her grave?"

"Yep, and we found the secret container in the tombstone with stuff in it and we have what Mr. Carswell was going to give you. Also, don't you have her original diary? I think that's a start."

"Yes, we do have the diary." Virginia put her hand to her chest. "We may have the location of Maximilian's wealth right here. Someone else may have discovered the same information you did and is also looking for the treasure. I might have interrupted the killer trying to get whatever Carswell had to show me. We need to find the killer and the treasure fast."

Natalie beamed. "My thoughts exactly."

"Anything on the other ladies?"

"Yep." Natalie looked around. "I could use a cold beer."

Virginia gave her an exasperated look. "Really? Now?"

"Yes. But I'd settle for a cool Dr Pepper, especially if you're buying."

"They're free here and you know it!" Virginia stood and sighed. "Okay. You're not going to tell me anything until we get you your drink. Let's go to the kitchen. I'll get one, too. It's getting hot." She started for the kitchen when she suddenly stopped. "Didn't Mrs. Cochran hang and smoke Derwood Noble with the rest of the beef in her smokehouse? That's what her diary said."

Natalie nodded. "That's the story."

"The story was that he wanted the ranch and tried to force her to sell it. But when?"

"Probably before she set out on her adventure."

Virginia steepled her fingers with a searching look. "Or, maybe he knew about her commission as a U.S. Marshal and was trying to get the treasure. Maybe she killed him when he tried to get the treasure for himself." She stood. "Let's get our drinks and put together what we now know."

Natalie rose and started for the kitchen when her cell phone buzzed. She pulled it out of her pocket and glanced at it. "My room! Now!" She took off toward the stairs. Virginia hurried behind her. "What's wrong?"

"Someone just entered my room and is fiddling with my laptop. It's still doing the background checks."

Virginia pulled her gun from her messenger bag and rushed past Natalie. She bound up the stairs to Natalie's room. The door was slightly ajar. Virginia released the safety on her pistol and nudged the door open. She quickly stepped inside and swept the gun around as she inspected the area then looked in the bathroom and closet. No one was there. Natalie's computer hung by its power cord with a corner of it resting on the desk chair. The bedroom window stood open with the curtains billowing in the breeze. "The room's clear."

Natalie rushed past Virginia, scooped up the computer, and examined it. "It's still running the program. I had it locked so whoever was here didn't get anything."

"By the looks of things whoever it was must have heard us coming and fled." Virginia took notice of a disturbance outside and went to the window. Below, the uniformed deputy was holding a struggling woman by the arm. Virginia called down to him. "Hold her, Deputy. We'll be right down." She turned, put her pistol back in her bag, and walked to the door. "Finish the background check while I deal with the intruder."

"You know who it is?"

"Not sure, but Deputy Sanchez has her in custody."

"Good. I'll come down when I've got everything."

"Okay." Virginia went to join the deputy and the woman.

Inside the war room, Deputy Sanchez had handcuffed the woman to a chair. He sat on the edge of a table a few feet away. "What were you doing jumping out of a second-story window?"

She glared at him.

"Look, Agent Clark is on her way. She's going to ask the same question. Make things easier on all of us and just answer the question."

Virginia bound into the room and skidded to a stop. "Thanks for apprehending her, Deputy. Clara? What's going on? Why were you in Natalie's room?"

Clara's face scrunched in defiance. "You wouldn't understand. It's a family thing."

Virginia set her bag on the table and pulled out a chair. She turned it around and sat resting her arms on the wooden back and studied Clara Paterson, a fiftyish woman with white hair, about five foot three inches tall and 155 pounds. "Look, Clara, we're investigating two murders. Family thing or not, I need to know what you were doing in Natalie's room. You know, if she had been there when you broke in, she probably would have shot you."

Clara swallowed. "Okay. I'm sorry about going into her room. Colin's mother was my mother's sister. Colin Carswell was my cousin."

Virginia gave her a soft smile. "I know."

"You do?"

"Yes. Go on."

"Well… Colin inherited this ranch and an endowment from what was left of our grandmother's estate. I got a slightly smaller share of the inheritance and no ranch. That didn't matter." She tugged on the handcuff. "I don't know anything about running a ranch and what I did get was generous enough. I never have to work again. But Colin phoned me a month ago and said he discovered something about our long-dead relative, June Cochran."

"Did he say what it was?"

"No. Just that he found something that could be valuable to the right people and asked me to come to this retreat."

"What did he mean, that it could be valuable to the right people?"

"I don't know. When I talked to him last night, he said he wanted an expert's opinion and was going to show it to you before he did anything." Clara raised her handcuffed arm slightly. "Do we really need these?"

Virginia smirked. "Take them off her, Deputy. She isn't going anywhere." She waited while Deputy Sanchez released Clara. He stood a few feet away as Virginia continued. "Okay. So why were you in Natalie's room?"

"I heard Ms. North say she had some program on her computer that could look up stuff about people and things and she had left it running while she was talking to you. I went to see what, if anything, she had found out about me or whatever Colin had found."

Virginia nodded. "Okay. Thank you. That information is confidential until we sort all this mess out. Do you know anything about a treasure?"

"Treasure? Around here?"

Virginia nodded. "Maybe. Family lore perhaps?"

Clara shook her head. "Sorry. No. There are stories about some Indians who lived here back in the day and some artifacts have been found, but no treasure."

"Thank you. Remember, you can't leave the ranch without my permission. I'm sure you understand."

"Yes." Clara hung her head. "I'm sorry I broke into your friend's room."

Deputy Sanchez sat on the corner of the table. "When did you and Mr. Carswell get this inheritance?"

Clara rubbed her forehead. "It was about... eight or nine years ago."

Virginia frowned. "Clara, what can you tell me about Simon Cochran?"

"Who?"

Virginia let silence hang in the air.

"Simon Cochran." Clara slumped in her seat. "It's been a long time since I heard his name. He was a great uncle of Colin's on his father's side of the family. He disappeared in the early 1950s or so after the war. As I recall, he was discharged in Watertown, New York at Pine Camp, or what's now Fort Drum, as a captain in the army. I was very young when I saw him last, but I remember Simon being a nice man. I remember that he was inquisitive about the old days on the ranch. Why do you ask? Did you locate him?"

"Yes. He's the skeleton in the trunk I found in the attic. He was murdered."

Clara jerked back, her hand thrust to her heart. "My God. Simon's been in the attic all this time? Murdered?"

"Looks that way." Virginia took a breath. "Now that Colin Carswell's dead. Who inherits this ranch and the other items in his estate?"

Clara sat looking at the floor. "Poor Simon." She looked up at the deputy, then Virginia. "I'm sorry, what did you ask?"

"Who gets Mr. Carswell's estate now that he's dead?"

CHAPTER 13

Clare sat staring at Virginia. She swallowed. "I guess I do." She sighed. "My inheriting the ranch kind of makes me a big suspect in Colin's death then doesn't it?"

Virginia glanced at the deputy, then at Clare. "If I were you, I wouldn't plan any trips in the near future."

Clare's eyes took on a haunted look. "Should I get a lawyer?"

"You are not under arrest and we are not questioning you about Colin's murder, yet. If I were you, I would call one. Do not say anything to anyone without consulting a lawyer. I wouldn't say anything to the other ladies either. Oh, and don't leave the ranch without my permission." Virginia looked at the shocked deputy. "You see any reason she can't go now?"

He slowly shook his head. A look of disbelief formed on his face. "Ahh, no she can go but stay on the ranch."

Clare stood and looked at Virginia. "Thank you." She slowly walked out of the building.

Deputy Sanchez watched Clare shuffle out of the building then turned back to Virginia. "Why did you tell her to get a lawyer? Why tell her not to talk? We may need to question her later."

"Well, we didn't exactly read her the Miranda Rights, did we? She wanted an honest answer. I gave her one. She's scared. By being nice to her and truthful, I didn't alienate her. She'll be more likely to talk to me later than if we had been, by-the-book, with her now. Anyway, I don't think she did it."

Sanchez raised an eyebrow. "If you say so. You're in command." He glanced around the room. "Is there anything I can do to help besides guard this place?"

Virginia chuckled. "Kind of boring isn't it?"

He sighed. "You could say that."

"If you would, please get on that computer over there and dig up the history of this ranch. Also, dig up what you can find about Derwood Noble. He is supposed to have died here in the mid-eighteen-hundreds. He was allegedly hanged and smoked here on the ranch by June Cochran."

Sanchez grimaced in disbelief. "She hung him and then smoked him like a side of beef?"

"That's the story. Mrs. Cochran strung him up in the smokehouse." Virginia shook her head. "There's also the matter of some old woman who lived around here back then. She was said to be a witch."

Sanchez took notes. "Okay. I'd be happy to do it. Will this help find who killed Colin Carswell?"

"It may well do that. It may also help direct us to Emperor Maximilian's treasure. I think that is what is behind Colin's murder."

Sanchez's face brightened. "I'll get right on it."

"Okay." Virginia rose and walked out of the building.

Halfway to the main house she spotted Harriet Fisher. Virginia waved, and hurried toward her. "Harriet! Have you got a minute?"

Harriet stopped and turned. "Hi, Virginia. How's the investigation going?"

"We've uncovered a few leads. Do you have time to talk to me?"

"Yes. I just finished a class on binding variations. I'm free for a couple hours."

"Good. Let's go sit on the back porch. Those rockers look comfortable."

They walked to the porch and sat in two wooden rocking chairs facing the hills beyond the yard.

Virginia shaded her eyes with her hand. "That looks peaceful and beautiful."

Harriet set the large cloth bag she was carrying on the floor next to her and ran her hand over her dark hair. "Yes, it does."

Virginia estimated that Harriet was in her late 50s and stood about five-foot-five. She watched Harriet get comfortable, then said, "You're a quilter and a knitter, aren't you?"

"I've been a quilter for eight years, but I'm a new knitter. That's why I'm here. I like to get new tricks for quilting and I'm learning more and more about knitting. I'm looking forward to your friend Natalie's class."

"Yes, her class about making felted purses will be fun." Virginia's face turned serious. "I have a question. You worked on this ranch at one time, didn't you?"

Harriet stared off at the ranch, then slowly nodded. "Yes. I was single. My maiden name was Raineau back then. I'm sure you'll look it up. I met my husband while working here. Now I'm a housewife and the mother of two boys. They're in college now. Before you ask, I live in Cedar Park, Texas."

"I see. When was it that you worked here?"

"About twenty years ago. I've stayed in touch with Colin all these years. He was a good man. Honest. Hard-working." Her eyes teared up. "He always treated me nice and paid me probably more than I was worth. I had an abusive relationship with a man back then. Colin kind of rescued me and gave me a chance to recover and feel good about myself."

Virginia stopped writing and put her hand on Harriet's arm. "I'm sorry about your bad relationship. No woman should have to go through something like that. What happened to him?"

"I don't know. One night he came around drunk and threatened me. Colin heard him and came to my aid. Colin took him away and I never heard from him after that night. I never asked what happened, if that's what you were going to ask. I figured it was my good fortune."

"Okay." Virginia settled back in her rocking chair. "Can you tell me about anything that may have occurred around here back then that might have seemed out of the ordinary?"

"No." Harriet rubbed her forehead. "Wait, there were occasions, nights, when I'd see lights out by the cemetery." She pointed. "Sometimes there'd be lights down by the oak forest. And there were times Colin would lock himself in that old barn for hours. No one was allowed inside."

"Do you know why?"

"Not really. I got a quick look one day when I took him his lunch. There were maps pinned to the wall and papers on a large table in a small room in the rear."

"Maps of what?"

"I'm not sure. I know some were old, and he had modern roadmaps alongside of them." Harriet paused and closed her eyes for a moment. "I remember seeing what may have been large jewels and a gold coin on the table. There was a leather-bound book there, too. I just got a quick glimpse."

"Can you think of anything else?"

"Well, he did go on an extended car trip once. He was gone for two weeks. Never said a word about it when he returned. I thought that was strange. I asked, but he always changed the subject."

Virginia made notes, and then looked at Harriet. "Any stories about the old days on the ranch?"

"Colin told stories about the old witch. She was the one who put the curse on anyone who harmed Mrs. Cochran." Harriet took a breath and slowly let it out. "The witch and Mrs. Cochran were friends, at least that's the story."

"Did the witch have a name?"

"Yes, but I don't remember it. I think it started with an L." Harriet wrinkled her brow in thought. "Oh, yeah, one more thing. According to Colin, the witch disappeared in the late 1880s. I don't know if she moved or died." She gave Virginia a sheepish look. "That's all I remember. It was a long time ago."

"I realize that. Not a problem." Virginia rocked the chair for a minute. "What did you do here on the ranch?"

"I was kind of an all-around hand. Mostly I fixed things. Some of the male ranch employees didn't like it, but I was good with machinery. Like I said before, I was raised on a ranch and could fix tractors, trucks, cars, and machinery. Did a little welding and electrical stuff, too."

Virginia stood. "Thank you for telling me all this. If you think of anything else, please come see me."

Harriet stood and picked up her cloth bag. "I will. I hope you find Colin's killer."

"We will, trust me." Virginia watched Harriet slowly walk inside the building. Virginia walked down the steps into the yard when she heard Deputy Sanchez calling from the door of the war room building. She hurried to him. "What is it? Did you find something?"

"Yeah. I got some dope on Derwood Noble. He's in a few government databases besides Google and the normal search engines the Sheriff uses."

Virginia raised an eyebrow. "What government databases?"

"Well, since you said he died in the mid-1800s, I tried the US Army and the US Marshal's Service first. Figured if he was wanted back then for anything, they might still have the records."

"Okay, what'd you find?"

Sanchez glanced at his notes. "Derwood Noble was a gambler and made a circuit around Texas and as far north as Dodge City. He ventured into Mexico on occasion. He was also known to be a killer. A gun for hire. He had been a Confederate officer as well. A major."

"Quite a resume. Anything useful?"

"I don't know. But it seems he had connections south of the border. The old guy worked for the Mexican government as some sort of agent. The U.S. Marshal in Laredo had a warrant for Noble's arrest for the murder of a U.S. Government assayer."

Virginia shifted her weight to her other foot. "Did your database say exactly when he was killed?"

"No. It seems he dropped off everyone's radar between 1868 and 1872. There is nothing after that." He gave her an expectant look. "Was that helpful?"

"Oh, yeah. Good job. I think I know why he was murdered. Any luck on the witch?"

"Not much." Sanchez flipped the page in his notebook. "There were some old newspaper articles and according to an obscure historical record, there was an old woman who lived nearby who was a recluse and an herbalist. She was also a healer of sorts. She cured a number of people of ills the local sawbones couldn't. That didn't go over well with him. Of course,

Mysterious Threads

in those days if you were different than other people in the area, and a woman, you were victimized. She was called a witch, especially by some of the clergy, in the area."

"What happened to her?"

"I don't exactly know. Stories say she moved to a forest on or near a ranch where the owner protected her. She was supposedly killed by a wandering ex-confederate."

Harriet thought she may have moved or died. The dead part agrees with what the deputy said. Virginia gave Sanchez an impatient look. "Got a name to go with this?"

"No. Her surname started with an R. Rain something or other. She was referred to by some as The Witch Doctor. Before you ask, I don't know when she died or the exact ranch where she lived other than it was near here."

Virginia rubbed her forehead to hide her disturbed expression. *Harriet said the witch's name started with an L. Where'd the R come from?* "Anything else come up about her?"

"Only the curse."

Virginia looked at Sanchez with wide eyes. "Curse? You wait for last to tell me about a curse?"

He gave Virginia a questioning look. "You realize curses aren't real, don't you?"

"Of course, but back then they were real to a lot of folks. What's the curse?"

"It is some silly thing that says anyone who harmed the ranch owner or his or her descendants would die a horrible and painful death."

"Nice. Just what we need. Anything else?"

Sanchez shook his head. "No. That's it. Was it useful?"

"Yes. I think Derwood Noble was killed to protect Maximilian's treasure."

"Did Mrs. Cochran actually find it?" Sanchez slid his notebook into his pocket.

Virginia nodded. "I think so." Sanchez's eyes widened. "Where is it?"

"That's what Colin Carswell's killer wants to know, and so do I."

"What's the plan now?"

"We call Detective Alverez back out here and compare notes." Virginia looked around. "I'd better go find Natalie. Will you call Detective Alverez? Tell him I'm on to something." She started to turn then stopped. "Do you have the key to the locker in the war room with the evidence?"

"No."

"When your night replacement comes, does he have a key?"

"No. Detective Alverez has the only key."

"Okay. Find out when Alverez can get back out here. I'm going to find

Natalie." Virginia headed back toward the house watching Sanchez out of the corner of her eye. *Looks like he's calling Alverez now. Natalie and I need to do some rapid computer work, get our hands on the diary, the thick folded document that was in the tombstone, and Carlota's quilt.*

CHAPTER 14

Virginia sat on a padded chair facing Natalie who was sprawled on her bed holding her laptop computer.

"I asked Deputy Sanchez to round up Detective Alverez," said Virginia. "We need to compare notes. Then you, Alverez, and I need to take a close look at Mrs. Cochran's diary, the thick folded document that was in the tombstone, the letters she sent to her son, and Carlota's quilt."

Natalie set her computer on the nightstand next to the bed. "Good idea. By the way, while you were busy, I got to have an impromptu conversation with Marlene Bauer."

"Good. Marlene's one of the ladies I was going to question."

"Right. She's a knitter and a budding quilter. She's jointly teaching a knitting class in two days. She's in her early sixties and a widow. Marlene taught high school history and took early retirement due to a back injury."

"Good to know. Does she have any history with the ranch? Did she know Colin before coming to the retreat?"

Natalie slid backward and leaned against the headboard. "Yes. And even more interesting is that she helped him with some historical research. She said Colin was researching the story about old Max's treasure and she provided some details and documents."

Virginia sat spellbound. "Was she specific?"

"To a point. She helped him over an extended period of time, so some of the early work she doesn't remember very well. But she remembers locating old maps and archive research about the area around here." Natalie gave Virginia a funny grin. "But we don't need to go to New York."

"We need to find those maps." Virginia leaned forward. "What do you mean, we don't need to go to New York? Why?"

"No. It seems Mrs. Cochran went there to investigate one of the confederates who manned the treasure wagons. He was one of the injured men who escaped the Indian attack and slaughter. The others stayed in Texas and died, but he fled to New York. He died years later. Mrs. Cochran was extremely sick by then and after talking to the gentleman, she sent her notes home to her son. She died right after that. In her letters, she said the treasure is not in New York. It's here in Texas."

Virginia rose and walked in a circle. "Did the letters say where in Texas?"

"That information is in her diary and the quilt and folio we found in her tombstone."

"That document we recovered that we haven't looked at yet?"

Natalie swung her legs off the bed. "Yes, at least I think so."

Virginia stopped pacing. "I need to tell Alverez."

"There's another tidbit that you should know."

Virginia frowned. "Oh? What tidbit?"

"Remember the witch?"

Virginia nodded. "Yeah. The one Deputy Sanchez said her name started with an R and Harriet said an L."

"Harriet was right. The witch's last name was Lerfervre. Isabelle Lerfervre. It seems the old gal was French, not Hispanic."

"French?"

"Yep. As we know, she was a friend of Mrs. Cochran and lived close by. Isabelle was an herbalist and a healer. Isabelle had briefly studied medicine in Paris, France, before coming to this side of the big pond. She disappeared. One story is an ex-confederate officer killed her when she couldn't fix up a couple of his men. The tale says the officer met a drastic and painful death because of some curse. You don't suppose that ex-confederate officer is Derwood Noble, do you? And Mrs. Cochran was the curse?"

Virginia chuckled. "I'd bet on it. You got all this from Marlene Bauer?"

"Some of it. Starting from what she told me, I was able to glean more from my computer. I also cheated and called Tom at the Smithsonian Central Security Service. After I assured him you hadn't killed anyone, yet, he had their people do some digging."

Virginia glanced out the window. "Looks like Deputy Sanchez is leaving, and a new deputy is taking over guard duty. According to Sanchez, the new deputy doesn't have a key to the evidence locker either. I saw Sanchez make a call when I left him. I asked him to contact Alverez. I wonder if he did."

"You didn't mention anything about knowing where the treasure is, did you?"

"No, because I don't know." Virginia leaned against the wall next to the window. "I'll call Alverez and see if he's on his way here."

"Good idea." Natalie stood up. "I'll change for dinner." Virginia dialed Alverez. The phone went to voice mail. Virginia cleared her throat and spoke. "Detective, this is Virginia. I don't know if Deputy Sanchez was able to contact you or not. I'd like a brief conference with you on what we've

Mysterious Threads

discovered and see what you've managed to find. Compare notes. Please give me a call so we can set a time. Probably tomorrow as it is close to dinner time now."

Natalie looked over her shoulder from the closet. "I thought you wanted to see the materials in the locker tonight."

"I do, but it will be late."

"So, what? You have what... two classes to take tomorrow? What time is the first one?"

"Ten."

"Good, if he can come early tonight then we get to assess what we've got and still be up in time for class."

"Okay, I'll ask him when he calls back."

Natalie pulled a pair of slacks and a blouse from the closet. "Good. As soon as I change, let's go to dinner."

"Maybe I should change, too."

"You look great as is. Now sit tight while I slip into these duds."

After dinner, while it was still light, Virginia and Natalie hiked around the cemetery examining the various tombstones.

Natalie pointed out a couple whose faded dates were around the same time as Mrs. Cochran's death. Natalie stooped and looked at an engraving on a headstone. "I wonder who they are."

"What're the names on the monuments?" Virginia peered over Natalie's shoulder at the latest discovery.

"They're mostly too weathered to make out. If necessary, we could do rubbings. They might help read the names." Natalie pointed at another tombstone. "Look, here's a cute one."

"A what?"

"This says, 'Here lies James Baure, the second-fastest draw in the county'."

Virginia chuckled. "Someone had a sense of humor."

Natalie stood to her full five-foot height. "Remind me again why we're traipsing around in the cemetery."

"We're looking for a grave that does not seem to belong here. Maybe more than one."

Natalie examined grave markers as she walked to the end of the row of tombstones. She bent over and looked at one. "Like this one?"

Virginia caught up with Natalie and looked where she was pointing. "Yes."

Natalie knelt. "Here's one from about that time in question, the lettering is faint, but I can read it." She cleared dirt off the worn lettering. "You're going to love this."

"Why? Who is it?"

Natalie looked up. "Isabelle Lerfervre."

"Are you serious?"

"Yes. The witch is right here. Who would have guessed?"

"If you hadn't done your research, we would never have guessed who this grave really belonged to. But I'd like to know if there're other people under the other tombstones or if the treasure is buried here."

Natalie rose and brushed grass off her knees. "Want to dig it up?"

"We'd need a court order."

"Think you can get one?"

"Probably not."

Natalie looked toward the buildings. Her face brightened as she eyed the man walking to the war room. "He's the evening deputy? Nice."

Virginia yanked her cell phone from her pocket. "It's Detective Alverez." She answered the phone. "Hello, Detective. What can I do for you?" She listened as they walked back toward the main house. "Okay. I'll be there in a couple minutes." She hung up.

Natalie waited, then gave an exasperated sigh. "What did he say?"

Virginia stuffed the phone back in her pocket. "He's here and wants to compare notes."

"Good."

They walked into the parlor as Alverez entered. Virginia waved him inside. They moved chairs into a tight circle and closed the pocket doors. Virginia sat back. "Okay, Detective, what have you got?"

Alverez opened his notebook. "I did a background check on Colin M. Carswell. He was squeaky clean. He hadn't had so much as a traffic ticket. No wants or warrants. He owned the ranch outright. No loans. His bank balance was substantial but there are no signs of illegal or unusual activity. He wasn't in the military. His taxes are all up to date."

Natalie fidgeted in her seat. "So, he was a good guy."

Alverez nodded. "By all the available records, yes. But there is one little fact that stands out."

Virginia raised an eyebrow in speculation. "What's that?"

"I can't find any record of him before 1995. Nothing. No military records, no government-issued licenses, no school records, no tax returns, no passport, no birth records, nada. He's a ghost."

CHAPTER 15

Virginia frowned. "If he's a ghost, how'd he get a Texas driver's license or open a bank account?"

"That's the interesting thing. "There are records of a Colin J. Carswell who has the same birth date and has a college degree from Texas A&M. Even got a birth certificate. He has a life and work history and is also squeaky clean. It also mirrors Colin M. Carswell. From fingerprints, the FBI says Colin J. Carswell and Colin M. Carswell are the same guy and have the same Social Security Number. He also owns this ranch. The guy we have at the Austin morgue, his driver's license says Colin Carswell. It has no middle name or initial, but the photo on it matches the photos on records for both Colin J. Carswell and Colin M. Carswell." Alverez shook his head. "In my book, something about this stinks. Who the hell was this guy?"

Virginia crossed her ankles. "Maybe he was in the U.S. Marshal's witness protection program and when they relocated him, they gave him a new identity."

Alverez shook his head. "That doesn't work. The marshals would give him a completely new name and a traceable background. He'd get a whole new identity all the way back to the doctor who delivered him."

"Could be the FBI is right, and Colin J. Carswell and Colin M. Carswell are one and the same."

"Probably." Alverez shrugged his shoulders. "Maybe somewhere along the line just made a clerical mistake on his middle initial and it's in the records as a second person. It'll stay in the records forever. That's happened before."

"That makes sense."

He frowned. "I wonder how the IRS handles it."

"Good question. Maybe they have the right guy in their system." Virginia looked at her notes, then leaned forward. "I have a question for you, Detective. Do you know the name of the woman they called the witch who was around here back in the mid-1800s?"

Alverez gave Virginia a blank expression. "No. I don't think anyone does."

"We do," said Virginia. "Her name was Isabelle Lerfervre. She was French and a friend of Mrs. Cochran."

"Oh? French? How'd you figure that out?"

"Our outstanding investigative skills and the Smithsonian Central Security Service. We believe she was killed by Derwood Noble, Major, CSA."

Natalie nodded. "We thought Noble tried to muscle in on Mrs. Cochran's hunt for the treasure, but now we think his killing Isabelle Lerfervre was another of the reasons Mrs. Cochran killed him."

Alverez shifted in his chair. "Why would Noble kill Isabelle if she tried to save his men?"

"Noble was an ex-confederate officer, a major, and could have been the officer in charge of Max's treasure train."

"If Noble was in charge of the treasure train, then he'd know where the treasure was."

Virginia pushed a strand of hair from her eyes. "Yeah, we thought of that, too. We think Isabelle found the men after the Indians attacked, and Major Noble wasn't there. When they died, the Major thought they told her where the treasure was hidden. Noble went ballistic and killed her. Maybe in a fit of rage, who knows? Then again, he might have tortured Isabelle and got the location of the treasure. The U.S. Marshal in Laredo had a warrant for Mr. Noble's arrest for murder of a U.S. Government assayer. He was definitely not a nice man. Mrs. Cochran got to him and was not happy about her friend being, murdered and she killed him."

"That's all assumption." Alverez shrugged. "I guess it could have happened that way."

"Yeah, it fits what we know," said Virginia.

Virginia glanced at the fireplace then back at Alverez. "As a sheriff's detective, do you have to know a lot about the history of the county?"

"Some." Alverez set his notebook in his lap. "I'm not a historian or a member of the county historic commission. There're some books on the subject in the Georgetown Library and at the Williamson County Museum. I think they cover some of it in schools around here, but I'm not sure."

Natalie nodded. "Out of curiosity, where are you from?"

He sat and looked at the women and smiled. "I'm from California, like you two."

Virginia tilted her head questioningly. "You know where we came from?"

"You bet. So, for your information, I was born in Fresno. After high school, I went into the army. Served as a military policeman. While in the service, I went to college and got a degree in psychology. After I got my degree, the army offered to send me to officer candidate school to become a commissioned officer."

Natalie leaned forward. "Did you go?"

"No. After eight years, I had enough and got out. I did two tours in the Middle East and one in Korea. True garden spots. If they wanted me to stay, why not send me nice places like Germany or France or Italy? No, they sent me to two hell holes. One was hot as hell and had huge bugs and madmen who wanted to kill me; the other was frigid. I was posted at forts in Kansas and Alabama, too." He rubbed his chin. "I got discharged at Ft. Hood and stayed in the area. I got on with the sheriff's office and have been here ever since."

Virginia sighed. "Interesting background. Thank you."

"I thought you would have checked me out before this. You can have the SCSS verify my story."

"I don't think that will be necessary."

Alverez leaned forward and asked expectantly, "Since your detective work on the witch is well above par, do you by any chance know where Ms. Lerfervre's buried?"

Virginia smiled. "Yes, we do. She's out back in the ranch cemetery. Would you like to see her grave?"

He looked at Virginia and Natalie and smiled. "All those years of people saying she was a witch when she was a healer and them not knowing who she really was, or where she was buried. How awful. Poor woman." He sat staring at his feet, and then looked up. "Yes, I'd like to visit her grave. You found her name and information about her. You gave her identity back."

Virginia reached over and touched his arm. "It nice to see someone who cares."

"That's why I do my job, ladies." He cracked a grin. "I try to give the dead a voice and closure to their families. I also like to bring the bad guys to justice."

Natalie nodded. "I'd be happy to take you to Ms. Lerfervre's grave now, if you want to go."

Alverez held up his hand and pulled his cell phone from his pocket. "Alverez." He listened. "I'm on a case." More listening. "Okay, I'm on my way." He disconnected. "I now have a second murder to contend with. The captain said since this one is primarily your investigation, I can go investigate this new case and liaise with you on this one. Looks like you two are on your own." He rose. "Can we take a quick look at Ms. Lerfervre's grave before I leave?"

Virginia and Natalie rose. Natalie nodded. "Follow me."

As they stepped away, Virginia called to him. "Detective Alverez, can I have your key to the evidence locker?"

He sighed. "Yes. You're the principal investigator. You should have had one all along. So, I'll give you mine. Maybe we can look at the stuff in the locker tomorrow. I'll call you." He took the key off his key ring and handed it to Virginia. "I'll take care of the key transfer paperwork at the station tonight."

"Thank you, Detective; Natalie and I appreciate it." Virginia watched Natalie lead Alverez out the back of the house. *Detective Alverez is a nice guy.* She hid a guilty smile. *I don't want to wait for maybe tomorrow. Natalie and I can look that the evidence tonight. The sooner I know more about this treasure, the sooner we'll be able to find Colin's murderer.*

After showing Alverez the grave and watching him leave, Natalie returned to the main house. She and Virginia went to Natalie's room. Natalie sat on the end of her bed. "Okay, the detective left happy... well maybe not happy. He liked seeing the grave but he's not looking forward to working the other murder and being the remote second investigator on this case. He isn't too thrilled." She eyed Virginia. "I don't like that funny grin. What nefarious thing are you thinking of?"

"You know me so well." Virginia leaned against the wall and gave Natalie a determined look. "I don't want to wait until *maybe* tomorrow to look at the materials in the evidence locker."

"You want to open it and look at the stuff inside tonight?"

"Yes, I've got the key, so why not?"

Natalie gave Virginia a disappointed look. "After all we've been doing, I was hoping for a nice evening with the other ladies here at the retreat."

Virginia bit her lip, the smiled. "That's a good idea."

Natalie raised an eyebrow. "You're giving up too easy. What are you thinking?"

"We still need to chat with Daniele Webley. If my memory serves me right from my computer search, she's a retired country storeowner and sold supplies and equipment to Carswell for years. She sold the business for a huge amount of money six months ago. Not sure if she is a quilter or knitter, but I remember someone saying she's a gardener, too."

"She's a quilter and a knitter. So, we casually chit-chat with the ladies, separate her from the others, and interview her?"

"Yes. She may have information we need. And she has a history with the ranch and Colin Carswell."

Natalie rose. "Okay. Let's go see if we can find her."

"Before we go, let's see if we got anything new from Tom at the SCSS."

Natalie stepped to her computer and accessed her e-mail. "Looks like he sent a file to both of us." She downloaded and opened it. "Oh boy, check this out."

Virginia peered over Natalie's shoulder as she opened documents. Na-

Mysterious Threads

talie read; "By the looks of these files, our skeleton, Simon Cochran, was quite the guy. He was a captain in the army as Clara said. According to this army report, he was discharged because World War II was over, and his severe arthritis would interfere with any future assignments. He had a degree in electrical engineering from Syracuse University, and after the army he worked at a few companies."

Natalie moved the cursor over the document. "Most of the companies are in the northeast, like Stromberg Carlson in Rochester, New York. But there is one in Austin, Texas. According to this other document when he was working in Austin, he lived there, and then moved to this ranch in late 1947. He disappeared around 1948 or 1949."

Virginia straightened. "So, Simon Cochran disappeared in '48 or '49. I have to think he was killed. Why?"

"Maybe this will help." Natalie pointed at the computer screen. "It seems he was very interested in Texas and Mexican history and Mrs. Cochran. I'm thinking he was after the treasure. Simon was discharged, or resigned his commission, in New York. Maybe while working there he learned of Mrs. Cochran's trip to New York tracing the confederate soldier there in the eighteen hundreds. He somehow found out what she learned and came back to Texas to look for the treasure. That got him killed."

"But by who?" Virginia paced. "We definitely need to talk to Daniele Webley. She's the last one of the ladies here that we need to talk to that knew Colin. Maybe she can shed some light on this. If that leads to nothing, then we have to extend our search for suspects. But Colin was killed during this retreat, so I think it's someone here."

"Daniele Webley's co-teaching the workshop tomorrow that Marlen Bauer is doing."

"That's right. They're roommates, too." Virginia picked up her backpack. "Let's go talk to the ladies and Daniele Webley. Maybe we can start during dinner." Virginia turned toward the window when she heard the deputy outside yelling and a shot fired.

CHAPTER 16

Virginia hurried to the window and peered out. Someone was running into the dark in the direction of the graveyard. The deputy sheriff stood outside the war room building with his sidearm drawn. He looked toward the graveyard and the forest behind it. Virginia opened the window and yelled. "What happened?"

He looked up at her. "I don't know for sure. I heard someone and came out to investigate. Whoever it was fired a shot then ran into the woods."

"Did you call it in to the sheriff's office?"

"I'm doing it now."

"Wait there, Natalie and I will join you." Natalie had finished attaching her holster to her belt when Virginia closed the window and turned. "We need to go meet with the deputy and see what happened."

Natalie nodded. "I figured as much. Why don't you and the deputy do your thing while I go look around the building and talk to the other women?"

"Good. See if they saw anything then talk to the ranch hands. I'm sure if they saw anything, you'll get it out of them."

"Why am I always the one to weasel things out of men? You're just as qualified."

"Yes, but you're my deputy, remember?"

Natalie stuck her tongue out. "Deputy my ass." She sighed. "Okay, I'll talk to the ladies then go be a sex kitten and scramble some male brains."

Virginia chuckled as she followed Natalie down the stairs then went outside to meet the deputy. She walked up to him by a fence. "Did you find anything?"

"Yeah. Whoever it was dropped a 9mm." He pointed at the ground. "I must have scared him or her, and he ran. Looks like it was a random shot. I don't see any damage from the shot, but leaving this behind was beneficial for us."

Virginia shook her head. "This is the second time someone ran into the woods back there. In the morning, we'll have to search for any leads. It's too dark now to see anything and we could destroy any useful clues."

"I agree. I was going to check on the ladies present to make sure they're okay."

"Why don't you secure the pistol and then come inside. My deputy is talking to them and will handle the ranch hands."

"That the pretty short blonde?"

"Yep. You noticed."

"Hard not to. Is she married?"

"No. But she has a boyfriend. He's a university professor."

"A professor? Lucky guy." He turned toward the patrol car. "I'll get the evidence bags, forms, and gloves from my car and catch up with you shortly."

Virginia frowned. "Once you have it bagged and tagged, can you call for someone to come and get it and start working on it tonight?"

"I can get it to the station but whether someone will start on it tonight is a matter for those who outrank me."

"Get it ready but don't make that call. Just hang on to it. I'll make some calls and see what I can do."

"Okay."

Virginia walked toward the main house as she dialed Tom at the SCSS.

"Hello, Virginia," Tom said. "What do you need? Bodies removed maybe?"

"I'm in no mood for jokes tonight. And no, I don't need any bodies discretely disposed of. I haven't even shot anyone."

"Yet."

"Okay, yet. What are you doing in the office at this hour?"

"Catching up on paperwork. What can I do for my best special agent and her pretty deputy?"

"Someone was snooping around out here, fired a shot, and dropped a 9mm pistol. The sheriff's deputy with us is bagging and tagging it but isn't confident he can get anyone in the crime lab to look at it tonight. I told him to hold on to the gun and wait for me to talk to you. Anything you can do to expedite things?"

She heard a rustle of paper then he said, "I'll see what I can do and call you back. Make sure the sheriff's deputy keeps hold of the pistol there until I get back with you."

"Will do. Thanks, Tom." She hung up.

Inside the dining room, Virginia found the women sitting around tables eating and discussing the shooting. Virginia moved to the far end of the room and quieted the women. "Have you all spoken to Natalie about what you may have seen or heard?"

They all acknowledged that they had.

Virginia gazed around. "Has anyone seen Daniele Webley?"

Marlen Bauer raised her hand. "Ahh… she was taking a shower and said she'd be down. I haven't seen her yet."

Virginia's eyes narrowed. "What time was that, Marlene?"

Marlene looked at her watch. "About thirty minutes ago."

Virginia headed for the exit. "I'll go check on her." She hurried out of the dining room and to the stairs. She took them two at a time as she bolted to the second floor. She stopped to get her bearings then ran to the room Daniele and Marlene shared. She halted in front of the door, stood to the side, and knocked. No answer. She knocked again, but louder. Once more, no answer. She cautiously grabbed the doorknob and twisted it. The door creaked open.

The lights were on. She swung her backpack off, pulled her pistol from it, and pushed the door further. She could hear the shower running in the bathroom. Virginia cautiously entered and gazed around. No one was there. She stepped to the bathroom and knocked on the door. No answer. She heard a stifled moan inside. Virginia tried the door. It was locked.

She stood back and kicked the edge of the door and stumbled backward almost falling on her back. The doorframe split but the door didn't budge. She kicked the door again, then leaned against it, and pushed. Virginia felt resistance as she heard something slowly sliding across the floor. Steam came out into the room as Virginia wedged her way inside. Daniele Webley was on the blood-smeared floor next to the door. Virginia stepped over Daniele and turned off the shower, and then dragged Daniele out into the steam-filled bedroom. Daniele was bleeding from what appeared to be a bullet graze in her side. She was unconscious but still breathing.

Virginia punched 911 into her cell. When the sheriff's dispatcher answered, Virginia identified herself as a federal special agent and told him to send paramedics to the ranch. She determined that the wound was not serious and went to examine the bathroom. The tiled wall had a small hole in it. She inspected the hole. The projectile that made it came from outside. She looked around and found where Daniele had bumped her head on the sink as she fell.

Virginia returned to the bedroom and saw Daniele starting to regain consciousness. She knelt next to her and examined the bleeding flesh wound. Virginia returned to the bathroom found some gauze and tape in the medicine cabinet. Returning to the bedroom, she used the gauze to apply pressure to the wound to stop the bleeding. There was some congealed blood on her scalp where Virginia located a contusion. Virginia spoke to Daniele. "Can you hear me?"

Daniele moaned, then nodded slightly.

"You've got a nasty bump on your head and a slight… slight superficial gunshot wound. I've got medics rolling. You're going to be okay. I'll stay with you."

Daniele put her hand on her side and the bloody gauze and then raised it. She looked at the blood. "What happened?" When she tried to sit up, she cringed. "That hurts."

"You don't remember?"

"I remember hearing what sounded like a gunshot or a car backfiring, then a pain in my side and falling." She closed her eyes. "My head hurts, too." She winced as she sat up and looked at the bandage on her side. "For just a flesh wound, it sure hurts. So, does my head."

"You bumped your head when you fell. You've been shot, so you're seeing the medics and the sheriff's deputy here will talk to you."

Daniele sighed. "Fine. Can you get me something to wear?" She pointed at the dresser to their right and the closet. Virginia changed the bandage, helped Daniele get dressed, and laid her on the bed. Virginia returned to the bathroom and looked around. She spotted where the bullet dug into the wall. *I'll have to get the deputy to retrieve that bullet for the lab.* Virginia glanced at her watch. *It's been quite a while since I sent Natalie to talk to the ranch hands. I wonder how's she's doing.* Virginia turned to find Natalie standing by the door.

Natalie shook her head. "I see you use your normal method to open the door."

"Don't get cute. Daniele is wounded."

"I can see that. Oh, the ladies heard the shot but didn't know what it was exactly."

"I know. Where are the ladies now?"

"Still downstairs in the dining room."

Virginia leaned against the sink. "How about the ranch hands. Were they any help?"

"When Colin was killed, the sheriff's deputies interviewed them. Some of the ranch hands do not like to talk to the authorities. Better their existence isn't on the police radar."

"Let me guess. They were forthcoming with you."

"You guessed it. They were very friendly and gushed."

"Gushed? What did you do?"

Natalie straightened and ran her hand down the side of her outfit. "I was my normal charming self."

"In that outfit, you just need to breathe to make them happy."

"Well... it took a little more than that. I was propositioned three times, asked out four, and begged to play strip poker."

"Oh boy. You didn't play strip poker, did you?"

"When they lost three straight hands they quit." And, before you ask, yes, I cheated. Distracting them while I did my thing with the cards wasn't very hard."

"Okay, what did you learn?"

Natalie started to talk when they heard Clara Paterson leading the Paramedics into the room. Natalie pointed at Daniele on the bed. "Over here, boys." She and Virginia stepped aside to let the medics get to Daniele.

As they worked on Daniele, Natalie motioned for Virginia to step over by the window. "I found out from the ranch hands that Colin did go on an extended car trip once. He was gone for two weeks. Never said a word about it when he returned. When he got back, he started to use the same building we are using for some sort of project that involved maps, a quilt, and some documents. He kept the building secured. Colin spent a lot of time in the cemetery and out in the woods beyond it. They have no idea what he was doing but whatever it was, he spent a lot of time and money on it."

"No idea?"

"Not really. But one man did some work for Colin for his project. He's a young guy. Kind of shy but strong. He said Colin had him set up computer equipment in the building and assemble some metal detectors and a drone."

"A drone?"

"Yeah. Colin also sent him to get topographical maps of the area. Once when he went to see Colin in the building, he noticed what he thought were gold rings. He said Colin told him they were polished bronze."

Virginia bit her lip. "So, Colin may have found part of what he was looking for. But where?"

She turned as a paramedic approached. "Special Agents, we are done here. Mrs. Webley has refused transport to the hospital and signed a waiver. The wound to her side is superficial and we treated it. But she does have a mild concussion. Have someone keep a close eye on her for the next forty-eight hours. My partner said there're three sheriff's deputies outside the room who want to speak to you. He told them talking to Daniele Webley should be kept short. But, they have to investigate any gunshot injuries."

Virginia nodded. "Thanks, guys. We'll watch Daniel. Please send the deputies in when you leave."

"We'll be here a few more minutes."

"Okay." Virginia's phone rang. She pulled it out of her pocket and answered.

"Virginia. Tom here. I've arranged for the Texas Department of Public safety lab to examine the pistol you called me about. If you can find the bullet, that would be helpful, too."

"How do I get it to them and where is the lab?"

"It's in Austin. But they are sending a Texas Ranger to get them. He's been told you and Ms. North are federal agents and to work with you."

"Okay, Tom, thanks." She disconnected. She looked at Natalie. "A ranger is coming tonight to get the gun and the bullet for testing."

"A Texas Ranger?"

"Yeah, a police type ranger, not a ball player or Smoky the Bear type ranger."

    Natalie huffed. "I know what a Texas Ranger is. Think he'll be cute?"

    "Natalie!"

    "Just kidding. Here comes the local fuzz."

    Virginia turned as three sheriff's deputies entered the room.

CHAPTER 17

Virginia stood in front of the deputies blocking their entering the room. "Gentlemen. An unknown suspect fired a 9mm handgun here tonight and the bullet went through the bathroom wall and grazed a woman's side. It's a superficial wound and she is doing fine. The deputy on guard outside scared the intruder away and has secured the firearm. He, my partner, and I will search the grounds and the woods behind here at first light. I need to speak with the victim before any of you do anything." Out of the corner of her eye, she saw Natalie answering her cell phone.

The deputies insisted on talking to the victim. Virginia put her hands on her hips. "Gentlemen, this is an ongoing federal investigation. I will be investigating this shooting."

The oldest of the three deputies stepped closer. "Listen, lady, this is a shooting in our jurisdiction. You are a civilian and will step aside or we will arrest you."

Virginia shook her head then pulled her credentials out of her backpack and handed them to the deputy. "I'm a Special Agent of the Smithsonian Central Security Service. I'm a federal officer. The sheriff should have informed you."

He chuckled. "Right. You're a fed? Where'd you get these fake credentials and badge, on e-Bay? I've never heard of your so-called agency. Impersonating a police officer is a felony."

Natalie reached past Virginia and tried to hand her cell phone to the deputy. "Someone wants to talk to you, deputy."

He looked her up and down, then barked. "Not now. I'm busy."

Natalie shrugged. "Your call, but I'd take it if I were you. Your retirement may hinge on it."

He glared at her. "Yeah? Who the hell is it?"

Natalie gave him a warm smile and cooed. "The Governor."

His forehead wrinkled. "The Governor?" He smirked. "Really? Governor of what?"

"Texas." She thrust the phone at him. "You really shouldn't keep the

Governor waiting. Talk to him if you want to keep your badge."

He took the phone and spoke. "Who is this?" He stiffened. "Yes, sir. Sorry, sir. I didn't... I... I understand, sir. But this is... yes, sir. Thank you for calling, sir." He handed the phone back to Natalie with a perplexed expression. "You know the Governor?"

"I know a lot of men. Some are actually important, like him."

"I see." He looked at Virginia. "I'm sorry about this misunderstanding." He handed her credentials back. "Well, we'll be leaving. Do you want us to take the gun to our lab for evaluation, Special Agent Clark?"

A voice behind him spoke. "That won't be necessary, deputy. I'm to take it to the Department of Public Safety lab in Austin. The ballistics team is waiting for it." They turned to see a tall Texas Ranger holding the evidence bag and copies of the paperwork.

Natalie's eyes widened. "He's a real Texas Ranger."

Virginia grinned and whispered, "Yeah, a real live Texas Ranger."

"I can see that."

The ranger spoke to the deputies. "By orders from the Governor, the Texas Rangers are doing a special favor for Special Agents Clark and North here." He tipped his white cowboy hat at Virginia and Natalie. "I'll get the result to you as soon as we have something. If you find the bullet, give us a call and we'll test it, too. And, if you need any assistance, just call." He handed Virginia his card, then turned, and walked down the hall. The deputies slowly followed.

Virginia leaned close to Natalie. "You called the governor?"

"No, Tom did from Washington after he got the sheriff out of his sickbed. Tom figured the governor would make a bigger impression especially when the sheriff wouldn't cooperate."

Virginia swallowed. "The sheriff isn't going along on this? I thought he was."

Natalie laughed. "I guess he's been resisting but he is now. His choices were, let us do our thing and he'd get credit for the final bust, or the governor would have the Texas Rangers come and officially help us and cut the sheriff out altogether. The governor said if the sheriff didn't get with the program, the Rangers would get the credit. Politics." She peered around Virginia at the bed where Daniele was. "How's she doing?"

"It's a flesh wound. She fell when she was shot and bumped her head on the sink. She probably has a mild concussion."

A couple minutes later, the medics came out and found Virginia. "Agent Clark, the doctor at the hospital said to have someone monitor Mrs. Webley for the next forty-eight hours and bring her in if she has any symptoms of neurological nature. No stimulants, no sleeping pills, and no tranquilizers. Keep her still. You might want to take her to her family doctor tomorrow. Also, we left some more disinfectant, gauze, and tape to change her bandages."

Virginia nodded. "Okay, we'll watch her."

As the medics left, the deputy sheriff from outside walked up. "I like how you handled Senior Deputy O'Brien. He can be a real prick at times. I also found some footprints outside that may be from the assailant. I've secured them and will show them to you in the morning. Deputy Sanchez will be back then, too. I'll see if I can find the bullet in the bathroom and take it to the Ranger's DPS lab tonight."

"Yeah, go ahead. Natalie and I have some work to do here." She watched him enter the bathroom, then turned to Natalie and motioned for her to step over by the window. "Why would someone fire a random shot at the building?"

"I don't know. Maybe it wasn't random. Could the shooter have been aiming for Daniele?"

"Possible but why shoot through a wall?"

"Good question." Natalie pointed to the far corner of the room. "What are those plants doing here?"

Virginia ambled to the plants, bent down, and looked at them. "Do you know what they are?"

Natalie joined her, glanced at the plants, and frowned. "No."

"They're autumn crocus."

Natalie straightened and shrugged. "That's nice. So, what? I saw some of those growing in the cemetery."

Virginia raised an eyebrow. "Really? They are a source of colchicine."

"No kidding? My uncle took that for gout." She glanced back at the plants. "I didn't know the drug came from a plant."

"Yes, it's used for gout and other conditions but in very small amounts. Forty milligrams are lethal. Ask Colin Carswell. That's what killed him."

"Forty milligrams are deadly? That isn't much." Natalie wrinkled her brow. "If that's the case, how'd they get here?"

Virginia eyed Daniele resting on the bed. "Maybe she can tell us." She stepped to the bed and sat on the edge. Natalie stood at the foot.

Virginia touched Daniele's arm. "How are you doing?" Daniele opened one eye. "Okay. My side hurts a little, but my head is another matter." She touched her short red hair. "I've got a headache. The paramedics said the doctor at the hospital said not to take anything yet. I'm nauseated but holding up pretty well. The medics said I had a concussion."

"Yes. You need some rest."

"Marlene Bauer and I are supposed to teach a session in two days. I hope I'm up for it."

"Let's wait and see. Do you mind if I ask you some questions?"

Daniele nodded her head then winced. "That hurt. Go ahead. I figured you'd get around to me sooner or later."

Mysterious Threads

Virginia chuckled. "You're right. You're a retired country store owner and sold supplies and equipment to Carswell, is that correct?"

"Yes. He was a nice man. Always treated me well, paid on time, and was a good customer."

Natalie tilted her head. "I'm guessing you're only in your forties. Why'd you sell the business?"

"Severe arthritis. The store required a lot of heavy physical work and it was becoming too painful. My doctor advised that I find another line of work that wouldn't put me in a wheelchair by fifty. I had help but being the owner… well, I did a lot of stuff myself. I found a buyer from California who paid me a huge amount of money for it. Huge. I'm not sure he realized what he was getting into but that's his problem. Now I'm into quilting and knitting."

Virginia gave her a confused expression. "How do you do that with the arthritis?"

"I limit my time using my fingers and take some great drugs. It's worse in my hip, back, and knees. But I also have a nice sideline business."

"What's the new venture?"

"Exotic plants." Daniele smiled. "I'm into gardening but for exotic and unusual plants like birds of paradise, leatherleaf, anthurium, calla lily, African angel trumpet, and orchids. I have four greenhouses on my property now."

"How's business?" Natalie asked.

"Okay. It pays for my expenses and a small profit. I'm not really doing it for the money. I made enough on the sale of my store to live comfortably for the rest of my life."

"Who are your customers?" Virginia glanced around the room. "Anyone from around here?"

"A few. Most are online customers via my website. I have clients in Texas and across the south. I even sent a few plants to California. I had to be careful with those orders. California is persnickety about folks bringing plants and fruits into the state."

Natalie grinned. "Yeah, California gets right uppity about that. A friend of mine got busted by a government "police" beagle at an airport, for having a peach in her backpack while waiting for a flight from Hawaii to California. That's downright embarrassing. A big German shepherd police dog, okay, but a beagle? She took a picture of the dog. He had a cute green doggie coat that said K9 Federal Agent-U.S. Department of Agriculture, and he had a little gold badge on his collar."

Daniele smiled. "That's a great story." She touched her head. "Ohhh… now my hair hurts."

Virginia pointed at the plants in the far corner of the room. "Where did those plants come from?"

Daniele slowly turned her head. "Those autumn crocuses?"

"Yes."

"I found them growing in the cemetery out back and Colin said I could take some. They aren't too prevalent around these parts and those seem to be wild. So, I dug up a few to take home." She closed her eyes for a moment then looked at Virginia. "Why? What's so important about the plants?"

"A chemical derived from those autumn crocuses is what killed Colin."

Daniele rested her head on the pillow. "Oh. I see what you're asking about them. They're poisonous?"

Virginia nodded. "Yes. I wouldn't plan any trips away from here for a while."

Daniele put her hand over her mouth. "Am I under arrest?"

"No. But don't leave without me, Natalie, or a deputy with you."

Daniel's eyes widened. "Even to see my doctor?"

"That's okay as long as one of us is with you. I'm sure we'll get this worked out, but for now, no leaving the ranch without one of us."

"Okay. The way I feel right now, following that order will be easy."

"Good." Virginia rose. "We'll let you rest for now." She and Natalie started for the door when Daniele called to them. "Girls, there's something else you should know."

Virginia and Natalie turned. "What is it?" Virginia asked.

"Someone else around here is interested in the autumn crocuses."

CHAPTER 18

Virginia and Natalie both stopped mid-stride and headed back to Daniele. Virginia gave her a curious look. "Who else is interested in the autumn crocuses?"

"I don't know exactly. But someone else was digging them up and left a trail into the woods."

"Could it have been animals?" Virginia asked.

"No. I saw where the plants had been disturbed. Animals don't use shovels. And there were human footprints leading back into the forest."

Virginia pursed her lips in thought. "Okay. Thank you. Now get some rest." She led Natalie out of the room.

In the hall, Natalie asked, "Do you believe her?"

"For now, yes," Virginia said. "It looks like tomorrow we've got a scouting expedition. Dress accordingly, and bring your pistol."

"I'll bring my taser, too. What about the rest of the evening?"

"I think you and I need to study the stuff in the evidence locker tonight. Because of what's happened so far this evening, there's no telling what might still happen. Let's head over there now, don't forget your gun."

"Okay." Natalie hurried to her room.

Twenty minutes later they had Empress Carlota's quilt, Nature's Jewel, the maps, copies of Mrs. Cochran's notes, her diary, an old Mexican Peso, an emerald the size of a silver dollar, a ruby bigger than a ping pong ball, three Maximillian gold coins, the histories about Maximillian's treasure and the ranch, a couple of topographical maps, and marked up modern road maps all spread out on the table in the war room building. They examined each item and made notes on a large moveable whiteboard. Natalie constructed a timeline to track events.

Virginia plopped onto a chair and stared at the whiteboard. "Okay. From what we've got, we're pretty sure the treasure made it to central Texas, then vanished. I noticed that Colin had this area of Lake Buchanan circled on the topographical map and the road map that includes an area encompassing both Llano and Burnet Counties. There's still the question of the Indians, especially the length of beaded leather most likely made by Iroquois."

"Maybe they are items Mrs. Cochran brought back from New York." Natalie leaned against the table. "You know, they may have been souvenirs."

"Possible. I know we didn't think so, but maybe some of the treasure made it that far north."

"But you didn't think the treasure got to New York."

"Yes, but maybe some of it made it. We'll sort it all out I'm sure."

"I agree… I think." Natalie glanced at the table then back at Virginia. "Clara said there were occasions, nights, when she'd see lights out by the cemetery and sometimes there'd be lights down by the oak forest. There were times Colin would lock himself in that old barn for hours. No one was allowed inside. Then there are the stories about the old witch."

Virginia bit her lip. "Yeah, the witch. From the stories and the diary, we know she was a friend of Mrs. Cochran and probably treated the men bringing the treasure to the U.S. after they were attacked by Indians."

"Maybe one of the men actually did tell her where the treasure was hidden." Natalie pointed at the pictures of the tombstones of both Mrs. Cochran and Isabelle Lerfervre. "Look at these."

Virginia looked at the pictures. "Okay, what am I missing?"

"They're similar, and both are for women who were involved with people seeking the treasure."

"So?"

"We found some stuff hidden in Mrs. Cochran's tomb. What if there is something else hidden in Isabelle Lerfervre's tomb?"

"Wouldn't hurt to take a look. Add it to our list for tomorrow." Virginia watched Natalie write it on the whiteboard. "Wait a minute." Virginia jumped to her feet and leaned over the table pushing papers around. Then she pointed. "We need just a couple more pieces of the puzzle to find the treasure. Then things will get exciting."

Natalie yawned. "What are you talking about?"

"We have almost everything we need right here. In the morning we'll do five things." She counted on her fingers. "One, we examine Isabelle Lerfervre's tomb for anything we may have missed. I'm sure we need something else. Two, we examine the area where the autumn crocuses are and were dug up. Three, we examine the footprints the deputy found and go follow them into the forest. Four, we call the ranger about the gun that was used tonight that shot Daniele. Five, I need to call one of my anthropologists at the Georgetown Museum about this Iroquois beaded leather artifact." She snapped a picture of the artifact with her phone. "Then, I think

Mysterious Threads

we'll be able to locate Maximillian's treasure and flush out Colin Carswell's murderer."

Natalie gave her a quizzical expression. "How?"

"We need one more piece of the puzzle."

"Oh? Where does the final piece of the puzzle come from? For that matter, what is it?"

"Isabelle Lerfervre's tomb in a hidden compartment as you aptly pointed out."

Natalie looked surprised. "I did?"

"Yes. Very astute of you."

Natalie grinned. "Good for me. How do you know this… this piece of the puzzle is missing, whatever it is? What is it?"

"The key to the map that is hidden in the quilt."

"Right. I knew that. I guess. The map we can't see in the quilt, but you know is there?"

"Yes. I remembered I needed a type of key in another quilt that took me to the jungles of Mexico and Guatemala. I figured this one need a key as well. It's a matter of finding it. Then you pointed out the thing with the two tombstones. Good job."

"Thanks." Natalie looked at her watch. "It's eleven. I think we should lock all this stuff back up and hit the hay. We can get a fresh start at it tomorrow morning bright and early. Anyway, it'll be safer than running around in the dark."

"That's a good idea." As Virginia reached for the documents, the lights went out. "Oh shit… that's not good." She stepped back to the wall. "Natalie, take a quick look out the window at the main building. Is the power out?"

Natalie glanced outside. "No. The lights are on."

"Then we've been targeted."

"Oh boy." Natalie turned on her cell phone flashlight app and waved the beam around the room. She spotted an unusual lantern on a shelf and stepped to it. "Want me to turn on this lantern so we can see while we secure all this stuff. I've already erased the whiteboard."

Virginia pointed at the only window in the structure. "Do you have anything to cover that window with?"

"No. But I've got an idea. Wait a minute."

"What are you going to—" Virginia raised her hand to shield her eyes. "Oh my god, that's bright!"

"Yeah. I'll keep the spotlight aimed at the window. You gather the stuff up and stuff it into the locker. No one outside can see in."

Virginia gathered the items on the table and quickly restored them in the locker. She locked the metal cabinet when something hit the main door. "What the hell was that?" She speed-dialed the onsite deputy sheriff. He didn't answer. She moved to Natalie. "Looks like the deputy is out of commission. We're on our own. Keep your gun handy."

"What do you want to do?" Natalie asked. "Can I turn out the light now?"

"Yeah. But we need to protect what's in the locker."

"Okay. It's built like a safe, I don't think anyone is going to break in, do you?"

"If I could open it with my lock picking tools, so could someone else."

"Right. Do we stand guard until morning and then see what's going on in the daylight?"

Virginia scanned the room. "Let's tape that butcher paper on that shelf over the window. Then we can use the light in here for us."

"Okay." Natalie made her way across the room, grabbed the roll of butcher paper and some scissors while Virginia found a roll of masking tape.

They taped three layers of the brown paper over the window. Virginia stood with her hands on her hips. "Nice job."

"It looks secure but just don't do anything between the light and the window. Shadows."

"Right. Can you tone down the intensity?"

Natalie nodded as she fiddled with the light's controls.

She held it up. "This okay?"

"Nice. Where'd you learn about the window trick, about the shadows, and how to operate that thing?"

"It's an old, adjustable, theater light. They don't make ones like these anymore. And the shining it in the window prevents anyone from looking inside. I learned the stuff from a special effects guy in Hollywood."

"Special effects?"

"Yeah—wait, I know that look. What are you thinking?"

Virginia grinned.

Natalie dropped into a chair "I'm not going to like this, am I?"

"You know me so well." Virginia sat on the edge of the table.

"I know I'm going to regret asking, but what do you have in mind?"

"I was considering taking everything out of the locker and stowing them in that large, blue IKEA bag under that computer table and those shopping bags. Then you and I just race to the main house, guns drawn but we take separate routes. You go for the back porch and I'll run for the side door."

Natalie wrinkled her nose then said, "Okay, I'm game. You sure we can't just leave the evidence here?"

Virginia heard soft footfalls outside the door. She pointed at the door then her ears. She picked up a pen and scribbled: *Whisper from now on.*

Natalie nodded then sniffed the air. "Do you smell smoke?"

Mysterious Threads

Virginia stopped and sniffed. "I smell something. That's probably not good. We can't leave the evidence here if there's a fire. We can't stay either," whispered Virginia. "Like I said, if I were the villain, I'd get us out of here then open the locker. Grab the bags while I open the locker and transfer the evidence to them. We need to get out of here and take the stuff with us."

Natalie pushed out of the chair then glanced at the door.

"Better call the sheriff. If the deputy is down, he'll need help. We should have done that earlier."

"You're right. You call the sheriff and have firefighters and paramedics respond as well," said Virginia. "I'll start packing our evidence."

Natalie dialed 911 when she heard footsteps in the gravel walkway next to the door. "Better move fast. We may have company soon."

CHAPTER 19

When Virginia finished packing the evidence in the bags, she looked at Natalie near the door with her gun drawn. "Did you call 911?"

Natalie nodded. "Yes. Deputies, firemen, and paramedics are on their way. I figure the sirens will frighten our mystery person away for now. But we are at least getting help for the deputy out there." She jumped back as something thudded against the door. The sound of a brief struggle then another bump against the wall followed along with the sound of someone running in the gravel walkway. Then silence. Natalie turned and looked at Virginia. "What was that?"

"Someone else got involved maybe? I think we should check. I hear sirens. Turn off your lantern or we'll be good targets."

Natalie switched off the light, unlocked the door, slowly opened it, and peered out. She could see a large, dark-haired man clumsily trying to climb to his feet. Natalie looked around then turned her lantern back on. "Edward?" She stepped out and knelt next to him as he fell back to the ground. Blood was coming from his scalp.

Virginia leaned out, surveying the area with her gun. "I don't see anyone else. Who's that?"

Natalie looked up. "His name is Edward Josephson. He's the senior ranch hand and he's hurt."

"I need to stay close to the evidence. Find out what happened before the deputies arrive."

Natalie had Edward sit up as she examined his head. "Doesn't look too serious, but you've got a nasty cut and you'll have a beauty of a headache. What happened?"

Edward took a breath then half smiled. "I heard a noise and smelled smoke, so I came out to investigate. There was someone out here trying to see inside the building. I knew this building is off-limits to anyone but you and your friend and the sheriff. When I got here, someone was at the door and he or she was going to try and break in. I knew you were inside. I startled the person, and I was clobbered in the head with something. He ran

Mysterious Threads

toward the woods out back."

"I take it you didn't recognize the person."

He touched his head then looked at the blood on his hand. "No, I didn't get a good look at the person, sorry."

Natalie gave him a warm smile. "Thanks for coming to investigate and help us. But you should have called the sheriff instead of going it alone. Next time at least bring a buddy."

He put his hand on his head. "You're right. I hope there won't be a next time."

Natalie looked toward the front of the ranch. "Sirens. Paramedics are coming."

He looked at the blood on his hand. "Think I'll need stitches?"

"I don't know."

"I hope not. I'm not a big fan of needles."

Natalie chuckled. "A big, strong guy like you, afraid of needles?"

He gave her a sheepish look. "Yeah. Please don't tell the other guys."

She patted his hand. "Your secret is safe with me." Natalie looked up to see firemen, paramedics, and three sheriff-deputies rushing toward her. "Help's here." She stood and waved her arms. "Over here!"

Virginia stepped into the doorway as the sheriff's deputies, firemen, and medics arrived.

The lead deputy, Senior Deputy O'Brien, looked at Virginia, then Natalie and Edward. "You two again? Seems like I just left here." He looked at Edward. "What happened to him?"

Natalie stood and straightened to her full five-foot height and looked up at Deputy O'Brien. "Nice to see you again, too. My friend here got clobbered on the head while running off an intruder. You'd better look for our missing deputy. He isn't here, and we couldn't reach his cell. He may be over there by the cemetery. This gentleman and the deputy will need the paramedics. We smelled smoke inside. Can you have the firemen look for the source?"

"Yeah." He called to two firemen. "Take a look around the building for a fire. They smelled smoke."

The firemen nodded and started searching around the structure. The other two deputies and two other firemen went searching for the missing evening deputy while the medics examined Edward.

Deputy O'Brien bent down to talk to Edward. "Need to see some ID."

"It's in the bunkhouse, sir."

"I'll vouch for him, Deputy," said Natalie. "We checked out the ranch hands already."

"That's right, you're some kind of a fed. Okay." Deputy O'Brien looked back at Edward. "What's your name, and do you live here?"

Edward flinched when the medics applied disinfectant to the wound.

He glanced at the deputy. "Edward F. Josephson, sir. Yes, I live here on the ranch."

The deputy entered it into his iPad then frowned. "Well, it seems Mr. Josephson has a record. A couple of arrests and one felony conviction. Were you tormenting these ladies, Edward?"

"No. I was investigating a suspicious person around this building when I got hit on my head."

Natalie put her hands on her hips. "As I told you, Deputy, we already knew about his background. The arrests were for two fights in a bar and that conviction was for possession of four ounces of marijuana for his own use over ten years ago. He served his time. He wasn't selling it. That shouldn't have been a felony anyway. He's a good man."

Virginia stepped out of the doorway. "He's been employed full time at the ranch since then and has a spotless record."

Deputy O'Brien's radio crackled. He leaned his head to the side and pressed a button on the mic attached to his shirt. "Go."

The voice on the radio said, "We found Deputy Straight. He's in the cemetery and unconscious. Has a head wound. Send the medics."

"Roger. I'll send them now." He looked at the medics patching Edward's head. "Leave him and go to the cemetery out back. We have an officer down."

One of the medics grabbed a large, red box and hurried away. The second medic looked up. "I'll be right there. I need to finish dressing this wound and I need to give this man tetanus and antibiotic injections."

"Now?" Deputy O'Brien's asked.

"The doc in the emergency room said to do it now. He won't need transport."

Deputy O'Brien started to say something when Natalie huffed and glared at him. He clenched his fists, then after looking at her, relaxed. "Okay, but hurry." He looked back at Natalie. "You can be scary, little lady."

Natalie smiled. "Thank you, Deputy. If you tried to send this medic away without treating my friend, you'd find out just how scary I can be."

Deputy O'Brien held up his hands in surrender. "I believe you."

The paramedic finished the bandaging and prepared a syringe and gave Edward an injection. Edward passed out. The medic stood with a blank face. "What the hell…?"

Natalie looked at Edward then at the medic. "He's afraid of needles and shots. I'll get some of the ranch hands to take him to his bed."

The medic shrugged. "Wait, I need to call the hospital back."

Natalie watched the medic closely as he conversed with the hospital over the radio. He looked at her. "Since he's already out cold, the doc said give him the second injection and transport to the hospital. I've requested

Mysterious Threads

an ambulance." He administered the medication. "I need to go help treat that deputy in the cemetery. Can you stay with him until the ambulance arrives?"

"Yes."

"Good." He handed her a piece of paper. "That's my cell. When the ambulance gets here call me."

"Okay." Natalie watched him close his medical boxes and hurry toward the cemetery.

Deputy O'Brien looked at Virginia and Natalie. "We'll take care of Deputy Straight. Do you want another deputy here until the morning?"

"Won't be necessary but thank you. We've secured everything for the night."

They all turned as Clara came out of the main house and marched up. "What's going on?" She frowned at the deputy. "I see you're back again."

Deputy O'Brien looked at Clara. "Who are you?"

Clara, her white hair slightly mussed straightened her shoulders. "I am Clara Paterson. My late cousin owned this ranch and now I do. I want to know what's happened."

Virginia interrupted. "Clara, the deputy sheriff on guard here tonight, Deputy Straight, was attacked. These gentlemen are here to help him."

Clara pointed at Edward lying on the ground. "What happened to him?"

"He tried to intercede to protect us and was injured for his efforts."

"I see. Will he be okay?"

"The paramedics just patched him up. We're waiting for an ambulance to take him to Georgetown Hospital."

"Good. He's a nice man. I hope he's okay." She glanced around then looked at Virginia. "Will you be so kind as to give me a more detailed update in the morning?"

"Of course, Clara. No problem."

Clara nodded slowly. "Okay. We can tell the others something at breakfast after we've talked."

Virginia smiled. "Fine." She watched Clara strut back to the house. *She has mud on her shoes.*

Deputy O'Brien shook his head. "I thought we were going to have an irate citizen on our hands. She's quite stuffy. You handled that very nicely, Agent Clark."

Virginia nodded. "Thank you. Now, if you don't need us anymore, we have some things to do."

"Ahh, will you send me your statements before seven this morning? I have paperwork to do. I don't think your intruder will be back tonight after all this, but I'd still be on guard."

Virginia smiled. "I'll get you our statements, and thanks again for your help."

"Agent Clark, since this incident happened on your watch, you're going to find out who attacked our deputy, right?"

"You bet. I don't like it when those helping me get hurt. I tend to do nasty things to the perpetrators."

Natalie nodded. "Yeah, most die, some disappear forever, and a few live long enough to go to jail."

Deputy O'Brien smiled. "Great. I like your attitude. Fine with me but don't say that too loud. If there is nothing else, I'll go check on Deputy Straight. Don't forget the report." He handed her his card then turned and hurried to the graveyard.

The two firemen who went looking for the fire returned holding long hooks and a large, red fire extinguisher. One smiled. "We found a pile of leaves on the far side next to the siding that was smoldering. We put it out. Looks like someone had just started it. Either they didn't realize wet leaves don't burn well or just wanted a lot of smoke."

Virginia nodded. "Thank you, fellas. We're glad you got here so quick."

"We're from the Liberty Hill Fire Department. Same with the medics. We're the closest to you. Have a nice rest of your evening, ladies." The firemen returned to their engine and drove off.

Natalie looked at Virginia. "What were you doing while I placated Deputy O'Brien and got Edward treated?"

"I got Dr. Doverspike to agree to let us store the evidence in the safe in my office at my museum."

"Huh? You called your boss at this hour? Why take the stuff there? Can you transfer evidence to the museum? Your boss agreed to it?"

"That's a lot of questions. First, it's my safe, so the evidence is still in my custody. Second, the safe has an alarm, as do the buildings. Third, the place has armed guards. Safer than here and yes, my museum director agreed."

"He'd agree to anything you asked. Do you always make lists?"

Virginia shrugged. "You know I do. It also looks like you're picking up my list habit, too."

"Yeah. When do we take the evidence there?"

"Go get your driver's license and keys."

"Already have them."

"Good. Here comes the ambulance. You wait here with Edward and make sure everything goes okay getting him out of here. I'll get the evidence bags." She hurried back into the building.

"Right." Natalie waved as the ambulance attendants rushed toward her. She called the paramedic who gave her his number. Once the medic arrived, she watched the ambulance personnel and the medic load Edward

Mysterious Threads

into the ambulance and take him away. She then joined Virginia and assisted getting the bags into her SUV.

Fifteen minutes later Natalie, with Virginia beside her and the evidence stowed in the back of the SUV, drove down the dark, winding county road.

Virginia kept looking back to watch for anyone following. After a few miles, she relaxed. "I'll be glad when this stuff is safely locked up."

Natalie nodded. "Me too. But tomorrow, if we find more information in Isabelle Lerfervre's tomb, how will we compare it to all this stuff? Will we have to come back to the museum?"

"That depends on what, if anything we find."

"You have an idea where the treasure might be, don't you?"

Virginia slowly nodded. "Yep. But I need that last piece of evidence to accurately locate it."

"Care to share?" Natalie glanced at the rearview mirror. "Oh boy. Vehicle coming up behind us at a good clip. Want to call for help?"

"Won't be time for them to come to our aid." Virginia twisted in her seat and looked. "I see it. I'll climb into the back seat. If there are fireworks, I'll have more flexibility back there and you won't be in the line of fire. Step on it, that car is closing fast."

"Okay."

Virginia felt the acceleration as she climbed into the back seat and pulled her gun out of her backpack. She turned around and watched the vehicle get closer. She waited, her heart pounded in her chest. She rolled down the side window as the vehicle roared up next to them. The rear window of the other car started to roll down. She saw the barrel of a gun emerge when Natalie slammed on the brakes. The SUV swerved then skidded to a stop as Virginia fell on the floor. The other car shot ahead. As the taillights faded, it turned into a side road.

Natalie glanced over her shoulder. "You okay back there?"

"Yeah, I'm fine. Just wasn't expecting that sudden stop." Virginia climbed back into the seat. "That was quick thinking. Looks like they're gone. Maybe we can get to the museum without another confrontation."

Natalie sat stiff. "I'll relax when we get to your museum. I don't know where that side road goes. He could come out ahead of us down the road." She drove ahead.

"I love your positive outlook."

Natalie turned on the radio. "Thank you."

After another five minutes, Natalie leaned forward and stared ahead. "I was right. Look who just pulled out from that dirt road."

"Shit!" Virginia's heart raced. "That's not the same vehicle."

Up ahead, a huge pickup truck came to a sudden stop across the street, blocking the entire road.

CHAPTER 20

Virginia leaned against the back of the front seat and looked ahead at a large, jacked-up, dark-colored pickup truck sitting across the highway. Four men with rifles stood in the bed of the truck. Two armed men hopped out and were standing in the street waving for Natalie to stop. "The guys from before must have called for help. Any way you can you get around it?"

"Doesn't look like there's much room, but I'll see what I can do. Hang on." Natalie tensed, then stomped on the accelerator. She raced ahead. The men jumped out of the way just as Natalie's speeding white Toyota Land Cruiser approached. A few yards in front of the truck, Natalie suddenly cut to the left. The SUV tilted slightly and swerved, missing the truck tailgate by millimeters. She abruptly turned to the right and missed a tree by even less distance. Gravel and dirt spun up behind them spewing rubble across the truck and road. The SUV fishtailed a few times as she cut back into traffic lanes. Natalie put the pedal to the floor, as she let the big roar of the V-8 engine fill the evening air and roared away into the dark. One of the men jumped to his feet and fired a shot but missed their SUV as Natalie weaved from left to right.

Virginia still clutched her seatbelt. "That was some driving. You missed that tree and the truck by a hair's width."

"Yeah, I did some stunt driving out in LA."

"You were a stunt driver, too?" Virginia asked, surprise in her voice. "There's no end to your talents, lady."

"No. I wasn't an actual stunt driver. I dated one for a while, and he liked teaching me new things."

Virginia raised an eyebrow. "What did you teach him in return?"

Natalie chuckled. "How to talk to girls."

Virginia had a surprised look on her face. "Really? That's it? Nothing juicy?"

"No!" Natalie gave Virginia a sour expression. "I was a regular actress, not a porn star. Believe it or not, I was one of the few girls he could casually talk to. Women made him extremely nervous. He was a nice guy and I felt sorry for him." Natalie looked in the rear-view mirror. "I see our friends are following but at a discreet distance."

"I hope they stay back. I'm sure the museum's armed guards will be waiting for us. That way the transfer should be safer."

Natalie gripped the wheel like a vice. "Getting back to our earlier conversation, what last piece of evidence do you need to locate the treasure?"

"The key."

"Wait, you said that at the ranch."

"Right. Empress Carlota's brightly colored quilt, Nature's Jewel, has a map in it. The Mexicans knew where they were going to hide the treasure before they left Mexico and made a map and put it in the quilt. Like the one I used in Central America, you need a key to actually read it. That way the quilt alone wouldn't be able to be deciphered. I think the key is in Isabelle Lerfervre's tomb as you pointed out. With it and the quilt, we'll know for sure about where the treasure is. Then we use the more modern maps Colin had to accurately locate it."

"So, do you really have any idea where it is?"

"Yes and no. I don't know exactly where, and there are other obstacles. That's where the key and the quilt come in."

"But the story says it was going to the Port of Galveston. Old Max was reported to have used four Austrian officers and about a dozen Mexican loyalists, to get it to Galveston."

"Yes. That was a subterfuge. The Austrian officers and Mexican loyalists were used until the wagons got to Texas. Then Derwood Noble, ex-captain, Confederate Army, replaced the Austrian officers and took charge along with the Mexicans and a few fellow ex-Confederate soldiers. I think he used the Mexican guards for a while then killed them so he and his men could keep the treasure. I realized we needed the key tonight after examining the quilt again. I figured out where the key was when you mentioned Isabelle Lerfervre's tomb and that it may have a secret compartment." Virginia yawned. "I think Mrs. Cochran hid it there. That's what Colin figured out just before he was murdered."

"Wow. You're good at this stuff. How about the poisonous plants? The autumn crocus."

"I think they may have been originally planted by Isabelle Lerfervre."

"So, they were her plants."

"Yes. Mrs. Cochran knew her well. Isabelle took care of the ranch and treated people for their ills while Mrs. Cochran was gone looking for the treasure for the president. Isabelle probably used the autumn crocus to make a crude form of colchicine to treat rheumatism and gout and used other plants for her remedies. No doubt, she learned the location of the treasure from the ex-confederate soldiers she was treating before they died. Isabelle perhaps moved nearby after Mrs. Cochran returned and she told Mrs. Cochran where the treasure was hidden. Later, after Mrs. Cochran hung and smoked Mr. Noble for killing Isabelle, she told the local folks Isabelle had died. The wild autumn crocuses there now are the descendants of the original plants."

Natalie shook her head. "I need to be more observant. You got all that while we were in the shed?"

"Pretty much."

Twenty minutes later Natalie pulled through the security fence gate into the shipping and receiving area and backed to the loading dock of the museum. The outside security lights were on, but the surrounding area was dark. Virginia exited the rear of the Land Cruiser and, with her gun held in both hands, scanned the area. She heard another vehicle drive by. Not seeing any danger, she said, "Okay, let's unload the evidence and get inside."

The steel loading dock door rattled as it rose. Two armed, uniformed guards stepped out. "Need any help, Virginia?"

She looked at the oldest guard and smiled. "Hi, John. I see Dr. Doverspike contacted you."

"Yes. He said to be alert and give you any assistance we can. Do you expect trouble?"

"Maybe. If you guys would just keep watch, my friend and I can get this stuff inside. We had one attempt to steal these materials already tonight, and someone followed us."

The guards used a hand-held device to close and lock the gate then moved to the sides of the dock, guns drawn, and watched the yard while Virginia and Natalie unloaded the items from the car onto a cart. The guards followed Virginia inside, closed and locked the door, and went to the central guard station to monitor the security videos of the outside and the various areas inside the museum.

Virginia opened her safe and stuffed the evidence inside. She closed it, spun the dial then sat in her desk chair and yawned. "That's done. We can rest easy now." She used her cell phone to e-mail the picture of the Iroquois beaded leather artifact to one of the anthropologists at the Museum. "She'll get that when she arrives in the morning and can look at it. Now that that the evidence is secured, I can quickly write that report for the deputy." She glanced around and frowned. "Natalie?" *Where's Natalie?*

Virginia picked up her desk phone and dialed security. "John, can you see my friend Natalie anywhere on your monitors? She has to be in the museum someplace."

"Just a second, Virginia, we'll cycle through quickly. Okay, I found her. She's in the Native American room. She's doing something with one of the exhibits."

Mysterious Threads

"Thanks, John. I'll go get her." Virginia disconnected. *What is she doing? I better find out what she's up to before I file the report for the deputy.* Virginia locked her office, and strolled to the Native American room. When she entered, she found Natalie sitting in a diorama holding the Iroquois beaded leather artifact in her right hand and a similar object in her left. Virginia walked up to the display. "What are you doing in the diorama?"

Natalie looked up with a big smile. She held up her right hand. "This is the Iroquois beaded leather artifact Colin had." She held up her left hand. "This is an almost identical one I found in this exhibit. They're pretty close."

Virginia walked to Natalie, took the two objects, and compared them. "I see what you mean. This one you lifted from my exhibit is a Wampum belt. I sent pictures of the one we took from the ranch to one of my anthropologists to have her examine it in the morning. You may have beat her to the punch." Virginia stepped back and looked at the diorama. "This display is about the Iroquois."

Natalie glanced around. "I know. What's a Wampum belt? Money?"

"Pretty close. Because the Iroquois had no writing system, they communicated their history and traditions orally. The Wampum belts helped keep their memories intact so that they could retell their history. The Iroquois also used the belts as a person's credentials or badge of authority. You are right though; some were used as money. Originally, they were cloth or leather belts with shell beads hand fashioned from whelk shell and white and purple beads made from the quahog or Western North Atlantic hard-shelled clam. Some types of Wampum belts were also used by tribes as a means of exchange."

"Interesting. Now I can't wait to hear what your anthropologist has to say. If they tell a story, maybe it tells of part of old Max's treasure making it to New York State. That's where Simon Cochran, the skeleton in the attic that you found, and June Cochran both were at one time or another."

Virginia frowned and nodded. "Possible."

Natalie tilted her head. "What's wrong? I didn't break anything in here."

"No, it's not that. Something I saw in the notes at the ranch just flashed through my head and I can't remember what it was. It had to do with the Indians, I think."

"Zinochsaa?"

Virginia's eyes widened. "Yeah, that was it. How did you—"

"It was written on the back of the front cover of June Cochran's diary. I remembered it because the word looked so unusual. I thought it could be Indian. It didn't look Spanish. What's it mean?"

Virginia shook her head. "I don't know."

Natalie took the exhibit item from Virginia and put it back in the display. "We need to lock that one up don't we?"

"Yeah. It's getting late. Let's go back to my office and I'll put it in the safe." Virginia led the way back to her office and put the beaded leather artifact in the safe. She looked at the clock on the wall as she relocked the safe. "Damn it's late and I'm bushed. I'd better write the report for the deputy before we return to the ranch. Have a seat, this won't take long."

Natalie sat in a side chair and looked at a couple of magazines while Virginia typed on her computer. A half-hour later Virginia hit the send button on her email. "All done. Let's get back to the ranch and get some sleep. Then in the morning we can go explore the cemetery where the plants were dug up and the woods."

"I like the sleep idea. I'm pooped." Natalie rose and followed Virginia out of the office and through the museum to the rear entrance. They climbed into the SUV and drove to the gate, driving out after it automatically opened.

Virginia watched the gate close behind them. She turned around and settled into her seat as Natalie drove back toward the ranch. "I'm glad the evidence is stowed in the safe at the museum. Now I can relax. Sleep will be very welcome."

"Don't count your chickens quite yet."

Virginia looked at Natalie. She was tense, her eyes wide. "What's wrong?"

"Look behind us. That truck I dodged a while ago is back and it's coming up fast. This is getting old." Natalie accelerated.

Virginia twisted around and looked. The truck behind them was distinctive. The row of intensely bright spotlights over the cab were on as well as the truck's high beams, turning the dark road into blinding daylight. "He's trying to blind us. Probably will attempt to run us off the road."

"Why? The evidence is back at the museum."

"They'll try to use us as hostages to get the materials."

Natalie's jaw tightened. "I'm tired and in no mood to play games. I can probably out-run or out-maneuver them." She accelerated.

Virginia looked out the rear window. "Can you open that tailgate from up here?"

"Yeah. Why?"

"I'm going to get into the back. When I yell, open the tailgate. I can shoot from there. They make a great target."

"Are you nuts? That's illegal."

"You're worried about legalities now? Want them to run us off the road? I'm sure they won't be gentlemen when they capture us. Think of what they will do to your car."

"My car?" Natalie gripped the wheel. "Climb in the back."

CHAPTER 21

Virginia climbed into the rear seat and pulled her 9mm pistol from her backpack.

She turned toward the front when Natalie spoke. "Get my .357 Magnum out of my backpack."

Virginia pulled Natalie's backpack off the floor and opened it. "Your .38 special is in here, too. Why bring both?"

"A girl needs to be prepared. There's a taser in there, too. I don't think that'll work for this. The .357 will do serious damage, so use it."

Virginia took the big, heavy gun out and leaned on the rear seat looking out the rear window. "This is going to be very loud when I fire it."

"It'll hit them with a lot of authority, too. So, quit talking and shoot. I'm opening the tailgate."

Virginia watched the truck gaining on them as the tailgate opened. "That light bar across the top of the cab is bright. I think there are four men standing in the bed of the truck with what may be rifles. I'll see if I can dissuade them from shooting."

Natalie glanced in the rearview mirror. "They're gaining on us, shoot already!"

Virginia held the large pistol with two hands, aimed and fired at the light bar. It shredded in the center sending sparks and pieces of metal flying. The men ducked. A rifle flew from the vehicle as the lights went out. Next, she aimed at the front grill and fired three rounds. The truck swerved a little and mist started to appear around the front of the truck. She watched as steam suddenly erupted and the truck slowed then jerked to a stop. "I think they are out of commission." She didn't get a response from Natalie. Virginia set the revolver on the seat and leaned over and touched Natalie's shoulder. "You okay?" she yelled.

Natalie nodded then spoke loudly. "Can't hear well yet. That gun is loud outside but in a confined space like this car… hurts the ears. Did you get them?"

"Yeah, that thing is loud. But that truck stopped. Besides putting holes in the radiator, I may have damaged the engine. Those full metal jacketed rounds probably cracked or punctured the engine block."

"Couldn't happen to nicer guys." Natalie glanced into the rearview mirror. "They may have cell phones and will call for help."

"Maybe, but they'll be more careful now that they know we'll shoot."

"You going to call the sheriff about the shooting?"

"Are you nuts? Just what Senior Deputy O'Brien needs, more of us. I don't think the guys with the truck will be reporting it either. Let's just go back to the ranch."

The high beams from Natalie's Land Cruiser cut through the night as they continued driving to the ranch.

Morning came too soon for Virginia. She was awakened by a loud knocking on her bedroom door. She opened one eye and looked at the clock next to her bed. *It's only six. I need more sleep than this.* She rose up on one arm and yelled. "It's early, go away."

"Mrs. Clark. We need to speak, now," said Clara Paterson. "You said we could talk before breakfast so we can address the other ladies."

Virginia sat up. *Shit, I did say that last night, didn't I.* "Okay, just a minute." She swung her legs over the side of the bed and rose. She slowly walked to the door and opened it. "Come on in, Clara, and have a seat. I'm not awake yet. I was up late."

Clara entered, sat in a chair by the window, and crossed her arms. "I want to know what went on last night, and how the investigation into my cousin's death is going."

"You don't want to know about the treasure?"

"Oh, yeah. That." Clara gave a dismissive wave of her hand. "There's no treasure around here."

"You may be right, but that's what got your cousin killed. I think it was what got Simon Cochran, your old relative whose skeleton I found in the attic, killed as well."

"Really?" Clara frowned. "Maximilian's treasure?"

"Yes."

"That was lost well over a hundred years ago."

Virginia sat on the edge of her bed. "Right. But Colin had uncovered certain facts that were leading him to it. That's what he thought anyway. Someone else wants it, too. Trouble is, Colin didn't know exactly where the treasure was, but he was closing in on it when he was murdered. As for last night, Natalie and I were looking at the evidence when someone tried to interfere. One of your ranch hands, Edward, attempted to come to our aid and was hurt in the process. The perpetrator also attacked Deputy Straight. That's why the other deputies were here along with the firemen and paramedics. The attacker got away."

"Was it related to the shooting earlier?"

"I think so."

"I see." Clara nodded. "Thank you for the explanation."

Virginia let out a small sigh of relief. *That short and redacted explanation satisfied her, good.* "Later this morning Natalie and I will be going to inspect the cemetery and searching the woods to follow up on some clues."

Clara leaned forward. "What clues?"

"I can't tell you that at this time."

"Oh. Yeah, I understand." Clara straightened. "You said there was evidence in my cousin Colin's murder. Is it still in the building you and the sheriff are using as a headquarters? I saw you and Natalie carrying something to her car last night. I take it that was something else."

"Yes."

"Is the evidence still here on the ranch?" Virginia didn't answer.

Clara stared at Virginia for a few seconds and gave a knowing nod. "I get it. Can't talk much about an ongoing investigation. I watch TV."

Virginia leaned forward. "Clara, were you outside last night? Other than to talk to us and the deputy?"

"Ahh... no. Why do you ask?"

Virginia shrugged. "Just wondering." *Then why was there fresh mud on her shoes?*

"No. I only went out when I talked to you and the policeman."

"Okay. Well I need to get dressed."

Clara stood. "I'll leave you to it and go brief the ladies at breakfast. Some of them saw the excitement last night and are curious." She smiled. "I'll see you later at breakfast or in the retreat sessions."

"Right." Virginia stood. "I'll be down shortly." She watched Clara leave then hurriedly took a shower and dressed. After slipping into a red and black checked blouse and blue jeans, she pulled her hair back into a ponytail, put on her hiking shoes, grabbed her backpack, and put her baseball cap on. "This outfit should be good for tromping through the woods. Now to rouse Natalie. This'll be fun." Virginia walked down the hall and knocked on Natalie's door. She heard movement inside then jumped as the door suddenly flung wide open.

Natalie stood in front of her wrapped in a towel. "Hi. Come in. I'm just getting dressed."

"You normally answer your hotel doors dressed only in a towel?"

"Why not? I'm not naked." Natalie turned and started for the closet. "Now if you were one of those cute firemen, I could be."

Virginia entered. "You have a boyfriend."

"I was kidding." Natalie glanced over her shoulder from the closet. "Wait a couple minutes and I'll get dressed. I take it, from the way you're dressed, right after breakfast we're going exploring."

"Yeah. I figured we'd have nice breakfast, answer a few questions from the ladies, go look at the footprints the deputy found, then go to the woods."

Natalie slipped into jeans and a T-shirt and strapped on a belt with a holster and stuck her .357 Magnum in it. Next, she pulled her hair into a ponytail, picked up her messenger bag, and smiled. "Okay, let's go eat."

"You're wearing your gun to breakfast?"

"Yes. Where's yours?"

Virginia pulled her .38 special out of her pocket.

"Why the revolver? Where's your 9mm?"

Virginia stuck the revolver back in her pocket. "This baby doesn't jam. Anyway, today the 9mm is my backup weapon and is in my backpack."

"Okay. Let's go eat then explore. Who knows what we may find?"

During breakfast, Virginia and Natalie talked briefly with Daniele Webley and answered questions from the other women as vaguely as possible about the previous evening. After they finished eating, they escaped the dining room and went searching for the footprints the deputy had discovered.

Natalie looked around as they walked into the yard. "Where is Deputy Sanchez this morning?"

"I got a text message from him. He'll be here in an hour," said Virginia. "He's at the sheriff's station being briefed about last night. I told him things were quiet now, so he didn't have to hurry."

As they walked, Natalie pointed at the ground near a fence. "Looks like the spot the night deputy mentioned. He anchored an orange tarp over it."

Virginia stepped to it and removed the tarp. "Yep. Here they are. The prints look like they are from some sort of hiking boot."

Natalie knelt and inspected the prints. "More like hiking shoes. LL Bean to be precise."

Virginia turned with a raised eyebrow. "You know this how?"

"The imprint here is like the one on the bottom of my shoes, see." She sat and raised a shoe for Virginia to look at.

"You're right." She looked at the shoe print again. "Give me one of your shoes."

"Why?"

"To get an idea of the size."

"It could be a man's shoe."

Virginia glared. "Give me the damn shoe."

"Okay, okay." Natalie removed her hiking shoe and handed it to Virginia. "It still could be a man's shoe."

"Agreed." Virginia set the shoe next to the imprint. "It's larger than yours. What size do you wear?"

"Ladies size 7. Give me back my shoe."

Virginia handed Natalie her shoe then looked at the footprint again. "The shoe prints are probably a size bigger than yours and they have been worn more on the outside."

Natalie leaned over and examined the prints. "The person was also limping."

Virginia frowned then reexamined the prints. "You're right." She stood and looked around while Natalie took pictures of the prints with her cell phone. "I don't see any more footprints, but the rest of the area is dry. That spot was damp. There are a few other wet spots around but none toward the woods or the building we were in last night."

"The deputy said the person hightailed it into the woods." Natalie pointed. "Let's go search the forest."

"The cemetery is on the way. Let's check out Isabelle Lerfervre's tombstone again."

They walked to the cemetery and located Isabelle Lerfervre's grave. They examined the grave marker, pushing and poking various features. Nothing happened.

Virginia leaned hard against a six-pointed star on the back of the stone monument then jumped when she heard a soft click. "Something just happened. I poked that star twice and nothing happened. Now it decides to do something?"

"Probably need to put more pressure on it." Natalie walked around from the front. "It needed the extra pressure to prevent it from just opening at the normal touch of a person or animal. What did it do?"

Virginia looked around the tombstone. "There, at the top of the base, there's what looks like a drawer." She knelt and grabbed the stone and tugged. It moved slightly making a grinding noise. She pulled harder and with jerking movements. It slid out with a loud scraping sound.

Natalie stepped back. "Are their spiders in it?"

Virginia peered into the cavity. "I don't see any." She carefully reached in and withdrew an oil cloth-wrapped package about the size of an iPad. She gave it a gentle squeeze. "Something soft is folded in this."

"Want to look at it now?"

"Yeah. Virginia looked around then carefully unfolded it. "Looks like a piece of folded cloth. Let's wait until we go to the museum to examine it in more detail."

"Okay." Natalie handed Virginia her messenger bag. "Stick it in here so we can go look at the woods."

Virginia stuck the package into the messenger bag and handed it back to Natalie. "I'll close this, then we can go." She pushed the drawer back into place and heard the locking mechanism click. "I'm surprised this thing still worked." As she started to get up, she noticed another odd-looking section of the granite monument. *Looks like I was right. Now for the second piece of information we need.* She glanced at Natalie. "Did you bring the paper and soft leaded pencil I asked for?"

"Yeah." She patted the messenger bag. "They're in here."

Virginia studied the monument. "Hand them to me, please."

Natalie gave the items to Virginia and watched her make a rubbing of a design on the monument. "What are you copying?"

"I think it's another map."

"Huh?"

"This and the one in the quilt are what we need to locate the treasure. This one, being exposed to the elements, is faded." Virginia stepped away, folded the paper, and handed it to Natalie. "Stick this in your bag, too."

Natalie shrugged. "I'm glad you're confident." She stuffed the paper into her bag.

Virginia turned toward the forest. "Yeah, but now we need to see where our suspect has been going."

They hiked to the edge of the woods. Virginia looked at the path. "Nuts! It's dry here, too. No footprints."

Natalie looked back at the ranch house. "I can see the main house from here." She pointed into the trees. "The ladies we talked to said there were lights coming from this direction. Also, we've had a couple figures run into the trees about here, so wherever they went it can't be too far. I hope there aren't any snakes. I hate snakes."

Virginia looked at the dense stand of trees. She pointed to her right. "Looks like there are signs of someone going this way. The trees are less dense over there." She jumped as a deer shot out of the brush and into the trees. "That doe gave me a scare. I didn't see her."

"Let's follow the deer."

"Why? It can go through places we can't, and it's running away from us."

Natalie waved her arm. "Okay, then lead on through the woods, Mrs. Boone."

"This is Texas, Mrs. Crockett would be better."

"Right." Natalie laughed. "You and Davy killed a bear in Tennessee when you were only three?"

"Sure. Follow me. I think you're right, whoever was in here didn't go far if the light could be seen from the ranch house."

"I hope your—" Natalie dove for the ground as a bullet whizzed past her and slammed into a tree trunk. She raised her head slightly and looked around. "What the hell? I didn't hear a gunshot." She pulled her gun and waited. After not hearing anything, she started to get up when she noticed Virginia on the ground next to the tree, not moving. "Virginia!"

CHAPTER 22

Natalie slowly rose to her feet and hurried to Virginia's side. She gently rolled Virginia over and searched for any bullet wounds. She sat back on her heels when Virginia woke up.

Virginia shook her head then looked up at Natalie. "What happened?"

"You've got a nasty bump on your head. I couldn't find any bullet wounds. You okay?"

Virginia abruptly sat up. "Whew, that was too fast. What bullet wound? Who shot? I didn't hear a gun." She looked down at her torso. "I don't feel like I've been shot." She touched her head. "My head hurts and I think I sprained my ankle, it hurts like hell and is throbbing. That's why I fell and bumped my head against that tree."

Natalie pointed at the tree. "Look there. That's a bullet hole. I ducked as it went whizzing by my ear, and you went down. I thought maybe you were hit. You weren't shot. I didn't hear a gunshot either."

"Someone used a sound suppressor on a rifle and fired from some distance. Otherwise we would have heard something." Virginia tried to stand. "My ankle really hurts. Give me a hand."

"You sure it's safe to get up? Your ankle may be broken."

"Yeah. If whoever was shooting wanted us dead, they would have attacked us by now. I think we are being discouraged from looking in the woods. Now help me up."

Natalie took hold of Virginia's arm and helped her to her feet. "Hold on to me while I get you back to the ranch house. Our hiking today is done."

As they slowly made their way back to the ranch, Virginia pointed at the cemetery. "Do me a favor, and let's go back over to Isabelle Lerfervre's grave."

"Okay, but why?"

"That's where a small part of Maximilian's treasure is located."

Natalie froze almost causing Virginia to stumble. "What? The treasure is here on the ranch? How in the hell did you figure that out?"

"Not all of it. Just a small amount."

Natalie looked around. "Now? It's broad daylight. The killer could be watching us."

"I'm sure the killer is watching. Let's get to the grave."

"Okay, if you insist." Natalie helped Virginia across the field and into the cemetery to Isabelle Lerfervre's grave. She lowered Virginia to the ground next to the monument.

"Okay, where's the treasure?"

Virginia patted the granite. "Part of it is under here."

Natalie frowned. "You hit your head pretty hard when you fell. Maybe we should get you inside and to bed."

Virginia scrunched her eyes together. "I'm not crazy or hallucinating."

"If you say so." Natalie looked at the tombstone. "You found something else here, didn't you?"

"Yep. There is another concealed opening and some of the treasure is in it. That's where the gold rings, the gold coins, and the gems Colin Carswell had came from. It's a part of the treasure cache."

Natalie sat against a headstone. "Who put it here?"

"June Cochran. She actually knew where the rest of the treasure was buried."

Natalie wrinkled her brow. "How'd you figure that out?"

"From the materials we examined last night, the need for the key, your timeline, and seeing this other part of the tombstone. There were notes in Colin's files from Simon Cochran."

"The skeleton you found in the attic—that's Simon?"

"Right. Simon traced June Cochran's activities and investigated the treasure like we thought. But he, like Mrs. Cochran, located the treasure here in Texas and part of it in New York. But he couldn't get it. At least not all of it."

"Why not? Wait, if what is here is part of the treasure, how'd you know it would be under her grave?"

"Think about it. The people who knew about the treasure are all dead. From Colin's and Simon's notes, the stories about the witch, Isabelle Lerfervre, seemed to start well before June Cochran left to go to New York. Like I said before, Isabelle Lerfervre watched over the ranch while June Cochran was gone. The stories about the ranch-witch were spread more by Mrs. Cochran after Isabelle was murdered. It helped keep people away."

"How about Derwood Noble and the curse?"

"Noble's the one who hid the treasure in the first place. Remember, his men were ambushed by Indians somewhere around here. Most of his men were killed. A few, along with Noble were injured. He and his injured men came to Isabelle for treatment. Probably in pain or suffering the side effects of her medicines, they told her where the treasure was buried. The men died. Noble survived and killed Isabelle because she knew where the treasure was hidden. Mrs. Cochran returned and interrogated him about Isabelle's disappearance and the treasure until he finally told her where most of it was buried and that he killed Isabelle. She may have used some enhanced interrogation methods on him to get the details. Who knows? Mrs. Cochran killed him and smoked him in the smokehouse probably because he killed Isabelle."

"Then why didn't she just go get it?"

"At the time, everyone wanted it: the U.S. Government, the French, and the Mexicans. While she was commissioned as a U.S. Marshal by the President to locate it, gold fever may have taken hold. Once Mrs. Cochran found it, the lust for treasure and maybe financial needs got the best of her and she didn't want to part with it. She figured the government didn't really need it, and she did. Being a marshal didn't pay a lot. So, Mrs. Cochran would get little pieces of it from time to time to help keep the ranch going and provide for her in later life. This way she didn't arouse suspicion about where her money was coming from, and she had a legacy for her family."

Natalie shook her head. "That's quite a story. I saw what you saw last night, and I didn't get all that. I think you bumped your head harder than you think. Let's get you to the house. Maybe some nice hot tea and some acetaminophen will help. Maybe a couple of icepacks. Right now, you might be just a sandwich short of a picnic. I know a nice... doctor who may be able to—"

"I'm not crazy. You were too busy taking notes, using the whiteboard, and saving everyone's bacon to take notice. I'm sure you would have figured it all out." Virginia took a breath and slowly let it out. "But my head and my ankle do hurt. And, you were right earlier. We're being watched. Whoever is watching will hopefully think we're resting. Let's go back to the house and make my condition look worse than it actually is."

"It probably *is* worse than you think. You're in no shape to be your usual Energizer Bunny, but you still have a lot of explaining to do."

"Yeah, I know. We need to take the rubbing and the map key in your messenger bag to the museum. There we can unlock the quilt map and examine that rubbing we made at the grave to see what it says. We can do that later today." Virginia rubbed her ankle. "So, now let's go to the house and get me all propped up with bandages, ice, and the hot tea. And I could really use the acetaminophen. We need to talk to Deputy Sanchez as well."

Natalie looked toward the house when she heard someone coming in their direction. "Speak of the devil. The deputy is headed this way." She stood. "Over here, Deputy Sanchez."

Sanchez trotted to them and looked down at Virginia. "What happened? Do you need some help?"

Virginia smiled. "Yeah, that would be nice. I banged my head and twisted my ankle. Will you please give me a hand to the house?"

"Yes, ma'am." He bent down and picked Virginia up and carried her to the house with Natalie following carrying her messenger bag and Virginia's backpack. When they arrived, Natalie had him place Virginia on the couch in the parlor facing the huge stone fireplace. As soon as Natalie adjusted the pillows behind Virginia, Clara came rushing in. Clara looked at Virginia with a wide-eyed expression.

"What happened to you?"

"I had an accident. My fault." Virginia pointed at her foot now resting on an ottoman. "I twisted my ankle and bumped my head."

Clara's expression turned to one of concern. "Can I get you anything? I'll get some frozen peas from the freezer for your ankle. Do you want an icepack for your head?"

"The peas would be nice. Natalie is getting some acetaminophen."

Helen Chandler walked into the room and looked at Virginia. "I overheard what you said. Poor dear. I'll make you some hot tea. That's good for almost anything." She rushed out of the room followed by Clara.

Virginia looked up at the deputy standing next to the couch. "Thanks for carrying me inside. There are a few things we need to discuss."

"I was briefed at the sheriff's office about last night."

"I was told that. How is Deputy Straight? Have you heard anything?" Virginia asked with concern.

"Thanks for asking. He was hit pretty hard on the head. He's in the hospital but should be discharged tomorrow. He'll be on medical leave for a few days and re-evaluated by the doctors then. Is there more about last night?"

"Yes. Pull up a chair. and I'll tell you while we wait for Natalie and my acetaminophen."

Clara returned with a bag of frozen peas wrapped in a dishtowel. She gently removed Virginia's shoe and placed the frozen peas on Virginia's ankle. "Is this comfortable, dear?"

Virginia leaned back into the cushions and smiled. "Yes. That feels great. Thank you."

Clara nodded. "Good. I'll go see how the tea is coming." She hustled out of the parlor.

Natalie entered carrying a pill bottle and a glass of water. "Here, take two." She handed Virginia two tablets. "They are 650mg each. That should help."

She swallowed the pills and motioned for Natalie to sit next to her. "I told Deputy Sanchez that we had some more information to give him."

Natalie rubbed her nose. "I was thinking about that. We may want Detective Alverez in on this, too."

Virginia thought for a moment. "He's on another case right now, but I did promise him we'd keep him in the loop." She glanced at Sanchez. "Can you get ahold of him and find out when he can be here, so we do this once?"

"Yes. I'll try and find him now." Sanchez hopped to his feet and strolled toward the kitchen punching numbers into his cell phone.

Natalie watched him leave. "You going to tell them everything?"

"No. Just that we moved the evidence, I know where some of the treasure is, and we were attacked last night and again today."

"That sounds like everything." Natalie raised an eyebrow. "You sure you aren't seeing pink bunnies?"

"No bunnies. But I should tell him we know who's buried under Isabelle Lerfervre headstone."

Natalie's eyebrows shot up. *"We* do?"

Virginia nodded. "Yes."

Natalie regarded Virginia quizzically. "Who?"

"Derwood Noble."

Natalie twisted around. "Noble? How did you figure that out?"

"As I explained earlier, the story back then was that Isabelle Lerfervre left the area for places known only to her friend Mrs. Cochran. Remember the locals thought Isabelle was a witch, so after Mrs. Cochran returned to the ranch, Isabelle supposedly left. Mrs. Cochran found out that Noble killed Isabelle for the secret of where the treasure was buried."

"I got that part."

"Okay. So, when Mrs. Cochran hung then smoked good old Mr. Noble, she buried him and erected Isabelle Lerfervre's grave marker. That settled the neighbor's rumors about the witch still being around. Most people here abouts, either didn't know Noble, nor did they care about him."

Natalie nodded. "Go on."

"I don't know for sure, but I'll bet Isabelle is buried in the cemetery under one of the old wooden markers that is unreadable today. Probably placed there by Noble. The grave marker served as a place to store small amounts of the treasure and convinced the public that Isabelle Lerfervre was dead and buried. It also provided a way to get rid of Noble's remains without anyone suspecting. She was a sharp lady." Virginia glanced toward the kitchen. "Here comes Helen Chandler with my tea and the deputy is behind her."

Helen placed the small teapot on the side table and poured Virginia a cup. "I have some milk and sugar here too, dear. Let us know if you need anything else."

Virginia nodded. "Thank you, Helen. How is Daniele?"

"Much better. Daniele's up and working on her demonstration for the upcoming class she and Marlene Bauer are going to do."

"Good. I'm glad Daniele wasn't hurt badly."

Helen glanced toward the window. "I forgot, there are sheriff's people out back doing something with footprints in the mud."

"Probably the forensic team making casts and taking pictures," said Virginia.

Natalie glanced up. "Any word about Edward?"

"Yes." Helen smiled. "If all goes well, he'll be discharged from the hospital after some more X-rays later today."

"Good."

Helen looked toward the kitchen. "Here comes the deputy. I'm sure you all have a lot to talk about, so I'll leave you. Call if you need anything." Helen left the room.

Deputy Sanchez retook his seat and finished chewing something. "They have fresh donuts. Who would have guessed?" He brushed some crumbs off his uniform. "I called Detective Alverez. He can't come until the day after tomorrow. Is there anything more I should know now?"

Virginia and Natalie exchanged glances. Virginia picked up her cup of tea. "You tell him."

"Okay." Natalie slid to the edge of her cushion. "You know about the attack on us, Deputy Straight, and the ranch hand last night, correct?"

Sanchez nodded. "Yes. I checked the evidence locker when I got here, and it is still secure."

"Well, Virginia and I emptied it last night and took everything to her museum and locked it in her safe. The safe and museum have alarms and twenty-four-hour armed security guards."

Sanchez's eyes widened in alarm. "You did what?"

Virginia set her cup down. "I'm the lead investigator. The evidence is technically still in my possession. Also, I'm the only one with the combination. After last night, I was concerned about its safety. And even an amateur could pick the locks to the building's door and the locker out there."

His breathing slowed. "It's all in your safe at your museum?"

"Yes." Virginia gave him a reassuring smile. "But we ran into some people who seemed to know we were taking it there and tried to interfere with us on the way there and back."

He gave them a questioning look. "I see you made it okay. So, what happened?"

Virginia picked up her tea and sipped a little. "The first two attacks Natalie handled with her expert stunt driving skills."

"Stunt driving?" Sanchez looked curiously at Natalie. "I thought you were an actress."

"I am. But I learned some stunt driving tricks from some of the movie-stunt crews."

"That's great. You said the first two. Were there more?"

"Yes." Virginia returned her cup to the table. "The last one resulted in me shooting out a light bar on top of a huge, jacked-up pickup truck chasing us and shooting holes in its radiator and engine block. It may have been a Ford 350 or something like it."

Sanchez swallowed. "You… you shot at a moving vehicle on a public road? Where were you?"

"In Natalie's SUV on one of the county roads. They were trying to kill us, and they had guns. You want us to write them a traffic ticket?"

"You should have called 911." Sanchez sat, breathing heavily. "You shot a truck from your moving car?"

"Responding officers would arrive in time to investigate our deaths or kidnapping." Virginia gave him an innocent look. "I didn't hit anyone, just the truck. And Natalie and I are here safe and sound. Well… until someone took a shot at us this morning." She pointed at her foot. "That's when this happened."

"Someone shot at you today?" He jumped to his feet. "Why didn't you tell me this before? Where?"

"Down by the woods."

Natalie pulled a red piece of yarn from her pocket. "I tied a piece of this on a branch where the bullet went into the tree trunk if you want to get it."

"You were shot at out there?" He glanced at the women to the window and back to Virginia and Natalie. "How… how can you two be so calm about all this?" He collapsed back into his seat. "Someone… someone is trying to kill you."

Virginia nodded. "Yes, we noticed that, and it distresses us deeply."

"Distresses you? I'd be scared shitless!"

"Natalie and I aren't exactly thrilled about it. The person behind it also injured Deputy Straight and a ranch hand. I don't like people who hurt my friends. But, the son-of-a-bitch is going to pay dearly and painfully for it."

"The sheriff will—"

"We'll handle it. Trust me, there won't be anything left for the sheriff to worry about. Oh yeah, the men who tried to ambush us last night got their instructions from someone here at the ranch. There was no other way they could have known we were taking something to my museum and when."

Sanchez sat with his mouth open. He quickly recovered. "Someone at the ranch? Makes sense. I'll write all this down and—"

Natalie motioned for the deputy to sit back. "Relax, there's more."

Deputy Sanchez sat and rubbed his forehead with both hands then looked at Virginia and Natalie. "More? Wasn't that enough? Shouldn't we wait for the detective?"

Virginia shook her head. "Not if you want to know where some of the treasure is and who killed Colin Carswell and Simon Cochran, the skeleton in the attic."

CHAPTER 23

Deputy Sanchez looked puzzled. "Wait, the skeleton was of someone killed in the late forties or early fifties. Mr. Carswell was killed like… like now. You know who killed both of them?"

"I'm pretty sure, and I have a plan to catch them."

"I see." Deputy Sanchez sat motionless, then slid back in his chair. "How about the treasure? Is it part of your… plan, too?"

"You bet. That's how we're going to flush out the killer. Want to stop being a guard and help?"

Sanchez smiled and nodded. "Yeah, that would be great."

Clara stepped into the room. "Virginia, someone from The San Gabriel Museum is on the phone and wants to talk to you."

"Thanks." Virginia glanced at Natalie. "My ankle is still hurting. Will you please take the call for me?"

"Sure." Natalie rose and padded to the kitchen. After a couple of minutes, she returned. "That was Dr. Terry Sorenson on the phone. She said she examined the photographs of the beaded leather artifact you sent her. She'd like to see the actual specimen. She also sent you an email about what she found so far."

"Did she give you a clue as to what she discovered?"

"She wouldn't say, but she said when you read your email, you'll want to get your tail back to the museum PDQ."

Virginia picked up her backpack and rummaged through it to locate her cell phone. She pulled it out, turned it on, and opened her email. There was a message from Dr. Sorenson. Virginia touched the screen and opened the mail. The short note stated:

> *Virginia,*
> *I examined the photographs of the beaded leather artifact you sent me. I would like to see the actual article for better in-*

terpretation. From what I could make out, it is Iroquois.

The type of structure and beading makes me believe it is from the Seneca band of Iroquois in origin. It is similar to the one in the Iroquois exhibit.

You said it was from the 1800s. Good guess. You can think of this item as a sort of Indian pawn ticket. It looks like someone, a white man, left something of value with this band of Seneca Indians.

I might be able to glean more by seeing the actual artifact.

Call me. Terry.

PS. The word you included, Zinochsaa, means Genesee. It was used by early writers in the area.

"I thought so. Terry is very good at this stuff." Virginia showed the email to Natalie then to Deputy Sanchez.

Sanchez looked at the email then at Natalie and Virginia. He handed the phone back to Virginia. "I'm not up to speed on what you have been doing. I take it from your expressions this email is very important."

Virginia chuckled. "Yeah, it is. This is very important. If you're going to be part of our merry little band, we need to get you up to speed."

"That would be great. This case has gotten interesting and helping you two beats being on guard duty."

"I'll see if we can get the sheriff to expand your duties."

Sanchez looked down, then back at Virginia. "That might be a problem. I'm a relatively new patrol deputy. I think that's why I've been on guard duty. I'm not a detective."

Natalie pulled out her cell phone and looked at Virginia. "Time for a call to Tom at the Smithsonian?"

Virginia nodded. "Last time we asked, Tom got us what we needed, so give the man a jingle."

"This Tom sounds influential," Sanchez said.

Virginia nodded. "Yes. He's my boss at the Smithsonian Central Security Service in Washington. The man can do miracles when necessary."

Natalie chuckled. "He especially likes Virginia in spite of her methods."

Sanchez looked concerned. "In spite of her methods? What does that mean? Is that referring to things like her shooting from a moving vehicle?"

"Yes. Sometimes Tom keeps track of her by the locations of the bodies Virginia leaves behind and he has to... quietly dispose of."

"He has to... hide bodies?" He looked at Virginia with wide eyes then at Natalie. "She killed them?"

Natalie looked up from dialing. "Yes, but for really good reasons, I assure you. And, he can make dead bodies disappear and get us neat things from other agencies and stuff."

Virginia shook her head. "Guys, I'm right here."

Sanchez sat with his jaw dropped. "Make dead bodies disappear? Why? That's—"

"Don't ask and don't say it." Virginia waited, while Natalie quietly talked on her phone.

Natalie appeared giddy when she hung up. "Okay, Tom said he hopes you feel better soon and to stop running into trees. He'll contact the Williamson County Sheriff about detailing Deputy Sanchez to us for the investigation. We should hear back shortly."

Virginia smiled. "Good. That's settled." She turned as Clara led a tall man carrying a manila envelope into the room.

Clara cleared her throat. "This gentleman is a Texas Ranger. He has something for you ladies." She nervously glanced up at the ranger and hurried out of the room.

Virginia twisted around. "What can we do for you, Ranger?"

"I have some information for Special Agents Clark and North."

Natalie sat up. She patted the seat next to her on the love seat. "That's us. Have a seat, Ranger. Whatcha got for us?"

The ranger's eyes widened as he looked at Natalie twisting a strand of hair with her finger. He pulled his eyes away from her and looked at Virginia. "Agent Clark?"

Virginia looked up. "Yes, sir."

He pointed at her foot. "What happened?"

"I tripped and ran into a tree."

He chuckled. "Sorry. I... well, thinking of a federal agent running into a tree seems... unusual."

"I try not doing it on a regular basis."

"Someone shot at us," blurted Natalie, "and she ducked and ran right into the tree."

He stood silent for a second then looked at the deputy. "That's why you're here?"

"No. I just became part of their investigation. Her running into trees is something new to me, too."

"I see." The ranger shrugged then looked back at Natalie. "Agent North?"

She smiled suggestively and purred. "Yes."

He removed his white cowboy hat and sat next to Natalie and handed her the envelope. "Ladies, this is the ballistics report and lab analysis on the firearm you found here."

Virginia rubbed her nose. "What does it say?"

He looked at Deputy Sanchez. "Are you the officer who secured the weapon and bullet?"

Mysterious Threads

Sanchez took a nervous breath. "Yes, Sir."

"Well, you did an excellent job considering the environment. We were able to learn quite a bit."

"Like what?" asked Natalie.

"It's all in the report. But in summary it says: the weapon is a 45-caliber model 1911A1. This particular weapon was made for the army during World War II. The weapon was originally sent to Ft. Belvoir, Virginia."

"That's the Army Corps of Engineers headquarters," said Virginia. "How'd you find all that out so quick?"

"Someone tried to remove the serial number, but it was heavily stamped into the metal. We were able to retrieve the ID and then traced it to the manufacturer. Fortunately, they had the record of where it went in their archive. Also stamped on it was SA for the Springfield Armory. The SA was used when the weapon was refurbished by an Armory to designate a repaired or refurbished weapon and where the work was done."

"Any idea who owned it or how it got here?" asked Virginia.

"Not really." The ranger cleared his throat. "The engineer unit that received them new during the war was deployed to northern France. When they returned, the weapon went for service then was returned to the fort. Last information anyone could find was that an officer had it, but it was never returned to army inventory after the war."

"Did the army say who the officer was?" asked Natalie.

"No. They didn't have that in their records anymore. It was a long time ago."

Virginia looked disappointed. "So, we don't know who owned it."

"No. But there were trace materials on the gun."

Natalie's eyes sparkled. "There was?"

"Yes. That's why I said the deputy did a good job preserving it for the lab. The trace materials included olive oil, some dirt, clay, and a little plant pollen. There was also some sewing machine oil. We weren't sure what all this means."

"Did you ID the pollen?" asked Virginia.

"Yes. A little mountain laurel and live oak. Probably from central Texas. There was some sugar maple and birch in it, too."

Virginia raised an eyebrow. "Sugar maple and birch?"

"Yes. The lab said it was old. It was in a part of the weapon that hadn't been cleaned in years. That part of the gun is not normally taken apart when the shooter cleans it. I don't know how much help this is, but I was told to bring it to you as quick as possible." The ranger stood. "Do you need anything else?"

Natalie ran her tongue slowly over her lips, "Well... what—"

Virginia shook her head as she interrupted Natalie. "I can't think of anything right now, Ranger. We need to consider what you've given us. Thank you for bringing it out here and telling us the findings."

He put his hat back on. "No problem." He smiled as he looked at Natalie. "If you do need anything else just give me a call." He winked and handed his card to Natalie.

She looked at the card then with dreamy eyes, looked longingly at the ranger. "I can think—"

"We'll let you know, Ranger," Virginia interjected. "Thanks again for all your help."

They watched the ranger leave.

Natalie turned to Virginia. "Party pooper."

Virginia leaned toward Natalie. "Natalie, remember—"

"I know, I've got a boyfriend. But that ranger was sooo cute."

"Right, and you have a boyfriend."

"I know. But I can window shop. I just can't try on the merchandise. Guys do it all the time." Natalie flexed her fingers. "Anyway, it's fun to pull your chain."

"Just what I need, a prankster."

"Hey, I'm a fun partner and I'm good at shooting."

"That you are. Right now, we've got a lot of data. Now we need to turn that data into information we can use to find the treasure and flush out the killer."

Natalie sighed, then nodded. "I think Dr. Terry Sorenson is right. We need to go to your museum and pronto."

Deputy Sanchez gestured at Virginia's ankle. "Virginia, are you in any condition to go anywhere?"

Virginia cracked a smile. "Yeah. My ankle hurts but I can still function. Anyway, Natalie can drive."

"I've got a sheriff's cruiser outside. We could take that. Might dissuade anyone from attacking you on the way."

"Not a bad idea but maybe we should take both your car and Natalie's. I think the sheriff will want to talk to you pretty soon, and this way we won't be stranded."

"Right. Okay. I'll follow you." He helped Virginia to her feet and supported her as they went out to the vehicles. Helen Chandler caught up with them at the front porch. "Virginia, are you okay to go out quite yet? Your ankle is still swollen."

Virginia nodded. "The acetaminophen is helping and the tea was great. But I need to go to my museum to do some research."

"You sure that's wise considering the blow to your head and your poor ankle?"

"Natalie and Deputy Sanchez will be with me in case there's any problems. We'll be back before you know it."

Mysterious Threads

Helen glanced at the envelope and smiled. "Okay. I was just concerned." She turned to Natalie. "Don't forget, dear, your session on wool knitting and felting classes is tomorrow afternoon."

Natalie nodded. "I haven't forgotten."

"Good. Well don't overdo things, Virginia. We want you back safe and sound."

Sanchez watched Helen return indoors. "Her concern is nice."

Virginia turned back toward the cars. "Help me down the steps, please." She walked with the deputy to Natalie's SUV. "Deputy, how long would it take the sheriff's office to get a background for check on some of the ladies?"

"I'm not sure. A quick criminal background wouldn't take long. More detailed could take days or longer. Why?"

"When we get to the museum, I'll give you a list of names. Have your people run a quick criminal background check. Then I'll see what else we can come up with. Let's see if anyone stands out."

CHAPTER 24

Virginia sat with her backpack on her lap in the front passenger seat of Natalie's SUV as they drove to the San Gabriel museum. "I feel safer with the sheriff's car right behind us."

Natalie glanced in the rearview mirror. "You and me both. Last thing we need is a rerun of last night."

"I meant you're driving within the speed limit and not trying for orbital velocity."

Natalie shot her a quick glare. "You want to walk?"

Virginia held up her hands in surrender. "Just kidding. I'm glad the deputy is there because of what happened last night as well."

"I have a question. Did the Seneca Indians in the 1800s issue tribal pawn tickets?"

Virginia chuckled. "No. Terry was making a point. Someone, at some time, left something with the Indians. What, I don't know."

"Maybe treasure?"

"Possibly. We'll see what Terry says when I show her the actual beaded article." Virginia pointed. "There's the museum. Go around back like last night and I'll use my remote to open the gates. Deputy Sanchez can follow us in. We'll be safer once we're behind the walls of the yard."

They entered the rear walled yard and parked. The sheriff's car slid into a spot next to Natalie's SUV. Sanchez quickly exited his vehicle and helped Virginia out of the SUV.

"This way, Deputy." Virginia, leaning on the deputy, limped up the concrete steps onto the loading dock as the large steel overhead doors rolled up. Two armed guards stood in the doorway. "Nice to see you again, Virginia." said the larger of the two men. "What did you do to yourself? You brought the sheriff?"

"I fell, and Deputy Sanchez is helping us on our case. Will you tell Dr. Sorenson I'm here, please?"

Natalie chimed in gleefully. "She tripped and ran into a tree." She held her arms out wide. "It was a big tree."

"That's enough out of you," said Virginia.

One of the guards stifled a laugh. He lowered the big door while the other guard went to a wall phone and made a call.

Virginia limped to her office. Once inside she motioned toward the chairs. "Sit while I open the safe." She used the desk as support and worked her way around it to the safe next to the desk. She opened it, pulled out the Wampum artifact, and set it on her desk.

Sanchez bent forward and looked at the beaded leather belt. "That's the Indian pawn ticket?"

Virginia pushed a piece of blonde hair from her eyes. "It's not really a pawn ticket. Let's see what Terry says when she gets here."

They turned as Dr. Terry Sorenson knocked on the doorframe holding a large, black portfolio. "Hi, Virginia. I see you brought friends," she said stepped into the office. Dr. Sorenson leaned the portfolio against the wall and extended her hand. "Hello, Deputy, I'm Dr. Terry Sorenson, Senior Archeologist."

He rose and shook her hand. "Deputy Sanchez. Nice to meet you, Doctor."

Terry moved closer to the desk and glanced at the artifact. "That's the article in the picture?"

Virginia nodded.

Terry pulled white, cotton gloves from her pocket and put them on. She picked up the Wampum belt and examined it. "This is interesting. It *is* an authentic Seneca Wampum belt and it *is* pretty old. As you know, Virginia, they didn't exactly have a written language. This is as close as they came to one." She held it out so the others could see then pointed at an area on the belt. "This area indicates someone left something with them. And this section means the person was not Indian."

Natalie squinted at the belt. "Can you tell who the person was or when it was?"

"No. But by the construction, materials used, and the aging, I'd bet it was over a hundred years ago. More like over a hundred and fifty years ago."

Deputy Sanchez looked at Terry. "Do you know where this is from?"

"Yes." Terry pulled a map out of her portfolio and unfolded it. "The Seneca's were in the western part of New York mainly near the Genesee Valley. They held the region between the Erie and the Cayuga bands of Iroquois." She set the map on the desk and pointed. "In this area."

Sanchez glanced at the map. "Is there anything that can narrow it down more?"

"Not by the belt's construction. I could send pictures of it to some colleagues in New York and see if they can get more specific. We could run some tests here as well."

Virginia looked hopeful. "Go ahead and do what you need to do."

"Okay. Anything else I can help with?"

"What do you know about the history of Lake Buchanan?"

Terry looked puzzled. "Lake Buchanan? The one out in Burnet and Llano counties on the Colorado River?"

"That's the one."

"What does Lake Buchanan have to do with this?"

"We have some old maps that Colin Carswell had. The area that is now the lake was highlighted by him on the maps. Same with some newer ones."

"I see. Well, I don't know much. I've been there. While on a tour, I learned it was completed around 1938 or '39 by the Corps of Engineers and the Lower Colorado River Authority as the first flood control dam on the Colorado River. The others followed. I remember a guide saying the water behind it covered some buildings and a place called Buffalo, Texas. The drought a few years ago exposed some of it. The fishing isn't too bad. That's about it. Why?"

"We may have a field trip there."

"Can I go?" Terry asked excitedly.

"Yes, you're on the team."

"Good. Want me to pull some USGS topography maps? I can also see if there is anything microscopic on the Wampum belt that may give us a clue as to its place of origin."

"That would be helpful, thanks."

"Okay, I'll start on these things and see what I can find out. I'll have the department secretary pull the maps from the files and bring them to you." Terry hurried out.

Sanchez watched her leave then looked at Virginia. "*She's* an archaeologist?"

Virginia nodded and grinned. "Yep."

"Wow. She also very pretty. Not what I expected."

"You were thinking of someone like Indiana Jones instead?"

Sanchez shrugged. "Well... I... yeah. She sure seemed to know her stuff. She's going to be part of our team, right?"

"Yes."

"I noticed the doctor wasn't wearing a ring and... I'm sorry." He swallowed. "I shouldn't ask."

Virginia smiled. "No, Terry is not married. I'm not sure if she's seeing anyone at present."

Natalie eyed the safe. "Let's take a look at the quilt now that we have the key."

Sanchez looked bewildered. "A quilt has a key? I don't understand."

Virginia removed the quilt from the safe. She hoisted herself up by using the desk as support and limped to her conference table where she unfolded the quilt. "The quilt has a map in it, but we need the key to see it and figure out the details." Virginia looked at the colorful quilt then turned to Natalie. "Get the key and let's see what we have here."

Natalie pulled the oilcloth bundle from her messenger bag, moved to the table, and unfolded the package. Inside was another piece of cloth with holes cut in it and some writing. "This looks pretty good for being so darn old."

"Yes, it is in remarkable shape." Virginia held it up and looked at it. "Okay which end is up?" She examined the faded writing on it, then looked at the quilt. "Houston, we have a prob… no we don't." She spread the cloth key on top of part of the quilt. "I think it goes here. See the three notches on the edges? They line up with those images on the quilt. I think that's the alignment tool. Now to see what it says."

Virginia, Natalie, and Sanchez bent over the table and studied the quilt and key.

Sanchez straightened. "I don't see anything."

Natalie scrutinized the items carefully. "This is confusing. Looks like part of… I don't know, early Hill Country? If, I use my… Hollywood imagination, that line may be a river. The Colorado?" Natalie pointed at one of the quilt blocks and looked at Virginia. "And, this part of this quilt block may be a town. Burnet?"

Virginia, still examining the quilt with a magnifying glass, mumbled. "That's my guess." She directed Natalie's attention to an image on the quilt. "I don't know what that image is, maybe a village or small town. And this line over here might be the Llano River."

Sanchez stood looking bewildered. "You two are getting all this from that Mexican quilt and this old piece of cloth?"

"Yes. The quilt is from Mexico, but the additions are newer and so is the map key. They were added when the treasure was hidden. And look, X even marks the spot." Virginia pointed at a small, faint, X sewn into a quilt block. "That mark was added to the original quilting. Without the key we would never have noticed it."

Sanchez bent closer. "There's an X there?"

Virginia handed him a magnifying glass and pointed. "See, right there."

He bent over and used the magnifying glass. "I'll be damned! I see it now. You guys are really good."

Natalie stretched and arched her back. "Where is that X in reality?"

"Let's look at Colin Carswell's marked-up topographical map and road map of the area and see if we can pinpoint it."

"I'll get them," Natalie said as she made her way around the desk to the safe. She pulled the topographical map and a road map from the safe and handed them to Virginia. "Here you go."

Virginia took the maps, spread them out on the table, and tried to compare them to the quilt map. She looked at Natalie and Sanchez. "I think we may have a problem."

Sanchez shook his head. "This whole thing you're doing is a mystery to me."

Virginia pointed at the quilt then at the topographical map. "When the quilt map was made, Lake Buchanan didn't exist. I think the treasure is under the lake about here." She pointed at the topographical map. "The marked-up maps Colin had puts it in roughly the same location."

Natalie clapped her hands. "Can we get it?"

"Well, we don't have a precise location and it's been buried for well over a century and it's been underwater for over eighty years. The dam probably has built up silt on the lake bottom since it's been in operation." Virginia leaned against the table. "If the treasure was buried, the added lake silt would make it even deeper underground."

Sanchez frowned. "You also have the issue of who now would own the treasure. The property that is now underwater may have been public land or Indian land when the treasure was hidden in the 1800s. Maybe a ranch. Now it's under a government-owned lake. We'd have to get permission from the Lower Colorado River Authority at least, maybe the U.S. Army Corps of Engineers, the county, the state, and county historic commissions, and who know how many others. And each one would all say the treasure belongs to them."

Virginia nodded. "Good point. We'd also get claims from the Indians, various historical societies, and even private owners of the land prior to the river authority buying or taking the land claiming it. Then there's the U.S. government and the governments of Mexico and France to consider. And, we don't know exactly where it is. This map is not exactly a GPS." She looked at as Terry walked in. "I hope you have good news."

Terry grinned. "I have great news. I think so anyway. That Wampum artifact is from an area near Lake Ontario and the Genesee River."

Virginia's eyes shined. "Great. Ohmigod, that's Rochester, or at least close to it."

"Right. And it's near where the Erie Canal crosses the Genesee River."

Virginia's eyes narrowed. She bit her lip. "That... would... place... it... in..."

"What is now Genesee River Park," added Terry.

Virginia got a far-away look in her eyes. "When I was young, my family would sometimes visit my uncle and aunt during Christmas there. My uncle and my father would take me sledding in *that* park."

Natalie plopped into a chair. "It just went from bad to worse. The Indian pawn ticket is for something that may be buried in a city park fifteen-hundred miles from here? It would be a wonder that the city didn't find it when they made the park."

Terry shrugged. "You're probably right. But, the belt really isn't a pawn ticket. It is a record of something being left for safe keeping with the Seneca."

Virginia leaned back and grinned. "It's a beautiful park and it's big." Virginia looked at Terry. "How'd you get this information so fast?"

"From a couple sources." Terry leaned back against the table. "I sent the pictures to a friend of mine at the University of Rochester. Then I looked at it under high magnification and found some... substances. The SEM gave better definition."

Sanchez wrinkled his brow. "SEM?"

"Scanning electron microscope," explained Terry.

"Oh."

"The belt is from that region. My friend at the university was excited to see the Wampum pictures and quickly identified it with the type of work done by the Seneca in that particular locale. Their village where it came from was in the area that is now the park. They also fished the Genesee River and Lake Ontario and hunted in the region. Whatever was left with the Indians could be anywhere from the park to Lake Ontario."

Virginia limped back to her desk and sat. "This ankle is killing me." She took a breath and slowly let it out. "We don't know that any of Maximilian's treasure is actually hidden there."

Terry smiled. "My anthropologist friend said there are old legends or myths of some gold and other treasure being held or hidden by the Seneca Indians in the area in the mid to late 1800s. For that matter, the treasure may not have been buried. The Indians could have kept it in a lodge. Where or how they may have gotten the treasure, he doesn't know. There isn't any natural gold found in western New York. Could this particular legend be based on facts? This one may be real after all."

Sanchez shook his head. "How'd Maximilian's treasure get to New York? That seems a stretch to me."

Natalie sat. "I don't think all of it went there. Just part of it. My money is on Mr. Noble taking some of it there. But if he had some of the treasure's gold in upstate New York, why did he come back to Texas?"

Terry rubbed her hands together. "Maybe he got gold fever. If he was going to live in New York, maybe he took what he could on his journey there without being conspicuous and was going to come back to get the rest of it. Who knows?"

Virginia closed her eyes and rubbed the bridge of her nose. "In reality the Seneca village was in the park area. But, like you said, they could have hidden it anywhere from there to Lake Ontario. This lends credence to the fact that the gun that was used at the retreat also spent time in that area. The ranger said it had sugar maple and birch pollen in it. Those trees are native to New York state."

"The park is the closest we've got to an actual location and the rest is the built-up City of Rochester and its suburbs," Terry added. "They probably would have found it in the developed areas of the city if it was buried." She looked at Virginia. "You going to go get the treasure under Lake Buchanan and the treasure in New York?"

They all turned toward Virginia. The tension was electrifying.

Virginia opened her eyes, looked at the clock on the wall behind the others, and said, "Time for lunch."

"Virginia!" Natalie cried. "Lunch can wait. What are we going to do?"

CHAPTER 25

"Three things," said Virginia. "I'm getting some acetaminophen because my ankle hurts like hell and my head aches. I'm still having trouble concentrating."

Sanchez leaned close to Natalie. "If this is what she's like when she can't concentrate, what's she like when she can?"

"You don't want to even think of keeping up with her then."

He cringed. "Oh."

Terry Sorensen set the portfolio on the table. "You said three things, Virginia. What are the other two?"

Virginia looked up from rummaging through her center desk drawer. "Nuts, no acetaminophen. The other two? Oh yeah, we have lunch and then we flush out the murderers of Colin Carswell and the skeleton, Simon Cochran."

Terry tilted her head. "After all the hunting for the treasure you're going to just abandon finding it?"

Virginia held up her finger. "Just a second." She picked up her phone and called her secretary. "Ann, will you *please* get me some acetaminophen? The way I feel a dump truck-sized load would be really nice. Thank you." She hung up and looked at the others. "My main goal is finding the murderers. I plan on using the treasure to lure the killers out. Later we can see what we can do about actually finding the treasure."

Terry raised her hand.

Virginia laughed. "Terry, you don't need to raise your hand. We're not in school. You are part of this team."

"Yeah, well, I have an idea. And since your pain killer isn't here yet, I thought I'd toss it out for consideration."

"Go for it."

"You're operating under the authority of the Smithsonian, right?"

Virginia nodded. "Yes."

"Can we have them get involved with the search while we flush out the killers?"

Virginia sat back in her chair. "Great idea. After I get my meds and we have lunch, I'll contact Special Agent Tom Mason and bring him up to speed. Then I can ask him to have the Smithsonian get involved. I'd like you, Terry, to lead their efforts."

Terry looked shocked. "Me? I don't work for them."

"You helped me when we went to the jungles of Mexico and Guatemala a couple years ago on the *Trail of Threads* caper and Tom sanctioned you being with me. I'll handle all this with the Smithsonian." Virginia wrinkled her brow in thought. "I'd better inform Dr. Doverspike about my intentions."

"You think he'll go for it?" Terry asked.

Natalie chuckled. "She's got Dr. Doverspike wrapped around her little finger. He'd do anything for Virginia."

Terry smiled. "Yea, I think you're right about that. It'll be the Smithsonian that will be the tough nut to crack."

Natalie shook her head. "She'll finagle Senior Special Agent Tom Mason into agreeing to it, trust me. Handling the Smithsonian bureaucracy is his problem."

Virginia grunted. "You two know I'm sitting right here."

They smiled and said in unison, "Yes."

Sanchez's cell phone rang. He pulled it off his duty belt and answered. After a very brief and quiet discussion, he looked at Virginia. "I've just been assigned to work with the Smithsonian Central Security Service and liaise with the sheriff. I've been assigned to work for you, Mrs. Clark, for this investigation. Your man in Washington sure knows how to get things done. That was fast, and the sheriff isn't even upset. He's impressed that Washington specifically asked for me and the sheriff's office is being kept in the loop and will get the majority of the credit for the arrests."

"Good. This won't hurt your career any, that's for sure. Now, after lunch I want you to go change into civilian clothes. You are a plainclothes federal operative now."

Sanchez grinned. "Okay."

Virginia looked up as her secretary, Ann walked in and handed her a large bottle of acetaminophen and a glass of water. "Here you are, Virginia. And, Dr. Doverspike said you must go to the hospital and have that ankle x-rayed. It may be broken."

"But—"

"He said if you didn't do it soon, he'd call paramedics to take you."

Virginia sighed. "Yeah, he would. Tell Fred I'll go right after lunch. My team and I have some skull practice to do over lunch."

"I'll inform him, but he'll want a doctor's note after lunch, and you know it."

She took the pills. "I'll go, I promise."

Mysterious Threads

"Okay." Ann left the office.

Sanchez turned to Terry and whispered, "Skull practice?"

Terry shifted in her chair. "Scheming, conniving, planning, and noodling out a plan. It's a football thing, I think."

He nodded. "Thanks. I've got a lot to learn about how she operates."

"You'll catch on or go nuts. Welcome to the club."

"I vote for Olive Garden for lunch," said Natalie. "They've opened that new one near Wolf Ranch Shopping Center."

"The one across I-35?" asked Sanchez.

Terry brightened. "Yes. I'm game."

Sanchez's phone rang again. He answered it, listened, and then hung up. "The criminal background check on the list of ladies you asked for is complete. None of the women have any felony arrests and there are no warrants out for them. No criminal records at all. A few have had some minor traffic tickets, but a long time ago. They're clean."

Virginia nodded. "Thanks. That's a start. Shall we go for lunch? Once we have a plan, I'll go to the hospital to see about my ankle. It's just a sprain. I don't think they'll find anything, but that will keep Dr. Doverspike happy."

As they all rose, Sanchez looked around the room. "Are you going to relock that quilt, the key, and the maps in your safe?"

Virginia, halfway around her desk stopped and sighed. "Yeah, that's a good idea."

"You go ahead, Virginia, I'll lock everything up," said Terry. "I'll meet you on the loading dock."

"Why don't we go out the front door? I can drive around and pick everyone up," said Natalie. "That'll be easier on Virginia's ankle. No steps,"

"I'll meet you all at the restaurant," said Sanchez. "I need to bring my cruiser."

Terry touched the deputy's arm. "If you don't mind, Deputy, I'd like to ride there with you after I lock this stuff up."

Sanchez blushed and stammered. "Tha... that would... be great... doc." He grinned at her.

After lunch, Natalie took Virginia to the Georgetown Hospital emergency room. Once Virginia completed the usual paperwork and answered questions, she was taken to an examining room. Natalie followed her to the room and looked at the equipment and pictures while Virginia rested on the examination table.

A man dressed in green scrubs entered. "Hello, I'm Dr. Anderson. You're Virginia Davies Clark?" Virginia nodded.

"Nice to meet you Mrs. Clark." He pulled up a stool and sat. "Let me see your ankle."

Virginia removed her tennis shoe and raised her foot.

Dr. Anderson examined her ankle and felt around noticing Virginia grimace as he touched it. "Swollen. Does your foot hurt, too?"

"No."

"Can you put your body weight on it?"

"No."

"How did it happen?"

"I tripped over a tree root."

"Did you hear a crack or pop?"

"No."

Natalie ogled the doctor then said, "She ran into a tree and was knocked out. She couldn't hear anything."

"Oh." He pulled a penlight out of his pocket, stood, and examined Virginia's eyes. "Have you taken anything for the pain?"

"Just acetaminophen. We put ice... I mean frozen peas on my ankle right after it happened."

"Good. That was the best thing you could do for it. Do you have a headache, seeing double, tired?"

"Headache yes, the other stuff no."

"Okay. I'm going to order X-rays to see what's going on."

"It's just a sprain, isn't it?"

"I think you may have a broken ankle and might have a slight concussion. Let's see what the pictures say, okay?"

Virginia leaned back. "Okay." She watched the doctor leave and glanced at Natalie. "What do you think?"

Natalie grinned. "Grade A prime."

"Huh?"

"The Doc, he's a hunk."

"He's married, and you're taken."

"I know, and I do love Jeff, but I can still window shop, just can't go in, and try it on." Natalie frowned as she looked at Virginia. "Probably broken. You'll look good in a cast. I want to be the first to sign it."

Virginia bolted upright. "I can't be in a cast! I've got work to do."

"That's what deputies like me are for." Natalie turned toward the door. "Looks like radiology is here."

Two women in green scrubs rolled in a gurney and helped Virginia onto it. One looked at Natalie. "We're taking her to X-ray. We'll bring her right back."

Natalie tilted her head and looked at the technician. "Before you got here, I overheard a couple nurses in the hall talking, and they said radiology is backed up."

One of the techs smiled. "Yes, we are. But when someone is sent by

Mysterious Threads

the emergency department or the ICU, they go to the head of the line. We're first."

"I didn't know that. Thanks." Natalie hopped up on the exam table and watched Virginia being rolled away, then settled down with her iPhone to play a game when it rang. "Hello?"

"This is Terry Sorenson. How's Virginia doing?"

"They just took her to X-ray. I may have complicated things. I told them she was knocked out by a tree."

"You realize because of that, they may want to keep her for a while."

"Oops. I didn't think of that."

"Well, I'm with Deputy Sanchez. We're going to his place so he can change out of his uniform. Want us to come to the hospital?"

"No. If there are unexpected events here, I'll call you. Otherwise we'll meet at the museum when we're through. You have your assignments from our lunch meeting to start."

"Okay. Oh, one more thing, did Virginia talk to the Smithsonian yet about the treasure hunt?"

"Yes. She called Special Agent Mason while we drove here. It's a go. He'll get back with us as soon as he has everything in place. But he agreed to you being the senior representative on the treasure recovery team."

"That was fast. How'd she pull it off?"

"The Smithsonian has been in on this from the start. They told Virginia when they assigned her to the case that it has to do with Emperor Maximilian of Mexico, and... well... the laws about antiquities theft, international intrigue, and art smuggling and possible murders are involved."

"But there isn't any of that." Terry paused then said, "Well maybe some theft of part of the treasure and a couple murders."

"Theft of the treasure, multiple murders, attacks on Virginia and me and the deputy last night. I think we're about to uncover a hell of a lot more."

CHAPTER 26

Natalie looked toward the doorway. "They're wheeling Virginia back. Gotta go. I'll call you with an update." Natalie hung up.

The two women rolled the gurney into the examining room and helped Virginia back on the table then left.

Natalie stood next to the table. "How'd it go?"

"They wouldn't tell me much. And thanks to you, I got a few head X-rays. I guess we wait for the doctor."

A few minutes later Dr. Anderson returned and pulled up a rolling stool next to the table. "Okay, the results are in."

Virginia looked perplexed. "Good news? Sprain?"

"No. You broke your ankle. But the good news is, you just cracked some bones. And, you do have a mild concussion."

"I can't be laid up. What can you do to keep me mobile?"

"Your fracture isn't bad, so we'll fit you with a support cast. You won't be plastered up if that's what's bothering you. You'll need crutches and will need to keep weight off of it for about four weeks or so. You'll need to see your family doctor for follow up. I'll send the x-rays and my report to him. Another doctor will be here shortly. He's an orthopedics man and will get you your support boot and crutches. As for your head, rest is the best thing for it. Rest, no alcohol, and don't run into more trees. We should keep you for observation for the concussion for a day or two. But from your reaction to even being here in the first place, I think doing that would cause more problems than it would solve. If your headaches get worse or you start seeing double, get overly tired, or have any unusual symptoms, come back here at once."

Virginia frowned. "Do you think it will get worse?"

"No, but just be watchful." He pulled a prescription pad from his pocket. "I'll give you something for the pain. After you get the cast, you're good to go."

Virginia sighed. "Thanks, Doc."

Mysterious Threads

An hour later, Natalie drove Virginia back to the museum by way of a CVS drug store to get the pain medication. She parked in front of the museum, helped Virginia get her crutches from the back seat, and assisted her into the museum.

Virginia nodded at the receptionist as she went by on her new crutches and said, "Don't ask."

Natalie smiled at the receptionist. "She ran into a tree, broke her ankle, and banged her head. But not to worry, the tree is fine."

The receptionist chuckled. "I'll inform Dr. Doverspike that you are back from the hospital. He wanted to know if you went and when you got back."

"Tell him I'm fine," Virginia grumbled. She continued down a series of halls to her office. Plopping into her chair, she pulled out the bottom desk drawer and rested her cast on it. She picked up her phone and called Dr. Doverspike. "Hello, Fred. As I'm sure Melanie told you, I'm back from the hospital. Ankle's broken and I've got a mild concussion. Happy?"

"Yes, I'm glad you took my advice. No, I'm not happy you were injured. Now rest."

"Can't. I've got a couple murders to solve and a treasure to find."

"You have help, Virginia. Terry is going to assist you, and I know Ms. North is there with you, too. I understand there's a deputy sheriff following you around as well. Let them help you."

Virginia wiggled in her chair to get comfortable. "I am. But—"

"I want you to be their leader this time. Be the coach and let the players do their thing. I can't afford you getting worse or injured more. We need you to heal, Virginia."

"Okay, I get the picture, Fred. You're right, Natalie North is here with me, and trust me she's like a mother hen, and I'm her chick."

"Good. Say hello to Ms. North for me. Now get your team going. Oh yeah, the Smithsonian called. Dr. Sorenson is officially on the adventure with you and Ms. North. The Smithsonian is covering all her expenses and they increased the grant they gave us for this case when you went on active duty. Maybe I should rent you and Terry out to them on a steady basis. You two are a gold mine."

"Don't even think about it."

"Just kidding. Now get back to your case and don't forget to give me all the juicy details when you're done. It'll be a new chapter in the continuing saga of the Virginia Davies Mysteries I'm writing."

"Right. My saga. Gotta go." She hung up and glanced at Natalie. "Dr. Doverspike says you're to keep me out of trouble."

"He knows I'm shorter than Tom Cruise, doesn't he? I can't keep you out of mischief, I can't even stop you from running into trees."

"Will you stop about the tree thing? I don't usually run into trees."

Natalie chucked. "I know. But it's fun teasing you. And, now you get to tell your husband about it."

Virginia kneaded her forehead. "Yeah. That'll be a disaster. The sooner the better. I'll call him…"

Virginia and Natalie turned as Terry and Deputy Sanchez, now in civilian clothes, walked into the office.

Terry looked at the special support boot sticking out from behind the desk. "They usually don't put casts on sprains. I take it you broke your ankle."

Virginia looked at her. "You guessed it. Oh, it's called a support boot, but it feels like a cast to me. I'm supposed to direct the operation and let you foot soldiers do the grunt work." She bit her lip. "I'm not happy about it one bit."

"Yeah, you're usually in the mix." Terry sat in a chair next to Natalie while Sanchez pulled another chair in from an empty office next door and sat. Terry leaned forward. "Dr. Doverspike said the Smithsonian just negotiated for me to join the project. How'd you pull it off with Special Agent Mason and the Smithsonian?"

"Years of Catholic catechism classes and my grandmother taught me how to reassign guilt with the best of them." Virginia settled back in her chair. "The pain meds are kicking in."

Natalie glanced around the office. "It's cramped in here. Why don't we all go to the conference room and go over our notes from our lunch meeting while Virginia explains to her husband what happened?"

Terry spoke. "I think that's a good idea. Maybe we can have a detailed plan with action items by the time she gets back with us." She turned back to Virginia. "I know you'll handle him with kid gloves. Good luck."

"I'll need it," mumbled Virginia.

Thirty minutes later, Natalie, Terry, and Sanchez turned and watched as Virginia came limping into the conference room on her crutches. She plopped into a chair and looked at the marked-up whiteboard at the end of the room.

Natalie eyed her questioningly. "How'd it go?"

"It would have been better if I had stayed in the hospital. I might have gotten some sympathy. After a lecture about my crazy antics, concern about my safety and the safety of the local flora and fauna, my being hell on wheels, and him wanting to join us, I got Andy to calm down. Now I'm supposed to check in with him on a regular basis. You'd think I was a juvenile delinquent."

Natalie chuckled. "You are."

"Look who's talking. Oh yeah, guess who happened to be in Andy's office at the university when I called?"

Natalie's eyebrows shot upward. "Who?"

"Your boyfriend, Dr. Jeff Cummings."

Natalie's eyes narrowed. She folded her arms across her chest. "You told Andy *and* Jeff that I was with you when you got hurt, didn't you? You mentioned we were ducking bullets, too, didn't you? Did you also tell him about our misadventure last night as well?"

Virginia gave her a demure smile. "Yep. Had to deflect some of the incoming fire. Anyway, I told them you were my savior."

"How'd that work?"

"You need to call your lover before he storms in here. He's very concerned about you."

Natalie groaned. "Just what I need."

"Hey, he loves you."

Natalie smiled, her eyes looking dreamy. "Yeah, he does. And he likes me as I am and really cares about me. He can cook, too. Jeff's a keeper. He's not at all like the lazy, money-grabbing, self-centered, sex-crazed jackasses I dated in Hollywood."

Terry smiled. "Good for you. You deserve someone like him."

Virginia motioned for Natalie to go phone Jeff. "Call Jeff. You can use the phone in my office." After Natalie hurried out of the conference room Virginia studied the whiteboard. "Looks like you guys have been busy."

Terry stood and aimed her laser pointer at the board. "Yes, we have. We divided our attack in multiple approaches. First, we copy and repackage the information about Lake Buchanan for the Smithsonian and the proposed search area so we can keep the originals. Second, the Smithsonian team is starting to sort out the permission thing to officially explore the lake and get the required approvals. We'll compile a list of possible interested parties and send it to them ASAP. I'll lead that effort. But this will take time, so I asked the Smithsonian for some urgent field equipment for us to do some preliminary, under the radar, surveying."

Virginia looked intrigued. "Under the radar? What kind of equipment?"

"They are sending some underwater lights and sensor devices, gravitometers, high-resolution portable sonars, and warm dry-suits for diving for us to get started. I asked for dive equipment that allows us to talk to each other and breathe through our noses."

Virginia looked suspicious. "They agreed with all that?"

"Yes. They're sending it by... special delivery. Agent Mason put me in contact with another man in his office. He said they'd also send the *DSI* super masks. They have integrated *AquaCom* connections so we can all talk to each other. He's sending the usual SCUBA gear with *AquaCom* interfaces plus closed circuit *DRAEGAR LAR V* rebreathers should we need some serious clandestine dives. We're getting four SeaBobs to use as underwater propulsion units. He said those babies can do thirty-miles-per-hour for up to four hours."

"That's great." Virginia closed her eyes and sighed. "Wait. What kind of special delivery?"

"They're sending the stuff via an Air Force plane to Ft. Hood. The army will deliver it here to the museum the day after tomorrow," said Terry.

"Okay. That's quite a list and a great job. How'd you pull all that off so fast?"

"The guy I talked to at the Smithsonian had been briefed by Tom. He had heard about your and Natalie's trip to the Caribbean and undoing of a major drug distributor and smuggler of antiquities during the *Secret Threads* case. He knew about me from when you and I were in Mexico and Guatemala on the *Trail of Threads* adventure a couple years ago. He was on the navy aircraft carrier that pulled us out of Mexico. He actually remembered me. Fancy that." Terry smiled. "He was most willing to help. He mentioned something about liking the pictures from our expedition south of the border. Did you send any?"

"I'm sure he remembered you. We were the only two civilian women on the ship. And even in the shape we were in, you drew a lot of attention from the crewmen. I didn't send any pictures. But I think you gave some to an officer on the ship when we departed."

Terry blushed. "Oh yeah. I forgot about those. Anyway, he said to say hello."

Virginia propped her injured foot on the seat of an adjacent chair. "You're planning on some clandestine diving in the lake? We'll need a good-sized boat."

"I can get us one of the sheriff's large workboats," interjected Sanchez. "Just need the date, time, and where to have it sent. I'll also tell the state game wardens and the LCRA Rangers that we're doing something for a Williamson County Sheriff's investigation, so they don't get in the way of the 'under the radar' explorations."

Virginia looked over at Sanchez. "You can do that?"

"The Sheriff said he'd supply anything I need to assist with this joint federal-county investigation. I'll get the boat and handle the other law enforcement agencies."

"Good. When Natalie gets back, we need to do some detail planning for our underwater operation."

"Our underwater operation?" Terry leaned on the table. "You're not diving, boss. I will dive along with Natalie. You and Deputy Sanchez will remain topside to handle the surface equipment, operate the boat, and make sure no one disturbs us. You can't go diving with a concussion and a broken ankle."

Virginia sat back and bit her lip. "I don't like being on the sideline."

Terry relaxed and sat. "You're not. You'll be directing things from the surface and protecting our asses."

"Exactly where will you be diving? The idea of the expedition was to narrow the area of the hunt. That's a large lake."

"Your secretary brought in some old maps of that area and the Colorado River before Lake Buchanan was formed. There is a location along the old riverbed where there are some large caves. There are other caves indicated around the lake, but they aren't as big and weren't easy to get to. We figured if Mr. Noble hid the treasure, it would be someplace he could easily access. And burying wagon loads of treasure would be hard and not go unnoticed. These caves would make a good hiding place. They happen to be close to where we think the X is on the quilt map. Anyway, it's somewhere to start. We figure they're about twenty-five to forty feet under the surface."

Virginia frowned. "And I have to sit this one out in a boat."

Terry nodded. "Unless you want your husband interfering, I'd say yes."

Virginia shook her head. "You're right. The plan sounds like a good one."

Sanchez stood and pointed at another part of the whiteboard. "Continuing from earlier, third, since you know the area better than any of us, we thought you should figure out the New York angle and plan what we need to do there. Clandestinely locating a long-hidden treasure in a metropolitan area will be tricky. You may want the Smithsonian involved with that, too. The…" he made air quotes "…interested parties in New York will come out of the woodwork."

Virginia nodded. "Agreed."

Terry looked at the materials spread out on the conference table. "You still have that… rubbing you made?"

Sanchez frowned. "I'm sorry, what rubbing?"

Virginia shifted in her seat. "I made a rubbing of part of Isabelle's tomb marker. There were some highlights or reliefs in the stone. Some were pretty well worn. I put some paper over it and rubbed it with a soft pencil. That made an image of the relief on the tombstone on the paper."

"Oh. Then we need to figure out what that says and soon," added Sanchez. "That's number four."

Natalie entered the room. "How can I help?"

Virginia looked at Natalie. "Deputy Sanchez, you, and I will try and figure what the rubbings mean."

Sanchez's face brightened. "Okay." Natalie nodded and plopped into a chair.

Terry pointed at another part of the board. "Fifth, Natalie is going to drop hints at your retreat, especially during her presentation, about the treasure and the lake. She's going to also mention that you think part of it is located on the ranch and that you have developed some more clues. This should trigger whoever is behind your attacks to do something." She turned toward Sanchez. "Deputy, that's another area for you to monitor."

Sanchez nodded as he sat and sipped a cup of coffee.

Virginia scratched her cast. "So, we actively start looking for the treasure and put the word out at the retreat that we're closing in on it."

"Right," said Terry.

Virginia sat back. "You guys did all this while I was digging my way out of trouble with my professor husband?"

Sanchez sat straighter. "Ms. North and I have a plan on how to watch the ladies at the retreat. And, we'll make some noise about starting to explore the lake. We're going to mention that our maps are locked in the evidence locker at the ranch. We'll put some fake ones of the lake there. I've arranged for us to get some unobtrusive video cameras from the Sheriff. We can install them. They're battery operated and wireless. We can monitor them from our computers."

Virginia rubbed her forehead. "Besides the New York angle, what else do I do?"

Terry smiled. "Lead and get better. The stuff about the New York side of the case needs to be cleared up. And you will monitor and protect our dives from the boat. We don't know who will be lurking in the shadows."

Virginia laughed. "Okay, I'll buy into all this. But the dives will be just 'under the radar' exploratory ones to help narrow down the areas for the Smithsonian to handle and intrigue our murderer."

"Right. The equipment the Smithsonian is sending will facilitate diving clandestinely. If we need to do more diving later, it will be nice to have."

"I agree," said Virginia.

"So first we figure out the rubbing," Terry said. "I think you're right, Virginia, there is something important on it. Once we have the information, we figure out what to do with it. Don't forget, you're running interference for us with the Smithsonian, too."

"It sounds like you're doing fine with them. They're sending the equipment you asked for." Virginia turned to Natalie. "How'd it go with Jeff?"

Natalie rubbed her eyes with the palms of her hands. "You aren't the only one who can reassign guilt. After a lot of weasel wording and promising him some... never mind, my boyfriend has graciously decided he doesn't need to come and help after all. Trust me that took some persuading. And, the museum receptionist gave me this for you. She said someone dropped it on her counter when she took a brief break to get a cup of cof-

Mysterious Threads

fee." She handed Virginia an envelope.

Virginia opened it. A small gold coin fell out along with a small, hand-printed note. She read it to the others. "It says;

> *I want the treasure and I will get it at any cost.*
> *I've been hunting for it for years and it is mine.*
> *Others have been killed; you could be, too.*
> *Don't get in the way"*

Virginia held up the coin and looked at the others. "Looks like we've kicked the hornet's nest."

Terry picked up the phone and dialed security. "This is Dr. Sorenson. Can you look at the security feed from the lobby for someone dropping off an envelope for Virginia?" She listened. "Okay, thanks." Terry turned. "There were a number of visitors today but none in the past hour. They're continuing to look farther back and see if there is anything."

Virginia looked at the note. "I don't think they'll see anything. Whoever left this will be careful not to be recognized."

CHAPTER 27

Back at the ranch, Natalie helped Virginia navigate the porch stairs and hallway to the parlor then settled her in an overstuffed chair with her foot resting on an ottoman.

As Natalie sat across from her, Virginia asked, "You're going to dive with Terry?"

Natalie nodded. "Yes. She can't go it alone."

"Right, but do you know how to dive? Have you been through PADI or NAUI training?"

"The who training?" Natalie frowned. "PADI or NAUI? What are they?"

"The national organizations that certify divers to ensure proper training."

"No. I didn't even know they existed. I've never SCUBA dived before," said Natalie. "But Terry's getting the type of diving gear that I can just breathe normally and the diving suit is a dry suit. We won't be in the ocean with sharks and other beasties. It's a lake with... with bass and other small freshwater fish. How hard can it be?" Natalie gave Virginia a hopeful look. "I've snorkeled before, that counts, doesn't it?"

Virginia jerked upright. "No! Diving would be dangerous for you! You aren't trained. You shouldn't go. The water will be murky, so visibility will be extremely limited, and you don't know what else could be there. This isn't the ocean, which tends to be clearer. With limited visibility, you can get disoriented to say the least. You could easily panic and that's never good underwater. And no, snorkeling doesn't count. You must be properly trained. You can't go if you're not certified, period. Call Sanchez and see if he's a diver. He can replace you in the water and you can stay with me on the boat."

Natalie shook her head. "He can't dive. Something about his ears."

"Well, Terry can't dive alone." Virginia sat back and crossed her arms. "Water is buoyant. I'll dive with Terry. My ankle won't be a problem."

Natalie chuckled. "You can't wear a swim fin on that broken foot. You going to use only one frog foot?" She smiled. "You'd probably just swim in circles. Plus, you also have a concussion. Your diving is out of the question."

Virginia sighed. "You're right. I see what you mean. We need to think of something. Terry can't dive alone. And I wouldn't swim in circles."

Helen Chandler hurried into the room. She stopped and gasped as she looked at Virginia's support boot. "Oh, my. You broke it?"

Virginia looked up and nodded. "Just cracked. The doc wants me to take it easy. No running through the woods."

"Well, you do like he says and take it easy, dear. Would you like us to bring you dinner in here?"

"No, I'll come to the dining room." Virginia wrinkled her brow. "Helen, didn't you tell me you were originally from Batavia, New York?"

"Yes." Helen nodded. "It's between Rochester and Buffalo."

"I know where it is. I used to visit that part of the state when I was young."

"I'm eighty-five, so my dear, you're still young to me."

Virginia laughed. "I guess so. What got you to Texas?" *Helen would have been born in 1935 and would have been about fifteen when Simon Cochran died. Nuts.*

"I got tired of the cold and snow. After my husband died, I moved here. My husband and I were friends of Colin Carswell, and he kind of sold me on Georgetown and Williamson County. At my age, my joints didn't like the weather in the north."

Virginia tilted her head and smiled. "How'd you and your husband meet Colin? He was from Texas and you were in New York."

"Fishing." Helen got a faraway look in her eyes. "Colin and my husband were avid fishermen. They both liked fly-fishing and spin casting. Back in those days the Genesee Brewing Company, they make Genesee beer, would hold a New York state-wide fishing contest every year. Colin would come up from Texas, and he and my husband would enter it. They became friends. Funny, I haven't thought about that in years."

"Do you fish?" asked Natalie.

Helen nodded. "I used to. My joints are too stiff and hurt too much to do it anymore. How about you two?"

"Yes," Virginia said. "I used to fish the Sierra Nevada, San Bernardino, and Santa Rosa mountains for trout. I did some saltwater fishing, too. But with grad school and work, I somehow stopped doing it."

Natalie sighed. "Yeah. I got started while doing a movie. After that, like Virginia, I'd go to the Sierra Nevada Mountains to the streams and isolated lakes, the Tehachapi, San Bernardino, and San Gabriel and fish for trout. Sorry to say I haven't done it in years."

Virginia sat back. "How'd Harriet meet Colin? Do you know? She isn't a native Texan, either is she?"

Helen rubbed her forehead. "No. I'm not sure how she met Colin. Harriet moved here a little before me. She worked for Colin for a while before she was married. She's originally from France. Her maiden name was Raineau. She's in her late seventies, but don't let on that I told you that."

"Okay. Clara Peterson is from here, right? She was Colin's cousin."

"Yes, you're correct. She grew up in Austin. Clara and Harriet are also members of the same quilt guild I'm in and they're in my quilting Bee as well."

"Good to know. Thank you, Helen," said Virginia.

"If you don't need anything, I'll call you when dinner's ready." Helen turned and went back toward the kitchen.

Virginia glanced at Natalie. "That was interesting, but something is off. None of the ladies are old enough to have killed Simon Cochran."

"That doesn't mean a relative or old family friend didn't do it," said Natalie.

"Right. More questions. We need some answers." Virginia looked around. "Where's Deputy Sanchez?"

"Ready for this? Deputy Luis Sanchez is eating dinner with Terry. He wormed a dinner date with her while you were convincing your husband you didn't require his immediate presence."

Virginia's face brightened. "Good for Sanchez."

"He's smitten by Terry. I don't think he's met an archaeologist before. He thinks she's pretty and smart. He's impressed that she is going to do the diving."

Virginia's hand shot to her mouth. "That's it. Why didn't I think of this before?"

Natalie looked confused. "What?"

"Andy. My husband's a diver. I bet I could get him to dive with Terry. He likes her, and he'd probably jump at the chance to do it so he could keep an eye on things."

"Huh? We're back to diving again?"

"Yes." Virginia grinned. "Does Jeff dive?"

"I don't know. The subject never came up. But if Andy is coming, Jeff will be right there with him." Natalie had a worried expression. "I'm not sure having them both along will be a good idea."

"Why not? It solves the second diver dilemma."

"Yes, it does, but then they'll be asking a lot of questions and want to stay and help."

Virginia reached down and rubbed her boot. "We just point out to them that they have teaching and research responsibilities, and the university doesn't pay them to investigate crimes or find treasure."

Natalie sighed and shook her head. "Easier said than done. We have our work cut out for us."

"I know. I'll call Andy and see what he says about diving. Then I'll have Terry coordinate the date with him directly."

"Try to get him to not... never mind. He'll blab to Jeff anyway."

"I thought you'd want to be with him."

"I do but not when someone keeps trying to kill us."

"Good point."

Helen stepped into the room. "Dinner time, ladies."

Virginia looked up at Helen. "We'll be right there." She watched Helen leave the room, then turned toward Natalie. "After dinner, call Sanchez and have him meet us at the museum. We'll start on the rubbing tonight."

Natalie shook her head. "Can't do it. I need tonight to finish preparing for my presentation about wool knitting and felting. My class is tomorrow. Anyway, you should rest tonight. I'll have Sanchez or Terry pick you up in the morning and take you to the museum. You guys can start working on the rubbing, and I'll come there after my class."

Virginia bit her lip. "Okay. I'll work things out with Andy about the diving tonight while you prepare for your class." She pulled herself up and grabbed her crutches. "Let's go eat and off handedly mention the treasure hunt while we dine. That hopefully will get the ball rolling."

"Yeah, that or get us killed." Natalie followed Virginia to the dining room.

After dinner, Virginia went to her room and researched more about the Seneca Indians in upstate New York on her laptop. She let out a frustrated breath. *Nothing about any treasure, myth or not.* She turned off her computer and started to get ready for bed when her cell phone rang. "Hello?"

"Virginia, this is Terry Sorenson."

"Hi, Terry. I thought you were out with Deputy Sanchez."

"I am. We had dinner together then we came back to the museum."

"I see." *Some date. How did she talk him into going back there?* "What can I do for you, Terry?"

"I wanted to look at that rubbing you made, but it's locked in your safe."

"Yes. I was going to go there tomorrow to examine it with you while Natalie is teaching her class." Virginia sat on the edge of her bed. "Why do you want to see it tonight?"

"Well... I glanced at it when you had it on the table in the conference room. I saw something but it didn't register with me until a little while ago. I wanted to verify what I think I saw."

Virginia stiffened. "What did you think you saw?"

"It confirms what you said about the treasure story, but the bottom part was added later, and it may give the location of the New York part of the treasure, but I don't think it's still in New York."

CHAPTER 28

"I see." Virginia sat thinking for a second. "I'll come to the museum now."

"You can't drive with your foot in a cast," said Terry. "And anyway, you don't have a car there."

Virginia sighed. "You're right. Okay, so it confirms our theory about the location of the main part of the treasure here in Texas?"

"I think so."

"And you said it gives the location of the New York part and it may not be in New York?"

"It was just a quick look. But that's what I think. However, what I think I saw didn't quite jive with what Carswell was doing."

"Oh boy." Virginia's grip on her cell phone tightened. "Natalie and I casually mentioned at dinner here that we were on the trail of the treasure and Carswell knew where it was."

"Trying to get the murderer to show his hand?" asked Terry.

"Yeah. I hope this doesn't jeopardize the hunt for the killers."

"I'm not sure what I think I saw was what it really was. That's why I wanted to check it out."

Virginia swung her legs on the bed and leaned back against a pillow. "What doesn't jive with what Carswell was doing?"

"I think I've said more than I should at this point. You know me, I like to be sure of the facts before I give an opinion."

"Yes, I know. Oh, before I forget, you can't dive alone."

"I know that. Natalie is going to dive with me." Virginia moved the phone to her other ear. "She can't. Natalie doesn't have a PADI or a NAUI certification."

"Well—"

"I'm going to ask my husband, Andy, to go because he is certified."

"Okay. But I think we should study the rubbing before you ask him."

Virginia hesitated. *Terry is a good archeologist so if she's concerned about this, I'd better take her advice.* "In that case, I'd better join you and we'll examine the rubbing tonight. I'll see if I can get my husband to pick me up and take me to the museum tonight."

"Don't bother him. I'll pick you up in twenty minutes."

"Okay. I'll be waiting in front of the main house. I'll have my cell phone on in case you need to reach me."

Virginia sat for a second thinking. "Wait, you can't get here from the museum in twenty minutes."

"I can in a police car." Terry disconnected.

Virginia sat looking at her phone. *Whatever Terry saw spooked her enough to get the deputy to use his emergency signals to come and get me. I'd better tell Natalie.* Virginia slipped off the bed and limped on her crutches across the hall to Natalie's room. She knocked on the door then heard a loud commotion inside the room. Someone screamed and cussed. Virginia tried the door. It opened. Someone barreled into her knocking her to the hall floor. She turned in time to glimpse a person dressed in dark sweatpants, a black hoodie, and orange track shoes, holding his side and swaying as he hurried down the hall to the rear stairs. Virginia's ankle throbbed and the back of her head hurt. Grabbing for her crutches, Virginia tried to get up when she heard Natalie.

"Let me help you," said Natalie from the doorway. Natalie picked up the crutches and helped Virginia stand. "You okay?"

Virginia shook her head to clear the cobwebs. "My ankle didn't like being run over. What the hell happened?"

Natalie glanced down the hall. "I had an uninvited visitor."

"I noticed." Virginia glanced into the room. "How'd he get into your room?"

"I have no idea."

"You must have severely pissed him off by the exit he made."

Natalie led Virginia into her room and pointed at the bed. "Sit. You need to get off that ankle."

Virginia hopped to the bed and plopped down. She looked at the floor and the overturned chair. "Is that blood?"

"Yes. And before you ask, it's his, not mine."

"What happened? Who was that?"

Natalie looked out her window, then back at Virginia. "I don't know. I could tell it was a man by his voice and build. He had a mask on. Believe it or not, it was a plastic President Nixon mask. He wanted to know where the treasure is. When I told him to go to hell, he tried to hit me, but he didn't succeed."

Virginia stiffened. "Are you all right?"

"Oh yeah. I may be short, but I'm no pushover. Since I moved to Texas and met you, I've learned how to defend myself. My ah… visitor is now in need of serious medical assistance, and probably soon."

"He is?" Virginia tensed. "Why? What did you do?"

Natalie sat on her desk chair. "When he grabbed me and raised his fist to hit me, I stabbed him in his left hand with a stainless-steel knitting needle. That hurt him and made him jump back. He got really pissed. When he came at me again, I used these." She held up a pair of large, bloody, pointed, bird-scissors. "I tried to take out his appendix."

Virginia sat with her jaw agape. "You stabbed him in the abdomen with those scissors?"

"That wasn't my intended target. I was aiming for something else that would have seriously and painfully impaired his love life, but unfortunately, he moved." Natalie took a breath. "I couldn't get to my gun, so I improvised." Natalie raised an eyebrow. "Think I should call the sheriff?"

Virginia laughed. "Ms. North, you're one dangerous woman."

Natalie grinned. "He knows that now, too. About the sheriff?"

"Deputy Sanchez is on the way here with Terry. You can tell him."

Natalie looked puzzled. "Why are they coming here tonight?"

"Terry thinks she saw something in the rubbing I made and wants to see it again. She thinks it may change our approach to things. She and Sanchez are coming to get me so I can open my safe at the museum and we can examine the rubbing tonight."

Natalie stood. "I'm coming, too."

Virginia leaned back on her elbows. "You have a class to prepare for."

"Done. I've got my talking materials, visual aids, and samples all finished and have my demo stuff ready."

Virginia gave a slight nod. "That was fast."

"I prepared most of it before we came. I just put the finishing touches on it here." Natalie looked out her window. "Guess who's here? And he's got his emergency lights on, too."

Virginia slid off the bed. "I'd better go downstairs. I told Terry I'd meet them on the porch." She picked up her crutches and started for the door when she stopped and looked at Natalie. "Why do you suppose he attacked you instead of me? I've got the physical limitation, and I've been leading this investigation."

"I don't know. Maybe because I'm your partner, I'm short, and I look defenseless. His opinion might have changed now." Natalie grabbed her backpack. "Like I said, I'm coming with you."

Virginia eyed her. "Like that?"

"What's wrong?" Natalie looked down at her clothes. "I'm dressed."

"In a cut-off T-shirt that barely covers your unrestrained boobs, and you are wearing shorts."

"Who needs a bra? This is comfortable." Natalie slipped her backpack on.

"That outfit leaves almost nothing to the imagination. Now that you've got your backpack on, there's *nothing* left to the imagination. You might want to just carry it. When we go downstairs, you'll give the women here heart attacks, to say nothing about poor Deputy Sanchez."

"That's their problem." Natalie huffed. "A couple things I quickly learned in Hollywood are: imagination is highly overrated, and a woman does not need to be modest to be respected. Let's go."

They met Terry and Sanchez in the parlor.

Natalie recounted the story of her intruder and stabbing him while Sanchez tried to take notes as he struggled to not ogle Natalie. "Deputy, do I have to go to the sheriff's office about this?"

He shook his head. "No. I'll take care of it. Let's get you ladies back to the museum so we can figure out what's going on."

Virginia stopped and looked at Sanchez. "If Natalie's surgery was as bad as she thinks then her attacker might be at a clinic or hospital emergency room. Can you have the sheriff's office check?"

"Yeah. I'll call it in while we drive."

Virginia limped out toward the police car with Natalie beside her.

Sanchez and Terry followed. He leaned closer to Terry. "Does Natalie usually dress like that? I haven't observed her do this before."

"You noticed?" Terry chuckled. "Sometimes. She was an actress and got used to wearing almost nothing or being naked in the movies she was in. Virginia said she'd dress like this a lot, and sometimes even more risqué, when she moved here a few years ago. She caused quite a stir."

Sanchez swallowed. "I can see that."

Forty minutes later, they arrived at the museum. The guards met them at the front door and admitted them.

They proceeded to Virginia's office where she opened the safe and removed the rubbing. She set it on her conference table, sat, and looked at Terry. "Okay, here it is. What did you see?"

Terry moved closer and bent over, examining the rubbing. After several minutes of intense concentration, she straightened. "Look at this." Terry picked up a pencil and pointed. "This section seems to verify what we know about the treasure. Except the location. Nothing specific about that. But if you look here," she pointed at a section in the middle of the rubbing, "It tells that Isabelle was the one who found out the location."

Natalie looked at the rubbing. "Does it say what happened to her?"

"No." Terry moved a couple feet down the side of the table and pointed again. "This section was added well after the upper parts."

Natalie looked at the rubbing. "How can you tell?"

"The upper sections are worn and weathered more. You can also see the style of the letters and figures are slightly different."

Sanchez's eyes widened as Natalie bent down and looked at the

Mysterious Threads

rubbing.

Natalie looked up at Terry. "Yeah, you're right. They are different. I never would have noticed that. Who did it?"

"Simon Cochran."

"The skeleton?"

"Yes. Well, not the skeleton, but Simon Cochran did it."

Virginia looked skeptical. "If Simon Cochran made the additions in the early 50s, and he had been in New York looking for the treasure, then he was killed after that."

"I think, from this rubbing, Simon Cochran found it and returned to Texas with it." Terry indicated a section of the rubbing. "This suggests that Simon brought it back in the early 50s and hid it on the ranch. That's probably what got him killed."

Sanchez shook his head. "I'm glad you ladies can read that thing. But why would this Simon fellow carve the information on the tombstone?"

"I would hazard a guess that Simon did it as a way to ensure someone later could locate the New York part of the treasure," Virginia added.

Sanchez twisted in his seat. "So, Simon could read what was already on the tombstone?"

Terry nodded. "Maybe some of it but probably not all of it would be my guess. He knew his ancestor made the upper images, so he added to them. Nobody up to that point had discovered them but him, so he figured this would be a good hide the information. The way the newer figures are written implies he was a military man and probably an engineer. Thus Simon Cochran."

"So why didn't he just go get the rest of the treasure?"

Terry waved her hand dismissively. "He didn't have the quilt."

Virginia rubbed her hands together. "If Simon did this in the early to mid-50s, then, from what I saw of his bones, he'd have been in his mid to late fifties. I think he could read the tombstone markings. That's why he added his materials to it for safekeeping."

Sanchez frowned. "Wouldn't hiding it someplace be better than putting it in plain sight?"

Virginia chuckled. "My husband is an amateur magician. He has repeatedly said if you want to hide something, put it in plain sight. That's exactly what Simon Cochran did. It's been safe for over half a century and the other section on the tombstone for over a century."

Natalie leaned against the wall. "Where does it say the New York part of the treasure is?"

Terry sat. "A better question is, who killed old Simon Cochran and now Colin Carswell?"

CHAPTER 29

Virginia pulled a sheet of paper from her desk. "Let's take a look at the timeline. In the early to mid-fifties, Colin would have been in his mid to late teens. Old enough to kill but I don't think he did it. He was probably aware of the treasure stories and about Simon Cochran, Mr. Noble, June Cochran, and Isabelle. Colin, as a boy, probably knew Simon briefly. Since the stories of the treasure had been around his family for close to a hundred years, he likely considered them legends or old family ghost stories. After all, he was a teenager. His father was alive then as was his father's older sister."

Natalie arched a speculative eyebrow. "Colin's father had an older sister? How'd you come upon this factoid?"

"Clara mentioned it at lunch yesterday. Colin's father's sister is Clara's mother. That makes Clara and Colin cousins. That we already knew. And, Colin's father was quietly searching for the… *family* treasure." Virginia picked up a small, old, worn, brown notebook. "I found this in the attic when I discovered Simon's bones. It's Colin's dad's journal and was in the steamer trunk that Simon's skeleton was in."

Sanchez straightened. "Hold on. Did the deputies who responded to the ranch when you found the skeleton know about that?"

Virginia gave him a sheepish look. "Ahh… no. I kept it. Don't forget, when we found it, the Smithsonian made me the lead federal investigator. So, technically the lead investigator had this evidence in her possession."

"Dios mio," he murmured. "What'll I tell the sheriff?"

"Nothing. This is an ongoing federal investigation and he doesn't need the sordid details. At least not yet."

Sanchez looked at Natalie. "Does she always operate like this?"

Natalie shrugged. "Pretty much."

"She's successful catching crooks this way?"

"Definitely. The Smithsonian Central Security Service loves her."

"The criminal's lawyers must have fits in court," said Sanchez.

"No. Virginia's adversaries usually don't go to court. They mostly go to the morgue or... disappear. The few who actually manage to get their day in court are put away for a long time in a federal penitentiary."

"The morgue or... disappear?"

"Don't ask."

Virginia cleared her throat. "Guys, I'm right here."

Sanchez gave a slight grin and nod. "Sorry. You know, I've never heard of normal police officers operating like you two."

Natalie chuckled. "We're not normal."

Virginia set the book down. "From what I read, and I just started it, Colin's father is the one who killed Simon. It was during some heated argument about the treasure and the ranch. It seems Simon had allegedly hidden the part of a treasure he may have brought back from New York on the ranch. Funny thing though, there is no mention of Maximillian. Colin's father wanted to locate and get the rest of the treasure. But to do it he needed money. He couldn't just go out and sell the gold and jewels he had already found without stirring up a lot of questions, especially by the sheriff or local ranchers."

Virginia glanced at her foot. "Damn boot. Now my ankle itches." She regarded the group. "Where was I? Oh yeah, owning gold. In those days, gold was highly regulated and unless you had a good reason, like jewelry, under $100 in gold, or industrial plating, and alike, private ownership of gold was illegal."

Terry had a disbelieving expression. "If he had part of the treasure, wouldn't he have shown it to Colin's father as an incentive to fund finding the rest of it?"

"You'd think so, wouldn't you?" Virginia picked up a pen and waved her arms as she continued. "But, no. At the time, so far in the journal, Colin's father said Simon never admitted to having the treasure, let alone hiding it. Maybe he wanted it all for himself or there is still something we don't know. Probably had gold fever. Colin's dad figured the treasure story was just an old myth and didn't support wasting money searching for it. Simon disappeared shortly after that fight between them. There are a couple lines in the notebook that suggest that later Colin's dad somehow learned that some of the treasure *might* actually be on the ranch and he started to look for it. He never found it."

"That's some revelation. Seems a little hard to believe, but then..." Natalie stepped away from the wall, sat next to Sanchez at the table, and looked at the old notebook. "Why didn't you say something about the book before?" Natalie leaned back in the chair and crossed her legs.

Virginia sighed. "At first I thought it was like a lot of the other stuff we have accumulated about this case. Something to go over after we look at the important stuff, like the maps, quilt, and the materials now in the safe. I didn't think about it until Clara mentioned some more facts about her family at dinner tonight. Anyway, I had been thinking that someone at the ranch committed both murders. Then we discovered their ages weren't right. So, based on all that I glanced at the notebook." She put the pen down.

Sanchez blinked, then nervously tried to look away from Natalie's mostly exposed breasts. "Ahh... I guess we solved the murder of Simon Cochran about seventy years ago. Where is Colin's father now?"

Virginia waved her hand dismissively. "He died years ago."

"Hmm... okay then, who do we like for Mr. Carswell's demise?"

Virginia looked at the group. "I'm not sure. But we're going to use the treasure hunt to flush the person or persons out."

Terry raised an eyebrow. "Persons, as in more than one?"

"Yes. Someone attacked Natalie tonight. Someone attacked a deputy sheriff and a ranch hand and tried to barbeque Natalie and me in the outbuilding. Someone shot at us and actually did wound one of the quilters with an old army .45. That particular gun had been here and in New York and may have belonged to Simon. Unless Simon's ghost shot it, someone found it and now used it. Natalie and I were attacked on the road the other night, and again on the way here a few nights ago by a gang of men. That could have only happened if someone at the ranch tipped them off. Then there are the threatening notes we've received. I'm thinking the culprit has accomplices. Probably paid thugs."

"Did Colin have any children?" asked Terry.

"No."

"So, that someone... Colin's killer, is at the ranch?"

Virginia nodded. "I believe so, yes."

"So, assuming we're using the treasure hunt to flush out the killer, am I still diving in Lake Buchanan where we think the interesting caves are?"

"Yes, but first, let's find the part of the treasure that's on the ranch. That might be easier. That'll also whet the killer's appetite for gold and should get the killer to try to get the rest of the treasure."

Sanchez took a deep breath. "Since we're getting this thing into gear, I'd better go to the ranch and set up the surveillance equipment I got from the sheriff."

Virginia lowered her leg to the floor. "When can you do that?"

"When we're done here."

"Good. Let's finish examining the rubbing so we know where to look for the New York part of the treasure on the ranch."

Terry stood. "May I suggest that you three go to the ranch and set up the surveillance equipment and mingle with the quilters like everything is normal? Well, normal as much as it can be. I'm sure the ladies will have questions and you could interject more hints about the treasure hunt. I'll remain here. Interpreting this rubbing will take me some time. I'll catch up with you as soon as I have something to report."

Virginia bit her lip, then said, "Deputy, can Natalie and I hook up the equipment you got from the sheriff, or do you have to do it?"

"Yeah, you can do it. I can give you the instructions and show you what you need to do. Why?"

"I'd like to have you stay with Dr. Sorenson as much as possible. What she is doing is vitally important, and after all that has happened, I think her having a bodyguard from now on is critical. And I'm sure she could use the help."

Sanchez looked at Terry. His face brightened after she nodded her concurrence. "Okay. Glad to help. But, will you and Ms. North be okay?"

"Yes. We can take care of ourselves. After we set up the equipment, I'll make a list of candidates for being the murderer. Now let's split up and go do our assignments. We have the action items from earlier and the rubbing to interpret, so let's get going."

Natalie smiled. "Or as Sherlock would say, 'The game's afoot.'"

Sanchez cleared his throat. "Ladies, there is just one little detail you forgot."

Virginia eyed him quizzically. "What?"

"You and Natalie rode here in my cruiser. I'll have to drive you back."

Virginia held up a finger. "Hold that thought." She dialed security on her desk phone. "Ed, this is Virginia. Any chance I can borrow a museum vehicle tonight? I came here in the sheriff's car, and Deputy Sanchez will be staying here to help Dr. Sorenson." She nodded as she listened. "Okay, Natalie and I will meet you at the loading dock. Thanks." She looked at Sanchez and Terry. "We're getting a museum cargo van. We'll return it tomorrow."

Sanchez took a breath. "Please try not to shoot at people or vehicles while you're driving."

Natalie laughed as she stood. "No promises. But as long as other people play nice, we'll try to restrain ourselves."

Virginia gathered up the notebook, the quilt, and some papers and stuffed everything but the quilt in her backpack. She rose, put on her backpack, and then grabbed her crutches. She looked at Sanchez. "Can you get the surveillance equipment for us and show us what to do to install it?"

"Yeah. It's in the trunk of my cruiser. I'll get it and drive around to the back." He hurried out.

Natalie picked up the quilt and stuck it back in the safe. "You want to lock this?"

"Not right now." Virginia looked at Terry. "When you finish, put the rubbing back in the safe, and lock it, will you?"

"No problem," said Terry.

Natalie followed Virginia out of the office toward the loading dock. "Leaving Luis here with Terry was nice of you. He's got a thing for her."

"I know. Plus, I get some assurance that she'll be safe. Once we get the keys for the van from security, we'll load the surveillance equipment in the back."

They waited on the loading dock for Sanchez to drive his car around from the front of the museum. A guard helped Sanchez load the equipment into the van. Sanchez explained what they needed to do and gave them some written notes.

Natalie drove the van out into the street with Virginia in the front passenger seat. Natalie kept watch in the rear-view mirror as she drove. "I don't see anyone following."

"Good. But when we get closer to the ranch we'd better be on guard," said Virginia. "Someone could be anticipating our return."

CHAPTER 30

As they drove through the fading evening light, Virginia's cell phone rang. "Hello, this is Virginia."

"Virginia, this is Deputy Luis Sanchez, I just got word about Natalie's attacker."

"You did? Who is he and how is he? Wait a second I'm putting you on speaker so Natalie can hear."

"Okay. The Georgetown police found him just inside the city limits on Highway 29 near a church. His car hit a power pole. He was bruised, bloody, and unconscious when they found him. He's in surgery at the Georgetown Hospital for a severe abdominal wound, a broken hand, head trauma, and bodily injuries. The head and body stuff are from the crash, his hand and abdominal wounds are Ms. North's handy work. He's listed in critical condition."

Natalie grinned. "I hope he's in a lot of pain."

Virginia shook her head. "I see you're concerned about his welfare."

"Yeah, right."

"Luis, any idea who he is?" asked Virginia.

"Yes. They got a fingerprint match. He's John Royce Boyd, forty-seven. Born in Laredo, Texas. He's one sick puppy. Ten arrests for assaults against women, rape, robbery, and assault with a deadly weapon. He also hires out as paid muscle. A very violent and unstable individual. He's had seven convictions. He's also wanted in Louisiana for a knifing at a night-club."

"Why is he allowed parole?" asked Virginia.

"Why he's out on parole is beyond me. Unfortunately, for him, his attack on Ms. North was in Williamson County. The courts here aren't like those in some other counties. *If* he lives, he'll most likely get his day in court then a free ride in the sheriff's shuttle to the state prison at Huntsville to spend the next fifteen plus years. Our district judges have no sense of humor about parole violators. He'll have to serve his whole sentence and the rest of the one he was on parole for, then be sent to Louisiana."

Natalie spoke up. "I'm not in trouble for stabbing him, am I?"

Luis chuckled. "No, Ms. North. He attacked you and you justifiably defended yourself. The DA said he attacked a federal officer who defended herself, so you are in the clear. The DA also said that it was too bad you couldn't get to your gun. You could have saved the county some money."

"Thank you, Luis. And, please call me Natalie."

"Okay. If there is nothing else, I need to go help Dr. Terry." He disconnected.

Virginia stared at her phone. "I didn't get to ask how Terry's doing. I guess she'll call when she has something to report." She put her phone away and settled back in her seat. "Muscle for hire. I want to know who hired him."

Natalie switched on her high beams. "You can ask him *if* he recovers. But I'd put money on the idea that he was hired anonymously, paid in cash via a money drop or with gift cards, and was to call a burner phone with any information he got from you or me."

Virginia nodded. "You've been watching a lot of TV mysteries, haven't you? But I think you're right."

"Yep. And I acted in a number of them, too. Nothing like first-hand experience."

Virginia twisted to look at Natalie. "Acting in movie mysteries is first-hand experience?"

"No. I've been with you on some capers, remember?"

"You're right." Virginia leaned forward and stared out the front window into the dark, desolate, stretch of road. "What's that up ahead?"

Natalie let out a sigh. "Maybe a welcoming committee. How'd they know we'd be coming?"

"Someone at the ranch must have tipped them off that we'd left earlier, and we'd be coming back this way. They've been waiting."

"But we left in a sheriff's car. They wouldn't be stupid enough to attack a sheriff's deputy, would they?"

"We aren't in a police car now. And, it's been my experience that most crooks don't hold Mensa cards."

"Gotcha. Looks like they want us to slow down. That guy with the rifle is standing in the middle of the highway."

"They're not expecting a museum van, so maybe we can just bluff."

"After being attacked on this road before and in my room, I'm not in the mood to play nice." Natalie stomped on the accelerator pressing her and Virginia back in their seats. "Let's see how far he can jump."

Virginia clenched her seatbelt. "You wouldn't—Oh no-you are!"

"Don't worry." Natalie aimed the van at the man. "If I hit him and dent the van, I'll pay for the damages."

The man raised his hand motioning for them to slow down and stop. As the van roared closer, he frantically waved his arm, then dropped the rifle and leaped to the shoulder of the highway as the museum van shot past him.

"Nuts. I missed him." Natalie grinned. "I'm getting pretty good at this. Maybe I should include this type of driving on my resume."

Virginia looked in the side mirror. "He's picking up his rifle and limping toward the other guy and that beat-up pickup truck. I wonder if they'll try and chase us."

Natalie slowed the van down. "If they do come after us, what do you want to do?"

"Well, we could do the safe thing and hall ass to the ranch."

Natalie nodded. "Yeah."

"Or we could turn the tables on them if they pursue us," Virginia said in an upbeat voice.

"I like how you think. But in case you somehow forgot, you're on crutches."

"I know." Virginia had a mischievous smile on her face. "But I have a plan."

"Heaven help us."

"You of little faith."

"Oh, I have faith. Faith that you'll get us killed." Natalie held the steering wheel in a death grip. "What's our plan?"

Virginia reached behind her seat and pulled out a strange-looking weapon and affixed it to her right crutch. "Now I'm ready."

Natalie eyed the weapon then asked, "What the hell is that contraption?"

"It's a pneumatic, semiautomatic, dart gun. It has a magazine that holds seven tranquilizer darts and a CO2 propellant canister. They're intended for large animals like tigers or lions or bears and such."

"Why do you have something like that? Most of the animals in your museum are well beyond needing tranquilizers."

"You're right. But the museum does send teams into the wild to collect specimens. Most are not that big, but you can't be too careful. This way, if attacked, we just put a critter to sleep for a while and not kill them. The last thing we want to do is hurt or kill an animal unnecessarily. We're scientists and not paid to go around killing innocent animals."

Natalie checked the side mirror. "How about the jerks coming up behind us?"

"They're not innocent." Virginia patted the dart gun. "Them, we can kill for free."

"Okay." Natalie accelerated. "The truck's gaining on us and now there're two motorcycles coming up real fast."

Virginia leaned forward. "See that dirt road up ahead?"

Natalie squinted as she looked at the road ahead. "No."

"It's on the right just past that caution sign."

"I don't s... I see it. What about it?"

"Turn onto it. It winds around for a short distance then ends at a construction site with a massive pile of dirt. Charge up it but be prepared to stop when I say so and stop really fast."

"Okay." Natalie swung the van onto the dirt road. They raced down the road kicking up dust. After a minute, the van's bouncing high beams found the mountain of dirt. Natalie glanced in the rear-view mirror. "The motorcycles are coming up on both sides. What now?"

"They're going to flank us. Go up that hill and just before the top slam on the brakes and pray we stop."

"Pray we stop? I hope you know what you're doing." Natalie took a deep breath and pushed the accelerator down. At the base of the dirt pile, the rear wheels spun kicking up dirt then caught purchase. The van shot up the steep, dirt mound.

The cycles roared up next to the van. The riders pulled handguns and started to aim them at the van's front tires when Natalie slammed on the brakes. The van fishtailed to a stop at the crest as the motorcycles shot past flying into space before dropping out of sight.

Natalie looked over at Virginia. "What just happened?"

"This pile of dirt is about what, fifty or sixty feet high?"

"Yeah, about that."

"This refuse pile came from a pit on the other side. Those two assholes just had about a hundred-plus-foot drop into a dark, rocky hole they may never recover from." Virginia looked in the side mirror. "Where's that truck?"

"Back there at the bottom of this hill. They're starting up now."

"Okay let's get out and stand next to the van. Get your gun but be ready to... to be a diversion."

Natalie looked surprised. "A diversion? How?"

Virginia pointed at Natalie's skimp top.

"Now you like my outfit?"

"Yeah, you do have useful assets and they are men after all. I'm sure you can capture their attention."

Natalie sighed. "Okay. Next time it's your turn. Let's hope this works." She got out and stood at the rear of the van.

Virginia stood on her crutches on the other side.

The truck skidded in the dirt as it stopped a short way up the pile of dirt. The headlights illuminated the two women at the rear of the museum van. A couple of empty beer bottles tumbled out as two men exited the battered truck. The men staggered a little as they started up the hill. The rider in the truck waved his rifle as he clumsily hiked toward the two women. About halfway up they stopped. The man smirked. "We've got you now."

Virginia glanced at the top of the hill then back at the man. "Don't you want to know what happened to your motorcycle buddies?"

"They'll be ba... back," he stammered. "Tell us where the treasure is, and we'll let you go."

"You and I both know that's not going to happen," Virginia barked.

He aimed his wavering rifle at Virginia. "Tell us what we want to know or else."

Virginia leaned against the van pretending her injury was worse than it was. She smiled at the man as he continued stumbling up the hill aiming his rifle at her. She muttered to Natalie. "Show time."

Natalie straightened and hiked up the bottom of her short top exposing her 38D breasts.

The men's jaws dropped. They stopped and looked at Natalie with wide eyes. The man with the rifle lowered his gun.

Virginia raised her right crutch and fired. The first tranquilizer dart whizzed past the rifleman's right arm and hit the side of the truck, but the second dart hit him in his stomach. The next dart just missed the driver's head, but as he tried to turn around, the next tranquilizer dart caught him in his right thigh. Both men dropped to the ground and stopped moving.

Natalie raised an eyebrow. "That was fast."

"Yeah, real fast. There's enough tranquilizer in the darts to stop a five-hundred-pound tiger."

Natalie eyed the downed men. "Do you think they're dead or just knocked out?"

"I have no idea. Either way, they won't interfere with us for quite a while."

"Right. What now?"

Virginia watched them for a minute. "We should go get the darts."

Natalie stared at the downed men. "Might be a good idea but I have no clue where the stray ones went."

Virginia wrinkled her brow. "One is somewhere near the truck. We extract the darts that hit them and then move them and the truck to the other side of this mound of dirt."

"With your ankle as it is, and you on crutches, I guess I'll have to move them."

"Wait, you're not big enough to move those men. I have an idea."

"Oh, God." Natalie slumped against the side of the van. "We've probably already killed two motorcyclists and maybe these two. What other felonies can we commit tonight?"

"We haven't committed any felonies. They attacked us, remember?" Virginia placed her hand on her hip. "They shouldn't drink and play with guns and definitely shouldn't have attacked two defenseless women."

"Defenseless? That's a stretch. What do you want to do now?"

"Get my tranquilizer darts back. Like I said, the first one I fired hit the side of the truck, so it must be close to it. The other one that missed is way over there in those trees and brush someplace, so I don't think anyone will find it soon. Let's see if they have any booze in the truck."

Natalie sighed. "Okay, I'll get the darts. You stay here. If there is any alcohol in the truck, I'll find it. Want me to pour a little down their throats?"

"No. They're just unconscious, I hope. If they're still alive, pouring alcohol down their throats might kill them. I think they were already drunk so just splash a little on them and put a little in their mouths but not enough to swallow. Then we leave them here with the alcohol and we'll make an anonymous call to the sheriff from the ranch saying someone was racing around out here and shooting. Fire the rifle but don't get your fingerprints on it." Virginia tossed Natalie a pair of cotton gloves from the museum van.

"Okay. Wait here." Natalie carefully proceeded down the hill and retrieved the three darts. She called to Virginia. "They're alive, but man are they limp. Whatever was in those darts really relaxed them. They're out cold to boot. The beer didn't help, I'm sure." Natalie fired four shots from the rifle and went to look for more liquor. After a couple of minutes, she backed out of the truck's cab holding up two full beer bottles. She splashed some inside the cab, and then on the two men. Next, she looked in the bed of the truck. She dumped a case of empty beer bottles in the bed, then took six. She marched toward the men and scattered the bottles around the area where they were sprawled out. Natalie climbed back to the van and handed the spent darts to Virginia. "Can we go back to the ranch now?"

Virginia took the darts and returned them to the van's driver's compartment. "Nice job. And, yeah, let's go to the ranch, I'm getting tired. I'll make that anonymous tip to the sheriff about them when we get there." She glanced in the rear of the van. "And we need to set up the surveillance equipment at the ranch, too."

Natalie buckled her seatbelt. "You're tired? I did all the work."

Virginia smiled as she buckled in. "Home, Jeeves. We've still got work to do and tomorrow the fun starts"

"Very good, Madam," Natalie said with her best British accent. "I've got a class to teach on knitted wool felting tomorrow. While I do that, *please* try to stay out of trouble."

CHAPTER 31

The next morning at breakfast a harried Clara Paterson limped into the dining room. "Ladies, there was some excitement near here last night." She paused to catch her breath. "I just heard on the news that there was an incident at the construction site a few miles down the road."

Virginia finished munching on a piece of toast. "What happened?"

Clara dropped onto a chair at the nearest table. "Someone tipped off the sheriff about a party where there was drinking and shooting."

Virginia sipped some coffee. "Never a good combination. Was anyone hurt?"

Clara nodded. "According to the announcer, two armed men on motorcycles must have been racing and drove off from the top of the mound of dirt and fell over one-hundred-and-twenty-feet to their deaths. The announcer said they apparently didn't know about the sudden drop when they got to the top of the mound. Two other men there were drunk. One man had a rifle that had been fired. The paramedics and deputies at the scene said the men were unconscious when they found them."

Natalie finished her orange juice. "Were they arrested?"

Clara nodded. "The report said they were examined by paramedics and taken to the hospital. They regained consciousness there, but claim they can't remember anything about last night. They were cited and released." Clara stood. "I need to get back to work."

Natalie turned to Virginia sitting next to her and whispered. "I was hoping they wouldn't be able to talk."

"Me too. The drugs in the darts probably affected their memory. But, because of what they were doing, I don't think they will blab anything. Nice job fixing the crime scene last night."

"Thanks. We're pretty good at committing felonies." Natalie scooted her chair back. "Got to go. I've got my class to teach in thirty minutes. What are you going to do?"

"Finish eating then spread more rumors about part of the treasure being here at the ranch. Then I'll use my computer to check the surveillance equipment and see if we got any visitors."

"Wouldn't the alarms have told us if we had visitors at the war room?" Natalie asked as she picked up her notebook.

"Yes, but the cameras will tell us if we had anyone prowling around there and the cemetery. I'll check in with Terry this morning as well."

"Okay. See you at lunch." Natalie hurried then stopped. "Remember when someone told us Colin had a drone?"

"Yes. You told me."

Natalie looked surprised. "I did?"

"You said one of the ranch hands mentioned it when you were playing cards with them."

"Oh yeah. I forgot about that. Maybe we could use it to see what's on the other side of the woods. That way no one can shoot at us."

Virginia smiled. "Good idea. I'll see if I can find it and a pilot."

"Okay. I'll check in with you at lunch. Now I've got some felting to teach." Natalie hurried away.

Virginia stopped Clara as she limped by again. "You're limping. What happened?" Virginia patted her crutches. "I hope you didn't run into a tree like I did."

Clara shook her head. "No. I think I overindulged in dinner the last couple of days. My gout is acting up. I also think there is a low front moving in shortly. I have the gout and arthritis."

"Isn't gout a form of arthritis?"

Clara thought for a second. "I think they have similar symptoms, but gout is caused by excess uric acid in the body and the buildup of uric acid crystals in my joints. My arthritis I think is inherited. Rheumatoid arthritis."

"What are you taking for it?"

Clara gave her a dark look. "Why?"

"My husband has Rheumatoid arthritis." Virginia buttered some toast. "He's had it since he was young. Just curious as to what you were doing for it."

"I see. My doctor has me on an anti-inflammatory drug and Tylenol for the arthritis, some narcotics, too if it gets really bad, like now. The weather. It happens. I have another drug for the gout."

"That's good. Thank you for that report about the incident at the construction site. It was interesting. The motorcycle guys died?"

Clara nodded. "Yes."

"Why were they there in the first place? Seems like a strange location to party and race motorcycles at night."

Clara stiffened. "I wouldn't know. Now if you will excuse me, I want to go to Natalie's felting class."

"Have fun." Virginia ate her toast. *That question seemed to bother her? Why? Gout? What anti-inflammatory drug do they use for treating gout I*

Mysterious Threads

wonder? I'd better check in with Terry then go find that drone.

Virginia went back to her room and pulled up Google on her laptop. She typed in 'treatment for gout'. She watched to list come on her display. She clicked on the first entry. It said:

> During an acute attack of gout, anti-inflammatory medications such as Nonsteroidal anti-inflammatory drugs (NSAIDs), corticosteroids, are normally used to reduce the pain and inflammation associated with an acute attack. Xanthine oxidase inhibitors like allopurinol also reduce the amount of uric acid produced by the body.
>
> Patients with chronic gout can use behavioral modification such as diet, exercise, and decreased intake of alcohol to help minimize the frequency of attacks. Additionally, patients with chronic gout are often put on colchicine. Caution: The usual adult oral doses for gout and FMF is 1.2-2.4 mg/day; in acute gout 1.2 mg/day and for gout prophylaxis 0.5-0.6 mg/day three to four times a week. High fatality rate was reported after acute ingestions exceeding 0.5 mg/kg. The lowest reported lethal doses of oral colchicine are 7-26 mg.

Virginia sat staring at the screen.

Colchicine? That's what poisoned Colin. It comes from the drug store obviously, but it also comes from autumn crocus. Daniele Webley had some in her room. She said they grow wild around here and are the remains of some old plants from years ago. She's into exotic plants and has a gardening business. Could she be our killer? Virginia glanced out the window. *I doubt it. From what I've seen, she'd have nothing to gain and has a legitimate reason for having them. I don't remember seeing any around here. I'll have to ask her again where exactly she dug them up. She may have told me, but I forgot. Hmm... I think Colin weighed about 180 pounds, therefore a dose of... 43.3 mg or so would kill him. That isn't much. His cousin, Clara has gout and may have colchicine.*

Virginia carried her laptop to her bed and sat.

Prioritize. Call Terry for an update. Find the drone and see if one of the ranch hands can fly it. Send it looking for what's in or behind the wooded area. See if Clara actually has the colchicine. Hint more about the treasure.

She turned off the computer, dug her cell phone from her backpack, and started to dial Terry at the museum when her phone rang. "Hello?" she answered.

"Virginia, this is Terry. I've got news."

"Good. I was going to call you. What did you learn from the rubbing?"

"The so-called New York part of the treasure was a ruse. The treasure was never in New York in the late 40s or early 50s. It's still at the ranch."

"It was... it is?"

Terry sounded giddy. "Yes, and I know where it is."

Virginia sat stunned. "You... you know where it is? You sure?"

"Yes. I can be there shortly to show you. Luis Sanchez is on his way here to pick me up. I'll drive the museum van back here when we're done."

"Okay. Be careful. Natalie and I had a run-in with some men last night."

Terry's voice sounded strained. "You two are okay, aren't you?"

"Yeah, we're fine but the guys who attacked us aren't. I'll fill you in later."

"Okay. I'll see you shortly." Terry disconnected.

Virginia tucked her laptop into a drawer and grabbed her backpack and crutches. She carefully hobbled down the stairs and out into the yard, then headed for the bunkhouse. Stepping onto the small porch, she knocked on the door and heard a low voice. "Come in."

Virginia entered the building and found herself in the common room. A tall, dark-haired man sat at a computer. He glanced at her. "Hi. What can I do for you?"

"I'm Special Agent Virginia Davies Clark and I—"

"I know who you are. You're with that other pretty agent who can consistently win every hand at poker."

"That's right. You've met her."

"You could say that. She's either the luckiest gal in the world, or she's a great card shark. I've played a lot of cards over the years and if she was cheating, she's good. I couldn't see anything out of the ordinary."

"Yes, she's good." Virginia chuckled. "She wanted to teach the guys a lesson."

The man laughed. "That she did." He rose and stepped toward Virginia eyeing her crutches. "I'm Robert Sommers. I'm the foreman around here. Looks like you have a problem. Have a seat."

"Thank you." Virginia sat on a padded wooden chair. "Agent North said you have a drone and used it to help Colin with his research. Do you still have it?"

Sommers nodded. "Yes."

"Is there any chance we could get whoever flies it to do something for us?"

Sommers smiled. "Of course. We'd be glad to help. What do you want to do with it?"

"Well... Agent North and I went to investigate the woods beyond the cemetery when someone shot at us. I'd like to take a look there and thought the drone might be safer and give us a more complete picture of what's there."

Sommers thought for a second, then answered. "Yeah, we can do that.

Anything in particular you're searching for?"

Virginia eyed him. *That was fast.* "Well, besides the tour of the woods, one of the things we're looking for are autumn crocus. I understand they grow wild around here."

Sommers eyed her in confusion. "Autumn crocus?"

"It's a plant."

"I know what it is. Yes, there are some around here. There are, or were, a few in the cemetery and more in a clearing in the woods behind the ranch. Why are you curious about them?" He sat on a sofa across from her.

"Because the poison that killed Colin can be obtained from that plant."

"I see. Okay, Agent Clark, I'll be happy to take you to see them."

"Great. You said there *were* some in the cemetery? What happened to them?"

"One of your quilters dug some of them up and potted them. I think she has them in the main house. Colin told me she's some sort of garden specialist, and she wanted them because they're old and grow wild around here. She was pretty upset, though, because someone else had mangled some of the plants. The lady figured the person who did it was up to no good because of the irreverent way they attacked the plants. There still are a couple of the plants though."

"Thank you for the information." Virginia sat back. "Okay we'll go see the plants, but I'd still like to use your drone. Who's the pilot?"

Sommers grinned. "Me. I can have it ready after lunch if that works for you."

"That works. Agent North will accompany me."

His eyes lit up. "Super."

"I have a... well... a silly question."

"Shoot."

"Now that Colin is dead. Who's paying you and the rest of the men and the handling expenses around here? His cousin, Clara Paterson? I believe she inherits the ranch if she's his only living relative."

Sommers laughed. "No, Clara isn't paying us. The corporation is."

"Corporation?" Virginia frowned. "What corporation?"

"The Carswell Group. A few years ago, for some reason, Colin established the ranch as a corporation."

"I didn't know that. Why would he want to incorporate the ranch?"

"He was looking for something. We guessed it was some sort of treasure, but he never actually told us." Sommers glanced at a photo on the wall then back at Virginia. "He did mention that the ranch being a corporation offered him some legal protection, but from what I don't know."

"I see. Well I'll look into that later. About the drone. How long can it stay up?"

"Four hours."

"Good. We probably won't need it that long but it's good to have options." Virginia spotted the picture Sommers had been looking at. It looked like an archaeological dig. "If you don't mind my asking, what is that in the picture you were looking at?"

"That was… it was supposed to be some sort of archaeological dig site. But after probing around in the dirt, all we found were some Indian arrowheads, a few pieces of broken pottery, some rusted knives, some bones, a gold mask, and a little charcoal. I had the feeling that wasn't really what Colin was looking for because he abandoned the dig after a month. What you see in the picture is what was left."

"Can we see it from the drone?"

Sommers nodded. "Sure."

"I have an archaeologist on her way here to meet with me. Would it be okay if she joined us?"

"Does she work for you?"

"Yes. She's with the San Gabriel Museum and is consulting in our investigation."

"Okay. I would be more than happy to have her join us. She might like to see the dig."

"You're probably right. Tell me, if the ranch is a corporation, then can Clara inherit it?"

He shrugged. "I'm not sure. Maybe. I know she has stock. She might inherit Colin's shares. He had the most stock. I think if she inherits his then she'd basically own the corporation and the ranch."

"Do you know who the officers are and who has stock? Can I get a list?"

He grinned. "I can do better than that."

"Huh?" Virginia leaned forward. "How?"

"I'll show you a copy of the articles of corporation which list the officers and principle stockholders. It's a very short list. I'll make a copy for you."

"And how would you go about providing said documents? You do realize I don't have a warrant."

"You could probably get a copy of the articles of incorporation from the state anyway. And yes, I know you don't have a warrant. You don't need one if I voluntarily give it to you."

"Can you? Like I asked before, how?"

"I'm one of the officers and stockholders. I'm the corporate secretary."

Virginia stiffened in her chair. She gave him a quizzical look. "You are?"

"Yep. I've worked for Colin since I was very young, and he was the kind of guy who took care of those who worked for him and were especially loyal to him."

"Something like Howard Hughes?"

"Yes, like Howard Hughes. I want to help you catch Colin's murderer. If this can help, then I'll give you all the access you need. Colin was a close friend and I want his killer brought to justice."

Virginia sighed. "We're trying."

"I know you are." He rose and went to a safe tucked into a corner and opened it. He stepped to Virginia and handed her the black notebook. "Why don't you read it here first, then I'll make a copy of everything for you. I can give it to you when we fly the drone this afternoon."

"Okay." Virginia took the notebook. *Did he say they found a gold mask at the dig?*

CHAPTER 32

Virginia sat reading the articles of incorporation. She noted they were for an LLC. There was nothing unusual in the document that she could see. *Let's see who the officers are. The president was Colin Carswell. The treasurer is Noland Philips CPA, Robert Sommers is secretary. That's it. Hmm. I wonder who the stockholders are?* She flipped to another page in the notebook, one listing the stock certificates issued. *Okay, each of the officers has some stock with Colin having the lion's share. The other stockholders are... Clara Paterson, not unexpected, and... what the hell... Helen Chandler and Harriet Fisher? Why'd they get stock?* Virginia looked at the number of shares. *Hmm... Helen Chandler and Harriet Fisher have just a few. Colin's death wouldn't enhance their stock positions any. Clara would benefit though. But why kill Colin? Daniele had the autumn crocus, but she doesn't have any stock.* She closed the thick notebook and handed it back to Sommers. "Thank you, that was most interesting."

"Do you still want a copy? I'll make one for you," stated Sommers.

"No, not right now. I've got what I needed. If I need a copy, I'll ask for it later. That'll save you time today."

He shrugged. "Okay. Just let me know."

Virginia started to climb to her feet when Sommers reached out and helped her. She smiled. "Thank you again. I'll be back with the Agent North and Doctor Sorenson about one-thirty."

Sommers nodded. "See you then."

Virginia limped across the yard toward the main house then onto the back porch. She stopped as the back door opened. Deputy Sanchez and Terry stepped out.

Terry looked around, then at Virginia. "Where were you?"

"In the bunkhouse."

"The bunkhouse?" Terry raised an eyebrow. "Whatever for?"

"Information and to get the ranch foreman to fly their drone for us this afternoon. I told him we'd meet him out here at one-thirty."

Sanchez shifted his weight. "A drone? Can we watch?"

"I told him Natalie and Terry would be there I'm sure having you observe too won't be a problem."

"Great." Sanchez looked around. "Where's Natalie?"

"Teaching a class. She'll be done around noon."

Virginia turned toward Terry. "You said you know where the New York part of the treasure, that wasn't in New York, is now?"

"That was convoluted. But yes. The story about some of it going to New York was a smokescreen to hide it from some people who were also after it, and June Cochran didn't want them nosing around here."

"You got all that from the rubbing?"

"That and some of the old documents you had stashed in your safe. I take it you hadn't read them all yet."

"No, not yet."

Terry shaded her eyes and surveyed the ranch. "Where is the smokehouse?"

"Huh? The smokehouse?" Virginia sighed. "It doesn't exist anymore."

"Then where was it?"

Virginia turned and pointed. "Over there near the building we were using as a war room."

"Is the foundation still intact?" Terry asked.

Virginia looked at the porch floor for a second and smiled. "Yeah. It's basically stone... like tightly packed pavers. They are still there along with some stone bench-like structures, but they are pretty worn and broken up."

"The floor is still in place, right?"

Virginia nodded. "Yeah."

"Good. Let's go see it." Terry stepped down the two steps while Sanchez assisted Virginia.

Virginia led the way to the open area with the rows of tightly placed, worn stone foundation. "Here it is."

Terry moved around examining the flooring. She stopped a couple of times to take some measurements, then straightened. "Okay, can we dig here?"

Sanchez and Virginia moved closer and looked at the area Terry was pointing to. Virginia took a breath. "Why?"

"This should be where the New York piece of the treasure is."

Virginia looked at the ground. "The New York part that wasn't in New York, right?"

"Yes." Terry stood rooted in place. "Now, can we dig here?"

"I'll have to ask for permission." Virginia bit her lip. "But this could be the action we need to set things in motion to catch the killer."

Terry stood with her hands on her hips. "You get permission, and we'll get the shovels."

"Won't be necessary, Miss. I'll get a couple of the hands to get digging equipment and dig for you," said Sommers coming up behind them. He looked at Sanchez.

"Hello, Deputy. Nice to see you again." He nodded at Terry. "You must be the archaeologist Agent Clark mentioned. I'm, the ranch foreman, Robert Sommers."

Virginia spoke up. "Mr. Sommers, this is Dr. Terry Sorenson. You're right, she's the archaeologist I mentioned would be joining us."

"Welcome to the ranch, Doctor." He leaned closer to Virginia. "Two questions."

"Okay."

"Are all your female associates this pretty?"

"There are only Natalie, Terry, and me."

"My point exactly." He smiled at Terry then said, "Whatever you ladies need, just ask."

"What was the second question?"

"Do you think she'd like to see the old Indian ruins we dug up? You know, the one in the picture?"

Virginia glanced at Terry dusting off a paver. "I'm sure she would."

"Good. After your drone overview flight, I'll take you all through the woods to that dig site so you can see it up close." He watched Terry, then asked, "Why does she want to dig up this area?"

"Before I tell you that, I need to get permission. I guess that would be Clara."

"I think I can grant permission as a corporate officer, but to keep peace in the family, getting Clara to okay it is probably a good idea. You go see her, and I'll get a couple of the guys and tools." Sommers smiled at Terry, then hurried to the bunkhouse.

Virginia hobbled over to Terry and Sanchez. "I'll go find Clara. She inherited this ranch, so I'll ask her for permission to dig." She looked at the pavers. "You really think the treasure is down there?"

"Yes. At least part of it. That's what the rubbing indicated. I don't know if someone beat us to it or not. It doesn't look like it, but…"

"We'll find out." Virginia moved next to Sanchez. "Keep a close eye out and keep Terry safe. We're entering new territory, and things could get interesting fast.'

He nodded. "I'll watch out for her."

Ten minutes later Virginia and Clara walked out of the main house. Virginia spotted the men standing at the smokehouse site listening to Terry. They stopped talking as Virginia and Clara walked up. "Okay guys, Clara said we can dig. Terry, show the men where you want them to start." Terry moved to a set of pavers and pointed. "Start here, please, gentlemen."

Clara leaned close to Virginia. "This is so exciting. We may have treasure here on the ranch. How much do you think it's worth? It will be a wind-

Mysterious Threads

fall for us."

"What we think is buried at this location is only part of the Emperor Maximilian's treasure. We don't know how much of the original treasure was split off and ended up buried here. The whole treasure was said to be worth ten million dollars back in the mid-1800s. But there could be a slight problem."

"That's a lot of money. I wonder what it's worth today?" Clara eyed Virginia. "Wait. What slight problem? Is it because there is more someplace else?"

"Yes, there probably is more and we think it's at another location. But there are contenders for the ownership of Maximilian's treasure."

"It's on the ranch land. That makes it ours, doesn't it?"

"Normally yes." Virginia cleared her throat. "But the French, Mexican, and U.S. governments will automatically file claims. There could be others like the State of Texas and who knows who else. I'd advise you to contact your lawyer as soon as possible."

"What if someone jumps the gun and tries to claim it quickly and... and take it?"

"That's where Natalie and I along with the deputy sheriff come in. Because this is a historic treasure, and as a federal officer working for the Smithsonian, and having jurisdiction over it, I'll arrest what we find and hold it in federal custody. That way no one can just come in and claim it. We, and the federal court, will protect it."

Clara looked surprised. "You can do that?"

"Yes. The U.S. Marshals do it at times when the need arises. For instance, there was a Spanish galleon found off Florida a few years ago. The divers who found the remains brought up a cannon. The State of Florida tried to seize it and a U.S. Marshal arrested the cannon thus preventing the state from absconding with it until the ownership could be sorted out. In another case, the Resolution Trust Corporation, it was part of the U.S. Treasury, had a Caterpillar tractor and a large tract of land arrested by federal marshals to give them time to get a problem sorted out." Virginia looked at the activity at the floor of the old smokehouse. Three men were moving pavers and digging. Terry was in the middle of things supervising and helping move rocks.

Clara smiled. "I'm glad you and Ms. North and that other lady are here." Clara's expression turned dark. "What if the U.S. government tries to take the treasure after you arrest it? Can they do that?"

"I don't know. They'll have a federal district court to contend with. But after I arrest it, we'll secure it someplace secret, so no one tries to steal it. I'm not going to tell anyone where I hid it. Not even you."

"Oh! Not even me?" Clara swallowed, then looked hopeful. "You'll keep it safe, right?"

"Of course, Clara." *She's not acting suspicious, just giddy.*

Sanchez moved to see what the men were doing, then turned to Virginia. "How long will this take?"

Virginia shook her head. "I have no idea. That's Dr. Sorenson's territory."

Clara rubbed her hands together. "I can't wait to tell Marlene about this."

"Marlene?" Virginia asked. "Why will she be excited?"

"Marlene is a retired high school history teacher. She took early retirement due to back injury. She's a widow now. She did some research about Maximilian's treasure after she retired. Marlene's maiden name was Torres. Her family is from Michoacán, Mexico. Didn't she tell you that when you interrogated her?"

"I think so. I just forgot." *She mentioned being from Michoacán, Mexico, but didn't mention anything about researching Maximilian's treasure. That I'd remember.* Virginia stood looking at the digging. *Sanchez is also from Morelia, the capital of Michoacán State in Mexico. I wonder if he knows her or her family?* Virginia leaned on her crutches and watched the men dig as Clara limped to the house. She thought about the stockholders in the corporation. *Harriet Fisher is a stockholder. She worked on the ranch at one time. Harriet's a naturalized citizen. Her maiden name was Raineau. Originally, she's from France.*

Terry, frantically waving her arms, and with enthusiasm in her voice, called out, jarring Virginia out of her thoughts. Terry motioned for Virginia to come closer. "Virginia, come and see what we found!"

Virginia hobbled closer. "Did you find something?"

"Look!" Terry pointed into the gaping hole the men had dug. She pulled her auburn hair into a pony tail.

Virginia leaned over the pit and peered into it. "What's that?"

"It's a metal box. A big, riveted, and coated metal box. And the faded lettering on it is in Spanish."

Excited, Virginia stumbled backwards and almost fell but Sanchez caught her. "Thank you, Luis."

"No problem. Is this part of the Maximilian's treasure, Doctor Terry?" Sanchez asked.

Terry bit her lip to keep it from trembling. "I think so." She gave the ranch hands her brightest smile. "Can you boys get that box up here?"

One of the men put a crowbar under the crate and tried to lever it. "It awfully heavy, Doc. We'll need a hefty block and tackle."

The other man frowned. "Maybe we can use one of the John Deere's and attach cables to the bucket and lift it out."

The first man nodded. "It's worth a try. I'll go get the 400E. See if you can clear enough dirt to maneuver better down here." He climbed out of the hole. "I'll be right back. We'll get it out one way or another."

Terry's brown eyes sparkled with humor. "Great. We need to assess this find quickly."

"I'll get the tractor and be right back." He trotted off toward the large, red barn.

Virginia stiffened when she heard commotion behind her. She glanced over her shoulder. She watched Clara leading Harriet Fisher and Helen Chandler up to the pit.

They leaned over the hole and examined the box at the bottom. Clara asked, "Is that Maximilian's treasure?"

Virginia gave a slight nod. "We think so. Maybe part of it. The guys are getting a tractor and some cables to lift it out. We'll know more then."

"Good." Clara, bubbling with excitement, turned to the ladies. "Well ladies, let's go back inside where it's cooler and not get in their way. We can watch from the windows. You'll inform us of the results, won't you, dear?"

"Of course, Clara. As soon as we know anything for certain."

Clara turned and strutted, with a slight limp, toward the house with the other ladies following.

Terry stepped close to Virginia. "If this really is part of Maximilian's treasure, what are you going to do with it?" She glanced around the yard. "Can you secure it here someplace?"

"Not here. I thought we could move it to the museum and store it there. It would be secure and technically still in my custody."

Terry looked at the top of the box in the hole. "I don't think the museum van can hold it. It may be too heavy."

"We can ask Mr. Sommers to let us use one of the ranch's flatbed trucks."

Terry bit her lip and shuffled her foot in the loose dirt. "Think he'll go for it?"

"When Natalie gets done with her class, you, me, and Natalie will ask. I'm positive he would loan us the truck. He said he'd help us." Virginia knitted her brow. "Terry, I have a question."

"Shoot."

"Why would there be a gold mask in a dig site that looks like it was just an old, early American Indian site?"

"Around here there wouldn't be such an item." Terry looked confused. "Why?"

"Later today we're going to see a site that had one. I need to find out where Colin put the artifacts from that dig."

"That will be interesting, but the more important question is the use of a ranch truck to get this box to the museum."

Virginia let out a small chuckle. "The real question is can we safely get it to the museum."

"Isn't Deputy Sanchez following us in his cruiser."

"Yes. We're talking about possibly millions of dollars in gold and jewels in that box. I don't think a lone police car and one deputy will deter our adversaries. Trust me; they're very determined. Millions of dollars are quite a motivation. We need to be on our toes." Virginia added, "When Natalie gets here let's discuss my plan."

"Your plan? Terry shook her head. "Please tell me it's a good plan."

"Right now, it's more of a... work in progress."

Terry rolled her eyes. "You're winging it again aren't you?"

Virginia looked into the hole, then back at Terry. "No, just waiting for it to coalesce into the right form. What could go wrong?"

"A work in progress? Waiting for it to coalesce? What could go wrong?" Terry arched a speculative eyebrow. "Last time I did something like this with you was in Guatemala. That time I almost got eaten by a crocodile."

CHAPTER 33

Virginia and Terry turned at the sound of a tractor heading their way. The large green, John Deere 400E, with its bucket raised, roared toward them kicking up dust. It stopped a few feet from the hole.

The ranch hand climbed down, stepped to the pit, and looked down. "Jake, can we get some cables under it?" he asked the second man in the hole.

"No. The dirt is too hard, and I don't have enough maneuvering room."

The tractor driver scratched his head. "How about we drill and tap some holes and use eyebolts to lift it?"

"This thing is old, rusting, and heavy, Sam. I don't know if it can take something like that."

"Hmm. We've got a problem."

Virginia hobbled to him. "Can you dig a… a ramp down to it and just pick it up with the front-end bucket or pull it up?"

Sam rubbed his chin. "Maybe. The ramp we could do. Looks a little too big and maybe too heavy for the bucket to just lift it and carry it safely. Might have to put some lines around it and drag it up or maybe I could tilt it and we could get some cables under it." He smiled at Virginia. "Good ideas, ma'am. I'll get right on it." He stepped closer to the hole. "Jake, get up here, I'm going to dig a ramp."

"Okay, Sam." Jake climbed out of the hole, leaned against a fence post, and wiped his brow with a large red bandana.

Virginia and Terry went to the porch and sat in two white, wooden, rocking chairs to get out of the sun and watched as Sam started digging a ramp down to the box. About forty-five minutes later the ramp was complete. Sam and Jake stood next to the tractor as Virginia and Terry approached.

Virginia looked at the ramp as Terry walked down to the metal box. "Nice job, guys," said Virginia. "Now see if you can get that thing up here." She looked at Sam. "Do you know where Mr. Sommers is?"

Sam nodded. "He's getting a flatbed truck for you. He said you wanted to move this to your... you really work for a museum?"

Virginia nodded. "Doctor Sorenson and I work for the San Gabriel Museum. But I'm also a special agent with the Smithsonian Central Security Service in Washington, DC."

Sam swallowed. "Oh. Wow! Well, our boss thought you'd want to transfer it to a more secure site and is getting a truck to move it. He should be here shortly." Sam eyed Terry. "She's a doctor?"

"Yes. But don't get ideas about her examining you. She's an archaeologist. Unless you're dead, well over a hundred years old, and mostly bones, she's usually not interested."

Sam gave an angelic smile. He put his hand on his chest. "I would never—"

Virginia leaned closer. "Of course, you had only the most respectful intentions."

Sam eyed Terry and grinned. "Only the best, I assure you."

Virginia chuckled then looked at the box at the bottom of the incline. "Exactly how big is that thing?"

Sam looked down at it. "It's about four feet high and six feet in both directions. It's also very heavy."

"That's about a hundred and forty-four cubic feet. If it was full of gold, that would weigh thousands of pounds. When can you bring it up?"

Sam looked at her in disbelief. "Gold?" He shook his head to clear his thoughts "Ahh... now I guess." He looked around and spotted Terry hiking back up the slope. "Doctor Sorenson, how do you want us to move it? Try and get cables under it and lift it or drag it up?" He walked toward her as Jake joined them.

After a brief huddle, Jake walked down to the box with cables as Sam backed the tractor down the ramp. They looped a series of steel cables around the box and affixed them to the tractor's trailer attachment point. Sam started the tractor and inched it up the incline. The cables became taut. The tractor's engine whined as Sam slowly drove the tractor up the slope dragging the metal box. Three times they had to stop to examine it for damage and shovel dirt that had accumulated in front of the leading edge of the box as they dragged it up the ramp. Once the box was safely on flat ground at the top of the slope, Sam shut the tractor down and unhitched the cables.

Terry hurried to the box and examined it and the lock. "The lock's old and rusted," she called out to Virginia.

Sanchez moved next to the box. "Want me to shoot it off?"

Terry shook her head. "No. That only works in Hollywood movies." She reexamined the hasp and lock. "Luis, see if Jake still has his crowbar."

Jake stepped forward and handed Sanchez the bar. "Is she going to try and pry it off?"

Sanchez shrugged. "I guess so." He held the crowbar out to Terry.

Mysterious Threads

"Thanks, guys." Terry took the crowbar and banged on the hasp. Rust dropped off. She inserted it under the hasp and yanked it up repeatedly until she heard the metal creak. With a loud snap, the hasp and lock flew off. Terry fell backward into the tractor behind her, hitting her head on a steel edge.

Virginia and Sanchez rushed to where Dr. Sorensen lay motionless. Sanchez knelt next to Terry and examined her. He sat back and smiled as her eyes fluttered open.

Terry looked at him. "Hi." She put her hand on the back of her head. "Oh... my head hurts."

"You banged it on the edge of the tractor when you fell."

"Did I get the box open?"

"Unlocked yes, open, not yet. Now we need to get you inside the house. You have a head injury."

She jerked upright wavering as she put her hand on her auburn hair. "Oh, that wasn't a good idea. Everything's spinning. Help me up. I need to open this box."

"I don't think that's a good idea, Doc. You're hurt."

Terry smiled and touched Sanchez's cheek. "You're very sweet, Luis. But I shot a man in Central America while sick and severely injured to help Virginia. I can do this. Once I look inside, I'll rest. Okay?"

"Well..."

"She's stubborn, Luis," said Virginia. "Let her see what's in the box and then she'll behave. She's a lot like Natalie and me."

"I see this. Okay, let me help you up." He looped his arm under Terry's and assisted her to her feet.

Virginia joined Terry and Sanchez next to the box. The three of them grabbed the top and tried to lift it. Rust held it tightly closed. They tried again to no avail. Frustrated, Terry kicked the box. She hopped around, holding up her foot. "That hurts. This thing is in pretty good shape for being over a hundred years old." She stopped and stood shaking her head. "Now both my foot and head hurts."

Virginia touched Terry's shoulder. "Easy does it. Let me see what I can do."

Terry looked longingly at the box. "Okay."

"Terry, you need to move out of the way I have an idea." Virginia turned and walked to the tractor's cab and with Jake's help climbed on with Sam.

Terry and Sanchez moved away from the box. Sanchez watched Virginia, then turned to Terry. "What's she doing?"

"I have no idea."

Virginia had Sam turn the tractor around and raised the bucket. The tractor moved forward, then Virginia had Sam bang the bucket on the top of the box. The box shook. Rust and dirt flew off in all directions. A rivet popped off.

Terry turned white. "What are you doing? That can damage the box and contents."

"Got to knock some of the rust off and this is easier than with a hammer."

"We could use acid and…" Terry sighed. "Be careful, please."

Natalie nudged Terry. "This isn't like her. She's a museum curator."

"I know. Maybe the stress of all this and being on crutches has gotten to her."

"Possible."

Virginia looked at the box. Then, with Sam's help, climbed down and hobbled to the box. "I didn't do too much damage." Resting on her crutches, Virginia tried to lift the lid. It moved slightly but seemed to be still secured by the rust. She looked back at Terry. "Sorry. We may have to wait and get it to the museum."

Holding some tools, Jake stepped to Virginia. "These may help." Jake used the pry bar and a drill with a cutting wheel attached to fight his way through the rusted sections. Then he and Virginia grabbed the lid and pulled. Virginia swayed on her crutches as the lid jerked, screamed, and finally popped partway open. They struggled to raise it.

Finally, it opened enough for Virginia to peer inside.

Virginia gasped. "Ohmigod. This isn't what I expected. This case is getting more convoluted by the minute, but it's going to make Terry very happy. She'll be publishing for some time."

Jake looked at Virginia. "What's in it?"

"It's not Maximilian's treasure, that's for sure. It's better."

Virginia heard a noise behind her. She looked to see the ladies from the retreat gathered around and all talking at once. Terry stood with Natalie next to the front of the box.

Natalie gave Virginia a questioning look. "What do you see?"

Virginia shook her head. "Not what I was expecting. How'd your class go?"

"Great. But what's in the box that's got you so wound up?"

Virginia had Natalie lift the lid as far as she could. She told her and Terry to peer inside.

Terry gasped. "You're right. That contains some artifacts that look Aztec. I thought most of their treasure was looted by the Spanish. Now it seems the Aztecs managed to hide some of it."

Virginia looked toward the barn. A large flatbed truck was lumbering toward them. "Here comes our ride to the museum." She turned to Sanchez. "Keep everyone away from this."

He nodded. "Okay."

Mysterious Threads

Virginia motioned for Terry to join them and walked away from the crowd of women. "We were looking for Maximilian's treasure, right? Well, either old Max was a thief of Mexican heritage or we stumbled on something else."

"That explains the ruse about the New York treasure. The notes were correct."

Virginia shook her head. "It does? What notes? This is an unexpected development. Everything we've been researching pointed to Maximilian's treasure. Colin even had a Maximilian gold coin."

Terry turned and looked at the box. "Yes. Simon found *a* treasure and some other records. We assumed it was Maximilian's. It seems old June Cochran couldn't find Maximilian's treasure. During her escapades as a federal marshal, she must have stumbled on a smuggling operation operated by Mr. Noble. Some of the artifacts that were stolen from sites in Mexico were later sold to museums and private collectors, especially in the Northeast."

"He did?" Natalie knitted her brow. "How do you know that?"

"It makes sense. It was troubled times right after the Civil War. What we know of Mrs. Cochran's activities comes from Colin. I think he was on to June's activities. That's just a guess but it explains what we just stumbled upon."

Natalie glanced at the box them wrinkled her nose. "It does? How?"

Virginia took a breath. "Derwood Noble worked as a gambler and ventured into Mexico on numerous occasions. We know he had nefarious connections south of the border. He was also known to be a smuggler. The story about him hijacking Maximilian's treasure was what we learned from Mrs. Cochran's journals and other artifacts."

Natalie nodded. "So, she killed Noble and took over the smuggling operation?"

Terry folded her arms across her chest. "We also had the quilt that indicated the lake where the rest of this treasure is hidden. Then there's the rubbing and the other notes."

Virginia pointed at the metal box. "And all that got us to this box of Aztec artifacts."

Natalie tilted her head. "All Aztec artifacts and nothing of Max's treasure?"

"Yes. Well I guess so. We need to inventory what's inside." Virginia moved her foot in the dust. "This is what I think. Like you two said, June Cochran was no fool. During her investigations back in the mid-eighteen-hundreds, she found that Maximilian's treasure was indeed lost. Since she had come up empty-handed with Max's treasure, she told the President that she couldn't find Maximilian's treasure. It had disappeared. But she didn't tell him she had stumbled onto Noble's smuggling operation. She concocted the story that she was still looking for Max's treasure as a cover for the smuggling operation. So, she decided that she'd help herself to Noble's handy work and enterprise. She needed the money for the ranch. She probably used… advanced interrogation techniques to get Noble to spill the beans, then did him in. After all, she did murder him and smoke the poor guy.

"She kept what Noble had stolen from Mexico for herself. Maybe she actually continued the operation and sold some of the artifacts to interested parties. A combination of a real need and gold fever. But she left clues to Noble's stolen artifacts. Maybe there's more in June Cochran's note in the safe we haven't looked at yet."

Terry gave Virginia a curious look. "Didn't you say something about a gold Aztec mask being in a local Indian dig site here on the ranch?"

Virginia nodded. "It was in a clearing behind the woods. According to the information Deputy Sanchez found about this ranch, back in the eighteen hundreds it stretched north. To the west, just beyond the woods, was the start of Noble's ranch. After he disappeared, June Cochran bought it from the bank. That didn't seem important until now. Maybe she used the profits from the sale of the Aztec artifacts to buy it. We were going to see the site this afternoon, that was until we found this. It can wait."

"Where is the mask now?" asked Terry.

"I don't know. We can ask Mr. Sommers later."

"That mask being found where it isn't supposed to be, cinches it for me." Natalie swallowed. "This is a lot to take in. It fits with what we now have. Now how do we prove our new theory?"

Terry rubbed her head. "My head hurts. How about we get that box to the museum for safekeeping and figure this out over some wine? Either of you two got some Tylenol?"

Virginia eyed Natalie. "Why do we have to prove it? We were going to use Maximilian's treasure as a way to flush out Colin's killer. This would work just as well."

"Yeah, it would. It's still a valuable treasure." Natalie fished in her backpack and pulled out a small, white bottle of Tylenol and a short bottle of water. She handed them to Terry. "Here yah go."

Virginia nodded. "Let's get this box to the museum. We need to rethink what we're doing. And I need to call Washington."

Natalie looked at the group of women standing around the box with Sanchez holding them back. "You might want to tell Clara we're going to transfer the treasure for safekeeping, but don't tell her it's Aztec treasure."

Virginia watched the group. "Right. I'd better give her a receipt for it as well to keep things legal and provide a record. I'll have to list the box and assorted objects of value, some containing gold and gems to hopefully get her to let me take it to the museum. I don't know if she knows about

Mysterious Threads

that gold Aztec mask Colin found or not, hopefully not. This may also trigger an aggressive response like that last few times."

CHAPTER 34

Deputy Sanchez watched as the box was pushed up a steel ramp onto the flatbed truck and tied down. He guarded the truck and its cargo until Virginia, Natalie and Terry returned from the main house after talking to Clara. When they arrived, he asked, "Did Clara sign off on moving the box?"

"Yes. I told her we think we have part of *the* treasure in it. I... kind of forgot to mention it isn't Maximilian's treasure. But she's fine with us taking it to the museum."

"You forgot to mention...? He shook his head. "Oh. The box is secured."

Virginia examined the box and tested the tie-down straps. "Looks like we're good to go."

Sanchez leaned against the truck. "Who rides where? I'll drive my cruiser behind the truck."

Robert Sommers exited the truck's cab and walked to the group. "I'll drive the truck, but you'll have to give me directions."

Virginia looked at the box, then said, "I'll ride with you." She turned to Natalie and Terry. "You guys going to ride with Sanchez or are you also driving, Natalie?"

Terry glanced at the museum van parked near the war room. "I'll drive the van back to the museum."

Natalie surveyed the truck and the sheriff's car. "I'll ride with Luis in the cruiser."

"Everyone got what they need?" asked Virginia.

Natalie and Terry gave their backpacks a light touch and nodded slightly.

"Okay, saddle up. The sooner this cargo is safely at the museum the better."

They climbed into their respective vehicles, and with the museum van leading, rolled out of the ranch.

Terry called Virginia on her cell phone. "Should I be on the lookout for anything in particular?"

Mysterious Threads

"Yes, anyone looking like they want you to slow down or for you to stop. Just keep going, I have you covered," said Virginia. "Luis and Natalie are right behind us. Just don't get too far ahead. Remember our plan."

"Right," answered Terry.

Sommers listened to the call. "You're expecting trouble, aren't you?"

Virginia fastened her seatbelt. "You can never be too careful."

The caravan threaded its way down the two-lane county road. At a preselected site, Terry turned the van into a dirt side road and stopped at a wide spot. Virginia told Sommers to follow the van. He stopped the truck next to the van then Sanchez's police car turned and blocked the road. Terry climbed out of the van and opened the rear doors while Virginia and Sommers climbed down from the truck.

Virginia looked at the police car. Sanchez had his shotgun out and was behind the car.

Natalie trotted over to the truck. "Ready when you are, coach."

Sommers scratched his head. "What's going on? I thought we were going to your museum."

Virginia pulled her 9mm in its holster from her backpack and attached it to her belt. She pointed. "We're going to transfer the contents of that box to the van. Then we will continue the trip to the museum."

Sommers looked confused. "Why?"

"Because someone may try and hijack the truck to get the treasure."

"Hijack the truck? How likely is that?"

"Very likely. People have tried to waylay us before, so we're not taking any chances."

Virginia swept her arm in front of her. "Look around." Sommers glanced at Natalie strapping her .357 Magnum on her hip and Terry tucking a revolver in her jeans pocket. "I see you all came prepared." He did a double take looking at Natalie. "That pistol looks like a cannon on her hip. It's about as big as she is. Can she fire it without falling?"

"Yes, Natalie can put six rounds in the bull's eye at twenty yards with that thing without falling."

Sommers raised an eyebrow. "Ouch."

Virginia scrutinized Sommers. "You armed?"

He stepped back, holding his hands out in front of him. "Ah... no."

Virginia looked at Sommers. "Okay, Mr. Sommers, Terry, and Natalie will transfer the artifacts to the van. With these crutches I'm useless to help them, so Sanchez and I will stand guard. We have to be quick. Timing is everything to make our trip look real."

Sommers hopped onto the bed of the truck and pried open the box. He stood spellbound. "Good Lord. Gold? This is... all this is real, isn't it?"

Virginia nodded. "Yes. Now hand the artifacts down to Natalie and Terry."

After forty-five minutes they had moved all the artifacts to the van and closed the door. Sommers sat on the edge of the flatbed and wiped his brow with a bandana. "That stuff was heavy. You ladies did really well considering its weight."

Virginia smiled. "Great job, guys. Once we get this locked in the museum, I'll buy everyone a cold beer." She watched their faces brighten. "Saddle up and let's finish this run."

Sommers gave Virginia a hopeful look. "Do you still want me to continue to the museum?"

Virginia rested on her crutches. "Yes. We need you to continue so it looks like the treasure is still in the box. I want that box at the museum for study as well. And that way you get your beer with the others."

"Okay. Let's roll." Sommers jumped down, walked to the truck's cab, and climbed in.

Terry looked at the van. "It's riding a little low in the back due to the weight. I hope no one notices."

"I think you'll be okay, just take it easy," said Virginia.

She turned and hobbled to the police cruiser.

They all climbed back into their respective vehicles only this time Natalie rode with Terry in the museum van. They turned out onto the county road and proceeded toward Texas Highway 29.

The caravan moved slowly. As they approached a four-way stop Terry pointed. "Natalie, is the guy by that car signaling us to stop?"

"Looks like it. Do what Virginia said and keep going. I'll call the deputy so he's aware." Natalie called Sanchez and Virginia and told them what was happening.

Terry drove the museum van past the man and the car then slowed to a stop at the four-way intersection. Terry turned to the left. "We've got company." She gunned the engine and accelerated through the stop sign.

The flatbed stopped, then started through the intersection when a pickup truck rapidly approaching from the left forced Sommers to pull to the side of the road. Two men hopped out and pointed rifles at the flatbed. They jumped when they heard the siren from Sanchez's unmarked police car. When one man aimed his rifle at Sanchez, Virginia fired three shots from the police car's passenger side window. The man jerked to the side, then fell. The other man jumped back into the pickup and roared away.

"Luis, drop me off and go get that pickup."

Sanchez stopped his car as Virginia grabbed a crutch and hopped out. "Luis, go, go, go." Siren blaring, he sped off after the pickup truck.

Virginia hobbled to the downed man and aimed her gun at him just as the car from earlier roared up. Virginia kicked the rifle away and turned her pistol on the approaching vehicle. The driver aimed the vehicle at Virginia. As the car veered toward her, she fired two shots and hit the front right tire causing the car to swerve and crash into a culvert. As the driver got out and attempted to aim a gun at her, Virginia fired two rounds. The man dropped to the ground unmoving. The passenger climbed out, his hastily fired shot at Virginia went wild, then stood on the far side of his vehicle resting his gun hand on the roof trying to aim at her.

Virginia aimed and fired hitting him just below his ribcage. He dropped his weapon and slipped to the ground. *How is standing behind an open window really hiding? He should get a Darwin Award for sure.* Virginia turned back to the rifleman she had shot and looked down at him. "How are you doing?"

Through gritted teeth, he said acidly, "How the hell do you think I feel, you bimbo. You shot me." He grimaced. "I need a doctor."

Virginia moved closer. *He's bleeding. I'm no doctor, but the wounds don't look life-threatening to me.* "Before I even consider calling paramedics, you're going to tell me who you work for."

"Listen bitch, you don't know who you're dealing with."

Virginia smiled. "Look Bozo, right now you're bleeding to death and who knows, I may have hit a vital organ or two that will finish you off first. So, talk and maybe I'll be in a better mood and call medics for you." She glanced at Sommers walking back from the cab of the truck. *Why'd it take him so long to see how I was doing? Well, he isn't armed so... He's putting his cell phone away? Who'd he call?*

He stopped next to the man on the ground. "I'll watch him, you'd better check out that other guy."

"Good idea." Virginia moved with a lopsided hop on one crutch to the car in the ditch and examined the men she had shot. She knelt next to each one and felt for a pulse. Looking back at Sommers who was kneeling next to the man he was guarding. She shook her head. "Dead." She froze. *What's he doing?*

Sommers rose and held his hands out, palms up. "He's dead, too."

Virginia awkwardly used the single crutch to stand, then walked across the street to Sommers. "How'd he die?"

"Probably bled to death."

Virginia shook her head. "His wounds didn't look *that* bad. Painful, but not that bad."

"Well, he's dead." Sommers glanced around. "We have to do something... call the sheriff."

"Don't worry about it. I'll get help."

Sommers stared at Virginia. "These men are dead. We should call your deputy." Sommers' face looked dark. "We moved the treasure and the ladies are on their way to the museum." He waved at the men on the ground. "These guys failed to get the treasure for someone. They'll go after the van now."

Virginia tensed. "Why?" She tightened her grip on her weapon. "They should think the treasure is still in the box on your truck."

"I... ah... well they attacked us and didn't get far so—"

"To whoever hired them it only means they didn't get the treasure in the box." She looked at Sommers hardened expression. "What aren't you telling me? Who did you call before coming to see if I was okay?"

Sommers grabbed Virginia's blouse and yanked her toward him. "Look! I'm calling the shot—" His head swung around at a sound coming from behind him.

Virginia started to raise her weapon when Terry and Natalie charged Sommers like linebackers. They plowed into him knocking him and Virginia to the ground. Terry jumped on Sommers' back and wrapped plastic ties around his wrists.

Natalie took a breath, then looked down at Virginia. "You okay?"

Virginia sat up and dusted herself off. "You knocked me on my butt, but yes, thank you, I'm fine. Where did you two come from? I thought you'd be hightailing it to the museum."

"Terry noticed the action in the mirror, so we turned around. We parked down the road, locked the van, and came running. I called Special Agent Tom Mason in Washington. He said you had called him earlier and had *special help* on standby, just in case. He just activated them. Besides Sommers, is anyone else alive?"

"This man was. I shot him but his wounds didn't seem life-threatening. He's dead now."

Terry had a knee in Sommers's back holding the struggling man down. She yelled, "Mr. Sommers, why'd you attack Virginia?"

"Get off me, bitch. Get these plastic things off me, they are cutting my wrists." He looked up at Virginia and Natalie. "I don't know, I panicked."

Virginia's cell phone rang. She pulled it out of her pocket. "Hello?"

"Virginia, this is Luis. The pickup got away. Are you okay? I'm on my way back to you but I don't see the museum van ahead of me or pass me. Do you think Dr. Terry and Natalie are okay?"

"They're fine, Luis. We have a situation here and I'm thinking maybe you should just meet us at the museum."

"Do you need help? I can be there pretty quick."

"No. We have things under control. It would be better if you meet us there, trust me."

"Well..."

"We're fine, Deputy. I've got... outside help coming."

"The Smithsonian friend of yours in Washington is sending... ah... the special assistance you mentioned before?" asked Sanchez.

"Yes, and you really don't want to have to explain any of this to the sheriff. So just meet us at the museum, *please*."

Mysterious Threads

"That might explain the four, low-flying, unmarked, black, choppers that just flew over heading your way."

"It does."

"Okay. I'll see you at the museum then." Sanchez disconnected.

A couple of minutes later Virginia watched as the military-type choppers landed on the road. Armed men in unmarked camouflage uniforms jumped out and rushed to Virginia. Others blocked the roadway. The lead man saluted, then said, "Special Operations Unit Six, ma'am. Your *uncle* in Washington said you needed our unique support. How can we help you?" The man helped Virginia stand and handed her the crutch.

She pointed to the dead men on the ground. "These men need to… disappear. I'd like to know exactly how that one over there died. Get rid of the car, too."

The uniformed man looked around. "Yes, ma'am." He pointed at the flatbed truck. "What do you want us to do with that?"

"Nothing. We'll take it," said Virginia.

He looked at Sommers struggling with Terry. "That man on the ground with the feisty brunette sitting on him. What's with him? Does he need our services, too?"

"Believe it or not, he's with us. He said he panicked during the shooting and grabbed me. I think there is more going on. We'll handle him. My friends took him down."

He looked at Terry and Natalie. "They did that to him?"

Virginia smiled proudly. "Yep."

The man looked around. "Well, you can go do what you were doing while we handle this situation. I'll call you and let you know when we've got things wrapped up."

Virginia smiled. "Thank you, sir." Virginia eyed Sommers then looked back at the uniformed man, "Sir, you know, on second thought, why don't you take him with you and hold him until I can interrogate him later. And, don't let him—"

"He will be held incognito. He won't know where he is, how he got there, or who we are, and no outside communications. If we need to, I'll inform him that you can hold him for seventy-two hours without a charge."

Virginia gave him a questioning expression. "That won't be a problem, will it?"

"No problem, ma'am." He saluted and turned to his people shouting orders.

Virginia hopped to the flatbed where Terry and Natalie were standing guard over Sommers. "These men will take Mr. Sommers with them for now. We'd better go. Sanchez is waiting at the museum."

Terry climbed off of Sommers. "He's all theirs." She watched two uniformed men lift the complaining Sommers, pull a hood over his head, and take him to a chopper."

Virginia turned to Natalie. "Can you drive this truck? It's a stick."

"Yeah." Natalie nodded her head. "No sweat. You ride with Terry to protect the treasure. I'll follow you."

"Good idea."

Thirty minutes later Terry drove the van up to the museum loading dock. Natalie parked the flatbed across the yard.

Virginia talked to the guards then watched as Terry supervised the staff moving the artifacts into the museum. One of the museum staff got a forklift and removed the empty box from the flatbed and took it inside.

Sanchez walked out of the receiving area onto the dock and spotted Virginia. "Did whoever your friend in Washington call to help you arrive okay?"

Virginia nodded. "Yep."

"Do I have anything to report to the sheriff?"

Virginia shook her head. "Nope."

"Was anyone hurt?"

"Luis, it's better at this point that you don't know. You're a good, honest deputy and I don't want to do anything to compromise your position."

"So, someone was hurt or killed, right?"

Virginia smiled. "Everything is good now, Luis. Nothing for you to be concerned about."

"Virginia, if a crime was committed then…" Sanchez let out a sigh. "I think you guys are fantastic. A little unorthodox, but you seem to get things done. Whatever I see and hear will remain between us. I don't think anyone would believe me anyway. Then there are those nondisclosure agreements and national security papers I signed. What the sheriff and I don't know won't hurt us."

Virginia touched his cheek. "Thank you, Luis. Let's see how Terry is doing. Later I'll want you to stay with her while Natalie and I go to interrogate our Mr. Sommers."

"Mr. Sommers?" Sanchez looked around. "Where is he?"

"Not here."

"I can see that. Oh. Your special help took him?"

"Yes. I'll interrogate him later."

Sanchez's eyes widened. "You want me to help with the interrogation?"

"Aren't we a little too unorthodox for you?"

"Yeah, but… right… I… ah… maybe I shouldn't go. You can tell me later what he… *voluntarily* told you."

"Good idea." Virginia handed Sanchez Sommers' cell phone. "Will you find out who Sommers called and received calls from in the last hour… make that two hours?"

Mysterious Threads

He took the phone. "Sure."

Virginia turned and led Sanchez through the door toward Terry's lab. "Let's see what wonders Dr. Sorenson is finding." Virginia's cell phone rang. She looked at the caller ID. *Unknown caller.* "This is Virginia."

"This is Special Operations Unit Six, Agent Clark. The incident site has been cleansed. The gentleman of interest to you is restrained."

"Is he being cooperative?"

"He was unpleasant at first. We sedated him, so yes. Before we knocked him out, he said he wanted a phone call and a lawyer. Don't worry, he isn't going to talk to anyone outside of us. From what I've heard about you and your colleagues, I'm sure you'll make him more than willing to… converse with you."

"Probably. Where are you?"

"In the air. Would you like us to bring him to your museum or take him to Fort Hood?"

"Fort Hood would be best. But Agent North and I can't get on the base. And, he might hear something there that would give him an idea where he's being held. Do you have a possible alternative, obscure, and secure location?"

"Yes, ma'am. There are some abandoned buildings next to the railroad yard in Taylor, Texas that we sometimes utilize. Very discreet, secure, and exceptionally soundproof. We'll take him there. I'll text you the address." He disconnected.

Virginia glanced at Sanchez. "You didn't hear any of that."

"Hear what?" He shot her a conspiratorial wink. "I didn't hear a thing."

Natalie came rushing toward Virginia and Sanchez. "You've got to come to the lab quick. Terry found something interesting."

CHAPTER 35

Virginia, Natalie, and Sanchez hurried to Terry's lab. Inside, Terry and an assistant had spread out the artifacts from the box.

Terry turned as they entered and held up an oilcloth package. "Look what we found."

Virginia hobbled on her crutches to the table and looked at the parcel. "What is it?"

Terry set the oilcloth down then pointed at the papers on the large lab table. "I found the package stuck in a gold mask. These papers were in it." She indicated one resting on an adjacent table. "It's basically an inventory of what was in the box. The documents also have a destination for the artifacts. They were to be shipped to a Mr. Albert M. Chamberlain in Yonkers, New York. He paid June Cochran two million dollars in gold for them."

Virginia swallowed. "Two million dollars in gold?"

Terry held up the document. "That's what it says."

"If Mrs. Cochran was going to ship the box full of artifacts to him, how'd it end up buried on the ranch? Why didn't she ship it?"

"I have no idea. But somehow Simon Cochran must have found out about it and engraved the box's location on the tombstone. I got the location from the rubbing."

Natalie wandered around the tables examining various items, then looked at Virginia. "Maybe she tried to ship it, but someone caught on to her escapades, so she had to hide the box in a hurry."

Terry shook her head. "I don't think so. It was under the entrance floor of the smokehouse and was carefully hidden. That took some time and planning."

"Okay, so maybe not in a hurry. Do we care why she hid it?" Natalie looked at the papers. "Is there another list of customers someplace?"

Virginia and Terry exchanged glances. "The stuff in the safe," they said in unison.

Natalie's face brightened. "Is the safe open?"

"Yes," said Terry. "I had security open it when we got here so we'd

Mysterious Threads

have access to the materials in it in case we needed them while Virginia was still on her way."

"Okay, I'll go see what I can find while you experts do your thing." Natalie hurried out of the lab.

Virginia turned to Sanchez. "Luis, I have a couple jobs for you."

He grinned. "Good. What do you need?"

"Go to my office. You and Natalie get everything pertaining to this case out of my safe and take them to the conference room. I'd like you to go through them to see if you can find out anything about Mrs. Cochran or Simon Cochran's possible smuggling operations, potential customers, partners, or… anything else of interest."

"Okay. But before we do that would you like to know who Mr. Sommers called in the last couple hours?"

"Oh! I forgot I asked you about that. Yes, who'd he call?"

"Two numbers. The first is an unlisted number, but I had my friends at headquarters get the name on the account. He called Clara Paterson's cell phone. The second call was to a burner phone."

"Clara Paterson? Hmm. The second call may have been either to have the van intercepted or to call off an attack."

"I think it must have been to call it off." Terry sat on a lab stool. "Why don't I continue to go through this. You and Luis go find out how Natalie's doing?"

"Okay." Virginia nodded and started to walk toward the door with Sanchez when Natalie appeared carrying Empress Carlota's brightly colored quilt. Virginia looked at the folded quilt in Natalie's hand. "What's with the quilt?"

Natalie walked to an unused lab table and spread it out. "Based on what we now think happened, I thought maybe we should take a closer look at it."

"Why?" Virginia joined Natalie at the table and looked at the quilt.

Natalie nodded. "Some of the papers we found and what we were told, we came to the conclusion that this is Empress Carlota's quilt."

"Correct. It even had information about the location of Maximillian's treasure being hidden under what is now Lake Buchanan."

Terry, holding a dagger, looked up from a large round magnifying lamp. "Just a thought, but if that is… what did you say that quilt was called?"

"The Nature's Jewel," said Virginia. "It's also known as the Fiesta Jewel quilt. It supposedly belonged to Carlota. Why? What are you thinking?"

"Well, if it was made in Mexico for Carlota, how'd the directions to the buried treasure get sewn into it? I'm no expert, but it didn't look like a late addition when you showed it to me earlier. Whoever made that quilt had to do it after the treasure was found and hidden."

Virginia stood with her mouth open. "That's a great insight. Why didn't I think of that before?"

"Maybe because you guys were too invested in the conclusion you had already developed," said Terry.

"Invested?"

"Yeah." Terry set the gold dagger on the table. "Someone made the quilt later and then fabricated a story by putting certain evidence in front of you so you guys would come up with the theory you've been operating under."

"Hmm." Virginia steepled her fingers and looked at the quilt with suspicion. "Maybe Simon Cochran found the illicit Aztec treasure and uncovered Noble's and June's smuggling operation He documented what he found from the diaries and the tombstone and then he had the quilt made to hide the directions to the Aztec treasure. He used the tale about Max's treasure as a cover. Then Simon learned about the artifacts we found under the smokehouse and added the directions to the tombstone as insurance before he died."

"That fits." Terry smiled.

Sanchez nodded. "That it does. But I'd better get to work on the documents in the safe." He hurried out of the lab.

"You're the quilt expert, Virginia," said Terry. "Why don't you take a good second look at the quilt and see if you can figure out how old it really is?"

"Good idea." Virginia pulled up a lab stool and started to examine the quilt when Natalie tapped her on the shoulder. Virginia looked up. "What?"

Natalie raised an eyebrow in a quizzical expression. "When are you going to… ahh… interview Sommers?"

Virginia sighed. "I guess that's more important than examining the quilt right now."

"I have an idea. Why don't you stay here and figure out when this quilt was made, and I'll go interview Sommers?" suggested Natalie.

"I couldn't ask you to do that."

"Look, we want to get to the bottom of this quickly, right?"

Virginia nodded.

"Then we need to divide up the chores," said Natalie. "I'm not a quilt expert, you are. Terry's the archaeologist so she needs to see what's what with the artifacts. That leaves me. Trust me, I'll get him to talk."

Virginia let out a breath. "Okay, but don't leave noticeable marks on him, at least not where they can show."

Natalie put her hand over her heart. "Perish the thought." She grinned. "I know he'll just love to see me coming."

"You may be the last thing he sees. Okay you go talk to the man." Vir-

Mysterious Threads

ginia pointed. "Hand me my backpack. The security team sent me the safe house location in Taylor where Sommers is being held. I'll let them know you are coming."

Natalie wrote down the location of the safe house, grabbed her backpack, and strolled out. She ducked back in a second later. "Can I use the van? I don't have a car here."

Virginia looked up from the quilt. "Take the flatbed. You still have the keys, don't you?"

Natalie rummaged through her backpack then extracted the keys. "Yeah. Forgot about that." She hurried out.

Terry finished writing in a notebook then looked at Virginia. "Don't leave noticeable marks on him? What's with that? He's a hell of a lot bigger than she is. She wouldn't do anything to hurt him would she?"

"With her you never know," said Virginia. "But I meant it as a joke."

Natalie parked the truck under a road bridge near railroad tracks and walked toward the graffiti-marked, abandoned building. Three large freight engines were idling, their noise blending with the traffic on the bridge above. As she made her way across the street, she noticed two well-concealed security cameras following her movements. *They know I'm coming.* Natalie walked past boarded-up windows to the battered wooden door and was about to knock when it suddenly opened.

The lead man from the choppers stood looking at her. "Agent North. Nice to see you again. Come in, quickly."

Natalie stepped in as the man closed the door. She noted that on this side the door was steel and heard the locking bolts slide closed. She looked around. The room looked like the waiting room of a legal office. It had tile with expensive-looking Persian rugs on the floor, muted green walls with paintings of European landscape scenes. The furniture was modern Scandinavian in style. Comfortable, stylish, and understated. "Wow. Not what I expected."

The man smiled. "Thank you. I decorated it myself."

"Where is Mr. Sommers?"

"When we saw you arrive, we moved him to the interview suite."

"Interview suite?" Natalie asked.

"Yes, it has a nicer ring to it than interrogation room. He's shackled to the table with a chain. We didn't want him to attack you. From what you and your friend did to him before, I'm not sure the chain is all that necessary. But we can't be too careful."

Natalie looked around. "Which way to the suite?"

"Follow me. Oh, I need to ask you for your backpack. You don't want it in there with him."

Natalie chuckled. "Good call. Here." She handed her pack to the man and followed him down a hallway.

"There's a panic button just under the edge of the table on your side and a phone on the wall. If you get into trouble, hit the button. To get out, just pick up the phone, you'll be connected to the officer in the command center." He handed her a small recorder. "You might need this."

Natalie looked at the device then slid it into her pocket. "Does the room have videotaping capability?"

"Yes. We can do it if you like. That way we'll also have a backup voice recording."

"Good, please roll the camera when I get inside." She stopped at a metal door.

The man opened it. "In here, Agent North."

Natalie unbuttoned the top four buttons on her blouse then entered the gray, bare concrete room. A camera was hanging near the ceiling facing the table. In the center was a stainless-steel table bolted to the floor. Sommers sat on the side facing the door, his wrists cuffed and chained through a metal loop welded to the tabletop. She yanked the black hood off of his head then dropped heavily into the chair opposite him. "Hello, Mr. Sommers."

Sommers jerked his head as he looked around. "Where am I?" He scowled at her and rattled his chain. "Why am I here like this?"

"The security detail thought you might try to attack me like you did Virginia on the road. This way I don't have to knock you down again."

He chuckled. "Like that could happen."

Natalie smiled. "We'll never know."

He leaned forward and clenched his fists. "You can't hold me like this. I want my lawyer."

"Mr. Sommers, we can legally hold you for seventy-two hours without a charge and no lawyer. But you're not dealing with local, county, or state law enforcement right now. You're dealing with me. What happens to you depends on how this interview goes and especially on my mood."

"I know my rights." Sommers spoke in a cocky voice. "You're a federal agent. You have to honor my rights. I'm not talking without my lawyer present." Sommers crossed his arms over his chest.

Natalie leaned back. "I can charge you with assault on a federal officer later. But for now, you are going to answer my questions."

He glared. "You heard me lady, I'm not talking without my lawyer."

Natalie watched his eyes as she took a deep breath and slowly let it out. *This should be fun. I'll redo what Virginia and I did in my barn to a developer who threatened me when I first moved here.* "Let me explain your predicament in simple terms, Mr. Sommers." She leaned forward, her blouse falling slightly open. "You are being held by a clandestine unit of the government. They are *not* on any official organization charts. They do not exist. This place does not exist. I'm not here. No one knows where you are. You can be made to just disappear. Poof. Vanish." She took another breath and leaned back. "Or you can be cooperative."

Sommers stared at Natalie's chest. "At the roadside incident earlier, I heard Virginia tell those men outside this room to make the guys she shot disappear and to take care of their vehicle and cleanse the scene. You mean she didn't call the cops and they actually made everything, including those men... vanish? Like in spy movies?"

Natalie pointed at her face. "I'm up here, Mr. Sommers. Yeah, like in the spy movies. Only this is real. Very real. This is not a movie. There's no trace of those men, their car, or that anything happened." Enthusiasm was clear in her voice. "They're good at it. And, if I don't get cooperation from you, I can have them make you disappear, too. Think about it. No one will know what happened to you. Not even your friends or loved ones." She watched his face pale. "Can I get you anything? Coffee, tea?"

He looked startled. "Huh? Coffee? Ahh... N... no thank you." Sommers swallowed. "You're for real? You can make things and people just go away?"

"I can't. I tell the gentlemen you met earlier and brought you here to do it. But *most* of the people I interview get the message and cooperate. How about you?"

"What do you mean *most* of them?" Sommers wrung his hands. "Do you have those that don't talk to you disappear, vanish?"

"Well, to be honest," she held her fingers an inch apart, "Yes. It's just a few. I do need a *little* help with hiding their corpses. But corpses can't protest, sue, or complain that my methods are a little... how should I put this? Oh, yeah, harsh, painful, humiliating, and lethal. Can't have corpses stay around and draw attention, can we? After a few days, they smell. Not pleasant. The guys outside help me with that." *I think he's starting to buy this.*

Sommers turned green. "Corpses?"

Natalie's eyes sparkled. "Yeah, some men have no stamina for my... what's the politically correct term? Oh yeah, enhanced interrogation techniques. It sounds better than torture, doesn't it? Some just give up the ghost." She chuckled. "Give up the ghost, get it? They end up being the corpses I mentioned. They're ghosts." Natalie gave a small sigh, then her expression changed to one of curiosity. "How do you think you'll do?"

His face reddened. "You're shitting me! You can't do this! You said yourself torture is illegal. I have rights! I demand my lawyer! I'll sue!" He jumped to his feet and yanked on the chain.

Natalie hit the panic button. The door immediately swung open and two very large men stormed in. They grabbed Sommers and slammed him back into his chair and pinned his head to the table.

"You want us to remove him, ma'am?" asked one of the men. He winked at her. "We can easily dispose of him for you."

Sommers squirmed. His eyes bulged as he groaned. "No, not quite yet." Natalie motioned for him to come closer, and she whispered in his ear.

The man nodded "No problem, ma'am." He motioned for the other man to come with him. They released Sommers and exited the room.

Natalie ran her fingers through her hair. "You have distressed me deeply, Mr. Sommers. That isn't good for your... future welfare. I asked the nice gentlemen to bring me some tools. Since it appears you are not going to answer my questions voluntarily, I'll just painfully extract the information from you. Or, I could use drugs, but they aren't as much fun... for me."

"You... you won't torture me. I... I have rights."

"You're right, it is illegal. But look around. Do you know where you are?"

Sommers shook his head. "No."

"Well, like I explained before, wherever you are doesn't exist in the real world. Here doesn't exist. I'm not here. If you're not here and I'm not here, I can't torture you, can I? So, guess what?"

Sommers stammered but didn't say anything.

"You will talk, one way or another." She grinned as she stifled a laugh. "And to answer your next question, yes, I will enjoy it. I'm good at it. That's why *I* was sent to do this interview."

"You... you're a psycho! You can't do this!"

"Yes, I can, and I will. How much pain you have to endure is up to you." Natalie stifled another chuckle, then gave him a hundred-watt smile. "You could be a good boy and tell me what I want to know and there will be no pain and we can be friends, or else."

Sommers swallowed. "I could get killed answering your questions."

"You could get severely injured or killed not answering my questions. The only thing you need to think about is that I'm here now, and I can hurt you... *now*. What someone else may or may not do to you is in the future. Right now, your future isn't guaranteed."

The door opened. The two men returned with various hand tools. They laid out a battery power drill with a bit in it, a ballpeen hammer, Channel-lock-plyers, two long pointed steel rods, a propane torch, and a long soldering iron with a large arrow-shaped tip. They placed a pile of clean white cloths and a rubber apron and gloves on the table. The first man looked at Natalie. "Can we get you anything else?"

Natalie looked at the items on the table then at the men. "Is this room soundproof?"

"Yes, ma'am."

"Good. No, nothing else, this will do. Thanks, fellas." Natalie watched them leave. "Now to get down to work."

Sommers wilted. "Down to work?"

"Yes, down to work." Natalie glanced at her watch. "It's later than I thought. I guess I'll have to skip the usual polite part where I try and pleasantly get you to talk and jump straight to using these tools, otherwise I'll be late for my nail appointment."

"Late for your nail appointment? Are you kidding?"

"No. I hate being late for appointments," said Natalie.

"You're a psycho!" Sommers yelled.

"You already said that." Natalie watched him as she slipped on the rubber apron and gloves. She gave him a soft smile. "I need these because things are going to get messy, and I don't want blood on my nails." She tried not to laugh as she rolled the rods around then picked up the large soldering iron, smiled, then looked at the now shaking Sommers. "You ever had a prostate exam? You know how they work, don't you?"

CHAPTER 36

Sommers's face glazed with shock. "No, I've never had a prostate exam. But I've heard it is not something to look forward to."

"You're right. But, let me explain what I'm going to do. I'll have the gentlemen that just left return, strip you, and bend you over." She waved the soldering iron around in front of Sommers watching his eyes follow it. "Then I'll push this nice, big, soldering iron with the large, arrow-shaped tip up your rear end. Probably need two hands to shove it up your rear, twist it a little, then yank it out. I can only repeat it a couple times before I've ruined your ass. Doctors use a gloved, lubricated finger, but this is much larger and sharper. There will be a lot of screaming, pain, probable infection, and copious bleeding."

Sommers flinched. Blood drained from his face.

He's caving. I guess my acting skills are still pretty good. She watched his eyes. *Is he going to faint?* "The room is soundproof so no one will hear your loud shrieks. You'll have difficulty sitting and will probably require a soft pillow. And... well... you'll be wearing diapers or a colostomy bag from now on, if you get my drift. Something about torn intestines and a shredded sphincter muscle, whatever that is, being ripped apart and not functioning as they should." She stifled a chuckle. "I'm sure you get the picture."

He stared at the other tools on the table.

"Then, *if* you still won't answer my questions," Natalie waved her arms over the other tools, "we get to use my other playthings." She pointed at the sharp rods. "These I can shove into different orifices of your body. This always results in extremely loud screams and lots of pain." She picked up the pliers, looked lovingly at them, then set them back down. "I like the pliers. They are what I call ball busters or ball smashers. Extremely painful and, just for the record, no love life afterward. Sorry about that. They work as well for pulling out finger and toe nails... and teeth." She pointed at the hammer. "This I use break bones with, especially joints. Fingers, elbows, shoulders, knees, feet... you get the picture. The torch I use on the bottoms of your feet. It's extremely painful. The foul odor of burning flesh is hard to get over, but not to worry, I'm used to it. You'll be the captain of your own wheelchair after that. Because I'm nice, I'll buy you a captain's hat." She pointed at the drain in the middle of the floor. "That's for cleanup by the way."

Sommers cringed as he fell back in his chair. "I... I don't think... you can't use anything I might tell you in court. Torture is illegal. You've violated my rights."

"You're right. And I haven't started to violate you... yet," said Natalie. "After I'm finished with my toys and you tell me what I want to know, you do realize your remains will have to disappear."

"Re... remains? Disappear? Shit." His face drained of any remaining color as he looked at the tools, then his voice quivered with desperation. "If I tell you everything I know... please... you can't tell anyone you got the information from me." He sniffled. "I could get... Can you *please* at least promise me that? If I talk, *please* promise me you won't kill me."

Natalie sat and smiled. "Agreed. If you talk without my having to resort to using my playthings, I won't hurt or kill you. You will not disappear, either." Natalie set the soldering iron down, clamped her lips together, and did a zipping-them-shut-and-throwing-away-the-key gesture. "Remember, you were never here, this place doesn't exist, I was never here, so *you* didn't speak to anyone, okay?"

Sommers sat, deflated, a tear rolled down his cheek. "Yes, what do you want to know?"

Five of the uniformed men watched the TV monitor. The largest of them cleared his throat. "Who the hell is she? Where'd she learn that stuff? Chained or not, that guy is about six-foot-two and two-hundred and thirty pounds. She's... what, maybe five feet tall and about one-ten... one twenty? Man, when she calmly waved that soldering iron around and explained in explicit detail what she was going to do with it and the results, well, she had me puckering my ass all the way out here. The way she gleefully explained the use of those other tools... short or not, man, I wouldn't want her mad at me. She's got to be CIA. Would she really have used those tools on him? She's pretty, but hell, she's scary. I'm glad we're on her side."

The others laughed then abruptly stopped when their leader said, "She probably would have used them. But she was actually an actress in Hollywood and now owns a ranch here. She's been deputized by the Smithsonian Central Security Service to aid one of their female special agents. You don't want to mess with her either. She's the one who shot those three men we cleaned up a while ago. They were armed and shooting at her when she killed them while she was exposed and on crutches."

They quietly turned back to the screen and watched Sommers rapidly answer Natalie's questions.

Virginia sat on her lab stool examining the quilt. She straightened up and stretched. "I wonder how Natalie is doing?"

Terry set a jeweled-studded gold necklace on the table. "It's been a while. Maybe Sommers wouldn't cooperate."

"No. He'll tell her anything she wants to know."

"If he doesn't want to talk, what'll she do? Try to seduce him?"

Virginia laughed. "In his dreams. Natalie's an actress. My money is on her using that skill to convince him it's in his best interest to cooperate with her." Virginia looked at the artifacts now cataloged on Terry's table. "How are you doing?"

"I'm about a quarter of the way through all this. How are you getting along analyzing the quilt?"

Virginia kneaded her forehead. "Well, it seems you were right. We were so involved with the idea we were after Maximilian's treasure that we looked at everything in that light. This quilt might look like Carlota's quilt, but it isn't." She waved her hand over parts of the quilt. "The fabric here appears to be from the late forties or early fifties. The quality and thread count are more in tune with that time period than the mid-eighteen-hundreds. The thread in the quilting is too modern to have been used back then. And the actual quilting appears to have been done on a longarm machine. Quilts were hand done in the mid-eighteen-hundreds. I could be wrong, some hand quilting rivals what machines can do today, but I doubt it." Virginia pointed at various sections of the quilt. "These pieces were actually made from actual old cloth from the eighteen-hundreds to give it the appearance of being authentic. Like you said before, how could a map made in Mexico before the treasure was taken to the U.S. have the location where it was hidden? It couldn't."

"So, someone went to great lengths to make it look like it belonged to Maximilian's wife Carlota," said Terry. "Why would anyone want to hide the Aztec artifacts and make it out as another treasure?"

"I don't know. Maybe because people have looked for Max's treasure before and it's kind of long lost and old hat. No one is desperately searching for Max's treasure anymore. So, his looking for it has people saying he's wasting his time and don't take him seriously. Thus, they don't notice what he's up to. The quilt was a way to keep the map safe. Just a thought."

"Yeah. I think you're right. Simon Cochran had it made when he located the smuggled artifacts. And, you needed the quilt, the key, and the notebook to actually use the map." Terry stood and stretched. "He did a good job. Colin was sure he was after Max's treasure, and so were we."

Virginia looked at the clock on the far wall. She turned as Sanchez entered. "Find anything different in the stuff from the safe, Luis?"

"Yes, but before I tell you what I found, have you heard from Natalie? Maybe I should have gone with her."

Virginia's cell phone rang. She looked at the screen. "It's Natalie." She answered and heard what sounded like bar noise in the background. "Hi, how's the interrogation coming?"

"I'm finished," said Natalie. "It went well. Sommers gushed. I've got it all on video and a back-up audio file."

"I hear a strange noise in the background. Where are you?"

"At a watering hole with the guys from your cleanup crew. We're celebrating."

Virginia shook her head. "You're celebrating?"

"Yes. The guys watched me take Sommers from a big, hard-nosed ass hole to a whimpering, slobbering, idiot in what they said was record time. He caved and talked. I think he needed clean pants though."

"He needed what? Do I want to know how you managed that?"

"You'll see it in the video. I gave an award-winning performance if I do say so myself," Natalie responded. "Wait till you hear what he told me."

"What?"

"It'll be better if you see it on video. You can sit back and eat popcorn and watch it."

Virginia tightened her grip on the phone. "You can be frustrating, you know that?"

"Yes."

Virginia let out a breath. "Where's Sommers now?"

"Sommers is sleeping and he's on his way to some backwater place in West Texas," Natalie said.

"West Texas?"

"Yeah. From what I've been told, because of the drugs they gave him, he won't remember anything that happened here. He'll wake up with a hangover and wonder how he ended up in a sleazy motel in some dusty, one-horse town hundreds of miles from here. They'll make it look like he was with a prostitute and she rolled him. I kind of feel sorry for him, well, not too sorry. He said Daniele told him Clara wanted him to cut loose ends. Sommers killed that guy you shot at the roadside. He shoved a shive into the base of the guy's skull and severed the medulla oblongata. I think that's part of the brain. The man's body will turn up someplace out there close to Sommer's motel. There'll be an anonymous phone call to the local fuzz telling them where to find the body and a description of the man who dumped it there, meaning Mr. Sommers. The police will find evidence with the body to lead them to Sommers' motel room. There they'll find Sommers and the bloody knife with his fingerprints on it. There is no need for them to know what I did to him. So, the police out in West Texas can give him his rights. I'll be back at the museum shortly. But I think the guys are trying to get me drunk. They think I'm something special and want me to join their organization."

"Natalie!"

"Don't worry. I'm just having a little relaxing fun after the interrogation," Natalie said in a chipper voice. "And they make huge Margaritas here. They look like swimming pools."

"Oh, God. Okay, hurry back and don't drink and drive. I can't wait to see what you did to Sommers and what you found out." Virginia disconnected. She looked at Terry and Sanchez. "She got Sommers to talk. He fingered Carla as the person behind all the trouble and the killings."

"Good. Now to go arrest her." Terry smiled. "Wait a minute, where is she now and why would she drive drunk?"

"The men Washington sent to clean up after me took her out to celebrate. They're at some bar. She'll be here before long."

Sanchez sat listening then shook his head. "Maybe I shouldn't be here when Natalie gets back."

Virginia turned toward him. "Why not?"

"If she did something… ah… too creative, then maybe it would be better if I didn't know about it."

Virginia set her magnifying glass down. "I'm sure she didn't do anything too illegal."

"It's the *too* part that bothers me. You having him taken against his will and not providing a lawyer when he asked for one before questioning was illegal. If she didn't give him his rights, we can't use anything he said as evidence."

"No problem. He just disappeared, Luis. He'll turn up and be fine. Oh, he'll go to jail for murder, but that's a different issue. Now that we are sure who's behind all this, we'll get them to incriminate themselves."

Sanchez looked startled. "Murder? He confessed to a murder? A different issue? After what you guys did, anything he said probably can't be used as evidence in court for the murder either."

Virginia smiled. "Not a problem."

"Not a problem?" Sanchez looked confused. "Why not?"

"Don't ask."

"Maybe you're right, I shouldn't ask." Sanchez shook his head and sighed. "This is all new to me." He frowned. "Don't ask?"

"Luis, you're going to get credit for a serious investigation and the apprehension of a murderer, maybe two, the attack on a deputy sheriff, and possibly bring to light a smuggling operation. Just hang in there for a while."

He gave her a slight grin. "Okay. I have learned a lot, but this is stuff they don't teach at the police academy that's for sure."

Terry walked to the quilt examining table and sat on a stool next to Sanchez and Virginia. "Luis, did you have any luck going through the stuff in Virginia's safe?"

"Oh, yeah, I forgot." Sanchez sat straighter. "I found a list of customers for artifacts in Mrs. June Cochran's papers. There are museums in Philadelphia, New York, Boston, and Chicago. Believe it or not, there's even one in Mexico City. There's a list of her private collector's names and addresses, too. In another notebook I found the same list but this one has an inventory of what she sent them, what they paid, and their addresses."

Terry beamed. "That list can help the police trace the artifacts and maybe recover some of them for their owners' families. That won't go over well with the museums."

Sanchez beamed. "There are also the names of the people in Mexico who stole the artifacts from working dig sites, previously undiscovered ruins that the thieves raided, and from private collectors in Mexico."

"So, June and Noble were fences and got the artifacts from the thieves and then acted as middlemen and sold them to people and institutions here in the States. I'm not too sure about the laws about antiquities back in the 1800s but the stuff was smuggled into the country. The government doesn't like not collecting duty. The Smithsonian Central Security Service will take what we discover and then go after the artifacts and anyone who illegally purchased them," said Virginia.

"Aren't they all dead?" Terry leaned on the table and ran her hand across the quilt. "Noble and June did their thing over a hundred years ago."

Sanchez rubbed his hands together. "Some of them may still be alive. I found a notebook, or more like a ledger that Simon Cochran had. He had the names and addresses of *his* customers, what they bought, and for how much. Looks like the guy started to revive Mrs. Cochran's operation. The taking and possession of stolen antiquates and smuggling them into the country was illegal in the fifties."

"You're right." Virginia's eyes widened. "How'd he do that? I thought the treasure consisted of just the stuff Mrs. Cochran had hidden of Noble's enterprise. After all, the Spanish looted most of it. I didn't find anything in Simon's background that even hinted of him going to Mexico or being involved with smuggling."

"Simon found what she had hidden. Plus, it looks like he went into business for himself," said Sanchez. "Simon located questionable antiquities dealers, thieves is more like it, in Mexico that were to be his sources for the more artifacts. Got their names and addresses, too. At least what they were back in the fifties. That way there would be no trail of him going to Mexico. He actually purchased and smuggled a few artifacts into the country on his own but died before he could really get his operation going.

Maybe that's what the fight with Colin's father was about."

"Boy, did we get this whole thing wrong," said Virginia. "We should have looked at all that material earlier. So, the rest of the buried treasure is what Mrs. Cochran or Noble hid?"

"Mrs. Cochran or Noble's treasures are what's hidden in the lake and what we have here." Sanchez fingered a corner of the quilt. "But there's more to the story. It seems that Simon had another hiding place for the limited number of artifacts he acquired for sale. He mentions someplace on or near the ranch, but I don't know what it means."

Virginia leaned closer to Sanchez. "What was it?"

"Swagmar. At least that's what I think it was."

"Never heard of that. Is it a real word?"

"I don't know." He rubbed his forehead. "The writing was faded, but that's what it looked like."

Virginia glanced at the quilt, then said, "Now days swag is usually something given away for promotional purposes."

Sanchez nodded. "I think it has other meanings, too, but Swagmar?"

"Guys, swag can also mean bling," said Terry. "Mar is Latin for sea. Bling sea?"

"Bling? Something of value maybe?" said Virginia. "In the days of the pirates, swag meant treasure. Swagmar could also mean treasure lake or treasure sea."

Sanchez turned to Virginia. "It can? You've heard of a treasure sea? Where is it?"

"Probably on the ranch," said Terry. "Virginia, is there a swamp or bog on that ranch?"

"I don't know."

"Didn't you say there was a Native American dig site that Colin had been working on at the ranch? It had a gold mask didn't it?"

"Yeah, maybe Comanche," said Virginia. "We were going to go look at it when you arrived and wanted to dig up the smokehouse. It's beyond the woods behind the cemetery."

"Virginia, the Comanche didn't have gold masks," said Terry.

"You're right. They didn't. With all that's been going on, I forgot."

Terry's face brightened. "Looks like another road trip is in order."

CHAPTER 37

"You're right." Virginia wrinkled her brow. "We need to take a look at the site. I guess it would be possible for that area to have been at least wet or had a pond nearby at some point. There's a lot of vegetation around it."

Terry glanced at the tables with the treasure on them. "I bet Simon used an undeveloped section of the ranch to hide his illegal bounty. Someplace out of sight, not visited very much, but still easy to access. An area with a pond or spring or someplace hidden by the woods would be perfect. It being an old Native American site of some type, maybe a village would be a good cover. By now a pond could have dried up."

Virginia sighed. "What the hell have we been doing? All of a sudden we've got a family of smugglers and Mexican artifacts and no Max's treasure."

Sanchez looked at the quilt, then asked. "When's Natalie getting back?"

"Shortly I hope." She looked at Sanchez. "That was good work finding Swagmar, Luis. Anything else in all those papers?"

"Not much. There were some notes that Colin wrote. He suspected something strange had been going on at the ranch out beyond the woods, but since whatever it was didn't happen often, he figured it wasn't that important, and he'd follow up on it later. He was focusing on finding Maximilian's treasure."

Terry glanced at the Aztec artifacts. "That dig site on the ranch, did anyone say exactly what was found besides the gold mask?"

"It was supposed to be the remains of an Indian campsite," Virginia said, deep in thought "Some pottery shards, charcoal, animal bones, some shreds of cloth I think. There was the gold mask, arrowheads, what may be poles or spears, a rusty old rifle, a broken knife… you know the usual stuff."

"Hmm… could be Tonkawa or Comanche. Just depends on the time when the camp was made. We need to see it."

They turned toward the door when a man in a lab coat walked in carrying a clipboard. "Ladies, Deputy. I have some information about that big, heavy box you brought in."

Terry motioned for him to come closer. "What did you find, Cory?"

Cory consulted his notes. "The box is made from iron. It was coated with a bituminous resin to reduce the rate of corrosion. The resin originated in Pennsylvania. Obviously, the coating was rubbed off in certain sections due to handling over the years." Cory gave them a skeptical look. "And more recently by someone using a tool to remove the hasp and probably a lock."

"That would have been me," said Terry.

Cory chuckled. "I thought so. To continue, the type of metal and the construction methods used indicates fabrication sometime during or shortly after the Civil War. Our analysis indicates the iron was made at Tredegar Iron Works in Virginia. It was the single most important iron operation in the Confederacy. For being that old, it's in remarkable shape. The lid did show some recent deformation... denting. For some reason there were tiny bits of relatively new green paint in that area I assume that was either you again, Dr. Sorenson, or Mrs. Clark. I'll leave the full report on your desk, Dr. Sorenson."

Terry smiled. "Thanks Cory, good work." He nodded and left.

"Well, I think it's time to decompress for a while," said Terry. "Shall we adjourn for a coffee break?"

Virginia and Sanchez stood and followed Terry to the cafeteria.

After some snacks, they were ready to go back to the laboratory when Natalie burst into the cafeteria.

"Virginia, your secretary said you guys were here," said Natalie.

Sanchez jumped to his feet. "Are you okay? We were worried about you."

Natalie smiled. "I'm fine, Luis." She held up a small black box. "I've got my interview with Sommers on this disk drive. Where can we plug it in?"

"I've got a computer in the lab," said Terry. "Let's do it there. I can project it onto a screen so it will be easier for all of us to watch."

Sanchez eyed the black disk drive. "Should I watch that?"

Natalie stepped to him and kissed his cheek. "I don't think there's anything *too* illegal on it, Luis. But if you don't want to watch me in action, then..."

"Okay, I'm game," he said quickly. "I just hope I won't regret this."

They hurried to Terry's lab. After getting the drive plugged in and the computer set to project the interview, they sat on lab stools with bags of microwaved popcorn. The video started. They sat eating popcorn and laughing as they watched Natalie not so gently persuade Sommers to cooperate. After an hour and a half, the video ended. Natalie turned to Terry, Virginia, and Sanchez. "Well, how'd I do?"

Sanchez spoke first. "I... I don't know what to say. What you did to get him to talk was... well as long as I don't have to explain what you did to the sheriff or a judge. You had me squirming. Continuing to threaten him after he demanded his lawyer was not exactly legal... it was highly illegal. But I see what you meant about the police in West Texas finding the dead body and Mr. Sommers with the bloody knife. They'll have all the evidence they need to convict him without the information you got out of him and treading on his rights." He looked around at the three women. "You guys are scary."

"That we are, Luis." Terry laughed. "You were very convincing, Natalie. We got what we needed."

Virginia smiled. "I remember us doing a similar thing to a developer who harassed you when you moved here. Good job."

Sanchez looked shocked. "OMG. You two have already done this to someone? No wonder Natalie said she did this before and was good at it."

"Yes. That's where I got the idea," said Natalie. "An obnoxious real estate developer was constantly harassing and threatening me over the ranch I inherited. He wanted me to go back to Hollywood and sell him the ranch for peanuts. So, Virginia and I... re-educated him. We never actually did anything to him, but we got the results we wanted. He left me alone." Natalie finished her popcorn. "Okay, what did you guys do in my absence?"

Virginia filled Natalie in on what they learned. "From what Natalie got out of Sommers and what we've learned, I think we need a new plan. But this time we've got the real scoop."

Terry went to a corner of the lab and dragged over a rolling whiteboard. "We can use this to work out the new operation."

Virginia rose and went to the board, picked up a marker, and said, "Let's get to work."

An hour later Virginia studied the work on the board.

"Good. I think we'll be able to bring this investigation to a conclusion quickly. But first we need to take a look at the Indian dig at the ranch. That's probably Swagmar. But this time we'll have help." She went to the phone and called Senior Special Agent Tom Mason at the SCSS in Washington. After a brief conversation, she hung up, and looked at the group. "Tom said he'll deploy our Special Operations team to join us at the ranch first thing in the morning. Later we'll have armed agents with armored vehicles to help us and guard the old Indian site. After we take a look, we'll launch our plan including diving in Lake Buchanan."

Natalie glanced at the wall clock. "It's getting late. How about we grab some dinner then return to the ranch. We can all meet up in the morning and go see... what did you call it? Swagmar?"

Virginia stretched. "Yeah. That's the area beyond the woods we were going to when someone shot at us and I hurt my ankle."

Natalie stared. "Okay... Swagmar. I won't ask how it got that name. Where are we going to eat? I missed lunch, and the popcorn wasn't enough. I'm famished."

Sanchez tossed his wadded-up popcorn bag in a trashcan. "Cracker Barrel?"

Natalie jumped to her feet. "I'm game." She waved keys in the air. "I've still got the flatbed. Virginia and I can ride in that and then return it to the ranch after dinner."

Terry looked at Sanchez. "Can I hitch a ride with you, Luis?"

Luis beamed. "Yes, of course, Doctor."

"Luis, please call me Terry. Doctor is way too formal. We're friends and co-workers now."

"Okay. Shall we go? Terry and I will meet you ladies there." Sanchez and Terry followed Virginia and Natalie out of the museum.

Later that night Virginia and Natalie drove the flatbed truck to the ranch barn and then walked into the kitchen of the main house.

Clara greeted them with a startled expression. "Virginia? I've been worried. We hadn't heard from you all day and you and Natalie weren't here for supper. Did everything go well?"

Virginia leaned against the kitchen counter. "Yes. We got the treasure to the museum as planned. Research has started. Oh, we brought the flatbed truck back."

"Good." Clara made a quick glance out the window. "So, there were no issues getting it to the museum?"

Virginia shook her head. "Nope, things went smoothly."

Clara wrung her hands. "I... I see. Daniele thought there might be some difficulty with the box, you know, since it was so old and all. Did Mr. Sommers return with you?"

"No. We haven't seen him. He disappeared after we got the box to the museum. I'm sure he'll turn up." Virginia poked Natalie to stop her from chuckling.

Clara cleared her throat. "I almost forgot. A man called for you. He said his name was..." She pulled a small piece of folded paper from her pocket. "Yes, here it is. Major Boyd Garcia from Fort Hood. He said he has some equipment you asked for and would bring it here tomorrow. He said to call him and arrange for a time. Here is his number." Clara handed the paper to Virginia.

Virginia took the paper. "Thank you, Clara, I'll get right on it."

"So, the treasure. How much do you think it's worth?"

"Probably millions. But ownership will be tricky. Like I said before,

Mysterious Threads

I'm sure various governments will want it as well as you. But it's safe for now."

Clara cracked a smile. "Good. Well, if you will excuse me, I have a Happy Pumpkin class to go to. See you at breakfast?"

Virginia and Natalie answered together. "Yes."

Natalie watched Clara hurry out of the kitchen. "That stuff from the army must be the special diving gear Terry requested."

"Yeah. We'd better get it here and under lock and key." Virginia walked with Natalie toward the stairs. "Let's go to our rooms and call the Major. We can see if he can get the stuff here early tomorrow. Then after we look at the old Indian dig site, we can go diving."

Natalie stopped Virginia at the bottom of the stairs. "Who exactly is *we*?"

"I asked Tom to send a qualified diver to go with Terry."

"Good." Natalie let out a sigh. "I thought for a minute you were thinking of diving."

"I thought about it, but you were right earlier. With my ankle like this I can't go. Like we have in our plan, you, Luis, and I can be on the surface guarding them underwater."

"I'm sure the lake authorities will love this."

Virginia started to hop up the stairs on her crutches. "Why complicate things? What the lake authorities don't know won't hurt them. Let's go call the Major." Out of the corner of her eye Virginia saw Clara, Daniele Webley, and Helen Chandler whispering near the front door of the house.

CHAPTER 38

After a quick breakfast, Virginia and Natalie strolled out the front door of the house. They waited only a few minutes before an army truck rolled up the driveway followed by a Humvee.

Virginia shaded her eyes as she watched the vehicles come to a stop. A man in army fatigues with an oak leaf insignia stepped out of the Humvee and approached them.

He nodded. "I am Major Boyd Garcia. I'm looking for Special Agent Virginia Davies Clark."

Virginia nodded. "I'm Agent Clark." She pointed toward Natalie. "This is Agent North. You have something for me?"

He looked at Virginia and Natalie. "Yes. May I see some ID, please?"

Virginia fished her badge out of her pocket and displayed it and her credentials to the major.

He glanced at the gold badge. "Thank you. Where would you like the crates, ma'am?"

"If you will have the driver move the truck around behind the house, we'll meet you there and show you where we need the boxes."

"Yes, ma'am." He returned to the truck giving instructions to the driver.

Virginia and Natalie hurried through the house to the outbuildings. They waved as the truck lumbered toward them. When the truck had stopped, two soldiers hopped out, and with the assistance of a couple of ranch hands, Natalie had asked to assist, unloaded the crates into the war room building. Virginia signed for the delivery and watched the army vehicles leave.

Natalie locked the door to the war room. "Okay, that's done, the alarm is activated as are the cameras Sanchez gave us."

Virginia scanned the area. "We were obviously a curiosity because everyone was watching from the windows."

"Well it's going to be even more entertaining. Here comes Sanchez with Terry, and that looks like the Special Ops guys who helped us yesterday behind them."

"You mean your fan club."

Natalie shot her an innocent expression. "They were fun."

After they all gathered around Virginia, she mapped out the plan. The Special Operations Team brought up a Humvee for Virginia, Natalie, Sanchez, and Terry to ride in. Then the team leader, using Virginia's map, led the group toward the woods and to Swagmar.

They maneuvered around the perimeter of the woods through brush, elm trees, rocks, and a few scattered oaks to a clearing. The earth in the clearing looked like it had been worked in the recent past. Small wooden stakes with brown strings attached were laid out a grid pattern. In a number of the squares there had been some digging. Outside the pattern were small mounds of dirt. The Special operations team took up guard positions around the sight.

Terry jumped from the Humvee and walked around the site studying what had been done. Then she gingerly stepped into the grid pattern, went to a square, and knelt. She ran her hands through the loose dirt, picked something up, and examined it. She repeated this three times in various squares. Holding what she found, Terry jumped to her feet and hurried to Virginia.

Virginia climbed out of the Humvee, stood on her crutches, and watched Terry hustling toward her. "What have you got?"

"Normally I wouldn't have done this. Under normal circumstances, this would be really confusing." Terry handed Virginia an ax, a spearhead, and a rusted six-shooter. "Native American and a rusted, mid-eighteen-hundreds firearm." Then she handed her a small silver circle with a hole near one edge. "Not Native North American. From the appearance, most likely Aztec. Looks like someone mixed Aztec artifacts in with what was already here. This was once a campsite or settlement of either the Tonkawa or Comanche. I'll need to study the site to determine which. Based on our discoveries yesterday and these Aztec items, this looks like what we expected."

"Tonkawa or Comanche and Aztec?" asked Virginia. "If I remember my history right, they *all* couldn't have been here together. The Tonkawa or Comanche weren't here at the same time either."

"Right. Someone buried Aztec artifacts here to hide them. Simon? He or June or Noble mixed the Aztec items with the Native American. From what I can see, this site needs to be preserved and excavated. There could be a lot of valuable information and artifacts of the people who were here before us. But we'd need the owner's permission and some funding to excavate and..."

Virginia patted Terry's arm. "I bet I can get some Smithsonian support. I'll call Tom in Washington later." Virginia glanced down at the ground, then back at Terry. "Then we'll have to get the new owner's permission."

"Great." Terry beamed then frowned. "Why would someone want to keep you away from here?"

"Probably because of the Aztec stuff."

"Right." Terry looked around spotting Natalie clearing dirt from something. "What did she find?" Terry rushed to Natalie and looked over her shoulder at what Natalie was holding. "A gold necklace? Nice work. We're going to need this place guarded."

Natalie rose, handed the necklace to Terry, and dusted off her jeans. "I'll ask our Special Ops guys to watch over it until we can get security guards."

Terry examined the necklace with wide eyes, then looked at Natalie. "Take a look at this. There are numbers etched into the bottom of this section. Those are ID numbers for a museum outside the U.S. This item was probably looted from some museum in Mexico."

"Now we've got some real evidence of the Aztec items being stolen," said Natalie. "That'll make Virginia happy."

"Yes, it's just what she needed." Terry quickly glanced around. "Think your uniformed friends will guard this place?"

"If I ask nice, I bet they'd do it at least for a while. Maybe I can get them to secure longer term help for us." She looked around for Virginia. "If I didn't know better, I think Virginia is already getting them to be our temporary security."

Virginia hopped back to Natalie and Terry. "According to the guys, someone has been watching us from the woods."

Terry looked around. "Do they know who it is?"

"No. Whoever it was is gone now. But the leader contacted Agent Tom Mason in Washington about replacement guards. Tom told him the security detail we requested is already coming from Houston. They'll be here in about an hour."

Natalie raised an eyebrow. "We requested them earlier?"

Virginia gave a sheepish smile. "Yes. I don't know exactly who they are though."

"Oh. Glad we were so… proactive."

Terry rapidly looked around. "We'll need to provide them with a place to stay and tell them what we need to protect and we'll—"

Virginia poked Terry with her crutch. "Relax. I'm pretty sure the Special Operations Unit has given them a sitrep."

Terry wrung her hands. "This is so exciting. Do you think Clara would allow us to excavate the site?"

Virginia shrugged. "I don't know for sure, but my money is on yes. But, if push comes to shove, I'll point out that there are smuggled, therefore illegal, Aztec artifacts here. We need to retrieve them. The Smithsonian Central Security Service has jurisdiction in these kinds of matters and if necessary, we can get a court order. That's what the SCSS has lawyers for. I don't think that will be necessary."

"There is this." Terry held up the necklace. "Here is some evidence of a possible crime. The ID markings on this suggest it was stolen from a museum in Mexico."

"Good. Now we've got some real evidence of federal crimes having been committed."

Natalie listened, then interjected. "If more of the people at the retreat are involved, you may need that search warrant sooner than you think."

"You could be right." Virginia tightened her grip on the crutch handles. "Let's get the men to take us back to the house and see Clara."

The Special Operations Unit leader drove the Humvee back to the house. Virginia, Natalie, and Terry went inside. Finding Marlene Bauer in the kitchen, Virginia asked her Clara's whereabouts.

Marlene glanced at the kitchen clock. "She should be just getting out of a class. You could catch her in the parlor."

Virginia turned to Natalie and Terry. "Wait here while I talk to Clara. I don't want it to seem like we're ganging up on her." Virginia hobbled to the parlor. After a couple of minutes the women in the workshop started to stroll through the room. Clara wasn't among them. Virginia stopped one of the ladies. "Have you seen Clara?"

The woman pointed. "Right after class, she darted out the door. She was wearing hiking boots."

"Oh. Thanks." Virginia hurried to the kitchen finding Natalie and Terry sipping iced tea.

Natalie set her glass down as Virginia approached. "Did you find Clara?"

"No. She darted outside as soon as the class ended and was seen wearing hiking boots."

Terry finished her tea. "Could Clara be the person spying on us from the woods?"

"Or shooting at us?" asked Natalie.

Virginia nodded. "Possibly. Where is Sanchez?"

Terry twisted and pointed out the window. "Still at the dig site."

"Let's go back and get him," said Virginia. "We can get an update on the security team while we're at it. Then we can inventory what the army delivered."

Terry's eyes widened. "The diving stuff I asked Tom Mason for? It arrived?"

"Yes. It's locked in the war room."

"Great! Any idea who my dive partner will be?"

"Not yet. Let's get Sanchez, then I'll ask Tom." Virginia led them to the idling Humvee and Special Operations Unit team leader. "We need to get our deputy sheriff back from the dig site."

He checked his watch. "Unless you want to take another round trip out there, I'll go get him for you. Our replacement team is almost here. If I'm not back by the time they get here, will you greet them and show them where we are?"

Virginia looked confused. "They're almost here? I thought... ah... yeah, sure. We'll wait here. Who are they?"

"It's a special unit from the Smithsonian. They were in Houston and were about to go back to Washington but were redeployed here, instead. The leader is Special Agent Francis Bullard."

Natalie's face brightened. "A girl is the leader? I like her already."

"No. Francis is a male, Agent North."

"Nuts."

"I'll go get your deputy and will be right back." The leader returned to his Humvee and drove off.

Terry looked at her watch. "It's still early. I should have gone with him."

Virginia patted Terry's shoulder. "There'll be plenty of time to research the site. We need to introduce ourselves to the new security detail when they get here. They're part of the SCSS? I didn't know we had such a group."

"We're part time, remember?" said Natalie.

Ten minutes later four large, black, unmarked, heavy-duty trucks that looked like large armored RVs rumbled up the driveway.

Terry beamed. "They look similar to the vehicle we took into the jungle a few years ago."

"They do at that." Virginia smiled. "I bet ours was more comfortable."

They watched the vehicles come to a stop and a tall, muscular man with raven hair and a deep tan emerge from the lead unit dressed in what looked like a hunting outfit. He strolled up to the women and presented his credentials. "I'm Special Agent Francis Bullard, of the Smithsonian Central Security Service. I'm looking for Agents Clark and North." Virginia eyed the object of Terry's ogling and chuckled.

Terry's going to want to camp out at the dig site now. "I'm Agent Clark." She turned slightly and waved her hand toward the women. "This is Agent North and this lady is our archaeologist, Dr. Sorenson."

Agent Francis Bullard nodded. "Nice to meet you all." Fire sparkled in his emerald green eyes. "You're Dr. Sorenson? Dr. Terry Sorenson?"

Terry nodded. "Yes, sir."

"Oh, wow. I've seen your picture and read a number of your papers and hoped to meet you someday. It is a great pleasure to finally do so, Doctor."

Terry smiled and fidgeted like a schoolgirl. "Nice to meet you, too, sir.

Mysterious Threads

I'll be spending a lot of time at the dig site. Maybe we can get to know each other a little better then."

He nodded. "I'd really like that. The Smithsonian said your museum will be the lead at the dig with help from Texas A&M. We'll be providing security for *you* and the archaeologists." Bullard turned to Natalie. "The Special Operations unit team said I would easily identify you, Agent North."

Natalie tipped her head. "They did?"

"Yes. They said you are one dangerous lady but you're pretty enough to just stand on the side of the freeway and cause an accident on I-35."

"They did?" Natalie grinned. "They're nice boys."

He turned back to Virginia. "They also said you're the boss and to try and remember that in spite of how pretty you are."

"Thank you." Virginia gave him a skeptical look. "Trying to butter up the home team, Agent Bullard?"

He laughed. "Tom Mason said to get on your good side quick. He didn't want me and my team returning to Washington in long, narrow, wooden boxes."

"Smart man. Okay. Let's get you out to the site. Natalie and I will ride in the last vehicle if that's okay. I'm sure you'll want Dr. Sorenson to ride with you."

"Yes." Bullard smiled. "Saddle up."

They rode out to the dig site, and after meeting with the Special Operations Unit people and talking to Virginia, the new team set up camp. They arranged their rigs in a semicircle around the dig site, turned on their electronic surveillance equipment, deployed perimeter sensors and defensive weapons, and set up floodlights.

Virginia watched, then spoke to Agent Bullard when he approached. "Looks like you have everything under control. Let me know if there is anything else I can do for you, and if anything happens."

Bullard handed Virginia a small hand-held radio. "If you need to contact us, use this. If we need you, I'll call on this radio."

"Okay. If there is nothing else, we'll get one of the Special Ops guys to take us back to the main house."

"Okay." He handed Virginia another radio. "Will you give this to Dr Sorenson? When she wants to visit the site, all she needs to do is call me, and I'll come and get her from the main house. I wouldn't want Dr. Sorenson to hike through all that brush and brambles. She could get injured."

"Of course, you wouldn't." Virginia chuckled. "I'll give it to her." Virginia looked around. "Where'd she go?"

CHAPTER 39

Virginia hobbled on her crutches around the dig site looking for Terry. She stopped and glanced around at the sound of someone calling her name. Spotting Terry dancing around excitedly at the edge of the woods waving at her, Virginia carefully ambled her crutches around the staked grid pattern to her.

"What's up?" asked Virginia when she approached Terry.

"I need to show you something. Follow me." Terry quickly turned and rushed into the woods.

"Wait for me," called Virginia. She moved slowly over the uneven ground, through the low brush, and trees, following Terry to a small clearing about twenty yards into the woods. She stopped next to Terry and looked at the spot where Terry stood. "Okay, why are you so excited? Did you find more artifacts?"

A strand of her auburn hair waved in front of Terry's eyes in the slight breeze. "No." Something better. Look." She pointed at the ground.

Virginia looked where Terry pointed. "Those are shell casings. Someone fired a rifle from here."

"Yeah. And look that way." Terry pointed at a clear sight path through some dense trees.

Virginia stepped closer to Terry and looked. "That... that looks like about where Natalie and I were when someone shot at us."

"That's what I thought. Now look this way." She pointed at an area of less dense foliage.

Virginia squinted. "That's toward the main house. If someone had a light out here or even at the dig, you might see a faint glimpse from the house." She narrowed her eyes in suspicion. "So, that explains the strange lights we've seen and how someone was able to fire at us. This is good work."

Terry had a satisfied grin on her face. "Thanks. I'll get some containers from Agent Bullard and gather up the casings. Maybe the crime lab can find some fingerprints on them."

Ballard walked up. "I was wondering where you two went."

Virginia pointed. "Can you have someone bag these shell casings as evidence and see what the lab can find?"

Terry gave him her brightest smile. "These may have been the bullets that were fired at Virginia and Natalie."

Bullard looked at the casings. "You might want Deputy Sanchez to get the fingerprint work done. That would be faster than my sending them to Washington."

"Great idea," said Virginia looking around. "Where is Sanchez?"

Bullard waved his thumb over his shoulder. "He's inside of Unit Two examining the capability of our vehicles. I understand you two had the original prototype someplace in Central America a few years ago on a case called *Trail of Threads*."

"We had a prototype?" Terry looked at Virginia in shock. "Really? A… a… prototype? We risked our lives with a prototype!"

Virginia shrugged. "News to me." She turned. "Agent Bullard, can you have the casings gathered up and have Sanchez get them to the sheriff's lab as quick as possible?"

"On it." He turned and hurried through the low brush and trees.

"A damn prototype," Terry mumbled. "We could have been killed."

"We made it, and the unit performed very well, didn't it?"

"I guess so. We both got wounded though." Terry sulked as she walked alongside Virginia out of the woods.

"We didn't get hurt inside the rig, just when we were outside. And, in the end, it did get us to safety."

"Yeah, you're right. A damn prototype." Terry looked unhappy as she glanced around. "We either have to walk out of here or we need Francis to give us a ride."

Virginia raised an eyebrow. "It's *Francis* now is it?" Terry twisted a lock of hair.

"Oh." Virginia rolled her eyes and handed Terry the small radio Bullard had given her. "This is for you. *Francis* said it's for you to communicate with him if you need anything. He also said to call him when you get to the main buildings and he'll come and get you to supervise the digging."

Terry took the radio. "Thank you." When they reached the dig site Sanchez and one of the security details passed them heading for the clearing and bullet casings. "I hope Sanchez can find useable fingerprints."

"Me too." Virginia continued to the side of the security detail's number one vehicle and leaned against it. "Boy, hiking around out here with crutches is tiring. We need to get back to the main house." Virginia wiped her hands on her jeans. "Where's Natalie?"

"In here," came Natalie's disembodied voice from above Virginia.

Virginia and Terry looked up. Natalie stuck her head out of the open window of the armored vehicle.

Terry gave her a quizzical look. "What are you doing in there?"

Natalie looked down at them. "I was dying to see what these things looked like inside. Very high tech, flat-screen displays, bulletproof, storage space, and yet comfortable. So, this is what you two drove around in south of the border. To hear your stories, it sounded like you were really roughing it. And here I was feeling sorry for you. This thing's got all sorts of sophisticated communication gear, remotely operated weapons, sensors, night vision, air conditioning, water treatment, and it's even got a small kitchen with a microwave, fridge, and satellite TV. This is so cool. Our guards will be camping here in style."

"We know. We used the prototype," grumbled Terry.

Virginia closed her eyes and shook her head. "We'll never live this down. Okay, Ms. North, come on out. We need to get back to the house. I'd like to inventory Terry's new diving gear before it gets too late."

"Okay." Natalie scrambled out of the vehicle. She stepped down from the doorway and patted the side. "I want one of these. Maybe I can camp out here in one of them."

"Natalie, dear, you'd be sharing the space with a number of men," said Virginia. "I've seen what you call pajamas. You'll give the guys heart attacks or cause them to need frequent cold showers if you join them for a night. Anyway, they're on duty."

"Party pooper." Natalie gazed languidly at the vehicle. "I still want one."

Terry smiled affectionately as she watched Special Agent Bullard across the expanse. "I think I'll need to spend a lot of time here and maybe a few nights. All for science of course."

Virginia looked where Terry was staring, and chuckled. "For science, right."

Agent Bullard strolled up to the women. "Your deputy left a little while ago to take the casings to his lab."

"Good," said Virginia.

"I take it you'd like to return to the main part of the ranch."

Virginia nodded. "Yes."

"The Special Ops guys are leaving, you can ride with them. This way." Bullard led them around the staked grid to a Humvee the special ops team leader was leaning against.

The leader snapped to attention. "If you ladies are done here, I'll return you to the main buildings."

"Thanks, I need to get off this ankle." Virginia climbed into the Humvee with Natalie and Terry. After bouncing over ruts and small brush they arrived at the house and exited the vehicle. Virginia leaned inside.

Mysterious Threads

"Thanks again, sir. You and your men have been great. Don't take this wrong, but I hope we won't need to see you anymore."

"That's okay, Mrs. Clark. But our orders are to stay in the Austin area on standby should future aid be required. Just contact Agent Mason and we'll be available to assist you with anything you need." He saluted and drove off.

Virginia looked around then nodded toward the house where women were watching them out of the windows. "Since we've already caused a stir, let's go look at the new diving gear. No time like the present."

Natalie put her hand on Virginia's shoulder. "You go inside, get a tall glass of iced tea, and sit. You need to rest your ankle. Terry and I can see what's what with the diving stuff."

"But—"

"No buts, go get some tea and rest. I know that's against everything you're made of, but we need you in good shape, not in the hospital."

Virginia sighed. "Okay, I'll go. But let me know if everything is ready."

One of the ladies from the retreat hurried to the group. "Clara gave me this to give to you, Virginia. She said Daniele took the message." She handed Virginia a slip of paper then returned to the house.

Virginia read the note then nodded. "Looks like we can arrange a dive for tomorrow."

"Tomorrow?" Terry tilted her head. "Who's my dive partner going to be?"

"Someone Tom arranged to come. This note says your dive partner will be here tonight at six. You will meet him then. Maybe we all can go out for dinner and discuss our detailed plans."

Terry nodded. "I'm up for that. Are you going to tell Clara and the other women suspects we're going to dive in the lake tomorrow?"

"Yeah. I'll let it slip in conversation when possible." Virginia turned and hobbled up the steps and into the house.

At six that evening, a big roar of the Corvette supercharged V8 motor filled the evening air as the vehicle skidded to a stop in the driveway of the ranch's main house. The women there hurried to the front room and peered out as a tall man with lean hips and broad shoulders climbed out of the car and walked with a slow, cocky swagger affected by heroes of old westerns, like when they sauntered into salons filled with bad guys. He was dark: black hair and eyes, skin so bronzed he might have been part Indian. The coppery shade was not restricted to his face and hands; his shirt was open partway displaying rippled muscles. As he strolled up the walkway, he looked at the building, then at a piece of paper. He stuck the paper into his jeans and slowly walked up the steps and knocked on the door.

Daniele Webley, a knitter and quilter, and Clara opened the door and gasped. "Hel... Hello," Daniele said. "Can we help you?"

He smiled. "Yes, ladies. I'm looking for Dr. Terry Sorenson. Ms. Natalie North, and Mrs. Virginia Davies Clark. I'm expected." He handed Clara a business card and smiled. "My card, ma'am."

Daniele swung the door wide open. "Please come in..." Clara looked at the card, "Commander Miles St. John. I know Virginia was expecting someone, so I'll tell her you're here." She and Daniele escorted the commander to the parlor and had him take a seat then ushered the other gawking ladies out of the room.

Two minutes later Commander St. John rose as Virginia, Terry and Natalie entered. "Good evening ladies. I'm Miles St. John, Commander, United States Navy. I believe you're expecting me."

Virginia hobbled to him and shook hands then introduced Terry and Natalie. "You're right on time, Commander. We were hoping you'd like to go to dinner with us to go over our mission. Dinner is on us."

He eyed the three women carefully. "It would be my pleasure, ma'am. But my vehicle is a little small to take everyone. Would it be—"

Natalie interrupted. "We can all fit in my Toyota Land Cruiser. It's the size of a tank."

Commander St. John nodded. "That would be fine. Ladies, since we will be working together, please call me Miles." He handed each of them his card.

Natalie and Terry flanked the handsome naval officer, with Virginia following out to Natalie's car. Natalie had Miles sit in the front next to her. Virginia and Terry were delegated to the rear seats. They exited the driveway and drove down the county road toward Texas 29 and then to Georgetown and The Longhorn Steak House.

As they drove Virginia examined the officer's card. *He's a SEAL? How'd Tom manage that? I guess Terry will be okay diving.* She nudged Terry and pointed to the card.

Terry looked at it and grinned. She leaned close to Virginia and whispered. "I'll be in good hands."

Virginia eyed her. "I trust you mean for diving."

Terry blushed. "What else?"

As they drove Miles turned and looked at Terry and Virginia. "Who will be doing the diving?"

Virginia quickly spoke up. "Terry and you, sir. Natalie and I and possibly a deputy sheriff will be on the surface acting as security and to handle logistics."

Miles smiled at Terry. "I'm sure we'll be just fine. Have you dived much, ma'am?"

"Yes... well I try to go to the Gulf a couple times a year, and out to Catalina off the southern California coast regularly for dives." Terry wet her lips. "I've been on some marine archaeological dives off Florida and Mexico, and in the Med as well. We obtained special new diving equipment from the Smithsonian for this dive. It's back at the ranch."

"Good. I can't wait to see the special equipment."

Virginia nodded. "Yeah, we get help when we need it. I'm glad you showed up so quickly." *Tom didn't tell him about our special diving gear? Why?*

"Yes, ma'am. The Navy detailed me to your group very suddenly. I was to be deployed with SEAL Team One but got suddenly redirected here instead. May I ask what the mission entails?"

"They didn't brief you?" asked Virginia. *That's funny.*

"No. My orders are to contact you and assist in a dive that involves some risk to you and is important to the government. I was told you, Agent Clark, are in charge and would fill me in."

Virginia chuckled. "Yes, sir. We can discuss our mission as you put it over dinner. But let me say this, we are overjoyed that you have joined our little band." *I hope.*

"Thank you. I understand that there is a security detail somewhere on the ranch we just left. May I inquire as to their purpose?"

Terry leaned forward. "They're guarding an unusual archaeological site and keeping people from continuing to shoot at us."

Commander St. John's jaw dropped. "Shooting at you?"

Virginia nodded. "Yeah. We've become a little paranoid from being attacked a few times since we started this case. That's why I'm on crutches."

Miles' looked at Virginia's foot cast. "You were shot?"

Natalie laughed. "No. She broke her ankle and ran into a tree ducking a bullet. It was a big tree. But the good news is the tree survived without any damage. We also had to tranquilize some men who were going to shoot us, and—"

Virginia poked the seat. "That's enough out of you."

Miles rubbed his forehead. "This is stranger than I expected. I take it you will brief me on the rest of what's going on at the restaurant."

"Yes," said Virginia. "That's the plan." *Funny Washington didn't at least give him some mission background.*

Natalie glanced in her rear-view mirror. "Gang, we need to get there first. We've got a tail."

Virginia looked out the rear of the car. "Natalie, lose them."

CHAPTER 40

Natalie accelerated toward the intersection with Texas 29. She slowed only slightly to be sure there was no cross traffic and ran the stop sign. She glanced over her shoulder. "You might want to call Sanchez and get us some help." She drove across the highway and continued down the county road. At a bend, she suddenly swung the Land Cruiser skidding sideways onto a side road then punched the accelerator and flew down the road.

Virginia called out from the backseat, "Sanchez wants to know where we are so he can get us help."

Natalie chuckled. "I've got no idea except that we're in Liberty Hill someplace."

Terry clung to her seatbelt and sputtered, "I don't see the car that was behind us. Maybe you lost them."

Natalie let out a sigh. "I hope so. Another round of defensive driving or a shootout doesn't interest me right now. I'm hungry."

Commander St. John sat staring ahead. He finally took a breath. "Is this type of thing normal for you three?"

Virginia laughed. "When we're on a case, pretty much."

He twisted around in his seat. "This case is that serious?"

"It involves a century-old smuggling operation, stolen artifacts, murders, treasure, attacks on us and a sheriff's deputy, and who knows what else. So, yes, it's serious. That's why they redeployed you so fast and we've got an armed security team at the ranch."

He turned back in his seat. "I see. I can't wait for the briefing over dinner."

Terry watched their back. "No one behind us seems to have any interest in us. I'll call off Sanchez. Let's get to the restaurant."

Natalie drove on back roads toward Georgetown then hopped back on Texas 29 and continued to the Longhorn Steakhouse.

After dinner and returning to the ranch, they all went to the war room

Mysterious Threads

where the diving equipment was stored. They went inside and relocked the door behind them.

Virginia sat on a metal chair, removed her iPad from her backpack, and consulted the hidden cameras the sheriff had provided. She finally looked at the others. "Okay. No one has been around the building. The alarms haven't detected anything either, so I think we're good." She looked at Terry. "Let's inspect the gear and go over our operation with Miles so we can get an early start tomorrow."

Miles looked around. "This is some setup you have."

"Thank you. We've moved the evidence for this case to my museum though," said Virginia.

Miles nodded. "Okay, let's go over each piece of equipment so everyone knows what it does, how it works, and most importantly, who's doing what. We don't need any surprises underwater."

Terry's cell phone rang. "Hello?"

"Doc, it's Deputy Sanchez. Did your dive partner arrive?"

"Yes, Luis. He's here with us now going over the dive equipment and our plan."

"Is he law enforcement?" asked Sanchez.

"No. He's a navy SEAL."

"A SEAL? Great. I can't wait to meet him. I got a text from Virginia that the dive is tomorrow. I have one of the larger sheriff's workboat and truck we can use. I'll bring it to the ranch. What time do you need me and the boat?"

Terry looked at Virginia. "Sanchez wants to know when tomorrow to be here with the boat."

Virginia thought for a second. "Tell him 0600."

Terry spoke into the phone. "She said 0600. Can you be here by then?"

"Yes. I'll get the rest of my gear and be waiting for you outside the ranch. We can load your equipment on the boat and the truck before we head out."

"Okay," said Terry.

"Oh, one more thing, I... err... the lab got some useable prints off some of the rifle cartridges from the dig site. They belong to Daniele Webley."

"They do? Why would her fingerprints be in your system? Did she get arrested or something?" asked Terry.

"No. She was a substitute teacher from 2011 to 2014. Teachers are fingerprinted in Texas."

"Oh. Good to know. I'll pass this on to Virginia. Thanks, Luis." She disconnected.

Virginia texted Agent Tom Mason in Washington to let him know that Commander St. John had arrived.

At six thirty-five the next morning, the team pulled out of the ranch driveway. Sanchez pulled the workboat with a sheriff's pickup truck. Natalie and Virginia followed in Natalie's Land Cruiser as Terry and Commander St. John brought up the rear in a museum van. The small caravan headed west on Texas 29 toward Lake Buchanan. After a forty-minute drive, they arrived at a boat launch site on the west side of the lake. Sanchez backed the boat down the landing into the water, detached it from the trailer, and then parked the truck.

Terry sat in the boat's pilot chair and pressed the starter. The engines coughed, then fell silent. She pressed the starter again, this time the two big Evinrude outboard engines roared to life. The boat sent back a creamy wake as it sliced through the water. Terry drove it a short distance out into the lake then turned and headed toward the nearby wooden dock. Pulling alongside, the pier, Natalie jumped onboard, grabbed the bowline, and tossed it to Miles on the dock who quickly secured the boat to the dock. Natalie, Miles, and Sanchez loaded the remaining dive equipment from the truck onboard along with a map Virginia had drawn the night before.

They untied the boat and headed out into the lake. As Natalie steered the boat, they knifed through the water and the early morning patchy fog. Since they were not far from shore, when she glanced over the side, Natalie could see the greenish tops of jagged underwater rocks covered with waving seaweed slowly retreat and the bottom fall away. She piloted the boat along their previously agreed course.

Miles helped Terry slip on her dry suit and went over the operation of their equipment for the last time. He glanced toward shore. "Where exactly is Agent Clark?"

Natalie tried not to look at the shoreline. "She's found a spot where she can watch us and if necessary, take out any surface adversary. Sanchez and I will monitor you two from the boat. While you and Terry are under the water, you'll be able to talk to all of us and to hear us through those nifty toys the agency sent. If you… or we encounter any difficulties call out. If Virginia spots trouble, she'll let us know or terminate it." *As will I.*

Miles looked at Sanchez sitting at the stern fiddling with some equipment. "You good over there, Deputy?"

"Yes, sir. Now that we're in deeper water I've got our sonars engaged. Good readings."

Miles moved next to Natalie. "How much farther?"

Natalie eyed the Defense Department GPS equipment sent by the SCSS then chuckled. "You're asking if we're there yet?"

Miles gave her a sheepish grin. "I guess so."

"Because of the shape of the lake's shoreline, it's two miles to our target. Might as well relax. Virginia's watching over us like a guardian angel." As Natalie piloted the boat the last mile or so, storm clouds gathered like large spreading bruises across the sky. A grey pall cast itself across the water around her. A stray bolt of lightning wouldn't have surprised her.

Nearing the GPS indicated location Natalie piloted the boat near shore and idled the engines. "We're on-site, guys." She spoke into her throat mic and adjusted her headset. "Virginia, we're ready to go."

"I can see you," Virginia responded. "I hope the weather holds."

"Me too." Natalie watched Terry and Miles place their equipment in the water then they slipped over the side of the boat. "The weather seems to be changing. You two still want to dive?" She waited then heard Terry.

"Sound check. Can you hear me Natalie?" asked Terry.

"Loud and clear. About the weather."

"Miles said we'd be okay but to let us know if the weather starts to degrade."

"Okay. How's the water?"

"Cold and murky. Not the Caribbean, Gulf of Mexico, or the South Pacific that's for sure."

"Ready to dive?"

"Yeah. We're turning on the sea scooters and our lights now. We'll let you know what we find."

Natalie moved next to Sanchez and watched the sonar screen. "Is that them?"

"Yes." He pointed at the screen. "The SEAL slowly passed under our boat a minute ago then joined Terry. They're going down and heading toward that underwater embankment."

Virginia's voice cut in. "Guys. A car just pulled up south of my twenty. Not sure who's in it yet, the fog is just dense enough to distort my vision."

Sanchez answered. "Any threat?"

"Not sure. Hopefully, not. I'll investigate."

Virginia slid out of her hiding place and limped on her crutches through trees as stealthily as she could toward the idling vehicle. She crouched behind a large elm and watched. The car's engine shut down. Virginia stared as the car doors opened and Helen Chandler, Harriet Fisher, and Marlene Bauer emerged. Helen held a rifle with a scope on it. Harriet had a video camera with a telescopic lens. Marlene lugged an orange bag with an inflatable boat inside. They trudged through the brush toward the banks of the lake. Virginia kept watch as the trio moved silently as possible through the light fog and brush around them. She keyed her mic. "Natalie, our expected visitors have arrived armed and are taking up position along the shore."

Natalie called back. "What do you want us to do?"

"Nothing now, but be prepared to high tail it farther out into the lake if I tell you to."

"Roger."

Virginia watched the women settle into a site behind an abandoned, tumbling boathouse and rotted pilings of an old pier. Helen knelt, raised the rifle and aimed it at the boat, and observed it through the scope. Virginia pulled out the radio to warn Natalie when Helen lowered the rifle, leaned against a tree stump, and watched the boat. Harriet used the video camera to watch the boat. Harriet said something to Marlene. Marlene pulled the bag to the water's edge and opened it. She pulled out a package then pulled a strap. The compressed gas canister attached to it inflated the orange, rubber-sided boat. Marlene pushed it into the lake and held the line while Harriet climbed in then Marlene hopped in as well.

Uh-oh. Here comes trouble. Virginia frowned. *I need to neutralize this quick. I can find out what exactly they're doing later.* She untied the animal tranquilizer gun from her left crutch, aimed it at Helen, and fired. The tranquilizer dart hit her between her shoulder blades. Helen's body jerked, then she and the rifle next to her tumbled forward onto the ground. When Helen hit, the sound alerted the other women. Marlene twisted around in the boat and pulled a pistol from under her jacket. Virginia's second dart caught her in the shoulder. She froze then fell into the rubber-hulled boat. Harriet dropped the camera and tried to paddle away. Virginia's next shot hit her in her side. She dropped onto the bottom of the boat.

Virginia keyed her mic again. "Three down. Be careful out there."

Natalie called back. "You want to elaborate? How'd you stop them?'

"Remember the incident at the mound of dirt and the motorcycles and other guys?"

"Huh? Oh yeah. Got it. Haven't heard from Terry or Miles yet. I'll call them."

Virginia went to Helen and tied her wrists with plastic ties and moved the rifle away. She watched the inflatable boat drift just offshore. *Not much I can do with that right now.* She called Natalie. "Got a small problem. Just to your south do you see an old, dilapidated, boat shed?"

A few seconds later Natalie responded. "Yes."

"Can you leave your position for a couple minutes and come around the shed? There's a small, orange, rubber-hulled boat with two of our friends from the retreat in it. It's drifting and I can't get it."

"Okay, we'll come around. I'll tell Terry we'll be off-site for a few minutes."

Terry heard their conversation in her communication equipment. She told Natalie they were descending to sixty feet and moving along the edge of the shore drop off and to let her know when the boat would be back. With a large bass watching her, Terry maneuvered her sea scooter around rock outcroppings and decaying trees. She spotted and checked out five small caves then she noticed an irregularity in the side of the lake located on a shelf like structure. Terry called Miles. "Commander, I think that could be our cave."

He moved his scooter closer to the opening. "It's a good-sized cave alright. The opening has some debris blocking it. Let's see if we can move it and look inside." He watched as Terry stopped in front of the opening, shinning her scooter's light inside.

Terry goosed the motor to inch closer to the cave entrance and examined the rubble. "This could be the right cave. I can see what looks like some metal crates inside behind all these rocks." She backed her scooter up when something shot by her face. Terry swung her head around to see what it was. A speargun dart bounced off a rock a foot to her right. Fear rushed in a blood-pumping ripple through her. Time seemed to freeze to a crawl as she turned to see Miles reloading his weapon. Terry nosed the scooter down and gunned its motor. She could hear the increased whine of the scooter's electric motor as it dragged her away from shore with increasing speed and sped deeper into the cold, dark lake. Fish darted out of the way. Another spear gun arrow shot past her right shoulder. Terry glanced back. Miles was holding his spear gun and watching her, then took aim. She twisted the scooter to change direction as she felt her heart race. She wove the scooter back and forth as she continued to dive into the murkiness. She called out, "Under attack. Miles is shooting at me!"

Natalie responded. "Understood. Where's Miles?"

An arrow shot over Terry's head. "Behind me. He's shooting at me! Why? Hurting me won't do him any good with you guys up there."

"I don't know. Try and get away, we'll see what we can do from here to help," called Natalie.

Virginia cut in on a second radio frequency the divers couldn't hear. "Luis, push the purple button on the control module for Miles' scooter."

Sanchez watched the sonar screen and froze. "I see them. Terry's running from him taking evasive action, but he's..." Sanchez looked at Natalie. "Why would a navy SEAL do—"

"Luis, where is he?" asked Virginia in a harried voice.

Sanchez eyed the sonar screen. "He's behind Terry and closing."

"Luis, I just got a message from Washington," Virginia screamed. "Miles is not a real navy commander or SEAL. He's an imposter and a killer. Terry's in danger. The real SCSS diver is still on his way. Push the button!"

There was a low rumble, then a loud thump from the lake as a small geyser with red foam shot up.

"Threat neutralized," Natalie's calm voice said. "Terry, you can return to the boat."

Terry's shaky voice responded. "Thank you, Natalie. Boy, my ears are ringing. If it's okay with you guys, as soon as my heart slows down, I want to see what's in that big cave. I'll keep you informed."

CHAPTER 41

Virginia watched as Natalie used the workboat to push the rubber raft back to shore. Virginia grabbed the line from the raft and pulled it up onto dry land as Natalie sped back to Terry's location. Virginia turned at the sound of scraping come from the sheriff's workboat as it pulled out into the lake and then saw a package drift away from it. She untied the rifle attached to her right crutch, set it on the ground, hobbled out a few feet, and grabbed the waterproof package. She stood in the cold water and carefully opened it. *This is a bomb with a remote trigger and it was under the workboat. I could have set it off by accident. That's why Miles went under the boat before joining Terry.* Virginia's blood boiled. *After finding the treasure he was going to kill Terry and blow up the boat. I'm glad Natalie blew him to pieces.*

She waded back, picked up her rifle and tranquilizer gun, then placed the bomb into the raft along with her crutches, and climbed in. She tied the wrists of Marlene and Harriet, then she called Tom in Washington and told him what happened, and she needed help. She then glanced at her wet cast. *Shit, now my ankle really hurts. It will never heal at this rate.*

A short time later two, large, enclosed, trucks and a heavy lift vehicle arrived. The Special Ops team hurried to Virginia. They secured the unconscious women and the bomb then asked for a sitrep. Virginia explained what was happening. After a brief discussion, Virginia called Natalie. "How is Terry doing?"

"Last I heard from her she was swearing at a rock in the cave that's blocking her. You must have heard her."

"Yeah, but I was busy with the Special Ops guys. Bring your boat to the dock. Two of the Special Ops team members are going to join you."

"They're here?" Natalie asked enthusiastically.

"Yes. Two of them are going to come aboard the boat and will use the spare diving equipment to help Terry. They also brought marine heavy-lift gear to bring up anything Terry finds in the cave."

"On my way," said Natalie. "We need to do something pretty soon those clouds don't look friendly and the lake is getting choppy."

Virginia looked to the west as bolts of lightning struck downward in the distance like rows of upside-down trees. *We'd better get this show on the road quickly.*

Eight hours later, in the dark rain, a sheriff's car, and Natalie's Land Cruiser rolled into the retreat ranch. Virginia, Natalie, Terry, Sanchez, and a female deputy walked up the front steps and into the house. Lightning strobed the ranch.

Clara and Daniele Webley rushed to the parlor and skidded to a stop. Clara looked at them with wide, wild-eyes, and stuttered. "You… you're here? Already?"

"Yes." Virginia smiled. "I see your gout has improved, Clara."

"Ahh… yes, thank you," said Clara. She swallowed. "You're all okay? I was concerned when the storm hit. Did you find anything?"

Virginia gave a slight shrug. "Yes, and we're fine."

Daniele looked pale. "I thought… ahh… how'd it go?"

"We found the rest of June's and Noble's smuggled Aztec treasure," said Virginia.

"Aztec? Don't you mean Maximilien's treasure?" asked Clara.

"No. Aztec. As Harriet, Marlene, and Helen now know."

"Huh?" Daniele went white. "Wh… where are…?"

"They're under arrest." Virginia shifted her gaze to Daniele. "You will be joining them, Daniele."

"What? That's preposterous. I haven't done anything."

Clara looked confused. "What's going on?"

"Just listen, Clara, and all will be revealed."

"I need to call my lawyer." Daniele turned toward the phone on an end table. "You can't prove anything."

Virginia stepped in front of her. "Remember Mr. Sommers, Daniele? In case you were wondering, Mr. Sommers has been arrested for murder."

"He was?"

"Yes."

Daniele tensed.

"You and your friends thought it was Maximilian's treasure you were after," said Virginia. "Then you stumbled onto June's and Simon's old smuggling operations. But *you* couldn't find their loot. When Colin found the gold Aztec mask where it shouldn't have been, he got scared and confused. He knew something was wrong but didn't understand it. You and Colin were very close. He confided in you, Daniele. He trusted you. You were supplying him with goods from your store for years and saw yourself as the future Mrs. Carswell. You knew about the ranch being a corporation

Mysterious Threads

and Clara being a principle stockholder. If Colin found the treasure, especially if it was on the ranch, then you had to do something to make sure Clara and the other stockholders would not be in your way."

Daniele's eyes darkened Virginia continued. "He cared for you and was going to change his will and give you stock in the corporation. I have the legal documents from the files. You planned to kill him and have his death blamed on Clara then take over the ranch. What you didn't know was he never filed the changes. Then Natalie and I joined in because you stupidly killed Colin. You thought you were clever and wouldn't get caught by all your misdirection. You even tried to use us to find the treasure for you. We counted on that."

"Colin was poisoned," Daniele ranted. "You stated the poison was from the autumn crocus that grows around here. I know about the plant because I grow specialty plants as a side business as you know. But I'm not a chemist, how would I get the poison out of the plant?"

Virginia nodded. "The actual poison used to kill Colin was colchicine. While colchicine is derived from the autumn crocus, the compound that killed Colin wasn't from a plant. It was made in a laboratory by a drug company. The colchicine that poisoned Colin had the same chemical signature as the drug Clara's presently taking."

"So, Clara did it, not me," said Daniele. "It's obvious."

"I didn't kill anyone. Any... anyone could get it," Clara stammered.

"No, they need a prescription, like you have."

Clara collapsed in a chair. "But... I... I didn't kill my cousin."

"I know that, Clara. Daniele stole the pills from you, making it look like you killed Colin. You were an easy target. I had the SCSS run a financial check on all of you. Due to unexpected problems in the investment market and poor spending habits, you, Marlene, Harriet, and Helen were in need of a source of enhanced revenue and soon. Thus, the treasure hunt. Marlene was a history teacher and was infatuated with Maximilian's treasure. She even did a lot of research. But since she retired early because of a back injury, her teacher's pension wasn't enough to cover her debts."

Virginia lowered herself onto the armrests of the crutches. "Helen was also a close friend of Colin's and in need of money. Harriet needed the money, too but is originally from France. She may have seen getting Maximilian's treasure as some sort of patriotic thing. The three of them said they thought it was Maximilian's treasure they were after and didn't know anything about Aztec artifacts. You, Daniele sold your business for a boatload of money, but things haven't gone well for you financially either. Clara, Daniele and the others conspired to cut you out of the treasure and frame you for murder."

"Clara has more reasons to need the treasure than me," Daniele huffed. "She even has the fatal drug,"

"Yes, but while she needed money, she isn't a criminal. Let's just say the evidence against her was too perfect. Something didn't feel right. We suspected Clara was being framed." Virginia took a breath. "Daniele, your fingerprints are on the rifle cartridges we found in the woods. They are the same caliber as the ones used in the rifle Helen had at the lake. Helen was the one who shot at your bathroom window with the old World-War II pistol to make it look like you were a target. But the thick frosted window blocks defected the bullet and it accidentally creased your side by mistake. It was convincing at the time."

"That's not enough to arrest me. Helen had the gun."

"The biggest mistake you made, Daniele, was not informing me that the SCSS diver was going to be late. Having a fake SEAL come early was brilliant. We accepted him based on his business card and us knowing someone was coming. I wondered why he used a business card instead of displaying his navy ID. Business cards are easier to come by than military IDs. It worked for a while because we wanted to believe he was a SEAL. As you can see, he failed in his mission."

Daniele frowned. "Is he under arrest?"

"No. He's dead. He was going to blow up our boat after the treasure was located. He tried to kill Terry while diving. That was a fatal mistake."

Daniele looked at Terry with disdain. "Did *she* kill him?"

"No," said Natalie. "I did."

Daniele spun around. "You did? How?"

"The special sea scooters we got from Washington had mines built into them that could be remotely detonated," said Natalie. "When he attacked Terry, I blew him into itsy-bitsy fish food. Miles didn't know the scooters had mines built-in. If he was a real SEAL, he would have known."

"And, there were the people who kept attacking us. They were paid thugs, and as I'm sure you know, most of them are now dead," added Virginia.

Daniele looked like she was going to faint. "You... you have nothing."

Virginia shook her head. "That's not all. The guys from that rock quarry who tried to Shanghai Natalie and I were picked up again, and under the circumstances, they agreed to talk. The ladies confessed as well. They all implicated you and provided very damaging evidence. Promises of possible immunity or lesser sentences will usually get those arrested first to cooperate and implicate the person behind a murder."

Clara gazed at Virginia. "I... I could have been charged with a murder I didn't commit. I don't know what to say. Thank you for... for believing in me, keeping digging and proving I didn't do it. Somehow thank you doesn't seem like enough."

Virginia smiled. "You're welcome, Clara."

Sanchez stepped forward. "Daniele Webley, you are under arrest." He

Mysterious Threads

read her the Miranda Warning and winked at Natalie while he handcuffed Daniele. He then whispered to Natalie, "That's how it's supposed to be done."

Natalie kissed his cheek. "Got it, Deputy."

Natalie, Terry, Clara, and Virginia, along with the other women at the retreat watched as Sanchez and the female deputy led Daniele to his police car and drive off the ranch into the dark and rain.

Three days later Virginia and Andy were at home eating breakfast when the phone rang. She answered it. "This is Virginia. How can I help you?"

"Mrs. Clark. This is Captain Harris of the sheriff's office. I want to thank you for keeping your word and giving the sheriff's office the arrests on your case and giving us credit in the press and with the county."

"I told you I would. And we couldn't have done it without Deputy Luis Sanchez, Captain."

"Well, thank you, Mrs. Clark. We have some good things in store for Deputy Sanchez. He said he learned a lot from you and your team but won't elaborate on some of it."

"Good for him. Don't press him, sir. I have a SCSS nondisclosure agreement from him as well as government national security documents he signed. I'd hate to see anything bad happen to him."

"Don't worry. He won't disclose anything and that's adding to his mystique around here. The other deputies think he was acting as some sort of federal secret agent. He's loving it. For your information, the DA has started processing the women. Thank you again."

"No problem."

"Just so you know, our sheriff and the Williamson County DA said they'd be happy to cooperate with you any time on other cases. Thanks for what you did and helping our young deputy learn on such a difficult case."

"You're welcome. Good-by, Captain."

ABOUT THE AUTHOR

Dr. David Ciambrone is a retired aerospace and defense company executive, scientist, professor of engineering, and a business and environmental consultant and is now a best-selling, award-winning author living in Georgetown, Texas with his wife Kathy. He has published twenty-five (25) books: four (4) non-fiction, two (2) textbooks for a California university, and nineteen (19) mysteries and has two (2) new mysteries in work. He is the author of the Virginia Davies Quilt Mysteries.

Dave has been a speaker at writer's groups, schools, colleges, libraries, quilt guilds, writer's conferences, and business/scientific conferences internationally.

Dr. Ciambrone also wrote three newspaper columns and wrote a column for a business journal.

Dave is a member of Sisters in Crime, the San Gabriel Writer's League, the Writer's League of Texas, Mystery Writers of America, the International Thriller Writers Association, The Beacon Society, and DFW Sherlock Homes Society.

Dave was appointed a U.S. Treasury Commissioner and to the management board of the Resolution Trust Corporation (RTC) by President Clinton.

He is a Fellow of the International Oceanographic Foundation.

Visit David at

Author's Website: davidciambrone.com

Facebook: facebook.com/david.ciambrone?fref=ts

Twitter: twitter.com/mysterywriter5

LinkedIn: linkedin.com/pub/david-ciambrone-sc-d-fiof/11/ab5/bb3

Amazon: amazon.com/author/davidciambrone

Progressive Rising Phoenix Press is an independent publisher. We offer wholesale pricing and multiple binding options with no minimum purchases for schools, libraries, book clubs, and retail vendors. We offer substantial discounts on bulk orders and discounts on individual sales through our online store. Please visit our website at:
www.ProgressiveRisingPhoenix.com

*If you enjoyed reading this book, please review it on Amazon, B & N, or Goodreads.
Thank you in advance!*

www.ingramcontent.com/pod-product-compliance
Lightning Source LLC
LaVergne TN
LVHW010256260326
834688LV00044B/1318